ALEXANDER'S LEGACY

AN EMPTY THRONE

ROBERT FABBRI

CORVUS

First published in hardback in Great Britain in 2022 by Corvus,
an imprint of Atlantic Books Ltd.

This paperback edition published in 2022 by Corvus

10 9 8 7 6 5 4 3 2 1

A CIP catalogue record for this book is available from the British Library.

Hardback ISBN: 978 1 78649 804 5
Paperback ISBN: 978 1 78649 807 6
E-book ISBN: 978 1 78649 806 9

Printed and bound by CPI Group (UK) Ltd, Croydon CR0 4YY

Corvus
An imprint of Atlantic Books Ltd
Ormond House
26–27 Boswell Street
London
WC1N 3JZ

www.corvus-books.co.uk

In loving memory of Joyce Imogen Husbands.
'Joycie'. 1924–2019. A much missed family friend.

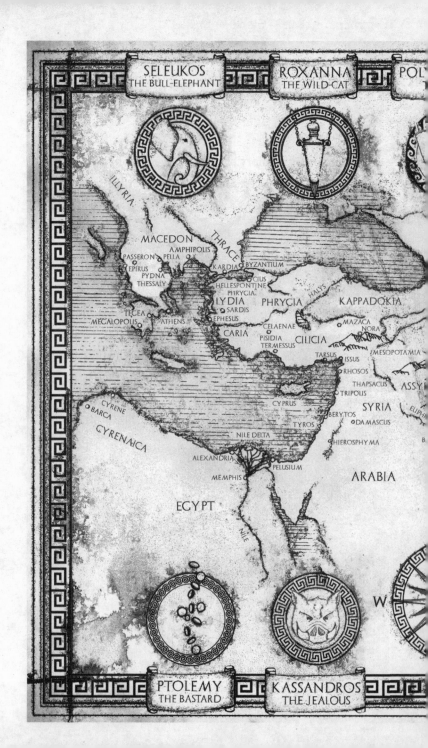

A list of characters can be found on page 412.

ANTIGONOS.
THE ONE-EYED.

MBITION, ANTIGONOS HAD learned late in life, is a motivation that feeds upon itself, growing fatter upon its own achievement; and he was in its thrall.

It had not always been so. Before the death of Alexander, the third so named to be King of Macedon, Antigonos had been content as the satrap of Phrygia, left behind to complete the conquest of central Anatolia by the great man as he rode east to steal an empire. And he had been happy with his lot, for nothing pleased him more than the sound, smell and thrill of battle; his campaign tent was his home, his men were his kin and his weapons his tools. For years he had lived for nothing but the joy of combat to the virtual exclusion of all else; yes, he had taken a wife, Stratonice, and yes, he had found time to father two children upon her, but this excursion into domesticity had been in his late forties and more an afterthought than a considered plan.

But now, fighting for fighting's sake, despite the deep pleasure he still gained from it, was no longer sufficient for Antigonos; for he had glimpsed an empty throne, and to seize it so that his eldest son, Demetrios, could inherit, thus establishing a dynasty, was now his desire. Granted, there were technically two occupants of that throne – or so he thought at the time – but one was a child and the other a fool. The child, named after his father, was the five-year-old issue from Alexander's marriage to the eastern wild-cat Roxanna, and was, therefore, tainted with non-Macedonian blood. The fool was Alexander's elder half-brother, now known as Philip, whose intellect had been damaged by a potion ministered by Alexander's mother, Olympias, to keep the path to the throne clear for her own progeny; it had failed to kill him but had left him with the mind of an eight year old. Antigonos could bow to neither; indeed, he could bow to no one since Alexander had drawn his last breath with his seven bodyguards around him straining to hear him name a successor. But he had only said, 'To the strongest,' as he handed the Great Ring of Macedon to Perdikkas – the most senior of the seven but not the eldest – and had neglected to say who 'the strongest' might be.

It had not been long before the empire had descended into civil war; Perdikkas soon fell to the assassin's blade.

Then there came the death, at eighty-two, of the last man Antigonos truly respected – Antipatros, the regent of Macedon in Alexander's absence. And Antipatros' replacement was not his son, Kassandros, but the nonentity Polyperchon, for whom Antigonos had no regard. So the seed of ambition had grown within Antigonos, as he had realised if Macedon was not to lose her empire it must be grasped by one man; and the seed had grown to fruition and was now in full bloom, for Antigonos was certain he could be that man. Indeed, he craved it with all his being.

However, there were many men who stood in his way; not the least of these his one-time friend, Eumenes. A Greek from Kardia whose loyalty to the Argead royal house of Macedon was absolute, Eumenes had recently reneged on an agreement with

Antigonos to serve under him. Eumenes had taken his army south from his satrapy of Kappadokia down into Syria to recruit mercenaries and build ships. Antigonos had given furious chase, for he needed to destroy Eumenes – there could never be trust between them again.

And thus it was with a mixture of emotions that Antigonos received his old friend, comrade and contemporary, Philotas, as he slaked his thirst with resinated wine, sitting beneath a canopy overlooking his army's coastal camp at Issos – the site of Alexander's stunning victory against Darius of Persia fifteen years previously.

'I assume, in the absence of Eumenes in chains – or at least his head in a sack – you weren't successful,' Antigonos observed, indicating to the pitcher of wine on the table next to him.

'I did what you asked: I infiltrated his camp with thirty of our lads and tried to persuade Eumenes' men to turn on him.' Philotas sat and poured himself a drink.

'And?'

'And he's gone, five days ago; heading east towards Mesopotamia.'

Antigonos grunted and held out his cup to be refilled. 'With his army or as a fugitive?'

'With his army. The news from the east is Peithon, satrap of Media, tried to install his brother as the satrap of Parthia, having executed the incumbent. Peucestas and the other eastern satraps formed an alliance and defeated him. I think Eumenes is hoping to unite the eastern alliance's thirty-thousand-strong army with his.'

'That would be a match for us.' Antigonos contemplated the news for a few moments, scratching at his thick, grey beard as if he were trying to remove a small rodent from it. 'And the Silver Shields weren't tempted to desert Eumenes?'

'I tried to persuade them, but no, they wouldn't. They've proved surprisingly loyal to him.'

'Considering he's a Greek; and a sly little Greek at that.' *How does the most elite unit in the whole army end up supporting Eumenes?* Antigonos mused as he glared out to sea with his one eye; his other, the left, a mass of scar tissue, the victim of a Greek arrow at the battle of Chaeronea, seeped a blood-tinged tear. 'What reasons did their commanders give you for supporting him?'

'Antigenes and Teutamus don't trust you not to execute them if they were to come over to you. They told me that because he's a Greek, Eumenes has few friends and is therefore more likely to keep the ones he does have alive.'

'My arse! They trust a Greek over me! My damp, hairy arse! They're Macedonian officers like me, and they don't trust me. Wait until I get my hands upon them, I'll...' Antigonos calmed himself with a deep draught.

'That's exactly their point, old friend; and I had to admit to them they were probably right.'

'You did what?'

'You heard.' Philotas reached over and once again refilled Antigonos' cup. 'Don't act so outraged, Antigonos; you and I have fought shoulder to shoulder in the front rank nigh on seventy times, certainly enough for me to know you. Of course you would have killed them. The Silver Shields are the most experienced and feared unit in the whole army, three thousand men in their sixties or over who have known nothing but war all their adult lives, and because of that they're the most opinion-ated and influential. It was they who forced Alexander to turn back from India; it was they who backed the fool, Philip, to be king and put us in this mess of having two kings. They rebelled against Antipatros for not giving them their back-pay, you

12

remember? Antipatros would have been murdered had you and Seleukos not saved him. Need I go on? No, of course not. They're trouble and, had I managed to persuade them to come over to you, executing their leaders and sending the unit to some out-of-the-way shithole on the fringe of the empire would have been the only sensible thing to do – for the benefit of the whole army's morale and not just your peace of mind. So no, old friend; don't act so outraged.'

Antigonos growled and glowered but said nothing for he realised all Philotas had said had been true. The nub of the issue was Eumenes could not survive without the Silver Shields at the heart of his army, but Antigonos could, and that was understood by all.

'Ptolemy had also sent representation,' Philotas carried on, 'but only to Antigenes and Teutamus, not the men, but with the same request: kill Eumenes and come over to him.'

'And they didn't fancy going to Egypt?'

Philotas shook his head. 'It was the same problem: they knew Ptolemy would have them dead in a trice and the Silver Shields would have been stationed as far down the Nile as possible and then forgotten by all but the crocodiles.'

Oh Ptolemy, you think you're the canniest of Alexander's seven bodyguards, safe in your fortress, Egypt; but I'll have you too, very soon. But even as the thought crossed his mind he knew that, of the surviving five bodyguards, Ptolemy was the most secure. Perdikkas, to whom Alexander had given the Great Ring of Macedon with those fateful words, had been murdered for his high-handed attitude in trying to force himself upon the empire; he had met his match trying to invade Egypt.

Leonnatus, arrogant and vain, had been killed in battle. He had tried to relieve Antipatros, who was besieged within the walls of Lamia by an Athenian army as the Greeks rose against

13

Macedonian rule, soon after Alexander's death. *But can I move against Ptolemy with Eumenes heading east to gather support there?* And that was the problem which now presented itself to Antigonos: should Eumenes gain the support of the former bodyguard in the east, Peucestas, satrap of Persis, and the eastern alliance, as well as Seleukos, the new satrap of Babylonia, an ambitious man on the rise – *in need of slapping down* – then the little Greek would have a formidable force indeed.

Antigonos got to his feet and looked out over the coastal plain at his army. Over fifty thousand strong, of which almost ten thousand were cavalry. Wafts of smoke, blended with the scents of roasting lamb and grilled seafood, rose from the thousands of cooking fires that punctuated the host. He breathed deeply, savouring the smell of an army in camp. *Gods, I love this life.* He looked north along the plain to where, all those years ago, he had commanded a part of the phalanx – sixteen ranks deep of pikemen, the anvil of the Macedonian army to the cavalry's hammer – when Alexander had turned his army and beaten the pursuing Persians. Darius, the Great King, had fled the field that day and his rule had been effectively finished. Antigonos closed his eye and relished the memory of a quarter of a million men in mortal combat. *Gods below, that was a day; I'll never see the like of it again. But if Eumenes is successful gaining allies in the east then the battle that ensues could be almost as big.*

Smiling at the thought, Antigonos opened his eye and looked at Philotas. 'So, what about Eumenes' fleet?'

'It was stationed in Rhosos, a couple of leagues south along the coast; I persuaded it to come over to you as soon as they saw your fleet fresh from its victory in the north. What's more, Eumenes had already loaded his treasury aboard to transport it over to Europe. A shame for him really.'

Antigonos rubbed his hands together, chuckling. 'How unfortunate. How much was it?'

'Thirty boxes of coinage, bullion and jewellery; we haven't counted it all yet. It's all in Rhosos.'

'At least five hundred talents, I should guess,' Antigonos said, looking in satisfaction as the treasurer opened the last of the strongboxes lying open on the treasury floor in the palace of the port of Rhosos, three leagues south of Issos. He slapped his nineteen-year-old son, Demetrios, on the shoulder. 'What do you think of that, my boy?' Bending forward, he pulled a gold necklace, with sapphires set around it, from the nearest box. 'That should do nicely for your mother; appease her for leaving her behind in Celaenae. Choose something for Phila; I'm sure she deserves it.'

Demetrios, now taller than his father, with a clean-shaven face that was far more appealing – although dominated by an impressive nose – and a full head of wavy, dark brown hair, looked down at Antigonos with pride in his eyes. 'She does, Father, most certainly she does; she's pregnant.'

This provoked a firmer slap and a hearty chuckle. 'Well, you've been trying hard enough, my boy; and there were you worrying because she's ten years older than you she would be difficult to manage.'

The look of pride turned into injured dignity. 'I've never had a problem with handling women.' Demetrios twisted away from his father's hand still clasping his shoulder. 'And I'll thank you not to imply it, Father; especially not in public.' He glared at the treasurer and his attendant slaves.

Antigonos put his hands up. 'Don't be so quick to take offence, Demetrios; I had to force you into the marriage, remember? It was a shrewd political move to marry one of Antipatros' daughters who just also happened to be the widow of Krateros.' Antigonos held his son's gaze for a moment and wondered what would have happened if Krateros, the darling of the army and Macedon's most successful general after Alexander, had not been killed by Eumenes in battle. *He was Antipatros' first choice to succeed him as regent rather than that nobody, Polyperchon; if Krateros were regent I'd still be just the satrap of Phrygia and taking orders from him. Perhaps Eumenes did me a great favour by killing him and I should be grateful to the little Greek after all.* 'Now choose a piece of jewellery for the mother of your forthcoming child and don't be so prickly.' He drew closer to his son, gestured to the treasure and lowered his voice. 'And remember, Demetrios: I'm funding Kassandros' war in Greece against Polyperchon. Some of this will end up with him; enough to ensure he wins and he'll be greatly in my debt. Knowing just how poisonous the man is, it's safe to assume he'll do away with the kings and try to take the throne of Macedon for himself. Your child will be his nephew and he, as yet, is without an heir. Once we have secured Asia…' Antigonos gestured for his son to finish the thought.

Demetrios considered for a moment. 'We would look west and take Macedon from Kassandros.'

'And in the process kill him.'

Demetrios smiled, cold. 'And my son will claim the throne and I will be regent.'

'No, Demetrios, you'll be king; King of Macedon and her empire; and your son will inherit the title, uniting Antipatros' family and our own, making the claim incontestable with the Argead heirs dead, and our dynasty will be founded.'

Demetrios' eyes widened at the sheer scale of his father's dream. 'You're aiming for it all?'

'Yes, my boy, all of it.'

'Even Ptolemy in Egypt?'

'Especially Ptolemy in Egypt, otherwise we'll be continually fighting him for control of Syria and Cyprus. The question is, do I defeat him before or after I take Eumenes and the east?'

'And what about Lysimachus in Thrace?'

Antigonos dismissed the name of the cruellest of Alexander's bodyguards with a gesture. 'He'll be content owing us loyalty provided we leave him to his own devices in Thrace; he's very happy fighting the northern tribes and making a big point about how he keeps us all safe from a barbarian invasion from the north. If we give him money so he can carry on building his fortresses up there, he won't bother us.'

'And Olympias?'

'That's where the value of good intelligence comes in. Come, let's walk.' He led Demetrios out into the palace courtyard, overlooking the port. 'You've heard of Archias the Exile-Hunter, have you not?'

Demetrios nodded. 'The one-time actor turned assassin, of course.'

'Well, a couple of months ago, Ptolemy, for an unbelievable price, persuaded the Exile-Hunter to travel to Macedon and reveal to Olympias his part in Alexander's death.'

Demetrios looked at his father with a mixture of curiosity and surprise. 'Which was?'

'When old man Antipatros sent Kassandros to Babylon to request confirmation of Alexander's wish to replace him with Krateros, Archias travelled with him as far as Tarsus. There, he procured a poison for Kassandros, who then travelled on to Babylon; Alexander died very shortly after his arrival. Iollas, Kassandros' younger half-brother, was Alexander's cup-bearer and therefore mixed his drinks for him.' Antigonos paused to let the implication of that sink in as he watched a sleek and fast *lembus* – a small undecked vessel – glide through the harbour mouth; his eye squinting in the sun, glittering on a gentle sea.

Demetrios did not disappoint his father. 'Olympias has always claimed Alexander was murdered by either Antipatros or one of his family but she has never had proof. Not until now.'

Antigonos grinned. 'Now she knows for certain in her mind; although it's circumstantial and not proof positive, it's enough for her.'

'She'll go all out for vengeance.'

'She will, and we all know what a vengeful bitch she is and yet no one can move against her because, as the mother of Alexander, she's sacred; not even Antipatros tried to have her killed as she plotted against him all the ten years Alexander was away. No one can kill her...' Antigonos left the thought hanging.

'Except for someone who hated Alexander with all his being; someone who knows if he doesn't kill her she will kill him and his entire family. Kassandros will have to kill her.' Demetrios looked at his father in appreciation. 'That was very clever of Ptolemy.'

'Yes, I will give him grudging respect. So you see, Demetrios,' Antigonos continued as he watched a figure leaping off the lembus onto the quay before the vessel had even docked, 'we have someone in the west who thinks he's advancing his own position by waging war against Polyperchon and, by default, Olympias, but is actually clearing the way for us once we finish Eumenes and Ptolemy; all in all a very satisfactory state of affairs. Now, why don't you choose a piece of jewellery for your wife who, even at her advanced age, is playing such an important role in our scheme.'

'Yes, Father, I will.'

'Antigonos!' Philotas called as he entered the courtyard, a scroll in his hand. 'This has just come from Kassandros.'

Antigonos took the letter and read it, mouthing the words. 'Well, things are beginning to move along at a fair pace.'

'What is it, Father?' Demetrios asked.

'Kassandros tells me his spies have reported that the fool, King Philip, and his troublesome wife, Adea, have been murdered by Olympias, along with hundreds of Kassandros' supporters and kin. She also desecrated his family's tombs and murdered his brother, stepmother and two young half-siblings. Kassandros will move north as soon as he has dealt with Polyperchon's son, Alexandros, in the Peloponnese and have his revenge.' He smiled, shaking his head. 'Olympias has just signed her own death warrant.' He handed the letter to his son. 'It would seem we've cause to be grateful to her. See for yourself.'

'Will you send more troops to help Kassandros?' Demetrios asked, having read the letter.

'My arse, I will; we don't want him getting too powerful. I'll send him money for mercenaries and bribes but that's it. And I'll remind him I want my men and fleet back as soon as he's killed Olympias and taken Macedon.'

'Do you think he will?'

'No, which will give me the excuse I need to invade.'

'And Ptolemy?'

'If necessary, an alliance of convenience could be forged there whilst I deal with Kassandros. This makes it plain to me what to do now: leave Ptolemy alone for the time being in case I need him later and, instead, follow Eumenes and defeat him before he manages to unite the east.'

'It's a bit late in the year to start another campaign, isn't it?'

Good lad, always thinking. 'It'll take a month to march to the Tigris. We'll winter there in Mesopotamia, using the time to resupply and have Nearchos build a river fleet so we can have the whole army in Babylon by the spring equinox. Then, using that as our base, we'll head east.'

'Meanwhile, Kassandros deals with Olympias for us.'

Antigonos beamed at his son and grasped his shoulder. 'Indeed; by the time we come back west, Alexander's mother will be dead and the Argead royal house will be one step closer to extinction.'

OLYMPIAS.
THE MOTHER.

BLISS IT WAS for Olympias to feed her lust for vengeance with the blood of her foes; and they were many, for throughout life she had found more pleasure in making enemies than cultivating friends. Why would she need friends when she was the mother of Alexander? Alexander was now dead but, despite that, she still made no effort to ingratiate herself with the people she effectively ruled over. For she now held the Great Ring of Macedon and was the regent for her grandson, the five-year-old king, the namesake of his father. Polyperchon, Antipatros' nominated successor to the regency, had abdicated the responsibility in her favour; she had grasped it, taking the ring and setting it on her forefinger to hold it high in the air as she admired such a compelling symbol of power.

From the heart of the palace in Pella, the capital of Macedon, Olympias had tightened her grip on that power so all but a few lived in fear of her. Now in her late fifties, hair dyed black and, save for a ringlet to either side, piled abundantly atop her head and set with jewels and pins of gold, she was still a striking woman; elegant and dangerous.

'I will not be spoken to like that, Thessalonike.' Olympias' voice was low with menace; her kohl-rimmed eyes slits – serpentine like the beasts she worshipped – as she looked down from her raised throne at the woman before her, barely in her twenties but exuding a force belying her years.

Thessalonike, the adopted daughter of Olympias after she had poisoned her real mother, a rival wife of Philip, the second so named, stood her ground against Olympias' rising wrath. 'You've not been listening, Mother; you're too focused on killing anyone who might have looked at you in a strange manner thirty years ago.'

'I take only the vengeance I'm due.'

'You don't have a monopoly in that. Kassandros will soon deal with Polyperchon's son, Alexandros, in the Peloponnese; the siege has been going on for four months now. Tegea will fall soon and when it does Kassandros will come north and he'll be looking for the vengeance *he* feels *he's* due.'

'Pah!' Olympias waved away the suggestion. 'Eumenes will arrive with his army before that and we'll crush Kassandros between us.'

'Where is he, then? We should've had news of him arriving in Greece days ago. He has the ships and the weather has been clement; there's been nothing to delay him.' Thessalonike paused for emphasis and held Olympias' gaze. 'Unless…'

'Unless what?'

'Unless Antigonos' fleet has left the Hellespont, come south and defeated him.'

She's right, Olympias considered as she tapped a forefinger on the arm of the throne. *It's been almost a month since Polyperchon managed to lose his navy by attacking Antigonos' fleet in the Hellespont. Antigonos would've had time to make his repairs by now.* 'If you're correct then we can't expect Eumenes at all.'

'No, we can't; and in that case there'll be nothing to stop Kassandros coming north as we don't have a fleet to counteract his.'

'Let him come; I'll gouge out his eyes, tear his balls off and ram them into the empty sockets.'

'Mother, you're putting emotion before pragmatism.'

'Of course I am! The pockmarked coward murdered my son. My son! The greatest man ever to have lived, murdered by him – a man who doesn't even have the right to recline at the table because he is yet to kill a wild boar in a hunt. Pah! Of course I respond emotionally.'

Thessalonike drew a deep breath and glanced over to Polyperchon sitting, hardly noticeable, at the throne room's council table.

'He won't help you,' Olympias sneered. 'He'll just do as I tell him like a good hound.'

'Then tell him to gather whatever ships he can find, muster the army, and garrison the passes from Thessaly into Macedon in order to halt Kassandros on ground of our choosing and there defeat him; if he enters Macedon the people will flock to him.'

'To Kassandros, the murderer of Alexander? Pah! The people of Macedon would never support him against Alexander's mother.'

'They would, Mother; they bear you no love and you know it.'

She's right again. They may fear me but it's not enough to bind them to my cause; they might hate Kassandros but they loathe me more. But what do I care for the love or opinions of the people? It's Kassandros I want, not love. She turned her gaze onto Polyperchon. 'Well? Will Kassandros soon defeat that useless son of yours?'

Grey and balding, a slight man destined always to follow rather than lead – thus his willingness to give up the ring – Polyperchon had little hesitation, for he was a master of detail; a consummate second-in-command. 'Without Eumenes coming to relieve Tegea, it will fall. Alexandros may escape but most of his surviving men will be drafted into Kassandros' army and then, yes, he will come north even more powerful than he was before. Without a fleet to oppose him he can sail his army past Thermopylae, making the very expensive deal we did with the Aitolians to hold the pass against him irrelevant.'

Olympias frowned. 'But we still have more than enough men to face him: we have your army, and my kinsman King Aeacides' army is still encamped to the west of the country and won't return to Epirus until after the betrothal of my grandson to his daughter. And then there are Aristonous' men.'

'Aristonous has gone back to his estates, taking his men with him, as you well know, Mother,' Thessalonike said, clenching her fists at her side. 'Your behaviour disgusted him, murdering Adea and Philip and all of Kassandros' prisoners.'

'They deserved to die!'

'For a man with Aristonous' sense of honour, they did not.'

'The man's weak; the only one of my son's seven bodyguards to retire back to his estates rather than take a satrapy.'

'Perhaps he knew what would happen and wanted no part of it.'

'Well, he is a part of it. I shall order him back to Pella immediately. Polyperchon, see to it at once.'

Polyperchon nodded.

Olympias glared at him. 'Why are you still sitting there, old man? I said at once. Go!'

Polyperchon jumped to his feet and scuttled from the room.

Olympias shook her head as she watched him leave and then turned her attention back to her adopted daughter. 'Aristonous can take care of our defence when he returns; I wouldn't trust that balding nonentity with it.'

24

'If Aristonous refuses to come, Polyperchon may be your only choice, so order him to start mustering the army and take it south to the border.'

Olympias fought against her reluctance to act upon a suggestion that was not her own before giving a grudging nod of assent.

'And tell Aeacides he had better not take his army back to Epirus because you are going to need it.'

'I'll speak to my cousin when he arrives tomorrow to celebrate the betrothal.'

It was far from a holiday atmosphere that greeted Aeacides, the King of Epirus, when he rode through the western gate of Pella the following afternoon, a kingly diadem upon his head and a gold-edged purple cloak about his shoulders. Many lined the streets, indeed the whole population had turned out to see the king, but it had not been out of curiosity or through any sense of love or respect: they had been ordered to. The edict had gone out the evening before and all who did not obey would face punishment unless they could prove they had an occupation that could not be forsaken for any length of time. Yes, they cheered as the portly young king rode into the city with his seven-year-old daughter, Deidamia, sitting next to her mother, Phthia, in a carriage at his side. Accompanying them, clattering behind, were an *ile* of two hundred of his Companion Cavalry – armed in the Macedonian fashion: with a lance and no shield – followed by a *syntagma* of two hundred and fifty-six phalangites, pikemen, again identical to the Macedonian equivalent. All the troops had flowers tied to their weapons and the horses were arrayed in high plumes and ribbons of many colours.

The soldiers waved as they progressed, calling out greetings to the crowd; but the return cheers of the citizens were forced and there was no joy in the people's faces despite the flautists, drummers and choir raising a rousing marching tune. On, along the main thoroughfare, straight as a spear shaft, towards the agora at the centre of the grid-planned city the procession went; there, among the throngs of spectators, their meagre enthusiasm waning by the moment, it turned north towards the palace on the edge of the city.

Olympias waited at the top of the main steps, the ancient marble worn with use, leading up to towering oaken double doors studded with bronze, both open, revealing a hall of grandeur within. An honour guard of elite Hypaspists in polished bronze cuirasses, helms and shields, the sixteen-point star-blazon of Macedon engraved upon them, lined the steps four deep, red horsehair plumes and cloaks fluttering in a light breeze, white-knuckled hands gripping long thrusting-spears held rigid, vertical, at their sides.

Olympias' hands rested on her five-year-old grandson's shoulders; the boy's mother, Roxanna, had been confined, screeching and lashing out with long-nailed fingers, to her quarters, and was now locked away and guarded by two huge soldiers. The scene had given Olympias much satisfaction, but there was very little satisfaction to be had from the present situation.

'Why are the people so sullen?' she demanded of Thessalonike, standing behind her right shoulder. 'They've been told to cheer and celebrate the coming betrothal. And instead, look at them.' She gestured to the crowd as Aeacides passed; with limp waves and shallow cheers their lack of enthusiasm was evident to all. 'I should have a few of them strung up to encourage the others.'

Thessalonike's sigh was easily audible. 'Oh, Mother, how little you know about the ordinary people of Macedon.'

'The ordinary people, as you call them, should do as they are told; and they've been told to be happy.'

'And what have they got to be happy about?'

'I'm just about to secure the future of the Argead dynasty through this betrothal.'

'They're not stupid; what they see is you securing your place as regent to rule over them for the next ten years and, seeing what you have achieved in less than a month and knowing your reputation, they don't like the thought of that.'

'My reputation?'

'As a power-hungry murderess, yes.'

Olympias swung around to face her adoptive daughter, knocking the young Alexander to the ground. 'How dare you talk to me like that; me, the mother of Alexander!'

'I dare, Mother, because you need to hear the truth about yourself. We both know you killed my real mother and she is just one of many on your list of victims; and we both know you spend all your time plotting, trying to obtain power, which makes you a power-hungry murderess and the people are wary of that. And no, being the mother of Alexander, as you ceaselessly and pointlessly keep reminding everyone, does not give you the automatic right to do whatever you wish and be loved or respected regardless.'

The blur of Olympias' right hand struck Thessalonike hard across the cheek; she reeled back, clutching at her face, stepping her left leg behind her to steady herself and then pulled herself upright and, with cold eyes and an iced smile, stared at Olympias. 'You will regret that one day, Olympias. I swear it.'

I may have been a little hasty with my reaction but the bitch had it coming. 'There's nothing you can do to frighten me.'

'Oh, I'll think of something; don't you worry.' She leaned over and pulled the crying king to his feet. 'Come, Alexander, kings don't cry, do they?'

Alexander looked up at her, suppressed a couple of sobs and shook his head. Thessalonike ruffled his black hair and then stroked his almond-skinned cheek. 'There's a good boy.' She eased him back into Olympias' grasp and held her gaze with flint eyes for a moment before resuming her position behind Olympias as Aeacides reached the foot of the steps and dismounted.

Olympias creased her face into a smile, cold and grim, and extended a hand towards him. 'Aeacides, King of Epirus,' she declaimed high and clear to carry far back into the crowd, 'we welcome you to Pella.' *He looks worse each time I see him.*

Bloated from excess of wine, his jowls sagging and his hair receding, with his blotched face looking ten years older than his twenty-three years, Aeacides made his way, none too steadily, up the steps and took the extended hand. 'Queen Olympias, cousin, it's a pleasure to be here.'

You can't stand the sight of me, as neither I can you. 'We look forward to uniting our houses with the betrothal of your daughter, Deidamia, to my grandson, Alexander, the fourth of that name of Macedon.' She raised both arms to the crowd encouraging a cheer and was, once again, both disappointed and enraged by the response. Stamping her foot, she turned and, with an abruptness that shocked all, withdrew within.

Thessalonike glanced at her adoptive mother's receding form and gave a trace of a smile before turning to Aeacides and gesturing that they should follow Olympias. 'Shall we?'

'And thus, before the gods and before this present company I declare this man, Alexander, and this woman, Deidamia, to be betrothed.' Aeacides, the father of the bride, stared down with bloodshot, porcine eyes at the two bewildered children standing before him. They held hands, symbolically tied together with a leather thong. Thessalonike and the handful of noblemen currently in favour with Olympias – in that they had

28

been permitted to live – stood by as witnesses. 'They will marry after my daughter's first moon. As agreed, for a dowry I will provide a thousand head of cattle and a hundred talents in silver and gold.'

As Aeacides continued to list the dowry, Olympias looked with distaste at the King of Epirus, her former ward who had come to the throne as a minor after his cousin had managed to get himself killed campaigning in far-off Italia. She had hated him ever since he had come of age and she had been obliged to stand aside as regent of Epirus. To compound the injury, he had then barred her from taking a seat at the council table, denying her the one commodity she craved: power. *With luck you'll drink yourself to death; unless, of course, I decide to poison you.* She considered the notion for a few moments. *Perhaps in a few years I'll—*

'What is this!' a shrill voice screeched from the chamber's door. 'Why have I been prevented from attending the ceremony as well as the welcoming?'

Olympias turned to see Roxanna, Alexander's mother, scratching at the face of a guard attempting to inhibit her entry. *How did she get out? There'll be some hard punishment for the two brutes I left on the door.*

'Get out of my way,' Roxanna hissed, clawing at the man's eyes with both sets of talons.

'Let her pass,' Olympias ordered.

Spitting at her victim as he stepped aside, his face bloodied, Roxanna stepped into the room, her dark eyes glaring out from between her veil and a high headdress. She stood and pointed at Olympias, a piece of bloody skin hanging from her long nails. 'You exclude me, you shun me and you steal my child from me. And now you don't allow me to see my son betrothed. I am a queen and a queen should be at the centre of everything.'

Olympias smiled without warmth. 'Oh, my dear, did your guards not get the message to allow you out? I shall have the slave bearing it whipped.' *The guards, more like.* 'Where are your guards, by the way?'

Roxanna's eyes betrayed a triumphant countenance beneath her veil. 'I took pity on them and sent my slaves out with food and drink.'

Fools to trust a gift from this wild-cat; how many times must I warn them but they still do it. 'Dead, then?'

'By now, yes.'

'Well, seeing as you are now here.' She indicated for Roxanna to take her place next to Alexander. The boy flinched as his mother laid a hand on his shoulder; his eyes, as dark as hers, looked around the room as if searching for a friend but finding none. *See how little love he bears you.*

Aeacides cleared his throat and carried on, anxious to get to the drinking part of the ceremony. 'In addition I will sign an alliance pledging the support of Epirus in defending my future son-in-law's throne from external and internal threats.'

'You'll do more than that, Aeacides,' Olympias said, 'you will leave your army here so I may use it against Kassandros.'

Aeacides blinked rapidly as he regarded her with shock.

'I'll send it back to you once Kassandros is dead.'

'But that'll leave Epirus undefended.'

'Try not to be so obtuse, Aeacides; it doesn't suit a king. Macedon is the only country likely to attack you and why would I do that? I think you can manage the odd incursion from the Illyrian tribes in the north with the garrisons you left behind.'

Aeacides opened his mouth to speak.

'I'll not take no for an answer.'

'I am the King of Epirus and I don't take orders from anyone.'

'Wrong, Aeacides, you take orders from me; that is, if you want your little son, Pyrrhus, to have a kingdom to inherit.'

'Are you threatening me?'

'A good observation. Yes, I am threatening you, again. Although I shouldn't really need to as it's in your own interests to leave your army here to help in the war against Kassandros.'

'How so?'

'Think. If Kassandros should take Macedon, he will certainly want someone on the throne in Epirus who has no connection with me, *cousin*, wouldn't you agree?'

Aeacides reflected on the thought, his face working hard as he calculated. 'Very well,' he said eventually. 'I have decided to stay with the army of Epirus within the realm of Macedon to safeguard my daughter's interests.'

Olympias smiled at her kinsman. 'That's a very good idea you've just had, Aeacides. You can stay with them in the west of the country, close to your border, in case Kassandros should try surprising us by launching an inland attack rather than coming along the coast.'

Aeacides muttered something inaudible. Ignoring him, Olympias looked down at the two children, who seemed even more bewildered than before; she unbound their hands. 'Now, my sweets, it's time for you to say goodbye to each other for the time being; and remember, in six or seven years you will be married. Say goodbye to Deidamia, Alexander.'

Alexander looked at his betrothed, two years older and half a head taller and far paler than him. 'Goodbye, Deidamia.'

'Tell her how pleased you are that she's consented to be your wife.'

'It makes me pleased that you will be my wife.'

Deidamia regarded him with grave, blue eyes. 'We shall see, Alexander; it's a long time away.'

The girl shows promise if she can reason like that at the age of seven. Olympias bent to kiss her on the cheek and then took Alexander's hand.

'Give him to me,' Roxanna hissed from behind her veil.

'What, so you can terrorise him and spoil him in equal measure? No, Roxanna, you are no longer involved in his upbringing; he's to be brought up as a Macedonian king and not some pampered eastern potentate with a penchant for boys and sherbets.'

Roxanna hissed, her veil flapping. 'I'll have my revenge one day, Olympias; I swear it with all the steel in my heart.'

'Be careful what you wish for, bitch; I'm the only person keeping you alive. The gods help you if you fall into Kassandros' clutches.'

KASSANDROS.
THE JEALOUS.

'T HEY SAID WHAT?' Kassandros'
thin, pockmarked face went puce
with indignation; his sunken eyes
burned to either side of his beak of a nose
as he stared at his younger half-brother.

'They said no,' Philip repeated.

'Then tell Crateuas and Atarrhias to act like generals with
backbone and send the assault in again!' Kassandros roared
down into Philip's face. 'And this time tell them any man who
falls back will fall back onto my sword.' Kassandros cursed and
looked over, across the siege lines and no-man's land, full of
retreating shock-troops, to the walls of Tegea, wreathed in
smoke from the burning buildings within them and lined with
the spectral figures of cheering defenders; before them was a
tidemark of dead and writhing wounded. 'We have to take Tegea
and defeat Alexandros before Eumenes arrives with his fleet and
army.' He turned his thin, hollow-eyed, beak-nosed face to his
half-brother, almost a head shorter and half a shoulder broader,
and grabbed him by the tunic edge protruding from above his
breastplate. 'We have to! Have to! If not we'll be surrounded:
Eumenes to the east with sea power and a land force; Alexandros
here, free to break out as soon as I move away; Aeacides to the

north west and Olympias with Polyperchon – and maybe even Aristonous – to the north-east. And what then?'

Philip grasped his half-brother's wrist and wrenched his hand away. 'Herding men to certain death is not how to take a city, Kassandros. Crateuas and Atarrhias are well aware of that and told me to tell you that these are their men; you are only borrowing them on Antigonos' orders. And I think they're right to refuse to try another attack.'

Kassandros drew up his lanky frame and sneered. 'What do you know about taking cities? You're just seventeen.'

'Enough to know that a defending force, one that's been under siege for over two months, can still push back a determined assault by far fitter men, and that threatening death to any man who refuses to go again to the walls will not lead to victory but mutiny.'

Kassandros drew a breath, ran a hand through his spiky red hair and relaxed, nodding slowly. It had always been a default position of his to threaten violence but he could see in this instance his half-brother was right – Philip had always been so much sharper than his twin, Pleistarchos. This had been the fifth assault to have failed during the course of the siege and the men were losing morale; killing those less enthusiastic for a fight would not put heart into the rest. No, something else was needed to winkle Alexandros out of Tegea and thereby remove the last threat in the Peloponnese, thus freeing him to turn his attention north to the real prize, Macedon, and his revenge on Olympias. 'So, Philip, the great teenage tactician, do you have any suggestions?'

'I know you don't like to think of him but ask yourself what Father would've done.'

The mention of his late father, Antipatros, was never pleasant for Kassandros; the memory of the man who had denied him

34

his birth-right and passed the regency of Macedon on to another pained him. *What would he have done? He wouldn't have consulted me; that I can say for certain.* His expression was grim at the thought.

His father had never loved him and, at times, only barely tolerated him, despite his efforts to please him. But it had been ever thus for Kassandros; he had never found it easy to be liked and soon gave up the attempt utterly. His contemporaries, learning from the great Aristotle in the palace at Pella, had despised him; Alexander, Hephaestion, Lysimachus, Peucestas, Seleukos, Nearchos, Peithon, all of them. His jealousy of their feats of prowess could not be contained and he had resorted to spiteful acts in order to even the score with them: hamstringing hunting dogs or drowning their pups or adding salt to their horses' feed at first. But then, as they all grew, and he was increasingly left behind in martial and hunting competition, it became more vicious: favourite hunting horses would be found dead in their stables of a morning; attractive slave-girls, kept for pleasure, would disappear and then turn up a few days later horribly mutilated; and then much worse still.

There had been nothing he would not do to ease his jealousy and sense of inadequacy which was manifest every time a meal was served; for Kassandros remained obliged to sit upright on the couch whilst all his peers had earned the right to recline at table. Only a fully-fledged man could recline and, to be one, one had to have killed a wild boar in the hunt. And Kassandros had not for he was not the martial type: gangly, skinny and, most importantly, a coward. Yes, he could admit it to himself, for what was the point of denial? It was obvious: should a threat come towards him his urge was to run and he was lucky if he managed to retain control of his bladder.

Thus scorned and shunned by all but his reluctant family, he had grown up with the great men of his generation; but he had not grown with them. And then Alexander had left him behind when he had set out on the greatest adventure of all time. But during the ten years Alexander had been away, Kassandros had learned to accept what he was, so he no longer found shame in it; easily and without embarrassment could he now take his place at the table, sitting upright like a woman or small boy. And yes, he had fought with his father in various battles and had managed not to shame himself by running away, but this had been through the expediency of never fighting in the front rank or, indeed, being anywhere close to danger.

Nevertheless, the shock and humiliation of his father's final act still burned within each time he was forced to think of him; and now, to consider what Antipatros would have done had he been in this same position was to remind himself just what a disappointment he had been to his father. He sat down on a folding chair outside his command tent and forced himself back into the mind of the man who had never shown him love. Above all, Antipatros had been a wily politician, and then a consummate diplomat, and thirdly he had been a good – although not brilliant – general. Kassandros looked up at his half-brother. 'He would have been clearer with his objective; my objective is to take Macedon and have our family's revenge on Olympias for the murder of our brothers and your mother, the desecration of our family tombs and the execution of many of our followers.'

Philip nodded his agreement. 'So why are we here?'

Kassandros looked across to the besieged town, its delineation becoming clearer as the smoke thinned. 'To rid ourselves of the threat to our rear when we turn north to our real objective.'

Philip smiled – a far more agreeable sight than when his half-brother attempted it. 'That's how I see it too; but do we have to kill everyone inside to ensure that? What you said about being surrounded just now made me think, Kassandros: yes, Alexandros is a threat to our rear but not a great one – fewer than ten thousand men. He would be a great boost to Eumenes' army but only if Eumenes actually arrives. Our spies in Asia reported that Eumenes was ready to cross more than ten days ago; but where is he? Without Eumenes, Alexandros is no threat to us in the south; he knows that, as well as we do. So let's negotiate; see what he wants.'

Kassandros considered the notion, rubbing the vivid scar on his right thigh – it, along with the limp it had caused, was another reminder of his cowardice and failure to kill a wild boar in the hunt. Ever since he had persuaded Antigonos to lend him men and ships he had been keen to prove himself a general to be reckoned with – albeit one who led from the rear, naturally. In his haste he had forgotten the principle his father had operated by: to use force as a last resort. *Father made most progress through diplomacy and bribery; I've been wrong and it's taken a lad half my age to point it out. I was too hasty to claim my first victory as a general. It would be far preferable to have Alexandros on my side; or, at least for the time being, just pursuing his own ends in the Peloponnese.* 'You have a point, Philip. Perhaps I was too quick to go to war; there're far easier ways of achieving your goals and we shall discuss them with Alexandros in the morning. Send a herald to ask for a parley.' He turned and walked away so Philip would not see the embarrassment written upon his face. It hurt Kassandros to take the advice of a younger sibling but he had seen enough of Philip's evident good sense to know it was in his interest to do so.

The hostages were led away to either camp, leaving Kassandros facing Alexandros across a table set just outside the open gates of Tegea. *From a position of strength, Father used to say. I wonder which one of us considers himself the strongest, me with an army of twenty-five thousand or him with his ten thousand safe behind these walls?*

For a while the two men sat and regarded one another, busy in their own thoughts as each formed an opinion of the other.

'Our fathers were good friends,' Alexandros, as nondescript as his sire, but with more hair, observed.

Kassandros winced. 'My father hated me.'

'Which is why he gave the regency to mine. A mistake in my view.'

That statement caused Kassandros to frown; he leaned forward, cocking his head as if he had not heard correctly. 'You surprise me.'

'Do I? Of course I think it was an error,' Alexandros confirmed. 'I know my father and he's the first to admit he's no leader; he loves to obey an order but is too unsure of himself to lead and so finds it hard to issue one. No, his joy is in well-turned-out, well-supplied soldiers ready to implement strategy and not to formulate it himself. That's why he gave the ring to Olympias; he's happy to be her lackey.' Alexandros smiled in a relaxed manner. 'I can't say I blame him for doing so; she would've killed him had he not.'

'Had I not have killed him first.'

Alexandros inclined his head a fraction. 'And you might have been in that position had you not wasted your time trying to deal with me.'

Kassandros frowned once more, this time not in surprise but in confusion. 'Why do you say securing my rear is a waste of time?'

'What could I have done to you, Kassandros? Really? Retake Athens with a small army like mine now you've executed or exiled the democrats and installed your creature, Demetrius of

Phaleron, as the leader of the oligarchy? Of course not. I could only have been a slight irritant at the most.'

Is my lack of experience so obvious? Does everyone take me for a fool blundering about, playing at being a general? 'You could've raised an army from the democratic Greek cities and come against me.'

'And why would I do that? The most I'll do is carve out a little patch for myself, here in the Peloponnese, in order to give me some sort of leverage with whoever wins in the north – you or my father and Olympias.'

'And when, not if, I am the winner?'

'Then we talk, Kassandros. You might find that I, and, indeed, my father, could be of great service to you; but we would both need insurance policies. I heard what you did to Nicanor of Sindus, executing him for being successful in your cause.' Alexandros tutted. 'Being jealous of success is not how to invite others to be your friends.'

Kassandros suppressed the urge to lean over the table and slit the man's throat for being so patronising; not least as it was impossible, for both of them were unarmed. *How dare he talk to me as if I were a belligerent youth!* He stood. 'I'll not sit and be lectured by you as to how to behave.'

Alexandros shrugged, spreading his hands. 'As you wish, Kassandros. But for the record: if you go north, I won't be following you, but I'll still be here in the Peloponnese when you come back. Whether we fight each other or join forces is up to you. But I promise you one thing: if you kill my father, we can never be reconciled.'

'I'd say that is a very good piece of advice,' Philip said, having listened to a summary of the parley in Kassandros' tent.

His twin brother, Pleistarchos, recently arrived by sea from Athens, nodded. 'I agree, Kassandros; we want to make as few enemies as possible in Macedon if we're to keep it. Yes, Olympias must die, but other than her we owe no one else any mortal vengeance.'

Kassandros brooded upon clemency. *I will have people fear me, though; for too long have I been dismissed. But I suppose there are other ways to assert myself and keep what's mine by right.* 'Very well; Polyperchon lives – should he survive the war, that is. We'll see if we can make use of him afterwards. Now, summon the commanders; I'm going to break off the siege and return to Athens to prepare for moving north before the weather closes in. I'll take the fleet and whatever troops we can transport; you two can help Atarrhias and Crateuas bring the rest of the army back overland.'

'The granaries are as full as can be expected after having two armies foraging in Attica,' Demetrius of Phaleron informed Kassandros upon the latter's disembarkation at Piraeus, the port of Athens. Tall with high-cheekboned and dark-eyed good looks, framed by black oiled ringlets falling to his shoulders, the de facto Tyrant of Athens – in that he controlled the oligarchy in Kassandros' name – grasped his master's proffered arm with a bejewelled hand, as, one by one, Kassandros' fleet glided, under oars, through the harbour mouth of the largest port in Greece.

'Enough to supply the army for ten days?' Kassandros asked, looking at the rings on his creature's fingers. *At least two more than the last time I saw him; he must be doing a good business in bribes. Excellent; it means the citizens see him, and therefore me, as the true power in Athens.*

'Yes, leaving just about enough to get the city through the winter.'

Kassandros disengaged from Demetrius' grip; the needs of the city were no concern of his. 'How are they taking the return of the oligarchy?' he asked while walking, his limp pronounced, along the quay; dockyard-slaves jumped out of his way and their Macedonian overseers saluted as he passed.

'There may be some opposition in private but very little in the assembly,' Demetrios replied, striding next to his master. 'Those democratic demagogues who haven't been exiled or executed have all fled.'

'Where to?'

'Mainly back to the colonies in Thrace where the disenfranchised were allowed to settle last time.'

'Hmm. They should be dealt with; I can't risk them coming back. Is there any news of Archias the Exile-Hunter? He would be perfect for the job seeing as his men are all Thracians.'

'It's said he's gone back to Ptolemy. No doubt he's hoping to have a repeat of the very generous fee he's rumoured to have received for facing Olympias and telling her about the poison he procured for you in Tarsus.'

'That was bravely done,' Kassandros admitted with grudging respect. 'What he said to dissuade the harpy from killing him I'd dearly like to know. It was a clever ploy of Ptolemy's; it must have enraged her beyond all endurance, knowing the bitch.' *And, as I've been discovering: if you let your emotions take control, you make mistakes. I've been taught a good lesson. I just hope Olympias is less willing to learn.* 'If Archias isn't available, find someone else to do the job.'

'I'll see to it immediately.'

'No, you'll be too busy preparing the fleet. The bulk of the army coming overland will be arriving in two days' time. I want the grain loaded onto the fleet; it should be ready to sail three days after that. Once I'm gone you can find your assassin.' Dismissing his creature with a wave, Kassandros limped off along a warehouse-lined street towards the fortress of Munychia, the home of the Macedonian garrison, which overlooked both the harbour and the ruins of the Long Walls that once connected Piraeus to the mother city, its towering Acropolis glowing multi-coloured in the sun, a league and a half away.

'Provided the rest are not gone for too long,' the garrison commander informed Kassandros as they walked along the high walls of the Munychia, 'I'm confident we can keep control with just five hundred men, especially as Eumenes' fleet has deserted to Antigonos and the little Greek is now heading east with his army.'

'What?' Kassandros said, halting mid-step.

'You haven't heard, sir?'

'Evidently not.'

'The news arrived this morning with a merchant—'

'I don't care when it arrived or who brought it!' Kassandros roared, his face redder than his hair. 'I want to know if it's reliable.'

The commander shrugged. 'I've not had it corroborated, if that's what you mean.'

'Then get it corroborated! And do it soon, otherwise you'll lose this cushy billet and find yourself guarding some shithole in the mountains on the Illyrian border.'

Helped by a boot up the arse, the commander scuttled away, the very real threat echoing in his ears.

Kassandros turned and rested his hands on the battlement's edge; he looked down upon his fleet, almost all moored now, and drew a couple of deep breaths to settle his temper. It had been his excitement at the news and his desperation that it was true which caused him to react so. *Gods above and below; let it be true.*

'We've heard it too, Kassandros,' Philip said, as, arriving with the army the following day, he and Pleistarchos reported to their brother, watching the grain being loaded onto the fleet.

'From whom?'

'As we passed through Eleusis, a wine trader from Salamis sold us a particularly fine vintage. His brother in Tarsus had sent it over; the news came with it but it was very vague.'

Kassandros' dark sunken eyes came as close as they ever could to gleaming. 'So it is true: Eumenes is now no longer a threat.'

Philip shrugged. 'Perhaps, perhaps not; I'd say it's still an unsubstantiated rumour. I suggest we send a ship over to Asia to find out the truth of the matter.'

'That may not be necessary,' Pleistarchos muttered, pointing to a vessel entering the harbour. 'She's flying Antigonos' banner.'

'Antigonos wanted me to show you this in person,' the newly arrived triarchos said as he led Kassandros and his brother down to the small cabin of his ship. 'This, he says, is a gift.' He bent down and lifted the lid of one of the four strongboxes taking up most of the cabin's floor-space. Within was naught but gold.

Kassandros' heart jumped as the means to buy victory presented itself.

'The others are the same,' the triarchos said, opening the second one's lid followed by the third and fourth. 'It was part of Eumenes' treasure that Antigonos captured when the fleet came over to him.'

'So it's true, then – Eumenes has lost his fleet and is heading east.'

'Yes, half a moon ago.'

'That makes going north so much easier.'

'Antigonos thought as much.' The triarchos shut the lids. 'The gold you can keep, the fleet and the army you cannot, Antigonos told me to say. Once you've taken Macedon, he expects you to send them back and use the men and ships you capture instead.'

Kassandros gave his most sincere look of agreement. 'Tell him it will be done.'

'I'm to sail back as soon as the gold is offloaded.'

With a smile and a nod, Kassandros turned and left. *I'll send neither my fleet nor my army back to Antigonos and he'll be far too busy chasing Eumenes east to come and get them.* 'Make sure that vessel never gets back to Antigonos,' he ordered his brothers as they walked back down the gangplank. 'Kill everyone on board and bring the ship back as a prize. The more Antigonos is kept guessing the better.'

Pleistarchos looked confused but Philip smiled, understanding and nodding in agreement. 'I'll send a couple of triremes after him.'

'Very good.' Kassandros looked at each of his half-brothers with an expression bordering on benevolence. 'Well, brothers mine, tell me how Atarrhias and Crateuas conducted themselves on the march overland.'

Philip frowned. 'What do you mean?'

'I mean, did they show any sign of disloyalty? Did they at all times try to get the best out of my men or did they try to sabotage the speed of the march? Can I trust them after they refused to mount another attack at Tegea? Why else do you think I sent you two with them? I need an assessment of how reliable they are – don't forget they are both Antigonos' men, foisted on me when he lent me the troops. So, tell me what you think.'

The twins looked at one another and shrugged.

'Their refusal at Tegea was because it was pointless,' Philip said. 'They didn't come to confront you themselves because they didn't want you to lose face, which was why they sent me. I would suggest that shows a respect for your position by two men who've both got considerable martial experience.'

'Meaning I haven't.'

'Meaning they're more experienced than you in the field and they didn't want to make an issue of it; and I think that shows respect.' He turned to Pleistarchos. 'Wouldn't you agree, brother?'

'Well,' Pleistarchos said slowly, giving himself time to think. 'I'd say I neither saw nor heard anything from either of them that would suggest they had anything but the success of this venture at the forefront of their minds.'

'However,' Philip added in a cautionary tone, 'once the objectives are completed they might well feel a pull back to Antigonos, especially as you intend to keep his army as well as his fleet.'

Kassandros looked surprised. 'What makes you say that?'

'Why else would you want to keep Antigonos guessing?'

'Indeed; why else?' Kassandros looked back at the strong-boxes being offloaded and allowed a faint smile to play on his lips; he turned back to his half-brothers. 'We now have the money and the strength; it's time to go and deal with Olympias and Polyperchon.'

POLYPERCHON.
THE GREY.

IT WAS ALL in the detail, checking, cross-checking and counter-cross-checking; that, Polyperchon believed, was the key to smooth-running military administration, and he revelled in pedantic detail. The mustering of the army was, for Polyperchon, a time when he could excel in a way no one else could, for his ability to retain facts and figures in his head was as no other. And so he had thrown himself into the work of bringing together, arming and provisioning the army as fast as possible, recognising that Thessalonike was right: Kassandros had to be stopped on the border. If he were to gain a foothold in Macedon he would gain much support, for Olympias was the cruellest of rulers.

But, despite her excesses and the way she treated him, Polyperchon was prepared to support her against Kassandros because he feared what Kassandros would do to him in revenge for his receiving the Great Ring of Macedon from Antipatros. Well did he remember the explosive reaction and the hatred in his eyes as Kassandros realised he was being passed over. He did not wish to witness that again; and so, for him, Kassandros triumphing was not an option if he wished to live more than his already fifty-seven winters and keep what was most important to him: a position of authority.

The crash of ten thousand men coming to attention echoed over the parade ground, beyond the northern walls of Pella, overlooked by the palace complex, whence, Polyperchon was perfectly aware, Olympias looked on.

Always watching, always waiting for me to make the slightest error and pounce upon it. 'Does she have the same effect on you?' Polyperchon asked Aristonous, sitting on his horse next to him as the shouts of officers inspecting their charges now rose in the air.

Aristonous glanced over his shoulder up at the female figure standing in a high window. 'What? Having a chill run down your back when you know she's watching you?'

'Something like that.'

Aristonous laughed; a dozen years younger than Polyperchon, he had been the eldest of Alexander's bodyguards and the only one who had wanted nothing for himself other than to be able to retire quietly to his estates. 'She's always had that effect on me.'

'So why did you obey her summons to come back?'

'I didn't come for her; I came for Alexander. The boy is our rightful king, whether we like it or not, and should Kassandros win then he will kill him. Once he's done that what would stop the pockmarked bastard taking the crown himself? And then where would we be?'

Polyperchon took off his helmet and wiped his bald head with a cloth. 'That would be the worst of outcomes.'

'It makes Olympias seem like not too bad a ruler when it's put in that context.'

'Indeed; still, I'm pleased you did come back and take on overall command. Since my defeat before the walls at Megalopolis, I've come to realise my limitations as a military commander. I was happy as a phalanx commander but more than that, well…'

Aristonous' expression was one of regret. 'Yes, to lose most of your elephants to the simple expedient of spreading caltrops on the approach to the walls was unfortunate to say the least.'

'How was I to know?'

'By scouting; it's a tried and tested method.'

He's laughing at me.

'And then for it to happen at the same time as losing your fleet; that can be construed as carelessness. Had we a fleet and a reasonable elephant herd, we would be in a very commanding position.'

Polyperchon nodded in regretful agreement as the inspection continued and each man presented his commanding officer with his kit and rations for close scrutiny; Polyperchon had insisted there should be no man who was not perfectly fitted out – for him it was a matter of pedantic pride, and each shouted rebuke pleased him as it meant another step closer to administrative perfection. Rank after rank of the phalanx presented first their helmets, some painted white, blue or turquoise and some left plain bronze, for the strap and inner padding to be examined and ripped away if deemed inadequate; then the buckles on the hardened-leather, -linen or -bronze cuirasses underwent the same rigours and after that the belts – both shoulder and waist. Greaves and leather sandals were then similarly investigated, as well as the straps on the small round, bronze-plated shield with which it was slung over the man's left arm in a way that he was still free to wield his sixteen-foot pike with both hands and yet receive a degree of protection. And then the sword and dagger were tested for keenness and their scabbards for cleanliness and ease of draw. After that it was the turn of the kit bag to be rummaged through and each item – cloak, cup, cooking pot, spare tunic and all the other accoutrements of military life – accounted for and seen to be up to standard. The man's pike was the final piece of kit to be examined and if the blade was deemed sharp and rust free, the socket that joined the eight-foot halves together tight and clean, and the soldier had committed no other infringements during the inspection, he was left to breathe a sigh of relief whilst his comrade next to him was put through the same misery. Behind the infantry, the cavalry went through their own ordeal similar to that of their unmounted comrades but with the added burden of their horse and all its tack coming up to official expectations.

Polyperchon revelled in the exercise, as it took his mind off his failings as a general, and stayed for the duration – long after Aristonous had declared that boredom was eating away at his innards – riding up and down the ranks finding fault, if he could, with the slightest detail.

'This man's shoulder belt is very loose-fitting; have him on extra fatigues for ten days,' Polyperchon ordered the miscreant's commanding officer before looking down on the man next to him who was, in his eyes, equally as remiss in the state of his shield rim: the bronze coming away from the wood in a couple of places; he too received extra fatigues. And thus Polyperchon spent his day making his men's lives even more miserable as he sacrificed them on the altar of military perfection; and it was with a sense of great achievement he came into the throne room as the light faded, to report to Olympias.

'The army will be ready to march south tomorrow,' he announced, sitting down at the council table already occupied by Thessalonike, Aristonous and Monimus, newly appointed to be the commander of Pella in their absence. 'We'll pick up a further eight thousand men who have been mustered at Pydna, in a couple of days, along with whatever vessels we've been able to collect in the south.'

'Have we any idea how many ships we can expect?' Olympias asked, tapping the arm of her throne with a forefinger.

Polyperchon looked sideways at Aristonous and Monimus. 'I don't; do you?'

'No more than a dozen,' Monimus replied; young for his position, late twenties, he had been appointed purely because his family was one of the few in Pella against whom Olympias had no grudge.

Aristonous shook his head. 'However many there are, it won't be enough to turn back Kassandros' fleet.'

'Which means he will be able to send a force around our army by sea and effectively surround it,' Thessalonike pointed out. 'Or, for that matter, send his whole army by sea and bypass you completely so you would have to attack him from the south if you want to get back into Macedon. Have you thought about that, Polyperchon?'

Of course I have. Why does she always have to try to point out the flaws in everything? 'I had thought of it but consider it to be most unlikely.'

'Why?' Olympias demanded.

'Well, why would he risk taking to the sea at this time of year?'

'You said yourself he'll use his fleet to avoid our Aitolian allies holding the pass of Thermopylae against him.'

'But that's a necessity; he has to take that risk if he wants to come north.'

'What you mean to say, Polyperchon,' Aristonous interjected, 'is that *you* wouldn't take that risk. We don't know what Kassandros is or is not prepared to do because we have never seen him at the head of an army in the field before. Just because the man has not even killed his first boar doesn't mean we should underestimate him as a military commander; he may well surprise us.'

Polyperchon looked puzzled. 'But no one in their right mind would risk taking an army to sea at this time of year. Think of it: he would have to take the narrow passage between the island of Sciathos and the dangerous coast of Magnesia and then continue north along that coast with no shelter until you come to the mouth of the Peneus River on the Thessalian border; and we're more than a moon past the autumnal equinox.'

'I know; and we've already had a few storms and it would make more sense to follow the road inland of Magnesia via Larissa and then meet up with the fleet again at the Peneus, but we can't be sure he will. You say no one in their right mind would take the risk; well, I say one part of the art of being a good general is to do the unexpected and the other two parts are doing it quickly and being lucky.'

He made me look a fool; but he's right: I was thinking about what I would do. 'What do you suggest then?'

Aristonous was in no doubt. 'We split our force. We'll leave a small force in Amphipolis guarding our eastern border should Antigonos send reinforcements by land to Kassandros. You go south as planned with the main bulk of the army, including the remaining elephants, but advance no further than the Peneus in case he does take the sea route and you miss him. I'll stay behind you with, say, five thousand men so if he lands his army in your rear we can trap him between us. On the other hand, if he marches through Thessaly and then embarks a small force at the Peneus to get behind you, I can deal with that smaller landing, whilst you take on his main force.'

'But then I have to face him alone.' *And have to make tactical decisions.*

Olympias turned to Aristonous. 'He's right; it should be you who leads the main army and Polyperchon should command the smaller force.'

Aristonous shook his head. 'With the main army it is just a question of going south and finding good ground to fight a pitched battle against Kassandros; but whoever commands the smaller force has to be able to make quick and bold decisions that our survival may well depend on.'

'Meaning he can't.'

Aristonous did not reply but, rather, shrugged.

I've never claimed to be a leader.

Olympias studied Polyperchon for a few moments, as if she were examining an unpleasant-smelling creature of unsightly aspect. 'Very well, Aristonous, I agree to your plan; you command the smaller force. I myself will come with you as far as Pydna and take command of whatever ships we have there; they may not be enough to turn back Kassandros' fleet but they'll be sufficient to prevent him from taking the harbour if he tries a landing there. I'll bring the king with me; maybe the presence of Alexander's son and heir will cause Kassandros' men to have a change of heart.'

Polyperchon felt the weight of responsibility begin to press down upon his shoulders and panic to rise within. 'But surely dividing the army is a basic tactical error. Antipatros and Krateros did it and it resulted in Krateros' death.'

'And that's what Kassandros will think,' Aristonous countered, his voice overtly patient, 'which will make it even more likely he'll attempt to land behind you, and then we'll be ready for him.'

'And what if he decides to completely surprise us and not take the road or the sea route but strike inland and come to Pella from the west?' Thessalonike asked.

Polyperchon rubbed his bald pate. *All these questions; just tell me what to do and I'll do it but don't leave me in command of an army, not after Megalopolis.*

'Then we'll need to act fast in coordination with Aeacides and his Eperiot army whom we'll leave in the west to counter that very move,' Aristonous replied. 'But first we need to find out what Kassandros is doing and we won't be able to do that until the armies are close enough for our spies to make contact.'

Olympias rose from the throne. 'Then we must hurry; sitting here and talking about what may or may not happen won't get the job done. I want Kassandros, and his two surviving brothers, dead by the full moon.'

Polyperchon felt sick; there was nothing he could do but go along with the plan, for to run away and seek shelter with his son in the south would bring shame upon him, and the eternal enmity of Olympias.

And so it was with a sense of relief, two days after leaving Pella with a force of twelve thousand men, that he reviewed the muster at Pydna, as it gave him an opportunity to once again indulge in what he excelled in: pedantry. By the time the combined force of over twenty thousand men were back on the march south there were very few who had not witnessed at first-hand what a martinet their new commander was, and grumbled about it whilst they were forced to do extra fatigues at the end of the day's march for some minor infringement involving a sandal strap or a peeling shield rim.

'The men are very disgruntled, sir,' Annias, who had been selected by Aristonous to be Polyperchon's second-in-command, informed him on the evening of the third day out from Pydna. 'There's too much attention to the detail of their appearances for their liking; they're not used to it.'

'I'm not asking them to like it; they must submit to it.'

In his late forties, Annias had worked his way up from the ranks, and was well aware of the thoughts and grievances of the common soldier. 'They understand there has to be a degree of inspection but it is very difficult to keep kit immaculate as if it's just been issued. The old sweats are complaining they've never seen it so strict, and my officers are telling me they don't like it one bit as the lads are blaming them for their misery as much as you.'

'Annias, I will have my men smartly turned out. If they kept their equipment clean and in good repair they would have nothing to gripe about.'

'There must be some leniency.'

Polyperchon drew himself up. 'I will not allow standards to slip in my army, Annias. Other generals may be lax in their approach to turnout, I know, I've served under them, but I won't allow a similar lackadaisical attitude; a smart army is an efficient army and let that be an end to it.'

And so it was by the time Polyperchon had left Olympias with her small navy in Pydna and had led his men south to the border with Thessaly, in the shadow of Mount Olympus, more of his men were on fatigues than not.

'He's bypassed Thermopylae as we expected,' Polyperchon said to Annias after they had debriefed the four scouts who had come in overnight. 'He's landed his entire army on the coast by Lamia and is marching north with the fleet keeping pace with him.' Polyperchon slammed his palms down on the desk. 'You see, Annias; I told Aristonous that Kassandros would never risk travelling the whole way by sea. He's going to arrive here in a couple of days with twenty thousand men and I'll have to face him alone unless I can persuade Aristonous to come south. We've split our forces unnecessarily.'

Annias shrugged. 'Can you be sure Kassandros won't suddenly re-embark his army to bypass us? Perhaps that's why he's keeping his fleet alongside him?'

Polyperchon dismissed the notion with a petulant wave. 'Why would he do that having just disembarked them? No, he's marching north along the road through Thessaly and we'll meet him here with five thousand fewer men than we could have. I'll write to Aristonous immediately and stress the urgency of him bringing his men south.'

'I doubt whether he'll come,' Annias said, pulling a couple of scrolls from a satchel.

'What makes you say that?'

'He considers you've got adequate numbers to deal with Kassandros; or, at least, should have, had there not been so many desertions in the last few days.'

'Desertions?'

'Yes, desertions; running away, either home or to join the enemy.'

'I know what desertion means.' *Do they all think I'm an idiot?* 'How many have we lost?'

'Nearly a thousand in the march south.'

'A thousand! Why wasn't I told?'

'I'm telling you now, sir.'

'Why so late?'

'Because, sir, there was only a trickle at first.' Annias consulted one of his scrolls. 'Twenty or thirty a night; but three nights ago we lost almost a hundred and then the following night another hundred, but then, last night it was over five hundred including an entire ile of Companion Cavalry, all two hundred of them, and a *syntagma* of two hundred and fifty-six phalangites, both units with all their officers.' He handed the scroll to Polyperchon.

'Five hundred? That's impossible!'

'Is it?'

'Why are they doing this? Where's their loyalty to Macedon? We're meant to be saving her from invasion.'

'Are we? Or are we just trying to keep a ruthless, power-crazed woman ruling over the country with an army that has more men on a charge than not, because of the unreasonable standard of turnout expected by its general?'

Polyperchon rose from his seat, indignant. 'A smart army is an efficient army, Annias.'

'As you keep on repeating, but no, sir, it's not. An efficient army is one where every man feels valued for his fighting ability and not the condition of his sandal straps. A smart army is only of interest to the finicky.'

'Are you saying my insistence on a smart turnout is contributing to the desertions?'

'Yes; the lads are being pushed too far for a cause most of them don't support and, what's more, this was found.' Annias handed Polyperchon the second scroll. 'And where there's one there are bound to be more all over the camp.'

Polyperchon opened it and read its contents, his eyes widening with each word. 'The bastard! He can't do this.'

'Why not? Offering money to the enemy to desert is common practice.'

'Yes, but this amount per man is outrageous. How can he afford it?'

'Does it matter if he can or can't? The fact is he's making the offer and to a lot of the lads it sounds much better than fighting in an army rigid with discipline for a woman who has just murdered a king and five hundred prisoners including Kassandros' brother, not to mention the desecration of Antipatros' family graves and the murders of his wife and their two youngest sons. What were their ages again? Two and four, wasn't it? When you look at it from the lads' point of view, Kassandros seems like the sensible choice.'

Polyperchon stared at his second-in-command, aghast. 'Unless we do something, the whole army will be deserting to him.'

KASSANDROS.
THE JEALOUS.

'IF OLYMPIAS IS in Pydna with a dozen ships and a small garrison, where's Aristonous and his subsidiary force?' Kassandros asked.

The *chiliarch* of the *syntagma* of Companion Cavalry, who had deserted Polyperchon two nights previously, took a couple of sips of wine, looking in turn at each of his five interrogators sitting around the table in Kassandros' tent. He contemplated the question. 'It took us all yesterday and most of today to reach you from Polyperchon's camp to the south of Heracleum on the Thessalian border, that's about twenty leagues. Messengers who travel between Polyperchon and Aristonous usually take three days to complete the round trip; however, they're very tight-lipped about where exactly they've been. But I do know they have to pass through Pydna, which is just over a day to the north of Heracleum if you're using the messenger relay.'

'How do you know they pass through Pydna, Menelaos?' Pleistarchos asked, reaching over and refilling the officer's cup.

'Ah, well. That's because they never use messengers who come from around Pydna; it's always lads from Pella or other parts of the country who get the job. They aren't tempted to take a few hours out to go and see their families or sweethearts and then claim the horse went lame and they had to walk it to the next station, if you know what I mean.'

Kassandros nodded and rubbed his chin. 'Yes, I see; that's an interesting point.' *I'll make a mental note of that; you can't trust anyone.*

'So Aristonous is somewhere beyond Pydna,' Philip said.

Menelaos inclined his head. 'I would say he's to the north of Methone, which is about a three-hour ride north of Pydna, and my guess is that he's inland.'

'What makes you say that?' Atarrhias asked. Of an age with Kassandros, he was everything that his commander was not: broad, dark and rugged; a life-long natural soldier.

'Because they would be using ships to communicate, not mounted messengers,' Crateuas answered before Menelaos could reply; he looked at the cavalry officer with respect. Older and more grizzled than his colleague, Crateuas had served with Antigonos throughout his tenure as satrap of Phrygia, thus had not been a part of Alexander's great adventure, unlike Atarrhias – or, indeed his, Crateuas', son, Alexander's former bodyguard Peithon, now the satrap of Media, who shared his father's physical prowess if not his intellect. Crateuas looked at the rudimentary map spread out on the table and pointed to Methone and then to a crudely drawn depiction of a mountain. 'That's Mount Olympus; north of it is Mount Pierus, part of the Cambunian Range that heads west all the way to Epirus.' He then traced his finger north along the coast until it came to a river. 'That's the River Haliacmon skirting to the north of Mount Pierus, and then following the course of the Cambunian Range through the region of Eordaea. If Aristonous is inland, he will need a good water supply and this would be it. Now, I come from Eordaea and if I remember correctly from my youth there's a small town about two leagues from the coast called Alorus; I would wager he's camped there. It's perfect for taking us in the rear should we try to land a force behind Polyperchon. It's also well placed to relieve Pella or Pydna if we were to make a landing at either. What's more, it has reasonable connections with the west of Macedon where Aeacides is lurking with his Eperiot army. Here Aristonous, who, let's face it, is in overall command of the enemy, can keep in contact with his two sub-generals. He's the one we need to get. After that everything will fall into place.'

'And how do you recommend we do that?' Kassandros asked, agreeing with his general's assessment.

Crateuas looked at the map and rubbed the back of his neck, musing upon the issue, and then indicated to Menelaos to leave them. 'We're here at Larissa on the Peneus River,' he said, pointing to the main town in Thessaly. 'Aristonous is expecting us to do what every army travelling either to or from Macedon always does: keep to the road that heads north-east back to the sea. Once it passes to the north of Mount Ossa, at the head of the inaccessible coastline of Magnesia, it brings us to Heracleum, where Polyperchon awaits us in an excellent position with the sea on his left flank and the foothills of Mount Olympus to his right. When we're back at the coast Aristonous expects us to use the fleet, embarking a force at the mouth of the Peneus to get around Polyperchon in order to attack his rear; to counter that he remains inland to the north.'

Crateuas glanced around his audience to check they were all following his reasoning; satisfied, he continued: 'So we make Aristonous think he's anticipated our moves correctly and then do something completely different. We divide our force into three.'

Kassandros was astounded. 'Three? I thought it was the height of folly to split an army.' *Is he trying to sabotage me?*

'Normally I would agree with you, sir; but consider this: we've already had nearly a thousand deserters from Polyperchon joining us, and the money you've offered will bring many more. He may have twenty thousand or so men but those numbers will reduce daily. It's in our interest to delay facing him. So what I suggest is we send seven thousand men, slowly, towards him, have them rendezvous with the fleet and go through the motions of embarking as if we are going to do exactly what's expected of us. Meanwhile, we head north, as fast as we can, to this river.' He pointed to the Europus River, a tributary of the Peneus. 'We follow that to its source in a pass in the Cambunian Range. At this time of year the pass should still be negotiable; it'll bring us down past the town of Phylacae to the River Haliacmon to the west of Aristonous, cutting him off from his Eperiot allies. We leave Atarrhias with a holding force of three or four thousand men to prevent Aeacides coming to Aristonous' aid, and then take him in the rear with eight thousand men to his five. Even if Polyperchon still has an army by then – which I doubt – the news of Aristonous' defeat will bring most of the rest over to us and Macedon will be yours.'

He makes it sound so simple. 'How long will it take us to get to the Haliacmon?'

Crateuas pursed his lips. 'If we move fast we could be there in three days and then be at Alorus in another three, before Aristonous realises the fleet is a feint.'

'Issue the men with six days' rations.'

And it was with a heart beating swift with nervous excitement that, six days later, Kassandros peered over the crest of a rock-strewn hill and looked down onto the town of Alorus bathed in soft dimming sunlight; there, outside its long-shadowed walls, stood Aristonous' camp exactly where Crateuas had predicted it would be. 'They still have no idea we're here. We should take them in their camp and not chance a set-piece action.'

Crateuas scrutinised the position for a few moments. 'I agree, sir.'

Kassandros smiled to himself: achieving his goal was that much closer; in fact, it was tantalisingly within sight. Leaving Philip and Pleistarchos, under the watchful eye of their kinsman Callas, to command the feint to the coast, he had led his army north as Crateuas had suggested. He had driven the men at a blistering pace and they had complied willingly, for they trusted their two generals, Crateuas and Atarrhias. Having reached the Haliacmon, Atarrhias was left with three thousand men to intercept any aid or messengers coming from Aeacides in the west on the Epiriot border. Kassandros and Crateuas had crossed the river on rafts with the horses swimming alongside, and moved east at speed with mounted patrols screening the advance and killing or capturing any rider found upon the road. Total secrecy had been kept; their attack would be a surprise.

'We must move fast,' Crateuas said in a hushed tone, crawling back down the hill. 'The longer we leave it the more chance we have of being spotted by a foraging party.'

'We go in at dawn,' Kassandros said to his assembled officers gathered around him; no tents had been pitched nor fires lit in the makeshift camp, two leagues from Alorus. 'Crateuas will take in the infantry, the heavies in dispersed order, just swords and shields, to surround the camp as the light troops and peltasts sweep through it. I'll stand back with the cavalry ready to contain any attempt to break out.' He searched a few eyes to see if anyone registered surprise at him taking the lesser – and safer – role. *Good, they don't know my weakness; I'll endeavour to keep it that way.* 'Now remember, the objective is to kill as many of them as possible so as to scare the rest of the army of Macedon into submission.'

'These are our fellow countrymen, sir,' Menelaos objected. 'Many of our lads will have kinsmen in that camp, especially those recently come over to you.'

'And I want them dead.' Kassandros held the man's stare but he did not back down.

'If you kill more than necessary,' Crateuas whispered in his ear, 'you'll be setting yourself up for many blood-feuds and your life will be in constant danger long after this is over.'

Maybe he has a point. But how can I back down now without losing face?

'May I make a suggestion, sir?' Crateuas asked out loud.

Kassandros gave a curt nod.

'Just kill those who show any resistance; remember, Olympias murdered your kinsman Nicanor and his men in cold blood; we need to appear better than her.'

This is intolerable, I'll have to give ground otherwise my order will just be ignored. It was through gritted teeth Kassandros said: 'Just get me Aristonous.'

The moon had long since set and the only light in the sky was a faint glow to the east. Kassandros mounted his horse at the head of a column of two thousand cavalry, who had walked their animals the two leagues to Alorus in the slow hours since midnight. Slow, too, had been their progress but it had also been quiet. Ahead of them, Crateuas' infantry, divided into two units side by side, walked in open order. All extraneous kit had been removed. What did remain was muffled with rags as far as possible. A soft breeze blew down from the foothills of the Cambunian Range to their right, wafting the clean scent of fresh running water, gurgling in the Haliacmon, whose course they followed. It swept away the tiredness Kassandros knew he would normally be feeling, having been awake all night after six such gruelling days. But it was not solely the quality of the air that invigorated him: the prospect of revenge was creeping ever closer. All those sleights, insults and humiliations would be assessed, weighed and paid back with interest. The notion kept him warm despite the pre-dawn chill.

Ahead the sky began to glow with more vigour so the outline of distant hills could soon be made out: black in contrast to deep purple. Here and there birds chirruped, welcoming in the new day. And then the first tower on the walls of Alorus etched itself against a reddening sky. Now, Kassandros knew, events would have to move swiftly. And as the thought crossed his mind, the infantry broke into a jog, splitting apart as one command veered left, to circle inland around the town, and the other, under Crateuas, swept underneath the walls along the river, through the fish markets and river port, attracting the cries of those already awake and at their work. But Kassandros was not concerned now by the shouts of a few people; that would be nothing unusual for the time of day. He kicked his horse forward to circle around the town, outside the arc of the infantry, to provide the cordon that would seal off any escape to the coast for Aristonous' trapped army.

His horse changed from a trot to a gentle canter – the light insufficient for faster progress – and the breeze began to tug at his cloak. A knot started to form in Kassandros' stomach, a knot of fear. The same feeling that beset him every time he neared danger. He could not fight it, that much he knew. He could but steel himself and try to hold his limbs rigid to prevent them shaking and advertising his mounting trepidation.

On he led his cavalry, through the growing light, clearing the northern walls of Alorus and coming to within sight of torches burning within Aristonous' camp. And the torches betrayed movement, much movement, as they flickered dark and bright with the passing of many figures before them. To keep his mind from his fear, Kassandros strained his eyes towards the camp. Through the gloom he could now make out a cordon of heavy infantry around the periphery. And then the first cries of pain and terror broke on the dawn air.

Surprise was complete.

Faster he pushed his mount as the light grew and footing became surer. Behind him his men followed. The wound in his right leg throbbed with the effort of clamping his thighs and calves against the flanks of the horse and letting his feet dangle free. The pain added to his intensifying terror. He gritted his teeth and prayed it would all be over soon.

Screams were now the constant backdrop to the beating of hooves upon firm ground and flames now raged, consuming tents and soaring above the camp. Figures, silhouetted by fire, struggled in combat, in pairs or groups, tangled in mortal conflict as the tide of the assault swept through the encampment.

Kassandros veered to his right, judging he had reached beyond the furthest eastern extent of the camp, heading for the river. After a few hundred paces he slowed his mount, raising his fist in the air, and then brought the beast to a halt. 'Form up on me here!'

The order was relayed through all the units; within a few moments a wall of horseflesh, four deep, blocked any escape towards the rising sun, now bursting over the horizon in a symbolic daytime rendering of the sixteen-point star-blazon of Macedon. *This surely is a sign*, Kassandros mused as he turned his head to look at the wonder, squinting his eyes against the deep red rays. At the sight he felt the knot within him slacken.

He looked to his left and saw Menelaos and his men next to him. To his right were more heavy lancers, their helms gleaming pearl-like in the dawn light. Steam issued from the nostrils of their mounts as they shook their heads and stamped their hooves, tack jangling in the still air. A light mist swirled above the river and thinly carpeted the ground to either side.

Turning back to the smoke-hazed camp he was aware of a lessening of the clamour of battle. Here and there, groups of prisoners were being led out from the destruction and made to kneel in long lines. Resistance, it seemed, had failed. Kassandros began to relax.

It was but a few shouts at first but then the noise grew into a cacophony of cries, equine screeches and hoof-beats. On they came, scores of riders out of the camp, crashing through blazing tents and fleeing figures, heads low over their beasts' necks, legs pumping to encourage their mounts into greater effort in order to escape their overrun encampment. Out past the infantry cordon they burst, knocking aside all within their path, their numbers growing as more escaping cavalry gravitated in their direction. Backlit now by flames and facing directly into the rising sun, they glowed a fiery red; mythological creatures from the depths of time. At least, that was how Kassandros saw them in his terror as they barrelled directly toward him. *What do I do? How do I not run?* There was no time. They were scarcely a hundred paces away, forming into a rough wedge formation, lances or swords waving in the air that carried their cries of rage to Kassandros, piercing him to his core. All around him, orders were being shouted as officers urged their charges into a trot to combat the frantic incoming charge. Menelaos' men moved forward, leaving Kassandros still, panic rising in his gorge, his bladder beyond control. The troopers behind him moved forward, passing to either side; to

65

turn and run would be to pass through them, declaring his cowardice for all to see.

It was then, with the threat but fifty paces away, he saw what he should do. He pulled on his mount's reins, causing the beast to rise up on its back legs, as if it were out of control, and at the same time move to its left. Again he hauled on the reins, making a show of struggling to restrain his horse as he urged it away from the line of contact, into Menelaos' lancers now all moving forward, disordering their ranks and creating a gap where he had been as horses shied away from his rearing mount. His terror transferred itself through to the animal and, already skittish from rough handling, it reared again, high and abrupt, casting Kassandros from the saddle to thump to the ground amid a forest of equine legs.

A hurricane swept through as the escapees hurtled into his disordered men, knocking them aside as the point of the wedge penetrated deep in the gap Kassandros had created and then expanded, widening the rend, forcing passage, driven by desperation.

Scrabbling on his knees, Kassandros fled for his life, negotiating moving legs and then rolling beneath bellies to scramble another few paces. All around him, panic ensued as the wedge burst through the rear of the formation into the open ground beyond.

And none chased them for there was no one to order them to do so.

And so through they passed, unharmed by their foes, a stream of fugitives, hundreds, some naked for they had been roused from their beds; and as they departed so did the pressure within Kassandros' ranks ease and he was able to rise to his feet and push through the confusion in search of his horse and of a reasonable excuse for his behaviour.

'The brute threw me,' Kassandros explained to Crateuas as they met by the long lines of prisoners. 'One moment I was going forward and the next I was on my arse.'

Crateuas looked at his commander, his face neutral, and offered no opinion on his misfortune. He pointed to the prisoners. 'Aristonous is not amongst them so I assume he was leading the breakout.'

Kassandros nodded. 'I believe he was.'

'How did they get through? They were totally outnumbered.'

'I don't know; but I've a shrewd idea. I want Menelaos arrested if he's still with us and not fled with his friends; I'm sure he was shouting to let them through. Someone was and they did get through us far too easily.'

Crateuas frowned. 'Why didn't you send men after them? We might have been able to pick a few off, even get them all; there couldn't have been more than three or four hundred of the bastards.'

Kassandros bridled at being asked questions on his conduct. 'We deal with the situation as it is. How many prisoners have we got?'

'About four thousand, I'm told; and most are willing to sign up with us.'

'Execute a few of the unwilling and see if that changes the others' minds. Do it quickly as I want to move east to come up behind Polyperchon as fast as possible. Bring Menelaos to me when you have him.'

'You know perfectly well that I didn't shout anything of the sort,' Menelaos said, a sneer on his face as he stood, between two guards, before Kassandros and Crateuas. 'You also know perfectly well that Aristonous only escaped because you yourself moved aside, creating a small gap in our formation that the tip of the wedge penetrated.'

Kassandros scoffed at the accusation. 'My horse panicked and began rearing.'

'Really? Some of my lads say you were doing it on purpose.'

'I'll not listen to this nonsense. I heard you shouting to let them through, and through they went; that's good enough for me.' He pointed an accusatory finger at Menelaos. 'You were the one who was squeamish about killing too many of them. You were the one who said there were a lot of the men with kin in the enemy's ranks. Did he not, Crateuas?'

'He did,' Crateuas confirmed in a tone that was less than enthusiastic.

'I'll not have treachery in my ranks. Take him away and execute him.'

Menelaos spat at Kassandros' feet as he was hauled off. 'It'll take a lot more than killing me to silence the rumours about you shying away from a fight, Kassandros. Because that's what it was, wasn't it? Shying away.'

'My horse panicked!'

'Of course it did,' Menelaos shouted over his shoulder as he was pulled out of the tent. 'Because it knew it was about to go into battle with a coward on its back.'

Kassandros turned to Crateuas. 'Find out who it was in Menelaos' unit spreading lies about me; I want them punished.'

Crateuas looked at Kassandros, doubt in his eyes. 'Is that wise, sir? They're going to be angry enough that Menelaos has been executed without interrogating each one as to who said what.'

'Just do it.'

Crateuas' expression was blank; he departed without a word.

He doesn't believe me. Gods curse this affliction; I need to do something that'll put an end to the rumour. Kassandros took a deep breath and closed his eyes. *Either that or conquer my fears.*

It was still with trepidation that Kassandros beheld the army formed up outside Pydna, in the shadow of Mount Pierus with Mount Olympus looming beyond it, as they headed south along the coast on the second day out from Alorus.

'Our scouts are certain it's Polyperchon who has joined up with Olympias and the Pydna garrison?' he asked Crateuas, riding next to him.

'They say so.'

'What makes them so sure?'

'There are a couple of elephants. Only Polyperchon in Europe has elephants.'

'But he had at least a dozen left after his defeat at Megalopolis. What happened to the rest?'

Crateuas shrugged. 'I've no idea.'

'And nor do you care by the sound of it.'

Crateuas shrugged again.

Kassandros ignored the insolence. With Atarrhias still behind them, covering their rear against a surprise attack by Aeacides, he needed Crateuas, however much their relationship had deteriorated since the execution of Menelaos. Menelaos' men had stuck together and none had admitted spreading any rumours about Kassandros' conduct on the day of the raid. Yet he still felt there was a degree of malicious gossip circulating in his army, now bulked by the four thousand prisoners signed into its ranks.

But even with the extra men, his numbers only amounted to twelve thousand and the force facing him was at least that amount, if not more; and Kassandros needed to be sure of victory. He shaded his eyes. 'They're sending out a delegation; they want a parley.'

Crateuas remained silent.

And it was with growing relief that Kassandros watched the delegation approach; relief because as it came nearer he recognised the figures of his twin half-brothers.

'Polyperchon withdrew into Pydna with what was left of his army yesterday,' Philip said. 'You've just missed them. A pity, as together we would have crushed him. Over half of his men had come over to us already; we even got a couple of elephants.'

'He had to go before the rest joined us,' Pleistarchos said.

Kassandros stared at the twins. 'If he went into Pydna yesterday, why are you here? Why haven't you started building siege lines?'

'We were only just arriving when our scouts reported your position,' Philip said. 'We weren't sure if it was you, Aristonous or Aeacides so we thought we ought to form up for safety's sake.'

'Only just arriving? What kept you? Why weren't you harassing Polyperchon every step of the way?'

'His men were deserting in droves; it seemed to us pointless killing men who could just as well be fighting for us. We were integrating the new arrivals into our ranks, splitting them up and spreading them about so as not to have less reliable units. We only began to move north two days ago.'

'And in the meantime, Polyperchon's got safely into Pydna and could sail away with at least some of his more loyal men.'

Philip shook his head. 'The fleet's been blockading the harbour ever since he went in. Also, we gave orders that every evening they should send men into Pydna to persuade more to desert. About a hundred came out last night; soon he'll hardly have enough men left for a personal guard.'

'Olympias will shortly have nothing left to fight with,' Pleistarchos added.

And Kassandros could see the truth of it as he looked over to Philip and Pleistarchos' men. He felt the excitement growing within him for now he had a real army, just shy of thirty thousand including Atarrhias' men, and it was still growing. Now he had Macedon in his grasp. 'Well, we had better start building; there's no time to lose.'

'Building what?' Pleistarchos asked.

'A wall around Pydna; we're going to trap that harpy, Olympias, in her lair.'

OLYMPIAS.
THE MOTHER.

O LYMPIAS LOOKED OUT from the tower atop Pydna's gatehouse at the scene unfolding before the town: the parley taking place between the two armies. And it was with a growing sense of foreboding she watched, for the army she had hoped was Aristonous' was far larger than it should have been. Unless Aeacides had linked up with it, there was only one conclusion to be drawn.

'If that's Kassandros' fleet blockading our port,' she said, turning to Polyperchon and Thessalonike next to her, and pointing to the ships rocking at their stations on a sun-sparkled, bronze sea, 'then it can't have transported a large force around us. And you are sure Kassandros wasn't with the army that chased you, to your everlasting shame, so disgracefully back into Pydna, Polyperchon? You are sure of that at least, aren't you?'

Polyperchon, smarting from the ceaseless jibes and insults he had received since his arrival in Pydna the previous day, closed his eyes and took a deep, calming breath. 'Yes, that army was commanded by his younger twin half-brothers, Philip and Pleistarchos, along with their older kinsman, Callas, left to keep an eye on the two youngsters.'

'Youngsters! Yes, you've said it: you were whipped by young-sters.' Olympias hissed at him in contempt before turning her attention back to the newly arrived army. 'Then I can only assume that's either Aristonous reinforced by Aeacides, which is unlikely given Aeacides' desire not to stray too far from Epirus, or Kassandros has somehow got to the north of us by another way.'

The parley broke up and horns blared out from the newly arrived army as it began to move forward in column rather than form into line of battle, and Olympias' worst fears were confirmed. *It must be Kassandros; I'm cornered. Still, better here than in Pella; and I still have the king with me, which might well count for something.* She turned to her adopted daughter. 'What's the state of our supplies, Thessalonike?'

'Water in the two wells is plentiful,' Thessalonike replied without looking at Olympias. 'The granaries are full and, including the supplies that Polyperchon brought in with him, we have enough to last the population and the troops for the winter and enough fodder for the horses and elephants for that time as well. In spring we'll have to start eating them, though.'

'And what if we just feed the troops and let the population fend for themselves?'

'Then the army alone might be able to hold out until midsummer, if we're lucky; although the horses and elephants won't make it that far.'

The question is do I reduce their rations bit by bit or do I refuse the citizens food right from the beginning and hope we can last long enough to break out or until Eumenes sends relief? Olympias contemplated the situation as she watched Kassandros' army link up with that of his half-brothers on the narrow plain between the coast and the foothills of Mount Pierus, just out of artillery range. Amid cheers, much embracing and slapping of backs, the men, thousands of them, greeted one another before the walls of Pydna as the final stage of the battle for Macedon began.

She did not notice it at first but from the milling crowds a horseman emerged; swiftly he traversed the open ground towards the gate, his head low along his mount's neck, the flat of his sword beating the beast into even greater exertion. 'Open the gates,' Olympias cried, as her eye fixed on the fleeing rider. 'Bring him to me in the throne room as soon as you can, Polyperchon. Thessalonike, come with me.' She turned on her heel and hurried away.

'Defeated! What do you mean defeated?' Olympias' serpentine eyes drilled into Aristonous, covered in the dust of travel, sitting with Thessalonike and Polyperchon at the council table.

'I mean Kassandros got around behind us and, in a surprise attack just before dawn, overran my camp and killed or captured most of my men. I managed to break out with about four hundred cavalry; I sent them on to Pella and then I infiltrated Kassandros' army in order to report the disaster to you in person. That's what I mean by defeated.'

Olympias hissed, her hands tight on the arms of her throne, knuckles white. 'How did you let that happen?'

'He was clever. He sent a feint to the coast to meet up with his fleet. Polyperchon sent me regular reports – as I'm sure he did to you – saying Kassandros was doing exactly what I expected him to do; so I let him do it. Never interrupt the enemy when he's making a mistake. Only he wasn't making a mistake, he was keeping me occupied, staring at his right, whilst, on the left, he came over a pass in the Cambunian Range and got behind me without my knowledge.'

'But surely you had scouts.'

'He must have captured or killed them all; nothing came in from Aeacides for three days before Kassandros attacked.'

'Aeacides? What news of him?'

Aristonous shook his head, forlorn. 'The last I heard he was still on the western frontier; however, I was told that a lot of his men are getting restless and want to go home; some have already deserted. They don't understand the point of sitting around on a hill doing nothing with winter approaching.'

'They should do as they're told.'

'They won't, that's the problem. Aeacides is weak. Without you with him, bolstering the army's morale, it gets restless. I don't think you can rely on him coming to our aid, even if Kassandros hasn't left a force to prevent that, which I very much believe he would have done. I completely underestimated him just because he has no battle experience as a commander. It was an elementary mistake.'

'One you accused me of,' Polyperchon pointed out.

'Pah! Enough, old man,' Olympias snapped. 'Slinking in here with your tail between your legs and more than half your men deserted to the enemy means you've no right to criticise anyone.'

'Reminding people of their failings is not going to get us anywhere, Olympias,' Thessalonike said in measured tones. 'At least he still has part of his army.'

She never calls me mother any more; not since I slapped her. I must try to regain her trust.

'How many men do you have left, Polyperchon?' Aristonous asked.

'Eight thousand,' Polyperchon said without relish.

'And with the forces we still have in Pella and the garrison I left in Amphipolis against Antigonos attempting to send reinforcements overland, plus the smaller garrisons from places like Apollonia and Aegae, we could still put over twenty thousand into the field. We could stop him yet, provided we can break out by either land or sea.'

Olympias tapped the arm of her throne with increasing impatience. 'And how do we do that?'

'Alexandros,' Aristonous replied.

Polyperchon looked at him in disbelief. 'He won't want to bring his army north, just ten thousand of them to face almost thirty.'

'You'll have to make him,' Aristonous said. 'We need him to come north in the spring and join forces with us, which would bring our combined number up to around thirty thousand as well. It's too late in the year now, therefore early next year is the time we need to muster all the available troops we have, down to the very last man.'

Olympias chewed on her lip, deep in thought. 'Very well; we risk leaving the approach from Thrace open; it shouldn't be for too long. Aristonous, you go north and collect the Apollonia garrison and all the others up there over the winter. Have them ready to fall back on here as soon as Alexandros arrives. Polyperchon, you can redeem yourself by bringing your son and his army up from the south as early in spring as possible. We'll sneak you both out by boat as soon as we have a favourable moon and an overcast sky. If we can manage to time a breakout with Alexandros supporting us from the south and the garrisons from the north hitting him from behind, we'll rip the balls off that murdering son of a toad. Earth Mother, grant me my desire.'

And it was Gaia, the Earth Mother, to whom Olympias sacrificed soon after in hope of her desire being satisfied, giving the goddess the blood of a black lamb as the priestesses chanted her slow, sacred hymn that echoed around the dimly lit, unpainted walls of the cavernous temple.

'Oh goddess, source of gods and mortals, all-fertile, all-destroying, Gaia, mother of all who brings forth bounteous fruits and flowers of all variety; mother who anchors the eternal world in our own; immortal, blessed and crowned with every grace.'

But it was alone she sacrificed, she reflected, as the priest-esses continued the hymn and the blood of the lamb drained into the silver bowl set before the altar. *If Thessalonike continues to refuse my invitations to sacrifice with me I'll be forced to consider her loyalty as suspect. But enough of her.* 'Come, blessed goddess, and hear the prayers of your children.'

However, throughout the ceremony her mind kept returning to the subject of her now-distant adopted daughter. Olympias could find no peace in, nor gain any comfort from, her devotions and, indeed, felt no closeness to the goddess as she had always done when worshipping her together with Thessalonike. As the rites continued, Olympias' focus wandered and she grew impatient, wanting the final dedication to come, forcing herself not to leave the temple early for she knew all the good she had achieved with her sacrifice would be null and void. *The harsh truth of the matter is I miss her friendship.* And it pained her for she realised the estrangement was of her own doing, and if they were ever going to bring their relationship back to as it was before the slap, it would involve her doing something she had never in her life done before: apologise. *Can I really ask her to forgive me without feeling humiliated? Impossible. But even so it is what I must do if I'm not to feel completely alone now my daughter Kleopatra remains in Sardis. I need her strength.*

And so it was that Olympias sought out Thessalonike in her rooms at the conclusion of the ceremony.

'You're sorry?' Thessalonike looked at her adoptive mother in open-mouthed bewilderment. 'You're telling me you are actually sorry you slapped and humiliated me before the entire population of Pella?'

Olympias swallowed her rising fury. *Why does she have to make this worse for me than it already is?* 'Yes, I am. I can see it has come between us and I would like it not to.'

'Oh, you would, would you? And why would that be? Because it doesn't suit your needs for me not to be the obliging little daughter any more?' Thessalonike stared Olympias in the eye. 'You've spent your life thinking only of yourself. I'm not saying that's a bad thing, in the final analysis everyone does it, but thinking only of yourself doesn't mean you can treat other people any way you like, especially people like me, the daughter of a king. What you did to me was unforgivable. I have never been so humiliated, never! If you want to have a comfortable mother and daughter relationship then your natural one is just across the sea in Sardis; go and seek Kleopatra out. Although, judging by the fact she has no real reason to be there any more, and might just as well be here in Macedon, I think her continued voluntary exile speaks volumes as to her desire to spend time with you.'

'How dare you speak to me like that when I came here to apologise for something I now regret!'

'You've never regretted anything in your life, Olympias, because everything you've done has been for yourself, so don't start pretending to do so now. You slapped me in public because you wanted to show me you could and I wouldn't be able to do anything about it; you did it because I was telling you the nasty truth. Well, Olympias, I *can* do something about it: I can carry on telling you the nasty truth, especially when you don't want to hear it and I can also make sure others are aware of a few facts concerning you.'

'Like what, for example?'

'Like what you're really doing here.'

'And what am I really doing here other than organising the defence of the port?'

Thessalonike smiled in disbelief. 'You really don't think your motives aren't transparent to me, do you? You're not here to take command of a little navy in order to save Pydna. No, not Pydna but, rather, yourself, should it all go wrong.' She pointed through the window, over the town walls to where Kassandros' combined armies were now setting up camp under a haze of cooking-fire smoke. 'As it seems it already has gone wrong. But you could've made a stand in Pella and yet you chose not to – why?'

'You tell me.'

'Because to escape Pella by ship you have to sail three leagues down a narrow inlet to the open sea, plenty of time to be intercepted; whereas here it's out of the harbour under the cover of a foggy night and, provided you can slip through the blockade, there you are, two days' sailing to Sardis and the protection of Kleopatra where you can start your scheming and plotting afresh. That's why you're here and I've made sure that both Aristonous and Polyperchon know the exact reason.'

'You little bitch!'

'Ha! So you don't deny it, do you, Olympias?'

'Why should I deny it to you? Yes, of course I have an escape plan in mind, and yes, it is easier to escape from here than it is from Pella, if you wish to go by sea. But that's not the main reason why I'm here, and giving that lie to my two generals is more than counterproductive, it's sabotage.'

Thessalonike looked at Olympias with suspicion. 'So tell me, *Mother dear*, what excuse have you given yourself for taking the safer option rather than remaining in the capital?'

With an intake of breath, Olympias shook her head and sat down on a well-appointed couch, leaning against its arm. 'Won't you offer me a drink?'

Thessalonike paused before clapping her hands and ordering a pitcher of wine from a slave-girl.

They waited in silence until its arrival.

'That's better,' Olympia said, placing her cup on the table whilst savouring the vintage. 'How much do we have, enough to see us through to next year?' She essayed a smile. 'We'll surely be needing it.'

Thessalonike was not to be warmed. 'If you refrain from your wilder, Bacchic excesses, it may just last. Now, Olympias, I've no wish for small talk with you; what do you want to tell me?'

'You're being too hard on me.'

'Not as hard as you are on everyone you have contact with.'

'You might think that's a fair point.'

'Just get on with it.'

'Very well.' Olympias paused for another sip. 'My safety, although it is always of utmost importance to me, was, in this case, a secondary consideration. It seemed, with the way we had this planned, we had a very high chance of success; I think even you would agree with that?'

Thessalonike inclined her head. 'I would. And I would also say, whatever you might think of Kassandros personally, it was a stroke of military genius coming through the Cambunian Range and dashing our plans with one move.'

'That'll always be a matter of regret. But I would not give the credit to Kassandros without being certain of the facts; he has some very able men with him. But I digress. I needed to be at Pydna, or rather I needed myself, the king and you to be at Pydna because Kassandros' army is borrowed from Antigonos. They are men who, in the main, have not been home to Macedon for years; some have been in Asia since Alexander first invaded, fifteen years ago. Now, say we defeated them, as we thought we would, what chance would there have been of swearing them into our army, to fight for us, truly fight for us with all their heart, when most of them now have wives and children over in Asia? Eh? Tell me.'

Thessalonike pursed her lips. 'Very little.'

'Very little indeed. Unless the mother, half-sister and son of Alexander were to appeal to them directly in the hour of their defeat. If we three were to have offered them a new life in Macedon, fighting for Macedon, imagine the army we would've had with them and our existing troops: it would have been enough to hold the Greek cities in check and then move across to Sardis and, with the addition of Kleopatra, we would've been the army of the family of Alexander; completely legitimate. No one could have stood against us and been morally in the right. We could have linked up with Eumenes and taken the empire.'

'And you could have had ultimate power; your son's power.'

Yes, that's always my dream.

'But now Eumenes has gone east so your dream is slipping away.'

'It can still happen when we break out of here; Eumenes will come back west.'

'He has no fleet and nor do we.'

'I'll capture Kassandros' fleet. As the mother of Alexander I'll appeal to them and they won't resist me.'

Thessalonike lowered her eyes as her shoulders began to shake. She looked up from her cup as a laugh escaped her. 'You just can't stop yourself, can you, all this scheming and plotting? And as you conspired to gain the Asian troops' loyalty, so you could rule the world, you forgot one thing, one tiny thing. Forget Kassandros' brilliant move, through it all you forgot the men you inherited in the army of Macedon are, in the main, men who were loyal to Antipatros and who were then transferred to a nonentity, Polyperchon, upon his death.' She paused for another burst of laughter. 'Why should they remain loyal to him and you in the face of Antipatros' son? That's where their loyalty is: to Antipatros' family; not to you, you who ordered the execution of Nicanor, the kinsman of Antipatros and Kassandros, and all of his followers. No, Olympias, they didn't feel a stronger loyalty to the mother of Alexander than they did to the son of the regent they had fought under for years.' Her mirth was now hard to control. 'All this relying on being the mother of Alexander, expecting it to make everything happen for you, is over. Most of Polyperchon's army, your army, deserted to Kassandros, whom you consider to be a pockmarked son of a toad, because they love him far more than they do you. How does that make you feel, Olympias?'

'Macedonians will always love the mother of Alexander!'

'Wrong, Olympias, they won't; not above all things, not any more. Times are different now: five years after his death, Macedonians are fighting Macedonians; you have only to look out the window to see the truth of that. Only Alexander could hold them all together and now as his memory fades so does their loyalty to him. They will re-attach themselves to what always bound them before Alexander: their tribal loyalties. Kassandros' men will always be Kassandros' men and Antigonos' will always be his, until they die or until someone offers them such a large bribe they can't refuse it. Just being the mother of Alexander doesn't count for much since this civil war started.'

Olympias jumped up, dashing her cup to the ground, shattering it, and strode to the window. The proof of what Thessalonike had said was staring her in the face. She clenched her fists and gritted her teeth, suppressing her rage; her heart beat fast as she reconciled herself to the veracity of all she had heard. In stages she calmed. Once she was mistress of her emotions again she turned to Thessalonike. 'So this is your vengeance, is it?'

Thessalonike smiled, ice in her eyes. 'Telling you the nasty truth? Yes, and it's a pleasure. I'll stay here and be with you and offer my advice, because I've nowhere else to go, as yet; but we will never be friends again, you and I, Olympias, not after what you did.'

I won't give her the pleasure of seeing my disappointment, the little bitch. 'Very well, if that's how you want it to be.' She turned, walked to the door and paused, looking over her shoulder. 'But remember this, Thessalonike: you are in my power. I can keep you here just as I keep Alexander and his eastern wild-cat of a mother.'

Thessalonike's ice-like smile had not thawed. 'Perhaps one day I'll test the truth of that.'

'Pah! You can try but you're as much my prisoner as Roxanna is.'

ROXANNA.
THE WILD-CAT.

I T WAS INTOLERABLE for a queen to be treated thus. Lamenting her lack of freedom, Roxanna paced her apartments – not nearly as lavish as her suite in Pella – high in the royal palace at Pydna; for, although she was technically allowed to leave her rooms to walk in the town, she could not do so without guards. Since she had poisoned the two men keeping her to her chambers during Alexander's betrothal, none of the other guards would volunteer and, much to her ire, were not forced to do so by their commanding officers. Therefore her only contact with the outside world was via her slaves, all of whom lived in fear, for all knew the lick of her whip and all had witnessed the sudden disappearance of colleagues who had seriously displeased their mistress.

Why is this taking so long? A queen should never be kept waiting. I'll have a finger off the girl when she gets back.

And the urgency of the girl's mission was clear to Roxanna. She had only to step out onto the terrace of her apartments to be aware of it: to look west was to see the beginning of a great palisade, now four days under construction, that would semi-circumvallate the harbour town from the north coast to the south coast. To look east was to see the fleet completing that circumvallation with their wooden walls. No, it was intolerable to be placed in such a position of danger. She had even thought she had seen Kassandros, the man who would have her dead should she fall into his clutches, surveying the town, and a cold dread had run through her. And how could she not become his victim, she wondered. Now that the siege was under way, who or what would prevent him from prevailing?

Thus it was obvious to Roxanna she had to escape and her escape must be soon, but her chances of success were slim and almost non-existent if she tried to take her son. But then what use was Alexander to her now? Now he had been stolen from her by Olympias, he no longer guaranteed her safety. No, it was best for her to leave him behind and for her to find another protector. She had to escape alone and tonight would be her best opportunity, for tonight there was no moon and clouds covered the sky. Tonight, she knew, Aristonous and Polyperchon would both attempt to break the blockade and leave by ship. And Roxanna intended to be on Aristonous' vessel; and what was more, she intended to have her revenge before she left. But to do that she needed the girl to arrive quickly for there was little time.

She went back to the table that acted as her work bench, scattered with small bowls full of various herbal and fungal ingredients, and leaned over to smell the contents at the bottom of a stone mortar, a mush of purplish red. Satisfied, she then ground it with a pestle. She sniffed it again. *That's about ready; where is the girl? The little bitch probably stopped off to get herself fucked by one of the guards, rubbing it in my face that no one comes near me.* She picked up the small, bulbous vial awaiting the results of her potion-making; her vengeance would be sweet. She stroked the vial's length with undue affection. When she was away from here she would finally have a man again for the first time since the half dozen nights that Alexander came to her chamber. Finally, after all this time of longing to feel the firm embrace of a man since Alexander's untimely death cut short her nascent sexual awakening, she would gain satisfaction. She had made up her mind. She would have Aristonous for she had found herself thinking of him since he had so dominated her during their flight from Pella.

A knocking on the door made her put down the vial, hook her veil across her face and turn. *At last; perhaps I'll let her keep her little finger after all.* 'Enter.'

The door opened to reveal a middle-aged woman and a child standing between the two guards always posted outside her door – guards who had learned from the fate of their two poisoned colleagues.

'Your son, as you commanded, Majesty,' the woman said, stepping forward with one arm around Alexander's shoulders.

'Leave us and wait outside.' Roxanna waved the nurse away, not even deigning to look at her. 'Guards, don't let anyone else in whilst I talk with my son. Come, Alexander.'

The boy looked up with anxious eyes at his nurse, who nodded encouragement as she turned and left; he stepped into the room.

The little brute always looks so scared when he's alone with me. 'Come and kiss your mother.' Roxanna unhooked her veil, stretched out her arms but made no attempt to kneel down to the child's level.

Alexander approached, his hesitancy obvious, and stood before her. She leaned over so he could plant a kiss on her cheek by standing on tiptoe.

'There, Alexander; that wasn't so painful, was it?'

He looked up at her, his dark eyes moist and full of trepidation. 'No, Mother. Are you well?' His voice shook.

'I am. Come and sit beside me.' She led him to a window seat, overlooking the great endeavour that was a siege wall under construction. 'What do you see out there, Alexander?'

The child looked out and thought for a moment. 'I see lots of men digging and banging on wood.'

'Yes, and do you know why they are doing that?'

Alexander looked up at her and shook his head.

'They are doing that to build a wall to stop us from leaving.'

'Why, Mother?'

'Because they are led by a very bad man, a nasty man, called Kassandros. He is a man who means me harm. He's having that wall built so I can't escape and eventually he hopes we'll all be so weak in here that he'll be able to knock down the gate and come and get me.'

'What will he do with you, Mother?'

'He'll kill me, child.'

Alexander did not seem to register much alarm at the prospect. 'Why?'

'Because he wants to have you all to himself; he wants you to be his king.'

'Will you let him?'

'I can't stop him, Alexander. It's inevitable.'

'It's what?'

'Inevitable: it can't be stopped. That's why I must leave.'

'Without me?'

'Yes.' She looked into her son's eyes. *He doesn't seem too upset about it.* 'Will you be brave?'

Alexander nodded his head and then frowned in deep thought. 'What will this nasty man do to me when he finds me?'

'He will keep you safe because you are the king.'

'Where will you go?'

'I can't say in case the nasty man makes you tell him your secrets.'

Alexander digested this and then nodded again.

'How will you escape?'

'Again, I can't tell you for the same reason. It might give him a clue where I'm going.'

'Will I see you again?'

I doubt you'll survive. 'Of course, as soon as the nasty man has been killed.'

'Who will kill him?'

'I can't tell you that either. But you must say goodbye to me and go now, for I have much to do.' She proffered her cheek once more and received a perfunctory kiss. 'You mustn't say a word about this, Alexander; not even after I'm gone must you say you knew I would escape. Do you understand?'

Alexander nodded once more and got to his feet. 'Goodbye, Mother,' he said without a trace of emotion and then walked to the door.

Roxanna followed him, reaching out a hand to ruffle his hair but withdrawing it before she had made contact. She replaced her veil, opened the door and gestured to the nurse to take the child and then ushered the waiting girl in, slapping her face before the door had even closed. 'Where have you been?'

The girl fought the reflex to put her hand to her cheek; Roxanna dealt her another blow.

'Where?'

'I'm sorry, Majesty, I was as quick as I could be.' She held out a small jug sealed with a stopper of rolled-up cloth.

Roxanna snatched it and slapped the girl a third time. 'Did you stop off to suck your boyfriend's cock? Is that what took you so long?'

The girl kept her eyes to the ground. 'No, Majesty, I swear I didn't.'

'Look at me.'

With reluctance the girl lifted her gaze; she could barely meet Roxanna's eye.

'You're lying, aren't you?' Another slap, this time fuelled by jealousy and frustration, laid the girl on her back, and with one kick to her belly Roxanna returned to her work bench, leaving the girl trying to contain her sobs.

Pulling out the cloth stopper, Roxanna held the jug to her nose. *Perfect.* Tipping it with care, she poured a dozen drops of the clear, viscous liquid into the mortar, added a good splash of oil and then gave the contents a vigorous stir with a wooden spoon.

As she waited for the mixture to settle so the infused oil could be reserved into her vial, she contemplated what she must do that evening. She had always been active in her youth, far away in the east, riding, climbing, helping her brothers to break in the new season's colts as well as practising with bow and spear with them – girls in her tribe were encouraged to be more than fetchers of water, cooks, seamstresses and washer-women – so the prospect of a long descent on a dangling rope did not daunt her. Indeed, she was looking forward to the adventure. Yes, she enjoyed playing the queen and acting with the dignity befitting the widow of the great Alexander, but she also yearned for the adventure of her younger days. This night would be the beginning of a new stage of her life, one where she would not live in a cocoon of luxury, fighting all the time for the recognition she deserved and being forever slighted and shunned.

She glanced over at the window; the light was fading. The girl had got up and was, with a colleague, awaiting her pleasure, kneeling at the far side of the room, just as Roxanna liked it. 'Go!' she ordered, waving them away with the back of her hand. 'And don't allow anyone to come in here until I give the word.'

The girls fled. Roxanna smiled to herself, enjoying the fear she inspired.

Seeing her potion had settled, she tipped the infused oil into the vial with great care and then wiped it clean before placing it back down on the bench next to a scroll. She untied the ribbon binding it, spread the scroll flat upon the table and with a childish hand wrote 'Olympias' at the top of the otherwise blank page. Turning it over, she took her vial and poured some of the contents onto the equally blank reverse before taking up a rag and rubbing the potion in. Rolling it up so 'Olympias' remained visible, Roxanna dipped the ribbon into the remaining contents of the vial before fastening it around the scroll with a bow, taking care to only make contact with the wet end with the tips of her thumb and forefinger which she washed, afterwards, with vigour in a bowl of water. Satisfied with her work, she placed the doctored scroll on the work bench and then cleared away the rest of the bowls and other detritus into a sack which she left beneath it. She picked up the vial to leave the scroll alone on the bench and smiled to herself at the thought of Olympias handling such a deadly thing.

Now, with her revenge prepared, it was time to ready herself.

The knot was secure, she had no worries on that account; climbing had been second nature to her in her mountainous homeland. She slung a bag across her shoulders, hooked her veil across her face and then lowered the rope over the terrace down, two storeys, into the courtyard in the darkness below; over the side she went, gripping the rope with fists, knees and ankles as she slid down with measured control.

At the sound of approaching voices, she froze, at the height of the first-storey window, shuttered against the night. She kept rigid as two guards strolled, at a leisurely pace, in her direction; with breath held she watched them approach. Immersed in an in-depth discussion of the inventiveness of a certain whore at a local tavern, the guards passed beneath her, one treading on the rope's end as he assured his mate that the lady in question's ability to arch her back right over so both feet and hands were on the ground made for a very stable platform upon which one could get good purchase, provided one could deal with the difference in height of the two relevant pieces of anatomy. With the question mooted as to which end it was best to approach whilst the lady was in such a position, the men receded discussing the relative merits of both but coming to no firm conclusions.

Roxanna let out her breath and waited for the footsteps to disappear, the muscles in her arms straining. Safe, she slid down the rest of the way.

With no sound, her feet touched the ground; she stepped back, pressing her back to the wall, and listened for a few moments before running, at a crouch, across the courtyard to the outer wall of the palace. Built so that the complex could be defended should the populace turn upon its masters, the wall had wooden steps leading up to the battlements. Up them she crept, pulling a coil of rope from her bag as she did. Checking left and right for guards along the wall, she moved forward to the far side and peered over the parapet down into the street, the height of three men below. People came and went but she had known that would be the case. Now speed was of the essence.

Attaching the rope to the frame of the steps, she threw it into the street. She scrambled down, much to the surprise of the few passers-by going about their business. Ignoring the looks and pointed fingers, Roxanna turned and walked away, at a pace that would excite no comment, in the direction of the harbour. None impeded her passage as she weaved her way through unknown streets dimly lit, if at all, hoping her sense of direction was up to the task of finding her objective.

It was the smell that told her first that she was close, the smell of decaying fish; on she went, now following her nose, down a narrow alley between two warehouses until she came out onto a quay crammed with boats and ships caught up in the blockade.

It was now solely a question of patrolling up and down, waiting to catch sight of her quarry. She had assumed nothing would happen until after midnight, but she had arrived early as she did not want to miss her one chance of freedom. It had been Aristonous who had spirited her out of Pella to Epirus to what she had thought would be the safety of Olympias' protection; in that hope she had been entirely disappointed. But during the journey – a time in which she had found herself enjoying the dominant, masculine character of an older man – she thought she had detected in Alexander's oldest bodyguard a level of attraction to her person and, perhaps, a degree of sympathy with her plight. It was upon that attraction and sympathy she intended to play. Indeed, she did not need to play, for she desired him more than she had desired any man, even Alexander, and she knew that desire would be irresistible to him and he would take her for his own to hold and keep safe, provided she could sneak herself onto whichever ship or boat Aristonous was using to run the blockade. And so, keeping to the plentiful shadows, she began her vigil.

It was the arrival, an hour later, of forty or so men who split and went aboard two sleek lembi that gave Roxanna the clue she needed. The small, undecked ships with twenty rowers apiece, whose speed made them ideal for blockade running, were moored at the furthest end of the quay, closest to the harbour mouth. As the men prepared their ships, slaves went around extinguishing all torches throughout the harbour and making sure all windows with light seeping from them were shuttered. Nothing was to be allowed to give away the positions of the escaping vessels. Slipping through the shadows, Roxanna made her way to a pile of old rope at the further end of the quay and awaited her chance to board once she knew which ship would take whom. Rats scuttled about her, unseen but not unfelt, forcing her to suppress a loathing of the creatures so deep it made her want to shriek.

Soft voices from along the quay heralded the arrival of Aristonous and Polyperchon in the almost complete darkness.

'I'll have to think long and hard about it,' Aristonous was saying as they came close enough for their words to be audible.

'Personally I don't believe we've a chance against what's camped outside the walls,' Polyperchon observed as Roxanna began to make out their vague figures. 'I think we'd be better off trying to come to some sort of accommodation with Kassandros rather than lose more men fighting him.'

'There would be no room for Olympias or the king in that scenario.'

'That could be seen as an advantage: two fewer things to fight about.'

'I cannot countenance Alexander's death.'

'Then we try to smuggle him out at a later date; with Olympias if necessary. But coming back here to fight is madness.'

'As I said, I'll consider what you say, Polyperchon; but even now I think maybe you're right: even if you do persuade your son to come north, Kassandros will hear of it and be able to block his progress in advance. Pydna is lost and Olympias would do well to try to make it to Sardis with Alexander. I'll wait in Amphipolis for your message as to how successful you've been in persuading Alexandros to come north before I bring my troops south in the New Year.'

Interesting; I'll make sure he has no wish to return here. The thought excited her; she was soon to have a man once more and she would make sure that he had no wish to stray far from her bed.

Aristonous and Polyperchon parted on the quayside, each walking up the gangplank to their own ship. Roxanna braced herself for action.

The sound of pounding feet, many of them, suddenly echoed around the dim walls of the port; she had no choice but to run. With a sprint she ran to Aristonous' ship, racing up the gangplank and jumping down into the belly amongst the rowers now all sitting on their benches. 'Help me,' she said to an astonished-looking Aristonous. 'Take me with you.'

'Stop!' a female voice shouted. 'Do not cast off.'

Olympias! Why is she not dead? How did she guess I'd be here? 'I beg you, Aristonous; hide me and take me with you and you may have me in whatever way you wish, whenever you wish, for as long as you wish,' she said, as the image of herself bent backwards, like the whore, with Aristonous getting good purchase on her came to her mind, sending an all-powerful sexual thrill throughout her frame; she had never wanted a man more.

Aristonous looked at her, as if considering her proposition.

'Where is she, the poisoning little bitch?'

'She's here,' Aristonous shouted back.

'No!' Roxanna wailed, the betrayal hitting her like a low punch in the stomach. 'Don't you want me?'

'Roxanna, the very thought of saddling myself with a wild-cat like you is laughable. Whatever made you think I would?'

'You desire me; I know it, I see it.'

'I desire few things in life and to be poisoned when you have no further need of me is certainly not one of them.' His reaction was swift and his grip firm; he grabbed her wrist as the knife hissed from its scabbard. 'Trying to kill a man you've failed to seduce can only make him believe he's made the right choice.' He looked up to a figure standing at the top of the gangplank. 'She's here, Olympias; she just jumped aboard.'

'I thought this was where I'd find you. Take her.' Two guards jumped down into the ship. 'Disappearing just before two ships are due to break the blockade was too obvious.'

Roxanna struggled but Aristonous' hold on her was too strong; the knife fell from her hand as the guards seized her and dragged her away, kicking and protesting. Bodily she was hauled out of the ship as Olympias smiled at her desperation.

'You can't do this, you bitch!' Roxanna screamed. 'You can't keep me prisoner.'

'I can and I will,' Olympias said as the gangplanks were pulled inboard and the two ships cast off. 'I wouldn't have you free to cause mayhem. Oh, and you'll have to manage on your own now; I made all your slaves take a good look at that blank scroll you left me to see if they could make anything of it before I touched it. I'm sure you can imagine what happened.'

I'll have you yet, Olympias. And then another thought came to Roxanna and she looked over her shoulder at the ships, fading in the dark, now making their way to the harbour mouth. 'Neither of them will be back, you know.'

Olympias was puzzled. 'What do you mean?'

'I mean I heard them talking as they said goodbye. Polyperchon doesn't think he'll persuade Alexandros to come north and Aristonous isn't going to come south without him. Aristonous thinks your best chance is to break the blockade and get to Sardis.'

'Don't lie to me, Roxanna.'

'Why would I lie about this? I thought they were both completely loyal to your cause until I heard their conversation; it took me by surprise but it makes sense. Just look outside the walls: Pydna is lost. Why would either Polyperchon, whom you treat with contempt, or Aristonous, who despises you for the murderous serpent you are, wish to come back here to die?' The slap caused Roxanna's head to ring.

Olympias rubbed her hand. 'For the king, your son, whom you seem to be abandoning.'

'How can I abandon something which has been stolen from me and is no longer mine? No, Olympias, Alexander has but one hope and that's neither you, me, Aristonous nor Polyperchon. Let's face it: I may be your prisoner but you are now Kassandros' and neither Aristonous nor Polyperchon will be back to fight for a losing cause; in fact, Polyperchon suggested they come to an accommodation with Kassandros, and Aristonous did not dismiss the idea.'

Olympias' face crumpled in stages as she realised the truth of it; of how she was just clutching at a vague hope. She looked up to see shadow ships. 'Stop! Aristonous, Polyperchon, stop! Come back!' But no amount of shouting would bring the vessels back to the quay as they disappeared into the all-enveloping gloom.

It was a small victory, but at least it was something and it warmed Roxanna's battered heart. As she stared at where the ships had last been seen she knew what she had to do next: it was her final opportunity and perhaps she might even be able to save her son. She looked at Olympias; even in the dark her face was stricken as the futility of her position sank in. *I have one chance left of saving myself.* 'Perhaps you have need of me after all, Olympias.'

'What need could I possibly have for a poisoning little harpy like you?'

'To stand a chance of surviving this we have to persuade Eumenes to come west. If we write to him together as the mother and grandmother of the king, in Alexander's name, begging him for help, that would be far more powerful than you or me doing it separately.'

'Perhaps; but he has no fleet.'

'He doesn't need a fleet to get to Sardis.'

Olympias made to answer and then paused. 'But how will we get the army there?'

'Forget the army; leave it here. Face it, Kassandros has won Macedon. I'm suggesting that you, me and my son, with a few trusted men, run the blockade and get to Sardis and wait for Eumenes to come and take us under his protection.'

It took a while before Olympias answered. 'You may be an untrustworthy easterner, Roxanna, but you are also right: it's a straight choice between becoming Kassandros' prisoners or starting afresh in Asia with the help of Eumenes.'

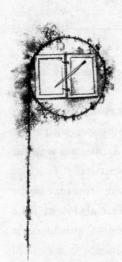

EUMENES.
THE SLY.

I T WAS NOT the arrival of the letter itself that surprised Eumenes, it was the thought, or rather the lack of it, which caused him to shake his head, his eyebrows raised, as he read it next to the comforting warmth of a brazier; the lack of thought and also the shocking news it contained. He handed the scroll to his fellow countryman, Hieronymus, and then, as his friend read the letter, rose to his not very great height from his camp-stool, walked to the entrance of his tent and looked out over his army's winter camp on the eastern bank of the Euphrates just within Babylonia, sixty leagues upstream of its capital.

The pre-campaigning season rituals had already begun, for the men could sense they would soon be on the move, and so the preparation of weapons and equipment was gathering pace as they responded to the rise in temperature by an escalation of industry. Not that it was ever particularly cold during the day in this part of the world; it was during the nights when the temperature plummeted. But now it would soon be time for Eumenes to take his army south. And the question was: to where?

It had been the news that Peithon, the satrap of Media, had been defeated by an alliance of the eastern satraps after he had summarily entered Parthia with an army, captured and executed the satrap and replaced him with his own brother, which had given Eumenes hope now that his power in the west had disappeared with his fleet. The victorious allied army, made up of troops from Persis, Bactria, Arachosia, Paropamisadae, Carmania and India, had chased Peithon west and was currently in Persepolis at the invitation of the satrap, Peucestas. Peithon had found sanctuary with Seleukos in Babylon.

To Eumenes' mind, the allied army had been sent by the gods: if he could persuade its leaders to ally themselves with him he would have the numbers to take on Antigonos. But first he had to get to the imperial treasury at Susa and withdraw the funds he would need in order to help those satraps come to the right decision. He was also anxious for Seleukos to join with him but that would involve him either executing Peithon or handing him over to the allied army as a demonstration of good faith; Peithon and his enemies could never be reconciled. *He will be no great loss to the world other than being a prime example of the Macedonian military mind working at its slowest.*

Eumenes had sent envoys to Seleukos asking for his cooperation against Antigonos, in the name of the kings – or king, as he now knew to be the case. He looked with regret at the scroll in Hieronymus' hands. *Olympias, why did you do such a thing? Now you have no legitimacy and so who can support you? That's why I can't go back west, even if I could; but without a fleet and with Antigonos behind me, how can I go back to the sea? No, it's onward I must go, as soon as I know where Seleukos stands.*

And that was his reason for delaying so long on the borders of Babylonia: to know Seleukos' mind. Would the satrap of Babylonia join with him and, with Peithon's life, encourage other eastern satraps to form an alliance, in the name of the kings – or king, as he had to keep on reminding himself – in order to take on Antigonos and crush his barely concealed imperial ambitions? The answer had been long in coming; and if, when it did arrive, it was negative, what would be his best strategy?

Such questions were becoming more urgent by the day as, with spring stirring armies from their season of slumber, Antigonos would soon be on the move south from his winter camp in Mesopotamia. Without the troops of the eastern satraps, Eumenes had not the numbers to face his huge army – over forty thousand if the reports from his spies were correct. The thought concentrated his mind and he came to a decision. *I'll move in two days whether I have an answer from Seleukos or no.*

With a satisfied and purposeful nod of his head he turned back to Hieronymus. 'Well?'

'Well, I think it shows naivety—'

'Of the highest order. I agree.'

'I do wish you would stop finishing my sentences for me.'

'I'm sorry, old friend, it comes from years of dealing with the Macedonian military mind; it can be tediously slow. But yes, Olympias is showing a naivety that surprises me; she must be getting desperate. For her to think that, rather than secure an alliance with the eastern satraps, I can somehow avoid Antigonos as I turn back west and then not be worried that I would have no naval support as I move along the coast to Sardis, assuming I even get there, is naivety at best, as you say, my dear Hieronymus. Now, I may be only a Greek, but I can tell when a Macedonian has less concern for my personal safety than I would think polite – even for a Macedonian.'

Of an age with Eumenes, Hieronymus, a martial man running to fat and balding, a soldier-historian, smiled at the understatement. 'She has no concern other than to get hold of your army and use it for her own ends now she's been utterly defeated in

Europe. Her murdering King Philip and his wife is proof of her ruthlessness.'

'Proof we didn't need as we've always been aware of it; what it's also proof of is her total lack of political vision. Kill Adea, yes, she was a problem, but murder the brother of Alexander who wanted nothing more from life than to play with his toy elephant and occasionally pleasure himself – admittedly in public – was folly, to say the least. I've always had the highest regard for Olympias and she, in return, has been heard to say something almost complimentary about me on at least a couple of occasions. I've always acted as her friend, despite the fact I know her to be a ruthless power-hungry harpy. But she is a ruthless power-hungry harpy who just happens to be the mother of Alexander and the wife of his father, the two men to whom I owe my whole life. But now she goes too far in relying upon my friendship. I can't go back west until the war in the east is won and to do that I need to build an alliance against Antigonos. With him gone, then, perhaps, we shall see.'

Hieronymus pointed to the childlike signature next to that of Olympias. 'And what do you make of that?'

'Roxanna? Other than the fact that I'm amazed she can write that well?' Eumenes grinned. 'Well, I suppose Olympias is using her, like she does everyone else, to bolster her chances of success. She thinks having both the mother and grandmother of the king appealing to me in his name will make it impossible for me to refuse the summons; but she's mistaken. Yes, my loyalty is to the Argead royal house of Macedon and yes, the boy Alexander is the heir to that house – unless Kleopatra decides to do something interesting – but the first thing to do in order to secure the future of that house is to kill the man who has now abandoned all pretence of supporting it. It's not to rush back west on a suicidal mission so Olympias can extract herself from the mess

101

she's got herself into. Frankly, I don't blame Polyperchon or Aristonous for abandoning her after the way she behaved in Pella. And I think stewing in Pydna, or even in Sardis if she manages to get out, will give her some time to reflect upon how to treat your friends and enemies alike in ways that don't come back to haunt you.'

Hieronymus handed the letter back to Eumenes. 'The trouble with that woman is she places so much store on being the mother of Alexander she can't countenance the possibility of having any faults whatsoever herself.'

Eumenes ripped the letter in half, crumpled it and threw it into the brazier. 'I don't think I'll bother to reply; if I refuse in writing she'll accuse me of treason so it's best to pretend I never received it. I'll make sure the messenger is kept with us.' He called to the guard outside the tent. 'Have Xennias report to me.'

'And there's a ship in sight coming up the river from the south,' Xennias said, having acknowledged the order to detain the messenger. 'The scouts reported it to be Babylonian.'

Eumenes brightened. 'Excellent. Summon the commanders to Alexander's tent; we'll hear Seleukos' reply in his presence.'

The great Alexander's presence came in the form of an empty throne, plated with gold, with his diadem laid upon it, his ceremonial sword lying across its arms and his breastplate leaning against its back. Raised upon a dais, it dominated the tent in which it stood. It had been Perdikkas who had first used the idea of holding counsel in its shadow so the decisions arrived at would seem to come from Alexander himself. Eumenes had copied the idea as a way of bending Macedonians to his Greek will, having claimed Alexander came to him in a – very convenient – dream and ordered him to set up the throne thus.

And so it was, beneath the shade of Alexander, that Eumenes and his leading commanders, Xennias, Parmida the Kappadokian, and Antigenes and Teutamus of the Silver Shields and Hypaspists, as well as Hieronymus, met the envoy from Seleukos.

'Seleukos sends his fraternal greetings,' the envoy said, standing before his audience seated beneath the throne.

That's code for he sends his greetings to Macedonians not Greeks; so the answer will be negative.

'My name is Patrokles, and Seleukos asks me to say that he is a royalist to the core and more than willing to be of service to the king.'

But he won't take orders from a Greek. 'That is most gratifying, Patrokles. Does he give me permission to bring my army to Babylon?'

Patrokles, in his mid-thirties with the dandified air of a Macedonian with a penchant for eastern luxury, looked down his nose at Eumenes. 'Seleukos fully expects you to do so; how else will you deliver it to him?'

Eumenes rubbed an ear with the palm of his hand, frowning, as if he had not quite heard what had been said; he gave the side of his head a couple of slaps, to clear a blockage. 'I'm sorry, Patrokles; I must be getting a little deaf. Would you mind repeating that?' He drilled a finger into his ear, examined it and then, satisfied that the obstruction was gone, sat up, head forward, full of concentration as the message was repeated. 'Ah, I thought that was what you said. I'd be grateful if you were to explain why Seleukos believes I'll be handing my army – the army loyal to me – over to him.' His face took on the countenance of wide-eyed, rapt attention.

'Naturally, Seleukos will be taking command of the enterprise.'

'And why do you say "naturally"?'

'Well, because he's a satrap.'

'As am I.'

'Yes, well, he—'

'Is Macedonian and I'm Greek?'

Patrokles looked directly at him. 'Naturally.'

'Naturally. And what will he do with Peithon?'

'He will be his second-in-command, naturally.'

'Will he now? And what position will I hold?'

'You'll command your Kappadokian cavalry and other foreign units.'

'But no Macedonian troops?'

'Naturally not.'

'And again there's that word for the fourth time. How free you are with it, Patrokles. It's how Macedonians justify to themselves their constant sense of superiority: it's natural.' He turned to his Macedonian commanders, Xennias, Antigenes and Teutamus. 'I would've thought you'd have to agree, gentlemen, naturally.'

Antigenes rubbed his bald pate ringed by a silver circlet of hair. 'Until someone defeats us, yes.'

'And what about my defeat of, firstly, Neoptolemus and then Krateros, eh? Two Macedonians beaten by a Greek.'

'Neoptolemus was Mollossian,' Teutamus countered.

Eumenes put up his hands in mock surrender. 'Of course, that makes all the difference.' He turned back to Patrokles. 'Tell my old friend Seleukos he's very welcome to join me in coalition against Antigonos and that Alexander is, in fact, in command.' He pointed over his shoulder with his thumb. 'Naturally.'

Patrokles scoffed. 'Seleukos anticipated this would be your unreasonable reaction and bade me to appeal directly to the Macedonians present. This Greek has been condemned to death by the army assembly for the killing of Krateros; he is unfit to lead an army made up of a large percentage of

Macedonians. Seleukos asks you to arrest and execute Eumenes immediately and to send him his head. I'll be only too pleased to take him the gift.'

Eumenes stifled a laugh. 'Seleukos has lost his manners of late; demanding the death of a man you're parleying with is ill-mannered to say the least.' He turned to his commanders. 'I'd say this man has just lost his herald's privileges; would you not agree, gentlemen? Or are you planning to decapitate me?'

Antigenes drew his sword, stood and took a pace towards Patrokles, stared him in the eye, nodding, and then looked back at Eumenes. It was with a flash of motion that his blade appeared at the herald's throat. 'Shall I take his head, Eumenes?'

Patrokles froze, shock and fear mingled on his face.

Eumenes stroked his chin for a while, making a show of contemplating a tricky conundrum. 'No, Antigenes, I think not; not now anyhow. Although, I must say, I'm touched by your offer; most generous it was. I think our cause is best served by sending him back intact to Seleukos. You can take the sword away from his throat before he pisses himself.' Eumenes smiled a faux smile at Patrokles. 'Now, my arrogant little chum, I had a perfect right to take your life then and you would do well not to forget that.'

Patrokles said nothing but gave a sullen nod.

'Go back to Babylon and tell Seleukos – who, by the way, I know to be a man of intelligence, and so he should be able to grasp this – that I hold the door open to him. I know he has very few troops of his own and as such will be an easy victim for Antigonos. Tell him to make no mistake about it, but when Antigonos arrives in Babylon he will like the look of that magnificent city and he'll want it for himself. Seleukos will find himself either running to me, where he will find little sympathy, or he'll have to rely on Ptolemy's charity, which is always expensive. I'm now going to make for Susa; Seleukos may join me on the road or wait for Antigonos to come south and kick him out of Babylon.' He paused for an exaggerated questioning look to check the herald had understood him; he had. 'Now, fuck off!'

Patrokles stood stock still for a moment before turning on his heel and exiting the tent with a lack of dignity that was the cause of much mirth for those remaining.

'Well, I think Seleukos has made his position perfectly clear. Our plans will not include him. I'll let Antigonos swallow him up. So, gentlemen, as soon as we can, we move east to the Tigris and find somewhere to cross. Xennias, take your lads ahead and locate a suitable place and enough boats.'

Eumenes looked with satisfaction at the large flotilla – boats of all sizes – that Xennias' quartermasters had assembled on the slow-moving, brown water, in the time it had taken him to march his army from the Euphrates. Downriver of the Tigris' confluence with the Dialas, the crossing point was just forty leagues to the west of Susa.

'We should be able to begin ferrying the army across tomorrow,' Xennias said. 'I calculate we can do it in three stages and then another two trips for the baggage and camp-followers; perhaps three if we can't get all the big wagons across in two.'

'Baggage, can't move with it, can't move without it.' Eumenes gazed over at the lush eastern shore, two hundred paces away, and at the plump farms on the rising ground beyond, a stark contrast to the forage-party-ravaged land he had just marched through; the victim of an army wintering. 'We'll camp on the other bank once we've crossed and send out forage parties whilst we wait for the baggage; we'll press on the day after. With luck, we should be in Susa in ten days.'

But the appearance of two triremes and two score of punts, coming up from the south the following dawn, delayed the start of the operation.

'Has he come to his senses at last?' Eumenes wondered aloud as he and Xennias watched the lead trireme turn, with considerable grace, towards the bank; standing tall on the prow with a body that could have been a model for a statue of Heracles was the huge figure of Seleukos. Resplendent in high-plumed silver helm, bronze muscled-cuirass and greaves and with a cloak of red linen billowing from his shoulders, he held onto a stay with one hand and leaned out over the water, muscles taut on legs and arms, as the rowers backed their oars, slowing the vessel until it came to a complete stop ten paces from the riverbank.

A Macedonian who actually thinks clearly, rather than just trying to hit everything with a sword; what a rarity. Eumenes walked forward to the water's edge and stood with hands on hips. 'Seleukos, you are most welcome, as are the punts.'

'Eumenes, if you think that I've come to help you cross then I must disoblige you. I've come to address your army in person seeing as Patrokles did such a poor job convincing your generals to choose the honourable and legal path.' Seleukos pointed a finger at Eumenes and raised his voice. 'That man is an outlaw, declared so by the army assembly. Are you, soldiers of Macedon, going to allow him to live when he stands so condemned? Answer me that!'

So, you're not a rarity after all; why am I not so surprised as to be disappointed?

Seleukos raised his voice as a crowd began to gather along the shore. 'This man is responsible for Krateros' death. Krateros! Our Krateros: the man who shared all our hardships and led us to victory in every battle he ever fought; the man in whom Alexander placed his deepest trust. Here stands Eumenes, the sly little Greek who caused the death of one of Macedon's finest. Are you, soldiers of Macedon, going to allow him to escape his punishment, a punishment that has been voted for by you and your brothers?' Seleukos finished his speech with a sweeping-armed gesture, leaving his hand high above his head. He stood absolutely still, an expectant look upon his face as he awaited his audience's reaction. Slowly the look of expectation dissolved, for not a sound of either support or opposition rose from the assembled troops. All just stood and stared at him.

Don't you ever give up? Do you really think they're going to cut off my head just because you think you look good posing on the prow of a ship? 'That was rather embarrassing, wasn't it?' Eumenes said in a tone full of cheer. 'You got yourself all worked up with righteous indignation at my continual existence and then found out that no one agrees with you. You see, Seleukos, I have been appointed the general in command of Asia by the regent, Polyperchon; how can I still be under sentence of death? That's all in the past now, old friend – although after that speech I would be rash in the extreme to consider you as such any more. And, for the record, I wasn't responsible for Krateros' death. He chased and attacked me when I was supporting Perdikkas, the holder of Alexander's ring and the guardian of the two kings – when we had two kings, that is.' Eumenes paused and looked at the men closest to him. 'Are there any of you here who wish me dead?' There was fierce muttering to the negative.

He turned back to Seleukos. 'Well, my one-time friend, bad luck, but it seems you'll be forced to endure my miserable little Greek life a while longer. Now, I'm going to cross with my army and go to Susa where I have a warrant giving me the right to draw upon the treasury there. With that money I shall receive the support of the eastern allied army which so pleasingly chucked that blockheaded fool, Peithon, out of Media, a satrapy he really did nothing to deserve. So you can either come with me, bringing Peithon's head, or, indeed, his whole live body, to give to my new friends, or you can slink back to Babylon and wait for Antigonos to take it from you. Which will it be?'

Seleukos gestured to a man behind him who put a horn to his lips and blew three long notes. Dark and intense, his eyes, to either side of a thin but prominent nose bisecting his angular face, narrowed as he broke into a smile. 'Neither, my sly little friend; you're going nowhere, as you can now see.' He pointed to the opposite bank as a force of over two hundred cavalry emerged from lush vegetation; leading their horses to the water's edge, the troopers mounted up and lined the riverbank to present a formidable obstacle for troops attempting to disembark. 'I'll leave you to contemplate the problem,' Seleukos said as the three or four men in each of the punts stood, produced bows and held arrows ready to be nocked. 'I have something to do that I think you might enjoy.'

Eumenes watched Seleukos' trireme back oars and manoeuvre to head north towards a left-hand bend in the river, followed by the other vessel, leaving the punts speckling the water, their pole-men working hard to keep them static as the archers stood ready to draw. *And there was I thinking I was dealing with a Macedonian of rare intelligence, like Ptolemy for example, but no.* 'How many artillery pieces do we have, Xennias?'

Xennias thought for a moment. 'Two dozen, or thereabouts; stone-throwers in the main.'

'Break them out and rig them along the bank as we begin to load the boats; I'm sure the lads will relish a spot of target practice if those archers try to impede our crossing or the cavalry try to stop us landing. Antigenes, get your lads aboard, the Silver Shields can have the honour of being the first to cross.'

As the first of the boats were ready to launch it became apparent something was amiss. Warning shouts from the upstream end of the camp, now mostly dismantled, quickly turned to ones of distress and then fear. 'Get them going, Antigenes,' Eumenes shouted, pointing at the boats, as he turned to sprint towards the incoming danger. Through the camp he ran, dodging slaves packing and loading, jumping rolled-up tents, bundles of pikes and other essentials of an army on the move as the sound of anguish grew. And then another sound met his ears: water; surging water. Ahead, men ran towards him, some jumping up onto already crowded wagons, some sprinting harder and some falling to the ground to be submerged by the chest-high wave inundating the camp. Grabbing onto the wheel of a cart, Eumenes braced himself for the impact and took a deep breath, for the wave may have been chest height for a normal man but it would surely swamp him completely.

It took his feet away as it hit, such was its weight and momentum; bodily he was lifted into the current, his arms straining as he held fast to the cartwheel, water tugging at his clothing and hair, until the cart itself was dislodged by the pressure to wash away with Eumenes attached. With a jolt, the cart met an obstacle, causing Eumenes to crash into its underside; water streamed around him as he tried to find his footing. Feeling firm ground beneath him, he pushed himself up so his face broke the surface. With an explosive exhalation he opened his eyes; he sucked in a chest-full of air, and then again and again as the pressure of the surge lessened and the water level, with surprising speed, declined. He looked around at the chaos that had, only a few dozen heartbeats previously, been a military camp. Men, sodden and grimed, picked themselves up from the mud, sharing looks of shock and surprise with bewildered comrades, as they trod their way carefully through the flotsam and jetsam strewn about them.

'He opened a sluice,' a voice said from behind Eumenes. 'Two, in fact.'

Eumenes turned to see Parmida astride his horse. 'He did what?'

'He rowed upstream of us and opened two sluices that both led into the same channel, which then opened up onto our camp; he was lucky we camped here.'

Eumenes shook his head, giving a wry smile in admiration for his opponent as the truth of the matter became apparent. 'That wasn't luck. He's prepared that because this is the first obvious place to cross the Tigris to get to Susa; any further upstream and you'd be north of its confluence with the Dialas and therefore have two rivers to cross.' *I'm sorry to have underestimated you, Seleukos. Although it's not as if you've caused me much damage other than to my self-esteem and perhaps the way the men look at me.* 'The main damage will be to our food supplies; I expect that's what his objective was: prevent us from crossing and leave us on this bank with nothing to eat; well, it won't work, my over-sized friend. No, it won't.'

Noticing with annoyance that he had lost a sandal in the deluge, Eumenes made his way back to the crossing point where the expected faced him: overturned boats and men wallowing in the river.

'We'll be all right,' Antigenes assured him as he helped some of his men to turn a boat over, tipping the water from it. 'We lost a couple of the lads, unfortunately, but all the boats are safe; we'll be ready to try again by midday.'

'And what about the artillery, Xennias?' Eumenes asked, looking with some relief at a dozen pieces that were relatively undamaged.

'We'll get the rest back into action and be ready before the Silver Shields.'

And, good to his word, Antigenes launched the first three dozen of his flotilla as the sun reached its zenith.

Out in the river the archers in the punts raised their bows and Eumenes held his breath. *Surely they're not going to sign their own death warrants by shooting at us?*

An arrow flew; high it climbed, until, lost in the glare of the sun, it began to fall to thump into the side of the lead boat. *A ranging shot.*

Then the sky filled with projectiles, streaking to the heavens; each archer releasing as fast and as fluidly as their life-long training made possible.

'Loose!' Eumenes shouted to the artillery as the Silver Shields hunched underneath upturned shields to brave the deadly hail.

With muffled thuds as the catapults' arms thwacked forward into rag-protected restraining arms, two dozen stones, each twice the size of a man's fist, hissed towards the punts. Heads exploded into red puffs of mist as the stones ripped through the lead punts and on into the rear ones, taking legs and plunging through the delicate hulls, sending the craft down. Within moments all archery had ceased as the surviving pole-men heaved for all they were worth downstream, away from certain death.

Eumenes' smile of satisfaction turned sour as, from around the bend upstream, two triremes, under full oars, came into view. He turned with urgency to Xennias. 'Fire is what we need; somehow in all this wetness we need to make fire. Seleukos is coming back.'

SELEUKOS.
THE BULL-ELEPHANT.

I'D LIKE TO *see how the sly little Greek tries to get across now.* Still standing in the prow of his trireme, holding onto a stay, Seleukos leaned forward over the water feeling every bit as much of a god as he looked. The fact his punts full of archers were fleeing worried him not one bit. He had brought them solely to hold the crossing whilst he took the two triremes north to break open the sluices in two specially dug channels designed to inundate the camp-site. Seleukos felt a surge of satisfaction as he congratulated himself on having out-thought Eumenes. This was the first point that would not involve crossing the Dialas as well, so Seleukos had guessed that this was where Eumenes would aim for, and he had had all winter to construct his trap. He had not sent his reply to Eumenes' offer until the work had been completed. As he had very little in the way of an army he was obliged to use all the forces available to him and nature was a very potent force. It had not been potent enough to wash his enemy away, but it would have done the next best thing: destroy most of his supplies.

All that remained for Seleukos to do was to trap Eumenes on the stripped-bare, western bank of the Tigris and let him suffer in a desolation of his own making. *Then we shall see just how many of your men remain loyal, Eumenes. I'll have your head on a pole by the equinox.*

Now all the punts had fled, more and more of Eumenes' flotilla entered the river; at least two hundred and fifty, he estimated, with the lead boats being over halfway across. He turned to the officer commanding the two bolt-shooters on either side of the deck, both protected by stout wooden walls against the artillery he had anticipated Eumenes deploying. 'Loose as soon as you are in range and then keep it up as fast as you can.' He stepped away from the prow and signalled to the triarchos, standing between the steering oars in the stern, in front of whom the ship's complement of marines crouched, keeping their heads below the line of the rail; the man nodded, he knew what he had to do. With a shout to the stroke-master in the oar deck below, the pace of the timing-flute increased and the grunts of human exertion amplified as the ship surged forward into attack speed. Satisfied that he could now be of little use to the operation, Seleukos settled, leaning against the left side of the main mast, protected from the western shore; he was ready to enjoy the spectacle of Eumenes losing his best men to the river.

Eumenes' artillery had now started to concentrate on the cavalry on the eastern bank with some success, but, again, that did not concern Seleukos, for enough would remain to repel or capture whatever few, if any, of Eumenes' men managed to make it across after his triremes had finished with them.

And the bolts fizzed away, two from his ship and two from the other, blurs across the water. Splintering through the side of a boat, one skewered together two veterans of many a campaign; they died, screaming, joined at the hip, as another bolt swept a man from his vessel and the last couple slapped into the river, spraying water over the two boats they so narrowly missed. With vigour and purpose did the artillerymen reload their weapons, ratcheting back the arms with rolling shoulders; with the bolt placed into the groove, the officer sighted it, ordering the wedge pulled out a fraction, lowering the trajectory now the distance to the enemy had closed, before pulling the release pin.

It was with pleasure Seleukos watched the missile smash into a boat containing a dozen men, shattering its side and capsizing it within moments; weighed down by gear, the ageing Silver Shields stood no chance as the next three bolts did similar damage now that the range had so diminished. *Now perhaps you'll change your minds about supporting Eumenes.* It was almost too easy.

Again four bolts flew, with the wrath of the gods, into the flotilla that was growing, despite the casualties inflicted, as more and more boats launched, but again that did not concern Seleukos for soon the triremes would be among them with pike and ram.

A couple of loud reports cracked out behind him.

'Fire! Fire!' the triarchos called.

Seleukos spun around to see a burning rag wrapped around a stone wedged into the shattered grating. Marines jumped up, running to extinguish it; two of their number immediately disintegrating into bloody mush peppered with smouldering rag. With hollow thuds a couple more burning missiles hit the hull, cracking timber but doing little damage as they dropped, hissing and steaming, into the water; but other shots were more fortunate, igniting fires on impact.

Still the marines kept the bolt-shooter active as their comrades braved decapitation to keep flames from spreading.

Now they were amongst the boats, driving through the heart of the flotilla, the triarchos swerving left and right as he strove to punch the ram through splintering wood, oars pounding on relentless. With the screams of the lost, a ten-man raft was shattered, disappearing beneath the surface in a welter of white water and lashing limbs.

Another set of screams, this time from the starboard artillery piece, now smashed and burning with broken men around it, from a lucky shot as the ship had borne to starboard, opening up the shield to the shore.

On through the crossing they surged, now causing little damage as the boats timed their runs so as not to collide with the great beasts of the river. But then Seleukos saw a group of half a dozen small vessels heading with intent towards the trireme; as they approached, another volley of flaming projectiles whooshed towards him, smoking tails describing their passage, to crash into the deck, hull and through oar ports. Men lay, shrieking with shattered limbs, as tunics burst aflame; cries rose from below and oars fouled as panic spread.

'Stop them!' Seleukos roared as he realised the objective of the incoming vessels.

But few heard his order and those who did had more immediate concerns.

And it was with a sense of helplessness that Seleukos grabbed a javelin, hurling it at the leading boat, for it was already too late: standing in the prows of each vessel was a man with an oil jar stoppered with a rag; and the rags were already alight. Into the chest of his target the javelin juddered, the jar falling into the river; but as it did, five others soared, from over-arms, up onto the deck to shatter, spurting flame over the already burning boards. Yet another artillery volley, blazing and fleet, whipped across the water, thundering into the ship, adding to the growing conflagration now battling with slopping blood and mangled flesh for ascendancy on a deck made mad by chaos.

It was then that the first of the oarsmen burst up from their now-burning domain, discipline having completely broken down; oars lay still and the ship began to lose way. There was one thing he could do; waving to the triarchos of the neighbouring, untouched ship, Seleukos ripped off his breastplate and greaves, and dived into the river. With strong breaststrokes he pulled himself beneath the water, to surface less than twenty paces from his objective. Backing oars, the trireme slowed for him. He grabbed a pike offered down and pulled himself up the side of the hull.

Seleukos looked back at the fires now gaining hold on the stricken ship and cursed the little Greek for his never-ending ingenuity as the triarchos got the undamaged trireme back under way. He then checked how his cavalry were doing in repelling the landing, but the artillery had now fixed their attention back to them; fire and beast did not mix and they were withdrawing. He sighed, resigned to failure, and turned to the triarchos. 'Get us out of here, there's not much we can do now to stop Eumenes.'

It was not so much the failure that irked him as they rowed away, it was the jeering of Eumenes' army as the crossing continued unmolested. It was that and the knowledge that as the army progressed east to Susa it would strip the other half of his satrapy of all the food it could find as Eumenes now had no reason to treat him as a friend.

And so Seleukos sent to Eumenes for a parley later in the day, once his army was across and he was awaiting the baggage.

'We lost quite a few good lads today,' Eumenes said as he and Seleukos sat beneath an awning, watching the tedium that was ferrying the baggage train across a river. 'And all because you wouldn't subject yourself to my command, even though your army consists of a few score bowmen and a couple of hundred cavalry – very lovely cavalry, I'll concede, but hardly numerous and even less so now after being introduced to my artillery.'

Seleukos dipped a hunk of bread in the bowl of olive oil on the table between them. 'I have many more men than that.'

Eumenes smiled, raising two questioning eyebrows. 'Oh yes? Then why didn't you bring them and really try to stop me rather than just giving me a soaking?'

Seleukos shrugged, popping the bread into his mouth, saying nothing.

'Because, apart from the few Peithon managed to bring out from his fiasco in Media, you have hardly any men ever since you sent back those Ptolemy lent you to kick Docimus and Polemon out of Babylon. Admit it, Seleukos, you have no troops and were trying to get hold of mine.'

He's at his most intolerable when he's right.

'And now all you've succeeded in doing is drowning a few good lads and ruining most of my grain and other supplies which will now be replenished by your own generosity – or, at least, the generosity of the farmers and townsfolk of your satrapy. Won't they be pleased with you when they find out.'

'That's what I came to talk to you about.'

'If you think I'm going to take gold in return for not feeding my army until I get to Susiana you are quite mistaken.'

'It would be a lot of gold.'

'Not as much as I can withdraw from the treasury in Susa, which will be more than enough for my needs. No, Seleukos, you should've joined me and not arrogantly insisted that I join you.'

Seleukos contemplated this in silence as he dipped more bread into the oil and watched the disembarkation of a boatload of pack-mules. Eventually he asked: 'How did you manage to start fires—'

'When the whole camp was underwater?'

'I wish you wouldn't—'

'Finish people's sentences for them? Yes, everyone wishes I wouldn't do that. But to answer your question, I had the mules' manes cut off. That proved enough to get a small fire going onto which we threw anything, from boxes or trunks which had floated and were reasonably dry, and added pitch. A few of my officers' wives will be less than happy with their husbands when they find out.'

Seleukos shook his head, eyes downcast. *I was a fool to underestimate him; but at least that puts me in good company.* 'So you won't spare my satrapy from your foraging parties?'

'On the contrary. I'm going to divide my army into three columns, side by side, three leagues apart, so as to take full advantage of everything there is to be had here. After all, Susiana is Antigenes' satrapy and why should his people suffer to feed his and my troops when yours will do just as well? Besides, why should I leave anything for Antigonos, who will be along very soon?'

'You little bastard.'

'Yes, you may have the semblance of a point there. You're half right: I am little but I'm not a bastard. I'm just a Greek who is doing everything he can for the Argead royal house and who, for some reason, is not appreciated by the people that house rules over, the Macedonians themselves. So fuck you, Seleukos. I'll do what I think best in that cause and if you don't like it then it's your own fault for not accepting my generous invitation. Now, unless you have anything meaningful to say, I suggest you get back to your navy, or the one trireme and two dozen punts you like to refer to as your navy, and retire to Babylon and advise the lovely Apama to begin her packing.'

Seleukos stood and looked down his nose at Eumenes, dislike smeared across his face. 'My wife won't be needing to pack. I will not be making the same mistake when Antigonos arrives, as I shall invite him to Babylon and serve under him wholeheartedly.'

'Then you are more of a fool than I thought.'

'Why so?'

'Because if you serve under him you'll be fighting me and therefore, whatever happens, you will lose. If I beat Antigonos then I'll take Babylon from you – granted I may spare your life if I'm feeling in a good mood at the time and manage to forget the fact you've twice demanded my death in recent days.' He paused to let the point sink in. 'But if Antigonos defeats me, he will, no doubt, execute me and then he'll look around for other people who may prove a threat to his progress towards ultimate power… You, with the wealth of Babylon behind you – although admittedly embarrassed for troops, but, thankfully,' he pointed to Seleukos' moored trireme, 'not a navy – would seem to him a risk not worth leaving in place. But I told Patrokles to explain that to you. Did he not do so?'

'Antigonos would never take Babylon from me.'

'You can think what you like, Seleukos. To be frank, your opinions no longer interest me.'

'He's right, you know, Husband.'

Seleukos looked at his wife, lying in bed next to him, and frowned. 'What makes you say that, Apama? If I swear to Antigonos then what problem will he have with me?'

'His problem is the fact you don't owe your satrapy to him, but, rather, to Antipatros and, therefore by extension, to his family, including Kassandros.'

'I'd never support that pimpled misfit.'

'Antigonos doesn't know that.'

'Besides, I want to carve out my share of the empire here.'

'Just make sure Antigonos never knows that. He's already removed four of Antipatros' nominations from the Three Paradises conference and replaced them with his own men. No, Seleukos, with hindsight you would've been safer joining with Eumenes.'

'And take orders from that little Greek? Never.'

Apama stroked her husband's cheek and snuggled deeper under his arm. 'You take orders from me, don't you?'

Despite all his concerns about his future, Seleukos smiled: he did take orders from his wife and very satisfying he found it too; indeed, he had just finished performing the last set of orders to her gratification, which was why they were both sheened in sweat – that and the humid weather with which Babylon seemed forever cursed. Still, the constant heat was small price to pay for the mastery of such a wealthy city and satrapy and he was not going to have it taken from him.

He ran his hand up Apama's back and thanked the gods Alexander had forced him to marry her at the mass wedding in Susa, seven years previously. He had forced all his senior officers to take Persian brides in his push to meld east with west. Few had liked the idea but Seleukos had fallen for his Sogdian beauty and had never been tempted to repudiate her as had most Macedonians after Alexander's death. Not even when Antipatros had wanted him to marry Kleopatra, Alexander's sister, had he been tempted. He kissed his wife's hair and held her closer, looking at the almost sheer drape hanging in the window to keep at least some of the burning midday heat from his high-ceilinged bedroom, the walls and floor of which were decorated with rich blue tiles with golden beasts and hunters upon them in an echo of the tiled walls of the city itself.

Through the window rose the Ziggurat of Marduk, partly dismantled by Alexander in his first visit to the city but now being rebuilt by Seleukos in a successful bid to ingratiate himself with the locals. It had certainly worked with the priests, who now supported him without reservation. It would be unthinkable to give all this up; this was the legacy he wished to leave his son, Antiochus, now six years old. He reached around and felt the swell of Apama's belly, ripe with child. *No, I'll not give this up. Here I stay and this will be the heart of my possessions. This will be my kingdom. Its throne is empty but I will fill it, as will my son after me.*

'So how shall I avoid Antigonos trying to remove me once he's defeated Eumenes?'

'I should have thought that was perfectly obvious.'

'Not to me it isn't.'

'Marduk save me from this husband.' Apama turned onto her side and laid her head on his chest, facing him. 'You have to prove your loyalty to him by exposing someone whose loyalty is not so firm.'

Seleukos thought for a moment and then a smile spread across his face. 'Peithon!'

'Exactly. Firstly, you had to stop him from incorporating those twenty-five thousand Greek mercenaries into his army, instead of killing them five years ago, then he tries to make himself independent in the east and annoys everyone so much they band together and kick him out. Once Antigonos has won, you give him Peithon. Make a good case against him and Antigonos will be duly thankful and leave you in place secure in the knowledge of your loyalty.'

'That's an excellent plan. I think I should send Patrokles to the resinated cyclops, pledging my support and offering the resources of Babylonia in his struggle against the traitor Eumenes.'

Apama reached forward and kissed him on the lips. 'I'm sure Antigonos will be only too pleased to accept your offer.'

'What I'll enjoy most is proving Eumenes wrong; not that he'll be alive to see it.'

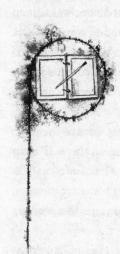

EUMENES.
THE SLY.

S USA, ON THE eastern bank of the Cheaspes River as it threads its way down from the heights of the Zagros Mountains to its confluence with the Tigris, just twenty leagues from the sea, was a welcome and familiar sight for Eumenes. The magnificence of its mountainous backdrop, verdant with forest and tipped by ice-laden peaks, made for a refreshing change from the flat lands they had marched across over the last ten days, taking everything edible they could find; stripping it bare. With temperatures made pleasant by cooling mountain breezes and with plentiful game in the foothills, it had always been a favoured residence of the old Persian dynasty and thus had two palaces: Darius' palace in the city itself, next to the Acropolis, and then that of Artaxerxes on the western bank of the river. More of a royal hunting lodge than a palace, it was here Eumenes had chosen to stay. For it was in this palace that his wife, Artonis, whom he had married on Alexander's orders at the mass wedding in Susa, lived. He had not seen her since their parting more than six years previously, when he had left her in Susa rather than have her endure the ravages of Babylon's climate as Alexander's court moved on to that city, shortly before his death.

Thus it was with much curiosity that Eumenes rode through the great gates of the palace into the shaded courtyard lined with almond trees, around which the whole complex was constructed. Curiosity because he did not know how warm his reception would be, having virtually abandoned Artonis in the years since Alexander's death, such had been his preoccupation with defending his legacy.

It was, therefore, with some surprise that he saw Artonis, flanked by statues of strange beasts, standing on the well-worn marble steps leading into the great hall. *That bodes well; a domestic issue is the last thing I need at a time of tricky negotiations.* He swung from his horse, and, handing the reins to a waiting slave, walked towards his wife.

Artonis stepped forward and, to Eumenes' eyes, glided down the steps. Veiled and clad in a high, brimless hat, circled with silver chains, a saffron linen mantel fell to her ankles that all but covered the deep-blue dress of finest wool. The cloth was embroidered with diagonal lines of gold thread crossing to create small squares at the centre of which was stitched a pearl: she was a vision of eastern elegance. Ever sensitive to his secretary's needs, Alexander had ensured the wife he chose for Eumenes would not tower over him, as so many Persian women would, and it was with pleasure that he took her hand and looked down into dark eyes lined with kohl and brimming with longing.

'Artonis,' he said, enjoying the sound of her name on his lips, 'I am so pleased to be back.' He rubbed the silken skin on the back of her hand and was reminded of the smoothness of the rest of her body.

'I am happy you have been able to make time for me, Eumenes. I know how hard you've been working to keep Alexander's line safe from those who would usurp it. As Susa is on the Royal Road I get news on a regular basis. I pray to Nanaya each day to hold her hands over you. Being in her temple gives me solace as I await your return, my dearest husband.' She lowered her eyes and bowed her head.

Eumenes decided all other business could wait.

Feeling invigorated – if an exhausted man can be said to be so – Eumenes rose from the bed and stepped to the window, stretching his arms out wide, enjoying the cracking in his shoulders as he did. Out across the river he gazed to the city beyond. There, in the Palace of Darius, he would be conducting the most important negotiations of his career, for if they were to fail, Antigonos would certainly triumph and Asia would fall into his hands. In the name of the king he had summoned the allied eastern satraps to Susa and, to his surprise, they had all written back agreeing to come – or, at least, send a representative. Even Peucestas had not baulked at a summons by a Greek. Breathing deep of the cool air and raising his eyes to the distant mountains, he wondered whether he should join his wife in the Temple of Nanaya on her next visit. *She is, after all, the goddess of warfare in these parts, as well as the goddess of voluptuousness and sexuality; it can't do any harm.* The idea intrigued him. Never having been the sort of man who went scurrying off to the gods at the approach of the slightest difficulty, Eumenes had little experience of any religion, preferring instead to use his own skills in navigating life rather than rely on what was, on the face of it to a practical man, the nebulous help of tenuous deities. Indeed, he had always been secretly amused by the Macedonians and their tendency to purify everything by cutting a dog in half and walking between the two sections, as if that would really be of help.

He turned to his wife, naked and lying on her back, her legs slightly apart, one hand behind her head and the other on her belly. He paused to enjoy the sight before going to sit on the edge of the bed and stroking her cheek.

Artonis opened her eyes and smiled at him. 'Come, Husband,' she said, taking his hand from her face and kissing the palm, 'lie next to me.'

'I've work to do.'

'So have I.' She pulled him towards her; he did not resist. She laid him on his back, her hands rubbing his chest as she straddled his waist and then leaned down to let her tongue play on his nipples before kissing her way down his body.

All thoughts of visiting temples dissolved in Eumenes' mind.

'I had missed that,' Artonis said as she returned to Eumenes' shoulder. 'Never let me be without you for so long again, Eumenes, if only so as I can do that for you.'

'It seems a very reasonable request to me. There was many a time in the past six years where I was in dire need of that particular service.'

'I'm sure that a man as powerful as you did not go without. There would be plenty willing to ease you that way.'

'Ah, but none as beautiful and lovely as you, Artonis.' And to Eumenes' shock, he found that he actually meant it. He had barely thought of his wife during the struggles of the last few years and now that he was reunited with her he realised just what he had been missing. 'If you don't mind the rigours of campaigning and the hardships of camping then you would be most welcome to accompany me when I go to face Antigonos. You could even come with me now, if you wish, on my visit to the royal treasury. Although I don't think I'll be requiring your services in that respect whilst I'm there.'

Artonis smiled once more. 'You never know, but I would love to, Eumenes. May I choose something? A necklace perhaps?'

Ah, women; they can never resist a chance to beautify them-

selves. 'Artonis, it would give me the greatest pleasure to pin something beautiful around your neck.' He leaned over to kiss her throat. 'And it will give me even greater pleasure to take it off this evening.'

'The five separate gifts of one hundred talents apiece are ready,' the warden of the royal treasury said as Eumenes stepped back out into the light, through the heavily guarded gate leading down to the strong rooms on the summit of the Acropolis.

'Thank you, Xenophilus,' Eumenes said, unnecessarily as the man had only been doing his duty – something he had been reluctant to do at first, until Antigenes, the man's commanding officer and satrap, had assured him Eumenes' mandate from Polyperchon was genuine. 'I'll take Peucestas' chests with me and give them to him personally now he's here. Have the rest of them delivered to each of the satraps as they arrive over the next couple of days with my compliments. And they are not gifts. They are to help them with the upkeep of their armies.'

'Indeed, sir,' Xenophilus replied in the tone of one who knows he is being lied to and cares not.

Ignoring the sarcasm, Eumenes took Artonis' hand, climbed the steps to the treasury wall and looked down over the ever-growing military camp to the south of the city along the river; his army had now been supplemented by the troops brought by Peucestas. Already, from this high vantage point, a black smudge could be seen on the horizon away to the south. His scouts had reported this was Tlepolemus, the satrap of Carmania, and his army, numbering over eight thousand. 'The question is,' he muttered to himself, 'will one hundred talents each be enough?'

'What was that, Husband?' Artonis asked.

'Nothing; I was just worrying about the negotiations.' Eumenes turned to his wife and held the emerald fastened about her neck in his hand. 'I have never seen larger, not even in India.'

Artonis stroked his cheek. 'It's beautiful, thank you.'

And it was beautiful. As soon as they had both glimpsed it in a chest full of assorted jewellery, they had known this was the piece that would suit her. After that it had just been a case of marvelling their way through the treasury. Eumenes had been there before with Alexander, almost seven years previously; despite the massive withdrawals made since, it was even fuller than he remembered it. The treasury at Cydna was impressive, he knew from recent experience, but it paled into insignificance compared with the riches of the entire east.

With one more glance over the force collecting before the gates of Susa, he led his wife around the walls of the treasury complex, one hundred paces square, inspecting their upkeep. Satisfied, he led her back down the steps to where Xenophilus was in conversation with Antigenes.

'He understands his duty, Eumenes,' Antigenes said, breaking off his discussion. 'No one will be allowed to withdraw a single drachma without a signed order from you as general in command of Asia.'

'Very good, Antigenes.' Eumenes gave a perfunctory smile to Xenophilus. 'In that case I think I can leave you in position if Antigenes feels he can trust you, provided you don't mind taking your orders from a Greek.'

Xenophilus' look was enough to suggest it would not be particularly easy. 'Not at all, sir.'

'Good; in that case I want you to start fortifying the treasury to prevent Antigonos – or anyone else for that matter – from taking it by storm. The city defences are in a good condition but a determined force could overrun them after a while so we must make sure the treasury walls are impregnable. We need stockpiles of weapons all around them and artillery pieces mounted upon them, not to mention braziers large enough to heat oil and sand every twenty paces or so. I also want you to start bringing in supplies so you could endure a lengthy siege. How many men do you have in the treasury guard?'

'Two hundred and fifty, sir.'

'Would you have enough accommodation for more?'

'Yes, sir; for twice the amount.'

'Antigenes, I'd like you to second another two hundred and fifty men to Xenophilus' command. I want to make absolutely sure that, whatever happens, Antigonos will not get his hands on any of this. Now, if you would excuse me, I'm going to visit the Temple of Nanaya with my wife before our meeting with Peucestas.'

And it was with remarkable intensity that Eumenes performed the sacrifice of a pair of quails to Nanaya. Never a greedy goddess, Artonis explained, Nanaya preferred the blood of beautiful things. It was a concept that appealed to Eumenes and, as he implored the goddess to look with favour upon his endeavours over the next few months, he felt his wife's favourite goddess might indeed hold her hands over him. He was full of confidence, therefore, when he entered the echoing audience chamber in the Palace of Darius soon after midday for his arranged meeting with Peucestas.

'Where is he?' Eumenes asked Antigenes, the only other person in the room, designed for the King of Kings of the Persian empire to be seen by his subjects and dispense royal justice. High, wide and long, it dwarfed all who entered it.

'He's waiting until you arrive so he isn't seen to be the lesser man,' Antigenes replied, taking a seat in one of the three chairs arranged in a circle around a table, beneath the raised throne dominating the far end of the room; mounted on a pedestal twice the height of a man, it was made entirely of gold. On it Eumenes had had placed the diadem, sword and breastplate so the meeting would, once again, be under the supervision of Alexander.

Eumenes sighed and, followed by a group of slaves carrying the strongboxes on wooden stretchers, walked the length of the chamber, his footsteps resounding off the glazed-tiled walls. Shafts of light, alive with motes, shone down from high windows and reflected off the polished marble floor, dazzling Eumenes. Signalling for the boxes to be set down at the foot of the pedestal, he dismissed the slaves, took the seat next to Antigenes and settled down to wait for however long the satrap of Persis felt was necessary to massage his dignity.

That Peucestas was a man who had ever rested upon his dignity, Eumenes knew only too well. He had always been a companion of Alexander's, educated alongside him at Aristotle's feet, and had proved his bravery and loyalty on many occasions on the battlefield. Indeed, he, along with Leonnatus, had saved Alexander's life when he had been pierced by an arrow in India, stranded on the walls of Multan, the Mallians' island citadel. They had sheltered the wounded Alexander with their bodies and shields until help had arrived and they were able to evacuate him. When none had been willing to make the incision necessary for the extraction of the barbed arrow, it had been Peucestas who had stepped forward and cut deep into Alexander's flesh. For this, and other services, Alexander had rewarded Peucestas with the satrapy of Persis when they had returned to Persepolis. Apart from being present in Babylon at the time of Alexander's death, he had remained there ever since, taking his pleasure in the luxury and wealth of the east, adopting its customs, dress and language as his own. It was now said of him that had you not known he was a Macedonian you would have never, for one moment, suspected it.

And the full truth of that assertion hit Eumenes with aston-
ishing force as, after half an hour, the doors to the audience
chamber swung open to reveal the satrap of Persis. Draped in a
wide-sleeved, deep-blue robe with broad edgings of white, embroidered with reds and gold, that almost completely masked his red
trousers and matching long-sleeved tunic, stood Peucestas. In one
hand he held a staff with a golden eagle's head, in the other, a
scroll. To the plucked strings of an instrument, hidden from view,
he came forward, his delicate calf-leather shoes, laced with red
ribbon, making no sound. Atop his head was placed a high tiara of
gold with a cloth of silk hanging from it at the neck to cover the
hair. But none of this surprised Eumenes unduly as he was
prepared for the outlandish use of costume for he had already
seen the first seeds of Peucestas' obsession sprouting in Babylon
at Alexander's deathbed. What he had not envisaged, though, was
the beard: ringletted and hanging long, Eumenes could have
accepted without a gasp, but reddened with henna was a step too
far. His mouth opened and the breath exploded from him as he
leaned forward in his chair, grasping the arms with white-
knuckled fists. Antigenes took one look, squeezed his eyes shut
and then looked again; accepting what he saw was true, he stared
in wide-eyed wonder that a Macedonian could be so attired.

Peucestas, giving no indication he was aware of the reaction
he engendered, progressed with stately dignity down the length
of the chamber, his eyes staring into the middle distance, never
straying to one side or the other. On he came and, as he drew
nearer, Eumenes regained control of his expression and rose to
meet him. After a few moments' hesitation, Antigenes did the
same, shaking his head and blinking as if coming out of a trance.

'My dear Peucestas,' Eumenes said, succeeding well enough
in keeping the amusement out of his voice, 'I'm happy to see you
here, ready to join us in our duty to the king.'

Peucestas kept his head level and looked down at Eumenes. 'My little Greek friend, each time I see you, your stature, or, rather, lack of it, makes me too want to gasp, only I have the good manners to restrain it. Antigenes, I'm pleased to see you back in the east. Your men will be a great aid in my struggle against Peithon.'

Eumenes did not correct Peucestas as to who the enemy really was, but indicated to the third chair for him to be seated; he clapped his hands to bring three slave-girls hurrying in as the music from the hidden instrument continued, soothing and melodic.

Their hands were wiped, and as wine and sherbet were set on the round table before them, Eumenes leaned over and opened the lid of the nearest strongbox to reveal a fortune in gold and gems. 'This is to help you with the maintenance of your army, Peucestas. I am not insensible to the fact that you've gone to great expense to bring such a force here.'

Peucestas again kept his head level as he looked down.

He's worried his tiara's going to fall off. That is too much to resist.

'Thank you for the small contribution,' Peucestas said, his voice dismissive. He proffered the scroll to Eumenes. 'Here are my orders.'

'Your orders?' Eumenes said, confused. 'Your orders from whom?'

For the first time Peucestas' neutral expression flickered, hinting at annoyance. 'They're not orders from someone to *me*, Eumenes. Are you deliberately trying—'

'To be obtuse? No, Peucestas, I can assure you I wasn't trying, it came naturally. If they're not your orders, in other words orders for you, then what are they?'

'They are my orders for *you*.' He still held the scroll out towards Eumenes, shaking it as if encouraging him to take it.

Eumenes held up both hands in refusal. 'I'm sorry, Peucestas, but I think you may have misunderstood: you do not command here.'

'I have the largest army. If not me then who?'

Eumenes gestured to the empty throne. 'Alexander; who else?'

Peucestas raised his eyes, still keeping his head level, and studied the throne and the diadem, sword and breastplate. 'That was Perdikkas' trick and look where it got him. No, Eumenes, I will be in command, little man.'

That is it; I've had enough. Jumping to his feet, he thrust a finger towards Peucestas. 'You are merely the satrap of Persis,' he roared, and then thumped his chest with his other hand. 'I hold the mandate as general commanding Asia from Polyperchon, the regent himself. As such, I am instructed to defeat the traitor Antigonos, who has gone against the authority of the king, and I have the power to issue what orders I see fit to achieve that. I summoned all the eastern satraps here to Susa so that we might take counsel here in Alexander's presence, beneath the throne upon which he sat on the day we all took our Persian wives. Here we'll decide together what to do – together! Understand? I won't have some puffed-up Macedonian coming to me, dressed as Xerxes going to a party, telling me he'll command because his army is bigger than mine and, besides, he's taller than me.' He thrust his face forward, close to that of Peucestas, causing his head to jerk back; off flew the tiara to clatter to the floor. 'Do I make myself clear?'

Peucestas stared at the little Greek in dumb disbelief for a few heartbeats until the wound to his dignity began to cause him serious pain. He rose to his feet and, with studied thoroughness, adjusted his dress before stooping to retrieve the tiara.

'If I were you,' Eumenes said as Peucestas made to replace the headdress, 'I wouldn't do that. It evidently gives you ideas above your station. No man is going to laud it over another in this army, but there has to be one overall commander to carry out Alexander's will in a logical and orderly manner and he will be decided upon when the rest of the satraps are gathered. Having made that decision, we will then devise a strategy for defeating Antigonos. Once we've defeated him, you are welcome to behave like some eastern potentate but until then I would be grateful if you would revert to being a Macedonian general.'

'Have you quite finished?'

Eumenes took a couple of deep breaths, looking thoughtful. 'Yes, I think I have.'

'Then I shall return immediately to Persepolis.' Peucestas turned and, replacing his tiara, began to glide from the chamber.

'If you go, Peucestas,' Eumenes shouted after him, 'what will you do? Join Antigonos like Peithon will be bound to? How will that go, do you think? Of course you won't, you can't. And if you leave the alliance you've already made with the eastern satraps, do you think they'll come to your aid when Antigonos attacks you? Of course not, why should they? You'll be all on your own in Persepolis. If you go now, Peucestas, you will lose your position whatever happens: if Antigonos wins he'll depose you, and if we win I'll make sure you have nothing. Now, go if you must but you can buy your safety by leaving the fourteen thousand men you've brought here.'

Peucestas carried on walking but slowed the further he got from Eumenes until he stopped just short of the doors and turned. 'The most annoying thing about you, Eumenes, even more annoying than your ghastly habit—'

'Of finishing people's sentences. Yes, go on, I'm all ears to learn what could be more annoying than that.'

Peucestas drew breath to calm his rising temper. 'What is more annoying is your ability to distil a matter down to its basic essence with utmost clarity. Yes, you are right: I cannot join with Antigonos, firstly because Peithon will be with him, and secondly because he will most certainly replace me with one of his own. Neither can I afford to leave this alliance solely because you are an affront to my dignity. So I'm stuck here if I want a chance to keep my satrapy. Very well, Eumenes, I'll stay but I want you to hold to your word that the overall commander will be agreed by us all.'

'I give you my word and Antigenes here is your witness.'

'Before the throne of Alexander,' Antigenes said.

'Before the throne of Alexander,' Eumenes said, 'we will choose one of our number to be the nominal leader of this alliance.' He looked at each of the six satraps and one deputy seated around the table beneath the empty throne. 'We will all make our nominations which must be someone other than ourselves. Although every morning we'll take counsel together before Alexander's throne so he may guide us as to the best course of action, we need one man to make the dispositions should it come to battle, and that same man should also be able to adjudicate on disputes between us. Are we all agreed?'

Androbarzus, deputising for Oxyartes, the satrap of Paropamisadae, leaned forward; weighty gold earrings tugged at his earlobes, the scent of rosewater enveloped him. 'Am I eligible?'

Eumenes had already considered the matter. 'Of course. You have brought twelve hundred infantry and four hundred cavalry in Oxyartes' name. Stasander here, from the combined satrapies of Aria and Drangiana, has brought fifteen hundred foot and a thousand horse, with some of them from neighbouring Bactria, and Azanes from Sogdia to the east of it has brought five hundred of his master's horse-archers and a similar amount of infantry archers.' He nodded at Azanes, fearsome, dark-eyed, full-bearded and garbed in leather and furs, and to Stasander, in his late thirties, clean-shaven and more conservatively dressed – for the east – in Macedonian uniform, before turning to another man, similarly attired. 'Tlepolemus also has fifteen hundred infantry and almost a thousand horse. You've all roughly the same amount of men and should all be treated equally.' Out of the corner of his eye he watched Peucestas' reaction. *Between them they have half the amount of men you do and yet you're keeping your mouth shut; perhaps you're not so stupid after all.* 'As should Antigenes with his three thousand Silver Shields, the same number of Hypaspists and the four thousand men in his satrapy's army stationed here.' Lastly he looked at the sun-browned face of Alexander's appointee as satrap of the Macedonian part of India, still recognisably Macedonian despite the native white headdress wound about his head. 'And Eudamos is eligible, for although he has brought but five hundred horsemen and three hundred foot-archers, he has with him one hundred and twenty elephants whose presence will reassure the army.'

Eudamos displayed his white teeth in what almost passed for a smile. 'I've made sure they have all been instilled with a taste for dealing death.'

Eumenes inclined his head with grace. 'Thank you, that is most considerate of you. Now, gentlemen, to business, your nominations please. Antigenes, you first.'

Antigenes passed a hand over his head as if smoothing hair he did not possess. 'One thing that has been forgotten in all this is that my Silver Shields are the most senior unit in the whole empire – surely their voice should be heard.'

Now is not the time to plead for special treatment, Antigenes. 'And their voice is being heard through you.'

136

'But I can't nominate myself.'

Gods, the Macedonian military mind is an impossible beast to deal with. 'No, you can't.'

'I insist my Silver Shields take precedence, and as I represent them it should be me who has command, especially on the field.'

Eumenes leaned his elbows on the table and rubbed his eyes before looking around. 'Let me put it another way for you all, gentlemen: let us each nominate ourselves seeing as that's what we all want to do. Antigenes here is nominating himself. Who will vote for him?'

A silence followed as Eumenes knew it would; he let it run until Antigenes began to fidget with discomfort.

'So,' Eumenes said, wearing his most earnest look, 'that was most interesting. Who wants to nominate himself next?'

'Enough of this!'

To Eumenes' surprise it was Peucestas who had made the intervention.

Peucestas got to his feet. 'We all know we'll never agree to a leader between us so either we sit here and bicker all day or we do the only other thing possible and elect Eumenes as he holds the mandate from the regent as general commanding Asia. That way my dignity is satisfied because, although he is a Greek, he has the authority of the king.'

Eumenes tried to hide his shock without much success. *Now that may be the first time since Alexander died I've ever heard a Macedonian say something making total sense.*

Around the table there were mutterings of grudging agreement that gradually became positive.

'Thank you, gentlemen,' Eumenes said, genuinely grateful, for now he had one less argument to pursue. 'In which case I think we should discuss our strategy in dealing with the traitor. By my reckoning Antigonos should be arriving in Babylon very soon. With him he has upwards of forty thousand men plus the camp-followers, all of whom have to be fed. I took the precaution of stripping as much food out of Babylonia when I passed through by dividing my army into three columns. I propose we now strip the food from Susiana and then draw him south into Persis, thereby extending his supply lines. We should leave Xenophilus in command of Susa itself, with just sufficient numbers to man the walls, and prepared to fall back on the well-fortified treasury complex should the city capitulate. Antigonos will have to leave a good few thousand here to lay siege to the city, as the treasury will be too big a temptation for him to resist; this will make us roughly equal in numbers out in the field. However, his supplies will be scarce and so his men's morale will not be as good as that of our lads. Then we wait for the opportunity to catch Antigonos off guard and crush him.' He looked around the table at pensive but, in the main, positive faces. 'Now, gentlemen, I've had my say, so, in the spirit of our new regime, you should all take it in turns to express your views as to the best way of dealing with Antigonos.'

ANTIGONOS.
THE ONE-EYED.

'**O**PEN THE GATES, Xenophilus,' Antigonos shouted, sitting upon his horse before the walls of Susa. 'And then give me the keys to the treasury. Things will go badly for you if you don't.'

'I have been ordered by Eumenes, the general commanding Asia, not to open the gates to the traitor Antigonos, and most certainly not to allow him to withdraw even so much as a drachma from the treasury.'

Antigonos suppressed the urge to point out it was Eumenes who stood condemned by the army assembly and he himself was not a traitor. *It will only make me look childish if I were to get into that sort of shouting match.* 'It looks like we'll have to leave a reasonable force here to lay siege to the place,' he observed to his son, Demetrios, next to him. 'Do you fancy the job, boy?'

Demetrios shook his head. 'I'd rather stay with you on the campaign, Father; it's a battle I want, not a siege.'

'Let me rephrase that: you will conduct the siege of Susa and there is to be no argument, understood?'

'But I know nothing of siege work.'

'Then it's time you learned.'

'From whom if you're not here?'

Perhaps I shall make some use out of Seleukos; and with any luck he might get himself killed storming the walls and rid me of an irritating problem. Indeed, Seleukos had been irritating Antigonos since he arrived in Babylon; it had become apparent that the priests' support for Seleukos and his popularity amongst the citizens, both due to his rebuilding of the Ziggurat of Marduk and his relaxed attitude to local customs and laws, had made him hard to remove without creating an unnecessarily dangerous situation. Yes, he would have to get rid of Seleukos somehow, because having seen Babylon, he desired it for himself – and needed it for his imperial ambitions – but it would be better if he himself were not to be seen to be the cause of Seleukos' removal. It had been to that end he had insisted Seleukos act as one of his generals during his campaign in the east where things could, perhaps, be more easily managed.

Antigonos turned in his saddle. 'Seleukos! Make a tour of the walls; I want to know how many men you think necessary to take the city and what is the minimum amount of time you need to do so.'

'Very well, Antigonos,' Seleukos replied, giving a sidelong look at Peithon.

If you're planning on keeping the contents of the treasury for yourself then I'd better leave a little insurance behind to ensure you won't be alive to do so. 'And report to me when you've done it.' He turned back to the walls. 'Xenophilus, you've just signed your own death warrant.' With a sharp pull on the reins, he turned his horse and headed back towards his headquarters at the Palace of Artaxerxes.

'How long will you stay here?' Demetrios asked as they clattered into the palace courtyard.

'I'll move south tomorrow, I hope. With the granaries and storerooms stripped bare for leagues around, we need to move on if you're going to have sufficient forage to conduct a siege. But I've a feeling it'll be the same story as we go south.'

'Then why go south, Father? You have control of all the satrapies west of the Tigris and now Susiana. Why not just take Susa, get hold of the treasury and leave it at that? Let the east go. With luck they'll fall to fighting amongst themselves and will be too busy to bother us.'

'Yes, I've thought about that, but Eumenes is still there and, as much as he is my enemy, I respect him. He's a cunning little Greek and I'd wager he's found a way to unify them. If we go back west then Eumenes will come after us, and I can't take that risk. No, here in the east is where it must be decided. Only one of us will make the journey back to the sea, and I intend for it not to be Eumenes.' He swung a leg across the back of his mount, jumped to the ground, handing the reins to a waiting slave, and looked up at his son. 'Make a report on the state of our supplies, Demetrios, and how successful the foraging parties have been around Susa.'

Demetrios' lack of enthusiasm showed. 'But, Father—'

'You will do as I say. I need to know the exact position before we move and you need to learn just how important that information is. You'll also need to work out how much food your siege force will need each day, once Seleukos comes back with the numbers.' Brooking no argument, Antigonos walked away, hands clasped behind his back, deep in thought.

And he had much to think about, for ever since he had broken his winter camp in Mesopotamia and headed south through Babylonia, he had been travelling in Eumenes' wake, through a virtual wasteland scoured of all that was edible. The lands around Eumenes' winter camp had been the worst but the route to the Tigris had also been ravaged by the passing of Eumenes' army; villages stood abandoned and starving beggars roamed the stripped fields seeking scraps. *Travelling in three columns so as to take as much as possible from the land, the sly little Greek is leading me on with the intention of starving me. Had it not been for Babylon he would be succeeding by now.* The fact Eumenes had not gone to Babylon had meant Antigonos had been able to take advantage of the huge city's supplies; Seleukos had little choice but to allow him to. He chuckled to himself at the memory of Seleukos' obsequious and transparent invitation to him to come to Babylon and his unremitting eagerness to be of service ever since, and then frowned as he recalled the strength of the satrap of Babylonia's position slowly becoming apparent. *But you won't be going back to Babylon, my friend.*

No, Seleukos could never be trusted, not again. And as for Peithon: his ambition to take the east had been surpassed only by his stupidity in setting himself against all the eastern satraps without first securing the friendship of some and turning others against one another. There was always plenty of time for betrayal and murder once your position was secure militarily, but Peithon did not seem to understand that simple concept and had managed to unite all his enemies against him and thus had been defeated. *Fool, but he may yet be a useful fool. He certainly knows how to command men on a battlefield even if he's too witless to understand basic politics. He'll fight hard for me if he believes that I will get him his satrapy back.* It was with this pleasant thought that Antigonos mounted the marble steps to the palace, barely noticing the bestial statuary to either side, and entered the great hall.

'You have an old acquaintance waiting to see you,' his friend Philotas informed him, striding to meet him.

'I'm not in the mood, Philotas; there's a lot to consider and not much time to consider it in.'

'I think it'll be of help to you if you spare time for a cup of wine with Babrak.'

Antigonos stopped. 'Babrak? Where's he come from?'

'Persepolis, master; and it's a place of great abundance at the present,' Babrak the Pathak merchant informed Antigonos as he sipped a sherbet in what had until recently been Artonis' suite of rooms; dark-skinned, hook-nosed and with sunken but twinkling dark eyes looking out from beneath a white headdress, he grinned to reveal red-stained teeth. 'Supplies from all over the satrapy of Persis, and beyond, are being stockpiled there.'

'Is Eumenes there?' Philotas asked from the window, looking out over Susa and the army setting up camp before its walls.

'No, master. He and his army are camped about twenty leagues south of the Pasitigris River. At least, they were when I left them eight days ago.'

Antigonos turned to Philotas. 'How far is the Pasitigris from here?'

'Ten leagues according to the scouts; it's the only major river between here and Persepolis other than the Coprates, which flows into it further south; from here we need to cross that river before we get to the Pasitigris.'

'So he's no more than thirty leagues from Susa; he's in no hurry it would seem.'

Babrak eyed the weighty purse as Antigonos placed it on the table between them. 'No, master; he's harvesting the bounty of the land. It's a very fertile region, the last one you travel through before the climb over the mountains and the journey through the Persian Gates down to Persepolis.'

'His supply wagons must be overloaded.'

'I believe the noble Eumenes was making a statement when he invited me to witness the feasts; a statement he wished you to hear.'

Antigonos put his hand onto the purse. 'There's nothing noble about that little Greek.'

Babrak inclined his head, placing one hand across his chest. 'Indeed, master, forgive my foolishness; there is nothing noble about him at all. He is barely taller than a boy and without the charms.'

'Indeed.' His hand left the purse. 'You believe he wanted me to know about his feasts. Why?'

'Ah, master... when a man has what another man desires it is but natural for him to flaunt his possession, be it the favours of an energetic boy or, as in this case, food during a military campaign. I was in the camp for two nights and on both occasions he feasted the entire army on oxen and sheep. And the bread, master – beautiful bread baked fresh, so light and melting in the mouth; it was evidently made from the finest grain.'

'Yes, yes; I can see why he wished to flaunt that when we're sitting here having to rely on what comes up from Babylon and what we can hunt in the mountains.' Antigonos paused in thought for a moment. 'You say you were there for two days, Babrak. Was Eumenes showing any sign of continuing to move south?'

'Yes, master; on the morning I left they were breaking camp.'

'Were they now? Did they seem to be in a hurry?'

'No, master. I have seen many an army break camp and it can be done with great alacrity, as one so great in the ways of war, such as yourself, would know. But this was done without speed, indeed, with reluctance, like a man dragging himself from the arms of his boy when business or one of his wives calls and passion must be interrupted.'

'Yes, quite.' Antigonos stood, shaking his head, and picked the purse up from the table. 'Just one more thing, Babrak.'

'I am yours to command.'

'You're everyone's to command and we all know it. But tell me, is Eumenes really leading them? Have Peucestas and the others accepted the sly little Greek?'

'He's doing Perdikkas' trick, master.'

'Meeting before an empty throne?'

'You have it exact, master.'

Antigonos lobbed the purse over to the Pathak merchant. 'Come and see me next time you're passing.'

'I see everyone, master.'

'I know; that's what makes you so useful.'

'Will you allow my caravan free passage in and out of Susa? I have much business there.'

'Negotiate that with Seleukos – he's to conduct the siege.'

'A noble man.'

Antigonos did not have the time to argue the point. Gesturing to Philotas to follow him, he walked from the room. 'We need to hurry – if we're quick we can catch him unawares. He thinks I won't come after him until I've taken Susa and secured the treasury, which is why he's taking his time foraging. But I'm leaving Seleukos here to lay siege whilst we press on.'

Philotas gave a look of surprise. 'How many men does he need?'

'Four thousand,' Seleukos said in answer to the same question as he reported to Antigonos shortly before dusk. 'Five hundred of which should be cavalry.'

Antigonos nodded his approval. *He seems to know what he's doing, that's about what I estimated it to be.* 'Very well, Seleukos; I'll decide who you'll have within the hour. You can go.'

A trace of resentment at being thus spoken to crossed Seleukos' eyes as he turned to leave.

'He's not enjoying being subordinate,' Philotas observed as Seleukos stepped from the room. 'I wouldn't trust him with the treasury.'

'I wouldn't trust you with the treasury, old friend; but what choice do I have if I wish to catch Eumenes when he least expects it?'

'Then let Demetrios do it.'

'He is, I'm leaving him here too, but he needs someone to learn from; he knows as much about laying siege to a town as my arse does – less, probably. So he will be able to keep an eye on Seleukos whilst at the same time learning about siege-craft from him.' He lowered his voice. 'Although, between you and me, I'm thinking about planning an unfortunate accident for our Titan-sized friend; once he's of no more use, that is.'

'A wise precaution.'

'Anyway, if we manage to surprise Eumenes, we can cross the mountains and take Persepolis and then be back here before the siege has progressed as far as the treasury.' Antigonos rubbed his hands together in anticipation of a fight. 'So, my friend, haste is our watchword. Tell Nearchos to have as many rafts made up overnight as possible; we'll need at least a hundred if we're going to get across the Coprates and Pasitigris with good speed.'

And speed had been Antigonos' obsession in the two days it had taken the army to march to the Coprates through blistering weather; so much so dozens of men had fallen by the way, suffering from the heat as the sun shone down with no thought of mercy. *But the speed has paid off*, Antigonos mused as he looked at the fast-flowing waters of the Coprates River about eighty paces wide; judging from the relenting sun there was three hours until dusk. *Now we need more speed to get across this.* 'Philotas, have Nearchos bring the punts up. I want you to take your lads across and spend the night digging a ditch and building a palisade long enough to shelter the whole army just in case we are caught mid-crossing.'

'Do you really think that likely?'

'No; but we're both old and grizzled enough to know how to do things properly. You should be able to get them all over in four crossings.'

With a pleasing sense of urgency, the rafts, each one twenty feet square, were offloaded from their transports; down the bank they were dragged to be launched into the river and moored to stakes hammered home into the soft earth on the shore. With few shouts and less intimidation, for every man knew the drill, the files of Philotas' command lined up ready for embarkation. With all of the hundred craft lying ready in the river, each with a rope attached long enough to span the width, Philotas gave the order to board; sixteen men to every raft, each fully armed and supplied with an entrenching tool or a woodsman's axe, they were laden but not beyond capacity. As the first of them, bearing Philotas, was loaded, the men struck out for the further bank, using their sixteen-foot pikes as punting poles. On they pushed out into the quickening current, forcing them ever downstream and playing with their varying speeds and trajectories so it was not long before collisions ensued; with shouts of warning and cries of fear, a raft, whirling around out of control, crashed into its neighbour, rocking it with savage force and dislodging two of its crew to tumble into white water. Hands clawed up from beneath the surface as if trying to catch hold of an unseen rope which would drag the drowning men to safety, but none appeared and the men were pulled under by the weight of their equipment. On the crossing went, more and more craft launching into the hazardous flow, now thick with troops on precarious wooden platforms. More cries and more death as a whole raft overturned; a couple of men managed to hang onto a neighbouring craft until their weight threatened its stability and their fingers were hacked away by unforgiving sword strokes. Under they went, the water turning red around them.

And still they pressed on and, as the last to launch pushed out into the river, so did the first come to the other side. Philotas and his relieved lads jumped into the shallows and waded ashore, pulling the raft after them and then beaching it. Slowly the rest followed, each man struggling to the bank, wet but alive, until all the surviving craft were on the shore. Antigonos squinted as he tried to make out the whereabouts of Philotas. Eventually he caught sight of his old friend supervising work to each of the rafts. For what seemed like an age, Antigonos awaited the signal. Finally Philotas waved.

'Bring them back, lads!' Antigonos shouted.

Men pulled at the ropes, hauling the rafts back across the river, but this time there was no driftage as further ropes had been attached to them on the far side; now they were secured to both banks.

Again with a pleasing sense of urgency, the craft were hauled back and the next wave of Philotas' command embarked. This time, with a rope securing each vessel to either bank and with a half a dozen men hauling on them, the crossing was less hazardous and proceeded at a steady pace with but few unlucky casualties. Twice more was the operation repeated and soon, as the sun neared the horizon, the last of the six thousand men under Philotas' command stepped ashore, sodden but still breathing.

The punts were hauled back one last time and then beached, ready for the crossing to continue at first light next morning, as Philotas set his men to work, digging a ditch and felling trees over a night of intense labour.

Rubbing his hands together in satisfaction, Antigonos turned away from the river in search of a jug or two of resinated wine.

With a satisfied grunt and wiping his beard with the back of his left hand, Antigonos thumped his empty cup down upon the table, put his feet up on a stool, poured himself another cup and looked around his tent as a slave lit the lamps within.

The first cries of far-off battle came as a shock to Antigonos' ears; as he leaped to his feet the officer of the watch burst into his tent.

'We need to get the rafts back over the river at once, sir,' the officer said without even a salute. 'Philotas has been surprised by Eumenes.'

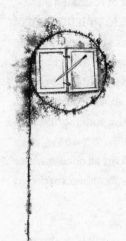

EUMENES.
THE SLY.

THE SURPRISE HAD been total. Eumenes would have laughed, as he and his Kappadokian cavalry surged through the rough perimeter of Philotas' bridgehead on the southern bank of the Coprates, had it not been former comrades who were falling beneath his blade. And slaughter it was, for all of Philotas' command had been occupied in the urgent business of making the perimeter secure against just such an attack.

But Eumenes had planned his ambush with great care and sly cunning. He had known Babrak the merchant would tell of all he saw in his camp to Antigonos and so he had tarried at the same place for the time Babrak was with him, making a show of collecting supplies and being in no great rush to move on. He had then allowed Babrak to see a slow breaking of camp, knowing Babrak's tale would tempt Antigonos. He needed only to hold on until the caravan was a couple of days' travel north before he turned his army around, crossed the Pasitigris with a readymade pontoon bridge and set to waiting a couple of hours' march from the Coprates.

And Antigonos had obliged him perfectly, even to the extent of commencing the crossing at the end of the day so Eumenes would be able to use the cover of dusk to surprise the small force trying to secure the bridgehead.

In his Kappadokians swarmed, dealing death in the last of the fading light, as Azanes' Sogdian horse-archers and the Thracian and Persian light cavalry followed them with Antigenes and Teutamos and their Silver Shields and the Hypaspists, in open order behind, armed with thrusting-spears, ready to do the really dirty work should resistance prove too dogged. But the ten thousand Persian archers Peucestas had summoned from Persepolis – by a system of shouted relay across the mountains – were seeing to it that resistance was softened. Over the heads of the cavalry they shot their arrows; Eumenes' horse had to avoid more than a few wounded, writhing on the ground.

Down he slashed his sword, slicing through the collarbone of a shrieking man stripped, as most of them were, to his tunic, far more prepared for fatigues than fighting. In a spray of blood he hit the earth to roll once before lying still, as Eumenes raised his blade and leaned to his right to slice the scalp from a veteran trying to defend himself with an entrenching tool.

Still the deathly hail of arrows fell on the bridgehead, working ever forward as the cavalry pressed on. On the riverbank, silhouetted figures in torchlight worked on the ropes, heaving the punts back across the Coprates; but there were too few craft to rescue all the beleaguered force. As the punts neared the shore many waded out to be sure of a place, desperate to escape the carnage rolling inexorably towards them. Onto the punts they scrambled, hauling at one another in their fear, pulling each other under or rocking the already unstable craft and dislodging men already aboard.

Now the archers concentrated their efforts on the river itself, strafing the bank, felling many of those trying to get to the punts as Eumenes and his men closed in, driving a stampeding mob before them. In the shallows, now littered with the victims of the Persian archers' deadly rain, a few punts managed to push off, men still clinging to their sides, as teams on the north bank, now in darkness, hauled them away.

But Eumenes did not care if a few hundred escaped; what was important to him was the morale boost his fragile coalition would gain from such a victory, for all the satraps had taken part, whether it be here on the river or away in the forest where Eudamos, Tlepolemus and Sibyrtius, satrap of Arachosia, were reaping the lives of those cutting wood for the palisade. And it was with great relief that Eumenes saw the first of Philotas' men sit or kneel in surrender. Down they went in their hundreds, huddling together in groups, once it became apparent there was no chance of escape and the choices had become either death in the river, death by the sword or enlisting into Eumenes' army. With the struggle now over, Peucestas' archers unstrung their bows, the Silver Shields, Hypaspists and other infantry sheathed their swords and the cavalry rallied back. Eumenes dismounted and, accompanied by Parmida the Kappadokian and an escort of a dozen men, strode through the field of bloodshed as the prisoners were rounded up in manageable groups. 'Who was in command here?' Eumenes asked a captured officer, sitting on the ground.

With sullen eyes, the man looked up. 'Philotas.'

'Was he now?' Grinning, Eumenes turned to Parmida. 'The evening has just got even better. Let's seek out our old friend.'

It did not take him long to find who he was looking for.

'I'm here, Eumenes,' Philotas said, getting to his feet as Eumenes approached the riverbank littered with bodies both on land and floating in the shallows. 'I assume it's me you want.'

'Ah, Philotas,' Eumenes said, in apparent good humour, 'the man who stole my fleet. Remind me, Philotas: had I not just spared your life when you did that act of sabotage?'

Philotas looked down his nose at the little Greek. 'A mistake you will—'

'Not make again? How very percipient of you. I am not a monster, however, and you will get a fair hearing before the army assembly.'

'How very noble of you.'

'I thought you'd appreciate it; you can also have safe conduct across the river for anyone whom you wish to speak for you.'

'I have known this man since we were boys,' Antigonos declaimed, facing the army assembly and pointing sideways at Philotas who was standing, disarmed but unfettered, between two guards beneath the empty throne raised on a dais. 'Nigh on seventy times we have stood, shoulder to shoulder, in the front rank of the phalanx. He is a Macedonian through and through and, as such, I fail to see how he can be condemned by a Macedonian army assembly for persuading a fleet to desert a Greek for a Macedonian. If you condemn this man, soldiers of Macedon, then you condemn a man who was fighting for his country.' With a final thrust of his fist in the air, Antigonos then pointed at his audience, the sixteen thousand Macedonian citizens in the allied army. Their non-citizen comrades watched the proceedings with curiosity from the side; across the river Antigonos' army looked on, witnessing the spectacle but unable to influence it. 'And if you do that, how can you ever expect to walk tall and proud in your towns and villages again, knowing that people will be saying behind your backs: "there goes one of the men who condemned Philotas for doing his duty"?' He brought his hand down to his side and glared at the assembly with his single eye.

Not a sound rose from them.

Very, very good, my resinated friend; just the performance I hoped you'd give when I offered Philotas the opportunity to ask you over.

Eumenes stood still, doing nothing to fill the silence growing more profound by the moment, enjoying the obvious puzzlement Antigonos was undergoing. *Finding it hard to believe my men don't equate Macedon with your cause, are you? Must be quite a shock. I'd better put you out of your misery.* He stepped forward, held out his hands and shrugged, questioning. 'How is our cause not Macedon's, comrades? How can supporting the king, the son of Alexander himself, not be in Macedon's interests?' He gestured to the empty throne. 'Every day, the satraps of the east and I meet beneath the throne of Alexander, that throne with his sword, breastplate and kingly diadem upon it; we discuss in his presence what we should do to further strengthen his son and heir's position. Despite my being appointed the general in command of Asia by the regent himself, the holder of the Great Ring of Macedon, before he passed it on to the sacred person of Olympias, we sit as equals before Alexander's spirit.' *There's nothing wrong with a little hyperbole, glossing over Olympias' true character.* 'How can that not be working for Macedon's true interests?' He paused to let a rumble of agreement rise from sixteen thousand throats. 'I have always striven to further the interests of the Argead royal house, whereas that man!' He thrust an accusatory finger at Philotas without looking at him. 'That man does nothing but strive to further the interests of that man.' He turned his finger on Antigonos. 'Antigonos! And his interests are in direct conflict with those of the royal house.' Pausing to let that sink in, he climbed the dais to the throne. 'Why are they so, I hear you ask? Because for Antigonos the royal house is an impediment to his route to power; because Antigonos wishes to make himself king and sit on the throne he claims is empty but is, in reality, still occupied.' He grabbed the diadem hanging on the back of the throne and presented it to the assembly. 'It is not an empty throne, it is Alexander's throne.'

The roar that greeted this pronouncement was abrupt and almost physical in its strength, pounding Eumenes' ears as he punched the diadem in the air before taking it in both hands and, with reverence, placing it back on the throne, bowing his head. This show of veneration drew yet more thunderous cheers from the assembly and also from their non-citizen comrades who had served with Alexander; even from across the river there were signs of appreciation for the gesture.

Smiling to himself as he watched the fury play on Antigonos' face, Eumenes descended the steps, backwards, keeping his head lowered but his eyes on his adversary. *Performing a full proskynesis in front of the throne would probably be a step too far; but I certainly seem to have our resinated cyclops worried.* As he reached the bottom of the steps, Eumenes turned, raised his head and gestured for silence; it took a while to become manifest such was the enthusiasm of his men, but eventually it was so. 'And now, soldiers of Macedon, you must decide what to do with this man who has done so much harm to the cause of the Argead royal house: in seizing our fleet with the treasure already loaded and preventing us crossing to Europe to link up with Olympias and Polyperchon, he effectively divided our forces. And now the royal army in Europe is under threat from Antigonos' puppet, Kassandros, and the royal army in Asia is hounded by the one-eyed monster himself; and it's all because of this man whom I had the decency to plead for the last time you demanded his death. I promise you, soldiers of Macedon, I shall not make the same mistake should you again find his life to be forfeit. So I ask you now: what doom do you pronounce on the man who stole our fleet?'

And it was unequivocal. 'Death!'

Philotas squared his shoulders and held his chin up; Antigonos looked at his old friend aghast as the mortal chant grew and then he stepped forward to be heard.

Gradually the din died; Antigonos cleared his throat. 'I am well aware, soldiers of Macedon, of the desire you have for vengeance for what you see as a betrayal of trust. Eumenes had spared Philotas' life and then he went on to steal his fleet and the treasure it contained. Yes, you are right, it was a betrayal of the man who had just pleaded for his life and won it back for him; Philotas should not have done such a thing and had I realised what had transpired, I would have returned both coinage and ships to Eumenes with apologies. But I didn't at the time. So now, with the benefit of knowing the truth of the matter, I make this offer: I will return the fleet and treasure to you, making good that which I have already dispensed. What say you, comrades?'

It was as much as Eumenes could do to stop himself joining the incredulous mirth that greeted this most unlikely offer; for all present knew it was a deal Antigonos would have had no intention of keeping once he had secured the life of his boyhood friend. All also knew Antigonos had been well aware at the time that Philotas had acted in bad faith. *I would have expected more from you than that; at least you could have made an attempt at an honest bargain.*

As if by a prearranged signal, the laughter turned back into the chant of death.

Eumenes turned to Philotas. 'Have you anything to say?'

Philotas met his eye. 'What is there to say to a little Greek who has got way beyond his station?'

'Yes, you may have a point there; you must find it painfully annoying to have to deal with a Greek like me; I suppose you really ought to thank me for putting an end to that unpleasant situation for you.' Expecting the response, he stepped back to avoid the globule of phlegm aimed at his feet. 'Guards, prepare him.'

Calloused hands grabbed Philotas' shoulders, and pulled his arms behind his back as they forced him to his knees.

I should at least have the courtesy to do this myself. Eumenes drew his sword and approached the condemned man.

'Wait!' It was Antigonos who shouted. 'Wait!'

'Are you going to plead for his life?' Eumenes asked.

'I wouldn't give you the pleasure. And nor will I give you the pleasure of executing my friend, Greek; if it is to be done I should be the man to do it. Do you not agree, Philotas?'

'I would deem it a last favour from a comrade with whom I've shared so much of my life, Antigonos. Spare me the shame of death from a Greek's hand.'

'That's all very touching if rather insulting to me, but then I'm used to that from Macedonians – being insulted, that is, not touched.' He contemplated the issue for a couple of moments. 'But you're right. I've no need to make this more painful for anyone than it already is. If you really want to know, I regret doing it, but I would have lost face with my men had I not punished Philotas once he fell into my hands. But that's by the by and probably of little interest to either of you.' He held out his hand towards the kneeling prisoner. 'Please, Antigonos, be my guest.'

Antigonos grunted and then looked down at his old comrade, as he drew his sword.

'Make it swift, Antigonos,' Philotas said, stretching his neck forward.

'I will avenge this, I swear.' Antigonos weighed his sword in his hand, closing his eyes and turning his face to the sky.

And swift it was: with a cry to the gods, Antigonos sliced his blade through the air and on through Philotas' neck, sending his head rolling, life still flickering in the eyes, until they were blinded by blood exploding from severed arteries.

I've never really enjoyed an execution but I think that has to be one of the more satisfying ones; Antigonos could not have been more obliging. 'You can take the body when you leave, Antigonos.'

'Try to stop me.'

'Actually, seeing as I have over forty thousand men on this side of the river and you only have yourself and your boat crew, I believe even I, a little Greek, as you so endlessly like to point out, would be able to do that; so why don't you just try saying thank you for being good enough to allow his remains to be returned to his wife?'

'Fuck you, Eumenes. You'll die at my hand one day.'

'If that's to be the case then I hope you will extend the same courtesy to me as I've shown to him.'

'I very much doubt it.'

'Then you would prove what I've always contended.'

Antigonos frowned. 'And what's that?'

'That refined manners are the preserve of Greeks and Persians. Guards, help him with the body.'

Bending down, the two men lifted the headless corpse by the shoulders and began dragging it towards Antigonos' waiting boat, leaving a gory trail.

'There is still time to stop this,' Eumenes said as Antigonos unfastened his cloak. 'We could still combine our forces and together we could reunite the empire and keep it safe for the rightful king.'

'With you in command, no doubt.'

'No, with Alexander in command.'

'I don't play those sorts of games.' Antigonos threw the cloak over Philotas' head.

'It's not a game; it's an effective way of getting everyone to act in unison, with a common purpose. If you and I were to unite, Asia would be ours for the king. Ptolemy would have to come to terms and accept the king's authority or lose everything he's gained, and Kassandros, your proxy, I think I'm right in guessing, would either submit to us or die – preferably the latter.'

'And then what?'

'And then we could all concentrate on making ourselves fabulously wealthy in peace in an empire ruled by the Argead royal house of Macedon.'

'My arse, we would. Macedonians would never countenance being ruled over by a child whose grandmother is not only the regent but also one of the most power-hungry bitches ever to have slithered out of a cunt; we would be at each other's throats within a year and you know it, Eumenes.' He reached down and gathered up the head in his cloak, tucking it under his arm. 'It will take a strong man to unite the empire.'

'And you think that man is you?'

'I know it is.'

'Well, that'll come as a surprise to a lot of people; a surprise most of them won't like.'

'They'll get used to it.'

'I doubt it; in fact I'd be willing to wager that, should you be successful against me – which is very much in the balance when you look at the numbers – then you trying to impose your will on the rest of the empire will lead to a coalition against you, just like what happened in the east against Peithon, and that will be your dying day.'

'My arse!'

'Is evidently what you use to do your thinking, Antigonos. Don't you see that there are only two possible outcomes: an empire united under the Argeads or an empire that fractures into three or four independent kingdoms?'

'It's pointless talking to you; I'll see you across the battlefield, Eumenes; and my eye will be the last thing you see as you die.' Antigonos turned and began to walk away, calling over his shoulder: 'And once I've finished you I'll take the others, one by one.'

'Ah, the Macedonian military mind.' Eumenes shook his head in exasperation and then shouted after the retreating figure: 'And don't forget when they are all lining up against you and somehow I am dead, that I predicted it; because they won't be able to bow their heads to you, not Lysimachus, not Seleukos, not even Kassandros who you so foolishly have helped to set up, and certainly not Ptolemy.'

'What do we do now?' Antigenes asked, coming to stand by Eumenes' side as they watched Antigonos cross back to the northern bank with the body of his dead friend.

'This is becoming quite an unexpected habit.'

'What is?'

'Macedonians asking my advice.'

Antigenes grunted.

'But to answer your question we move south and wait to see what Antigonos does.'

'He's gone north, into Media,' Xennias said, making his report to the satraps gathered around the table beneath the empty throne a few days after the victory at the river.

Eumenes frowned. 'Media?'

'Yes.'

'He's not chasing us?'

'No, he's not; I was surprised too when Azanes and his Sogdians came back in this morning reporting that.'

The Sogdian stepped forward, emanating a strong waft of horse sweat. 'He's left Seleukos with a token force to conduct the siege of Susa – but not enough to take the city, just contain it – and, with the rest of his army, is following the Zagros Mountains north; my guess is he's heading for the capital, Ecbatana.'

Eumenes rubbed the back of his neck, which prickled with heat. 'Peithon must have persuaded him to reinstall him as satrap and then he'll go on to secure Parthia.' His face brightened as he looked around the assembled company. 'That'll take him at least the rest of this year and probably some of the next. He will be wintering up there. This is excellent news, gentlemen.'

'How so?' asked Stasander, the satrap of Aria and Drangiana. 'We've only just managed to kick the arrogant idiot out; we don't want Peithon back in power in the neighbouring satrapy.'

'We can deal with that at a later date. The reason I say that it's good news is Antigonos has just made a grave mistake: he's expecting us to follow him in order to pursue the same strategy as we have been using against him and starve us of supplies. But we won't fall for that; no, we won't because he's given us the chance and the time to go back west and secure all the western satrapies, defeat Kassandros and unite with the king and, perhaps, even deal with Ptolemy. Then we can be there, with a much reinforced army, waiting for Antigonos when he comes back next year or the year after. We will choose the ground and we will defeat him together.'

Stasander waved the suggestion away. 'What is the west to us? Our powerbase is the east; if we leave it unguarded with Antigonos and his large army unchecked then he'll take everything from us.'

Peucestas stood, his head rigid as he balanced his tall tiara. 'The east is what we fight for and Antigonos is a direct threat to it at the moment. I for one will not lead my men any further west than Babylon.'

Eumenes banged the table in frustration. 'But the west is exposed to us – now! Antigonos, in going to Media, has left the door open. We have to grab this opportunity; it gives us the chance to end this once and for all and have an empire united under the Argead king.'

'No, Eumenes, it does not,' countered Tlepolemus, the satrap of Carmania. 'We might take the west but what if

Antigonos decides he's very happy with all our satrapies under his command and does not come to face our army? *You* will still have the western satrapies but *we* will have nothing. I, too, will not follow you.'

'Nor I,' Sibyrtius of Arachosia confirmed.

'If I were to go west for too long,' Eudamos said, 'I would have no satrapy to come back to as it would be part of India once again; and I would hazard none of you would help to win it back.' His dark eyes looked at each of his colleagues in turn; none contradicted him. 'So I stay in the east.'

'And my lord would have me on a stake if I were to take his men to places that have no relevance for him,' added Androbarzus, deputy for Oxyartes, the satrap of Paropamisadae.

'I would follow you,' Azanes said, surprising Eumenes. 'I've always wanted to set eyes on the great sea of the west.'

'Thank you, Azanes, but I fear you're in the minority.' Eumenes again glanced around the table; the rest of the faces were adamant. *I can see their point, but it is so short-sighted.* 'This is our best chance; if we don't take it, the only people who benefit are Kassandros and Ptolemy.' But even as he pleaded, Eumenes knew his cause was lost; sacrificed upon the altar of self-interest.

'None of us care about Kassandros and Ptolemy,' Peucestas said.

There were nods of agreement all around the table, with the exception of Antigenes, who remained neutral.

'What about you, Antigenes?' Eumenes asked.

'My satrapy is here in the east; I would defeat Antigonos here first before looking to the west; just as you had originally planned. But if the majority was for heading back west then I would go along with it, but it looks like that is not to be.'

Eumenes sighed, knowing when to abandon a forlorn cause. 'In which case, if we are to stay in the east and defeat Antigonos here, and given we don't want to follow in his wake through terrain stripped of all food, I would suggest we go to Persepolis and wait to see where Antigonos ends up. We can then approach him from the opposite direction, east, through your own satrapies which will keep us supplied.'

Peucestas glanced around his fellows, receiving nods of agreement. 'Very well, Eumenes, we accept your plan.'

Eumenes pointed to the empty throne. 'Alexander's plan.' *Although Alexander would have done what I first suggested and, before defeating Antigonos, knocked out both Kassandros and Ptolemy.*

PTOLEMY.
THE BASTARD.

MOVING WITH UNHURRIED precision, Ptolemy straightened up at the waist, stretched his arms wide and then, bringing them over his head, placed his palms together; inhaling deep, he bent first to the left and then the right, slow and deliberate, pressing down as much as he could, before leaning back so he felt a clicking in the small of his back. Up he came again, this time to turn to the left, arms extended; going down on one knee and crouching, head bowed, he placed his fists on the cool stone before, with muscles taut, rising back to his full height and then repeating the same move to the right.

His mood was excellent and had been improving day on day for the past six months, since he had returned to Alexandria from Tyros, expecting to have to withdraw his garrisons from Syria, only to learn a month later that Eumenes had headed east and Antigonos had followed him. Now spring had come and armies were free to roam that distant land in the reasonable expectation of being able to supply themselves, he was looking forward to a quiet year, or even two, getting on with securing his position without anybody bothering him. He reasoned whoever won the duel in the east would certainly not have the time in this campaigning season to come against him, and probably not even in the following as the distances were so great; this he knew for a fact having travelled the terrain with his putative half-brother Alexander – if he was indeed the bastard son of Philip, the second of that name of Macedon.

Easing himself upright with straining thighs, he sucked the air deep into his lungs and felt a rush of pleasure at his situation: with the east occupied, Kassandros blockading Olympias in Pydna and Lysimachus busy building his fortresses in northern Thrace and fighting off barbarian incursions, Ptolemy had concerns from only one direction: west. And thus he found his already excellent mood improved even further as he exercised on the terrace of his suite of rooms in the newly built palace on the eastern side of the Great Harbour of Alexandria whilst watching the ship, a trireme bearing the awaited Carthaginian embassy, sail towards the harbour mouth.

'My lord?'

Ptolemy did not need to turn to know Lycortas, his chamberlain, was standing in the doorway, his hands tucked into the sleeves of his long robe; plump, shaven-headed and with an unreadable expression on his face, he was, to Ptolemy's mind, the second most important advisor he had, after his mistress of many years, Thais, the mother of three of his children. 'Yes, Lycortas.'

'The bride is ready and the guests are all assembled.'

'Excellent, Lycortas.' It was not possible for Ptolemy's mood to improve as his arms described a downward circle and he began a slow and controlled crouch. 'Excellent!'

'There is, I'm afraid, one problem, my lord.'

There always is. 'Go on.'

'It's your wife, lord.'

It always is. 'She's refusing to attend my wedding?' He rose from the crouch, his palms coming together as he thrust his hands high and then held them skywards, lifting his face to the sun.

165

'Indeed, my lord; she is using her pregnancy as an excuse.'

'Well, that'll make it a more joyous occasion.'

'And she's refusing to allow the young Ptolemy to attend.'

'And that will make it a more peaceful occasion.' His son and namesake, now almost three, was a difficult child to say the least. *Too much of his mother in him. Now Antipatros is dead, what does Eurydike actually bring me other than making Kassandros my brother-in-law, which is not something to be relished?* He brought his head down, to look out over the harbour that was to be the mouth of the great city, founded by Alexander a dozen years previously and currently under construction, as he rested his hands, palms still together, first on his head and then his heart.

The question had occurred to him more and more over the past few months since he had, on Thais' advice, begun an affair with Eurydike's cousin, Berenice, with a view to taking her as his third wife – his first wife, Artakama, whom he had married at the Susa mass wedding, he had abandoned when he had left Babylon, so to his mind Berenice was just the second wife.

It had been Thais' talk of dynastic politics that had convinced Ptolemy the step was necessary. His children with Thais were not of the status to forge dynastic alliances, being the illegitimate offspring from a liaison – admittedly a long liaison – with the highest paid courtesan in the world, one with a single client; they would do for minor alliances with petty kings. Eurydike's children were legitimate and her pedigree was good as the daughter of Antipatros, a nobleman and the late regent of Macedon, and they would be suitable spouses for the sons and daughters of his peers; however, they lacked one thing: royal blood. This is what Berenice would supply for she was the daughter of Princess Antigone of the Argead royal house; he would father children of royal blood on her, and that, to Ptolemy's mind, was dynastic planning.

He shook his head, putting the raging jealousy of the pregnant Eurydike from his thoughts, and indicated to the approaching Carthaginian ship now passing through the harbour mouth. 'Have the embassy comfortably settled in their apartments. Send them my apologies, explaining to them the reason I haven't greeted them in person, and then invite them to the wedding feast; they couldn't have arrived at a more fortunate time.' He stretched his arms before him, palms out, muscles tense, before turning his hands over and relaxing into the final restful position of the ritual salutation of the sun, practised by the indigenous population of his domain for more years than could be remembered.

'Gods, that feels good,' he said after a few moments, enjoying the rejuvenating sensation of well-worked muscles. 'It gets every part of your body.'

'Indeed, my lord.'

'Do you do that or something similar, Lycortas?'

'Yes, my lord; only I have someone do it for me.'

'What good is that?'

'It preserves my dignity.'

'Ha! Very good!'

'Imagine me, with my weight, trying to rise from the crouch using only the muscles in my legs? I would be in need of a new robe after the effort and would still be in the crouching position – or saluting the water as I believe that movement is called.'

'It is. I'm surprised you know, seeing as you only do it by proxy.'

'I had younger days, my lord, days that have not been completely dimmed in my memory.'

'Of course you did.' Ptolemy turned to check the progress of the trireme as its sail was hauled down and the oars began to bite in the calm sea of the protected harbour, now in the process of being divided in two by the great mole, the Heptastadion, which would eventually join the island of Pharos to the mainland. 'It'll be very interesting to hear what they have to say, seeing as it was the Carthaginians who asked for this meeting.'

'Indeed, my lord.'

'Yes. But first I must go and get married.'

'No, my lord; first you must get dressed – or at least wrap a towel around yourself.'

It was with pleasant anticipation that Ptolemy dressed for his wedding, for he knew before long he would be shedding the garments to spend a very enjoyable afternoon with his new bride before receiving the Carthaginian embassy later. Over the past few months he had ensured Berenice was suitable for his extravagant sexual tastes and she had performed very pleasingly, showing much promise; so much so he had neglected Eurydike's bed more than was, perhaps, politic, thus causing the domestic disharmony he was currently enduring. Thais, however, had no such cause for jealousy as he was a frequent visitor to her chambers, firstly for advice and then, secondly, for the skills only a courtesan of her experience could provide: depravities he could only hope to teach Berenice, having already failed so dismally in Eurydike's schooling; she could but endure, not enjoy, and there was no satisfaction for him in that.

Thus it was with blood surging in his loins he lifted Berenice's veil, repeating the age-old form of words which transferred the bride from the family of her absent father into his own. He cupped her face in his hands and, surprising himself with his tenderness, kissed her mouth. In her mid-twenties, tall and dignified, with lithe limbs and smooth, pale skin, Berenice was a woman of extraordinary beauty and, as Ptolemy knew from experience, sensuality. As he drew away from the kiss he found himself gazing into hazel eyes, in thrall to their sincerity:

Berenice was not someone to say one thing and do another, she was direct and honest and Ptolemy admired her for those rare qualities – qualities he was well aware he lacked. What was more, she came with three children from her previous marriage, all of whom could also be used for diplomatic purposes. However, what excited Ptolemy most was that, despite her overt femininity in the form of her immaculate makeup and coiffure, subtle but thrilling scent and elegant choice of attire and jewellery which showed her body to full advantage – a body he would soon be getting to grips with once more – she was also a woman of deeds: whilst a widow, she had competed at the Olympic Games and won the chariot race, a feat none of her sex had ever before achieved. *I have much to thank Thais for in suggesting this match. Berenice is everything I could wish for as a wife: beautiful, adventurous, willing and, above all, I can trust her to give her honest opinion; much like Thais, really, but without the extra special ingredient that makes her such a charming bed companion.*

Pulling his gaze from deep within her, Ptolemy offered his arm to Berenice and turned to face the assembled guests, all two thousand of them, in the expansive central courtyard of the palace; he acknowledged them with a wave and a regal nod. It was the signal that well-placed agents in the crowd had been waiting for; cheering erupted in pockets that soon spread until the courtyard reverberated with the glee of his subjects, dressed in Macedonian, Greek, Egyptian, Persian and Jewish attire, creating a riot of colour and a truly cosmopolitan feel.

'They're happy to welcome you as my wife,' Ptolemy said, smiling at her and again surprising himself at the genuine pleasure he felt at this remark.

Berenice returned the smile, displaying remarkably white and even teeth. 'I hope soon they'll be equally happy to welcome me as their queen.'

Taken by surprise by this bald statement, Ptolemy covered by leading off the wedding procession, through the crowd of guests, in the direction of the great hall that would accommodate eight hundred of the most influential guests at a hundred tables whilst the rest would be feasted out in the courtyard.

'I take it you think that I should declare myself Pharaoh,' Ptolemy said to his new wife as the guests parted to let them through as the sea gives way to the bow of a ship.

'The throne is empty and you're the only man with a claim to it.'

'The throne of Egypt, you mean?'

'What use would any other be to us? This is the only one we can safely defend.'

'My thoughts exactly; but it is too early to make a formal break with the rest of the empire, which proclaiming myself Pharaoh would effectively do. Also, I think politically it would be best for someone else to claim a throne first so it can never be said it was I who broke up the empire – after all, there are many to claim. No, Berenice, we must be patient.'

'I've never been a patient woman.'

'Then that is, amongst other, more pleasurable things, something I shall have to teach you.'

'And when do my lessons start?'

'As soon as our guests have drunk our health and escorted us to the bridal chamber.'

It was not until the following day that Ptolemy managed to extract himself from Berenice's arms, such was the intensity of his schooling and the receptiveness of the pupil. The Carthaginian embassy, however, did not seem put out by their wait and, indeed, as he entered the audience chamber, surrounded by eight bodyguards, he detected a few knowing half-smiles amongst the twenty-strong delegation waiting on him, dwarfed by the double lines of columns, painted in reds, blues and golds, along each wall.

Although he had greeted each member the day before at the wedding feast, he had not said more than a few words to any of them and, apart from the Carthaginians raising their goblets to the newly-weds and catching Ptolemy's eye, there had been no other contact. And so after Lycortas had announced him, now seated upon high, and called the meeting to order, Ptolemy watched with interest as the leader of the delegation came forward. Of a muscular build, dark-skinned and -eyed with a slender but pronounced nose and thin lips, his hair and beard were tightly curled. He wore a knee-length robe of rich green and gold stripes, gathered around his waist by an embroidered sash of similar colour. With a deep red cloak, edged in gold, clasped about his neck, draped over just one shoulder, and with heavily ringed fingers and thick gold bracelets about his wrists, he looked at once outlandish and dignified.

A hardened killer for all his refinement, Ptolemy mused as he watched the way the man carried himself.

'To Ptolemy, ruler of Egypt, the two Sufetes of Carthage, the Supreme Council of Thirty and the Tribunal of One Hundred and Four send their greetings.'

Referring to me as ruler rather than satrap is almost recognising Egypt as independent; curious. This is a game I'm interested in playing.

'And they wish you a long and prosperous life.'

In other words: 'reign'. His Greek is remarkably good, if somewhat sibilant, to be able to convey such nuances. 'I thank them for their good wishes and would ask you to give them mine in return, as well as my sincere wish that peace and trade shall be the cornerstones upon which our two great nations will build a lasting relationship.' Ptolemy caught a look of understanding at the coded message flick across the ambassador's face.

'That our two *nations* should do so is the wish of my masters in Carthage.'

Good, by his accepting Egypt as a nation we have just established we're talking one to one without consideration for my former comrades or the regent, be that Polyperchon or Olympias.

'My name is Mago of the house of Barca, lord Ptolemy, and I have been empowered to speak for the Sufetes, the Thirty and the One Hundred and Four.'

Ptolemy indicated with a nod of his head that he accepted Mago's credentials.

'What I have to say is of a delicate and highly confidential nature and so I will send all of my delegation from the room other than two men who will be able to vouch for the conversation when we return to Carthage.' He turned and gave a sharp order in a tongue of which Ptolemy had never, in the few times he had heard it, been able to make out a word.

Once the delegation had departed, Ptolemy turned to his guards' commander. 'Ask my brother Menelaus to join us and then take your men away.'

Lycortas stepped forward.

'I know what you're going to say but the answer is no. I won't be alone, you can stay and I've summoned Menelaus so we will be equal numbers; but I would have thought if these gentlemen had wanted to kill me they wouldn't do it themselves in my own audience chamber but, rather, send their Carthaginian version of Archias the Exile-Hunter. Which reminds me: has he returned from Macedon to collect the other half of his fee yet?'

'I will make enquiries, lord.'

'Do so; I'm anxious to see him.'

Once Menelaus, Ptolemy's governor of Cyprus, here in Alexandria for the nuptials, was present and the guards had left, Ptolemy turned to Mago. 'So, my friend, now you may speak in confidence.'

Mago looked to his two companions, both similarly attired but in varying hues; they nodded; he turned back to Ptolemy. 'Our trading interests on the island of Sicilia are no secret. There is much to trade and plenty of towns to trade with, plus it is a staging post for the island of Sardinia to its north where, again, we have concerns.'

Ptolemy's knowledge of the geography of the west was hazy, but he knew the whereabouts of Sicilia and could picture another island to its north next to Italia. 'Go on.'

'We are a trading nation and wish only for peace so trade can prosper. We wish for the west of the inner sea to be seen as our sphere of influence. We have colonies along the Hispanic coast in the far west and along the African coast, both east and west of Carthage. There was even a time when we held sway over Cyrenaica, before we were forced to concentrate our gaze westwards. Indeed, as my family name indicates, we come originally from Barca in Cyrenaica. My great-grandfather, Hasdrubal, sold the family business in Barca and moved to Carthage when it became apparent we could not hold the east and the west at the same time.'

Where's this going? Surely they're not going to ask me to give them Cyrenaica back?

'But no,' Mago said, reading Ptolemy's mind, 'we are making no claim on Cyrenaica, far from it. My father, Hannibal, and my elder brother, named after my grandfather, both agree with the Sufetes and the Thirty, who have responsibility for our foreign policy, that Carthage's future is in the west. Even to the extent of the lands both north and south beyond the Pillars of Heracles. It is about who holds the east that we have come to talk.'

'I hold the east as far as Tyros and Cyprus, which my brother here rules in my name,' Ptolemy said, indicating to Menelaus.

'Indeed; and you shall, no doubt, be taking control of Crete soon.'

Ptolemy's face remained impassive. *Best to keep them guessing about that.*

Seeing he was to get no response on that subject, Mago pressed on: 'As a result of the last war we waged in Sicilia, over a period of more than sixty years, which finished badly for us twenty-three years ago, we now control only the south-western corner of the island. Our troops were gravely mauled both by disease and the army of the then Tyrant of Syracuse, Dionysus. But now we feel it's time to change the situation. We have waited a generation to rebuild our manpower and we have refilled our coffers. We have augmented our citizen forces with mercenaries from Gallia and Hispania, as well as local tribesmen in Sicilia. In short, we are ready to go on the offensive and try to do what our grandparents failed to: gain control of the whole island.'

'But?'

Mago raised his eyebrows. 'You are prescient, lord Ptolemy. Indeed, there is a "but". There is a new tyrant in Syracuse and from our sources he makes Dionysus seem like a reasonable man; having been banished from the city twice in his younger days, he came to power last year by entering Syracuse at the head of an army of mercenaries, having made a solemn vow to uphold the democratic constitution and keep it alive.'

Ptolemy sucked the breath between his teeth. 'Mercenary generals don't tend to mix very well with either democracy or solemn vows.'

'Indeed not; he ordered the deaths of the ten thousand most prominent men in Syracuse and took complete control through fear. None are now willing to oppose him as this man doesn't punish a miscreant by simple execution; rather, he executes his entire family and leaves only him alive and well, to suffer a living death of life-long mourning in solitude. This tyrant is truly a man to be feared. His name is Agathocles.'

'He sounds as if he could be a good thing for Carthage.'

'In that if we were to rid Syracuse of him the grateful citizenry would welcome our nomination with open arms?'

Ptolemy immediately saw where this was leading. 'Which is why you are here: the Sufetes and the Thirty have been analysing what he needs to do to keep power.'

'Exactly; they have put themselves in his place and what with their conclusions and what we know from his past behaviour, they have surmised that to keep his people supporting him, despite his crimes, he will embark upon an offensive war.'

'Nationalism is the weapon of all tyrants and demagogues.' *And I haven't been shy to use it myself; I think these Carthaginians have predicted Agathocles' next move correctly.* 'But what has that to do with me, seeing as I have no interests in Sicilia?'

'And very pleased the Sufetes and the Thirty will be to hear that, lord Ptolemy; but it was not what I meant. Yes, no doubt Agathocles will begin seizing independent towns in Sicilia, and no doubt come out and try to force our army on the island into a pitch battle on ground of his choosing, which may or may not be successful. But it is more than that, lord Ptolemy; we have seen our weakness when it comes to dealing with Syracuse.'

'And why would you tell me?'

'Our weakness against Syracuse is not the same as our weakness against you; not that our two nations have any reason to go to war.'

'Quite.'

'Quite.' Mago paused to collect his thoughts. 'What we have concluded is, with two armies in Hispania to expand inland as well as preserve what we already have, and with an army in Sicilia as well as the standing army around Carthage itself to keep the Numidians in order, the best way to attack us is where we don't expect a threat to come from and then go for our heart.'

'Ah! I see,' Ptolemy said, admiring the analytical abilities of this strange race. 'Recruit two armies, which would not be difficult for him given how many mercenaries are about at the moment and how much wealth he would've got from the people he's murdered. Land one on the North African coast, ensuring his rear by coming to an agreement with Ophellas, my deputy in Cyrenaica, and then advance on Carthage, supported by the fleet that transported them, from the lesser defended south.'

'You have it. By the time we would find out about it, it would be too late to withdraw one of our armies from Hispania. We would have no choice but to bring the closer Sicilian army home, thus leaving the island open to Agathocles' second army. He would then either withdraw the first because it would never be enough to take Carthage once our Sicilian army is back, or...' Mago let the sentence fade.

'Or go back on his agreement with Ophellas, which, as we know from his betrayal of Syracuse, he is prone to do, and take what he can of Cyrenaica before I can react. Hmm, interesting and also inconvenient.' Ptolemy studied the man before him; he respectfully lowered his gaze. *That was a sound lesson in strategy and an interesting insight into how these people think: don't fight for the limbs, go for the heart.* 'And what have you been sent here to ask me for, Mago of Barca?'

'A formal alliance of our two nations, recognising our spheres of influence.'

'The borders being where?'

'A line midway between Cyrene and Carthage with you renouncing any possible future interest in Sicily or any of the islands west or north of it, and us renouncing any possible future interest in Crete or any of the islands east or north of it.'

Ptolemy stood to show that the audience was at an end. 'Thank you, Mago. I shall consider the matter and you will have my answer shortly.' He walked from the room, leaving Lycortas and Menelaus to deal with the embassy, and made directly for Thais' suite.

'Did you hear it all?' Ptolemy asked as Thais knelt before him and washed his feet in a bowl of water of a pleasing temperature.

'Every word.'

'And?'

'And it was an impressive display of analytical thinking. Carthage will not be a straightforward conquest.'

'I never thought it would. But I didn't think they would be this wily. What do you suppose Mago meant when he said: "our weakness against Syracuse is not the same as our weakness against you"?'

'If you went to war with Carthage, you would go directly for the city itself.'

'And also to Sicilia to prevent the army there being withdrawn.'

'Naturally. But more to the point, seeing as we have had an insight into how they think, an invasion of Sicilia would also prevent that Carthaginian army being sent to Cyrenaica and—'

'Cutting our supply lines and line of retreat and even threatening Alexandria itself.' Ptolemy looked down at Thais, eyes wide as the implication of this sank in. Thais took a linen cloth and began to dry his feet as if she had said nothing of import. 'So Carthaginians are asking me to help them against Agathocles so they can keep Sicilia not just for trade but also as a base to launch a counterattack on me should I ever decide I want to expand west.'

'It looks that way.'

'They're basically asking me to help them in their own defence against me.'

'Clever, aren't they?' Thais began work on the other foot without looking up.

'Very. And you saw all this just as you listened from behind the screen?'

Thais carried on with her work. 'Ptolemy, my love, you are the canniest politician I know, but if you have one weakness it is in not assuming your opponent has already outguessed you, even before the negotiations have begun. Admittedly that happens very rarely, but it will happen from time to time and today is a good example of it. Sometimes you're just too forgiving.'

'It's always been my weakness.'

'I know. Now the question is: what answer are you going to give them that will make them think they're still outguessing you and leave them completely unaware you've outguessed them?'

Ptolemy reached down and cupped her chin in his hand and lifted her face, admiring the gentle curve of her nose and the pout of her lips, full and red against her pale skin framed by loose hair, red-golden as a late summer sunset. 'Gods, I'm lucky to have you.'

'I know. I'm surprised you remember, with all the distraction you've had recently.'

He leaned forward and kissed her; she responded with enthusiasm.

'I'll give them my answer tomorrow; I know exactly what to say and then do. The Exile-Hunter will be of great use in this matter, when he returns.'

Fortunately, it was only a couple of days later, after the departure of the Carthaginian embassy, bearing Ptolemy's undertaking to sign a treaty along the same lines as had been suggested, that Archias the Exile-Hunter was ushered into his private suite by Lycortas.

'I was beginning to worry you no longer wished to do business with me; it's over six months since I sent you to tell Olympias of your procuring the poison for Kassandros in Tarsus before he travelled to Babylon. I was very worried, seeing as there is the second instalment of your fee waiting here.'

Archias gave a theatrical bow, humorous eyes twinkling at Ptolemy from a round, almost boyish face, crowned by abundant black curls, which belied his forty or so years. '"Thus leisurely I hastened on my road".'

'Indeed,' Ptolemy replied, thinking the quote might be from Sophocles, but not sure enough to name him.

'And don't worry about the payment, lord Ptolemy; Lycortas has furnished me with the outstanding five talents and my men with half a talent apiece.'

'Indeed, lord,' Lycortas confirmed. 'He wouldn't do a thing I asked of him since he arrived this morning without payment. Fortunately for him, I was not leisurely in my haste to pay him.'

Archias grinned and shrugged. 'I always insist on prompt payment.'

'Prompt payment? I expected you back months ago.'

'Ah, I had business in Athens that delayed me past the end of the sailing season so my men and I wintered in Attica.'

'Very nice, I'm sure. Is there anything I should know about your business in Athens?'

'It was for Demetrius of Phaleron, Kassandros' creature put in place to make sure the oligarchy thinks in the right way. Suffice it to say there are two who will never think again; more I cannot say for professional reasons, client confidentiality and all that sort of thing.'

You can't help but like the man, if only for his impertinence. 'Extremely noble of you, Archias.'

'"What is noble is forever loved".'

'Quite. So Kassandros' hold on Athens is tightening?'

'I would say so. It's tighter than it was, at any rate.'

'I shall have to work out a way of destabilising it, in that case.'

'Now would be a very good moment to attempt such a thing as Kassandros is still occupied with the siege of Pydna. Olympias is defiant and determined to hold out, as I know from having popped into the city for a nose around on my way here. If I can be of service in the matter I would be only too pleased; I do so enjoy destabilising work.' Archias sat without invitation. 'Now, is Lycortas going to serve me some of your second-best wine he always feels I'm so undeserving of? I would dearly love a cup before we discuss what you wish me to do in Athens.'

'It's the third-best, actually,' Lycortas said, his face betraying the fact that he considered even that to be too good for the likes of Archias.

Ptolemy smiled, more at Lycortas' outrage than at the Exile-Hunter's cheek. 'And it's not to Athens I wish you to go at the moment, but Syracuse.'

'Syracuse? A beautiful city. I have some very pleasant memories from there, both personal and professional from my previous career on the stage as well as my present one.'

Ptolemy smiled despite himself. *He's a ruthless killer and yet an engaging and entertaining conversationalist; a thoroughly likable man.* 'But before we discuss the Syracuse business, tell me how you found Olympias coping in Pydna. For a price, naturally.'

'Naturally.'

OLYMPIAS.
THE MOTHER.

A
S SPRING TURNED into summer, the situation Olympias found herself in was not yet desperate, but her options were severely limited. Indeed, she had but three, and it was the third of those, after hold out or surrender, she had now decided to attempt: escape. And it was to this end she, Thessalonike, Roxanna and the boy-king Alexander boarded one of the three sleek and fast lembi, fully crewed and made ready for the sea, shortly after midnight on the last new moon before the longest day of the year.

Letters smuggled in and out of the city to and from her daughter Kleopatra, still sitting in Sardis, had convinced Olympias there would be no help coming from Eumenes. He had not turned his army around and headed back west; quite the contrary, and Antigonos had followed him into the vastness of the east. The last news Kleopatra had of him was that he had defeated Antigonos somewhere to the south of Susa and was campaigning even further east; although no one was sure where as news was sparse over the winter and spring, but now with the coming of summer more certain intelligence would surely arrive. However, it would be at least a year before he could be expected to be back on the coast, assuming he survived the duel with Antigonos now being played out with armies of growing magnitude – if the rumours and second-hand hearsay were anything to be believed.

My curse upon them all; Eumenes, Aristonous and that snivelling little nonentity, Polyperchon. Olympias had cursed her allies regularly since it had also become apparent Roxanna's assertion was true, that neither Aristonous nor Polyperchon would return with the help they had promised, having escaped by boat from the city soon after the siege had commenced. Long had Olympias waited, standing in the highest tower of Pydna, looking out over the huge wall and siege works hoping against hope to see the shadow of a host, proving the eastern wild-cat had misheard the conversation she had claimed to have witnessed between the two commanders, or had even lied about the whole thing in order to make herself more important to Olympias. But once two months of fine weather had gone by and no relief had appeared on either horizon, either military or naval, it became obvious Roxanna had heard correctly and neither Aristonous nor Polyperchon would be coming to break the siege. And now, as midsummer approached and all the livestock had been consumed, supplies were down to the scrapings in the granaries and were reserved for able-bodied soldiers only. The sick and the citizenry were left to fend for themselves or, more likely, starve to death, and so it was time for Olympias to look out for herself.

'We sail immediately,' she ordered the triarchos as she came aboard.

The man bowed his head. 'With respect, Your Majesty, we should wait until—'

'I said immediately!' Olympias was in no mood to deal with insubordinate underlings.

'But—'

The glare Olympias gave, even in such dim light, was enough to stop any objection the triarchos had.

'Immediately it is, Your Majesty. And what about the two decoy vessels?'

'They won't be much good as decoys unless they sail with us, will they?'

'No, Your Majesty, but it would be better—'

'I will decide what's best. Now, silence and get on with your job.'

Mumbling to himself, the man turned and went aft to order to cast off.

If he thinks he can expect my gratitude after that display, he will be bitterly disappointed. Olympias turned as Alexander let out a small yelp of pain as he stubbed his toe on a box holding many of Olympias' possessions. 'Quiet, child! Sit on that box and stay still. I don't want to hear another sound from you until we are through the blockade. Roxanna, for once in your life, do something maternal and comfort your son.'

With just a hiss from beneath her veil, Roxanna did as she was told and sat next to Alexander, putting her arm around him.

'He doesn't look like he's enjoying his mother's succour too much,' Thessalonike observed as the boy shook off his mother's arm.

'As long as he doesn't give us away with his whining I don't care what he enjoys. I just need him alive for when we get to Sardis. Eumenes will never be able to refuse my order to return west if the king is with me in Asia.'

'Assuming we get there.'

'We will,' Olympias asserted as the crew of all three lembi began casting off and setting their oars. 'We will because I have sacrificed to Poseidon and Dionysus as well as the Earth Mother; they will hear my prayers. And besides—'

'The snakes have spoken?'

Olympias looked hard at her adopted daughter in the gloom and saw mockery on her face. 'Don't be a little bitch.'

'Don't be a superstitious fool. I've never known the snakes give a correct answer; have you?'

Olympias turned away. *I'll not get into an argument here with her. She'll find out just how much I don't need her once I'm reunited with my blood daughter in Sardis. I'll make you pay for turning on me, Thessalonike.* Making her way to the bow, Olympias held fast to the rail as the ship slipped its mooring and the crew pushed away from the jetty with boat hooks so the oars could be spread. All lights were now doused and complete darkness reigned over the harbour. Despite the man's impertinence, Olympias found herself admiring the triarchos for being able to find his way through the harbour mouth without any point of reference. Slow the oars did beat; the gentle splash of their blades breaking the surface in unison and drops pattering back into the water as they were raised were the only sounds disturbing the still night. Not even the rowers allowed themselves their customary grunt at each stroke, for all knew the vital importance of complete silence.

At the beginning of the siege it had been a relatively easy affair to break the blockade, such was the inexperience of Kassandros' fleet and army. But now they had grown wise to the wiles of the besieged and very few ships had been able to get into or out of the harbour or men find a way through the great siege wall. Indeed, the last men who had managed both ingress and egress had been Archias the Exile-Hunter and his seven Thracians, and he had not been persuaded to say how he did it. He was just there one day and gone the next. But Olympias felt confident they would be successful this night for it was pitch dark and the decoy ships would make a willing sacrifice. *If only so as the crews can go over to Kassandros and get a decent meal.* Olympias was not unaware of the men's motives.

The waves grew as they passed out into open sea; the pace of the rowers increased, led by the man nearest the stern on the starboard side as no piping the beat was possible in the silence. Olympias strained her eyes into the gloom; the shaded outline of one of the decoy ships was just visible ahead to larboard. The other one, to starboard, was lost in the murk. On they ploughed through the growing swell, facing into a stiffening breeze that checked their progress more than Olympias would have wished. The phosphorescence playing in the bow-wave seemed blindingly bright in comparison to her shaded surroundings, so she closed her eyes and issued a stream of prayers to all the gods she had recently sacrificed to, urging them not to forget her gifts and to act upon them so she might come to safety and begin the vengeance she so craved. Oh, how she would make those who had abandoned her suffer.

The strain of rowing at such pace began to tell on the oarsmen and involuntary grunts and groans at each stroke issued, despite the hissed rebukes of the triarchos, but still they kept the tempo up, their backs straining as they heaved their oars time and time again, glad of the spray that flew inboard to cool their skin.

At first, Olympias thrilled at the sight, thinking a shooting star was a good omen, and well it might have been, had the streak across the sky been such a phenomenon. As it plunged into the sea with a hiss to starboard it showed it was not so. More streaks of flame raced to the heavens, originating from different areas of gloom. Shot at random, the fire arrows mostly plummeted harmlessly beneath the waves. But such was their number it was only a question of a few moments before one juddered into a vessel, briefly burning before it was doused, but those couple of heartbeats were enough for the unseen archers to get some sort of bearing. Skywards the streaks of flame rocketed to pause at their zenith before diving back down, peppering the starboard decoy ship and the sea around it. Flames caught with surprising rapidity, burning bright before being extinguished, hissing with steam; and again the archers renewed their aim, made clearer for them by the longer burn. Arrows began to thump into the targeted ship; in they came, staccato in their rhythm, with such rapidity that soon fire had taken a hold, silhouetting figures as they rushed in panic to save their boat and their lives.

The triarchos steered to larboard, veering away from the stricken vessel as yet more furrows of flame ploughed through the sky, dooming the lembus to fiery destruction and a watery grave.

Unable to restrain herself any longer, Olympias turned to the triarchos. 'Make them row faster!' she screamed, her hair wind-wild in the glow from the dying ship. 'I must escape, I must!'

'They go as fast as possible, Majesty.'

'It's not fast enough.' She lashed out with a foot at the back of the nearest oarsman. 'Faster!'

And so the man increased his stroke, but he was at the rear of his fellows and none saw what he had done, so within two pulls he had fouled the sweep of the man in front; the oar fell from his hand and was pulled back by the forward motion of the ship to tangle with that of the third man along. The boat slewed round as the triarchos bellowed for oars to be shipped before complete catastrophe occurred.

Alexander howled as his grandmother raced along the ship's length, pushing him from his box in her desire to get to the triarchos' throat with the knife she had pulled from within her cloak.

'Order them to row immediately or you are a dead man,' she shrieked into the triarchos' ear.

'Of course, Majesty. But please do not interfere again. Oars out!'

With a few moments to sort themselves out, the oarsmen managed to pull the first stroke together; with quickening heaves they accelerated away, making no effort to control the noise of physical exertion as the burning vessel nearby burst into a fearsome inferno. Now the probing fire arrows started their search for new victims, rising from many points of origin and flicking at random across the sky to fizz harmlessly into the sea. On the oarsmen pulled, hearts pounding, cheeks puffing; it was a shock to all as the first arrow thumped into the spine of a heaving rower, severing it and causing immediate paralysis. He slumped forward with the missile standing proud, its flame a torch.

'Put it out!' the triarchos cried.

The men scrambled for water, the stroke now completely forgotten.

But it was too late, their position had been marked; as the flame was extinguished, a dozen more flaming missiles thwacked into the ship with juddering reports.

'Water!' Olympias screamed quite unnecessarily, for the men were already scrambling for the bailing buckets.

But the damage had been done; the vessel was afire and had become a target for all with a bow out, unseen, upon the water, in at least two dozen ships.

'We go back!' the triarchos shouted, forcing the steersmen to push their oars to starboard. 'Half of you row and half fight the fire!'

Round the ship came to larboard with what little way still remained to it.

Realising that to escape the fate of their fellow mariners they needed to obey their captain's orders, the oarsmen set to their tasks, one half fighting flames with a will as the other rowed as if their lives depended on it, which, of course, they did.

'Why have you turned back?' Olympias demanded, threatening the triarchos with her knife.

'We are trapped, Your Majesty; who knows how many ships they have out there, at least a couple of dozen, probably more, and the closer we get to them the more they'll hit us with fire and the easier a target we will become. We'll have no chance. Better to try to extinguish the flame and blend back into the night and hope the archers find sport with the second decoy. Had we waited, like I was trying to tell you, then we would not have been in amongst all this and could have slipped away as the decoys did their job.' He looked up to the flames still streaking across the darkness and shook his head. 'This is new; I've never known them to use fire arrows at random like this at night-time.'

It was the last thing he said. The exposed throat was too much of a temptation for Olympias and she took out her frustration on it, ripping it open with her knife. 'Row!' she ordered the men as the triarchos flopped to the floor and the last of the fires hissed out. 'Row!'

And row the oarsmen did, for they had seen what their queen had done and all knew of what she was capable, and besides, she had made no order to return the ship to its original course. They were heading back to the relative safety of a harbour in a port under siege from both land and sea, but that was preferable to what they had experienced trying to slip through the blockade. The sight of the second decoy being strafed by fire arrows and suffering death by a thousand flames was enough to put yet more vigour into their tired limbs, and it was not long before they were back at the harbour mouth waiting for the great chain protecting it to be lowered.

With tears of rage and frustration in her eyes, Olympias stormed down the gangplank of the docked vessel with Thessalonike following – Alexander, too terrified of his blood-soaked grandmother to move, sat on his box hyperventilating as he stared at the corpse just a few feet away from him.

'You're enjoying this,' Olympias said, accusation in her tone, as she strode along the quay, once more lit by torches as there was no need now for secrecy.

'What gave you that impression, Olympias?' Thessalonike responded. 'I want to escape this place as much as you; the thought of slipping into a warm bath in Sardis with the knowledge of a good meal and decent wine awaiting makes me want to weep with longing.'

'Is that all you can think of? Luxury?'

'It's better than imagining different ways of killing people slowly. Face it, Olympias, you are stuck here and there's no one coming to your aid because you've alienated everyone who has tried to help you, with your viciousness and cruelty.'

Olympias swivelled, hand flailing, but Thessalonike caught it by the wrist just before it made contact with her cheek. 'No, Olympias. I won't allow you to hit me ever again, especially not for telling you the truth. You don't like it, do you? Good, I promised you that would be your punishment and it pleases me to see it hurt you so much.'

'You ungrateful little bitch!'

'Ungrateful? Ungrateful that you murdered my mother? No, Olympias, you have this coming from me. And whilst I'm giving you the hard truth let me tell you this: there is no escaping from here and soon we'll have nothing left to eat other than the few fish we manage to pull out of the harbour. So you have one option left: surrender.'

'Never!'

'Listen to me. It can be done through negotiation.'

'What, with that murdering little pockmarked pile of dog-dung?'

'He no doubt thinks exactly the same of you, without the pockmarked bit, perhaps. You did kill most of his family, after

189

all, didn't you? Oh, yes, and there were those whom you couldn't kill because they were already dead, so you desecrated their graves instead; I'd say you are both murderers in the other's eyes. So negotiate. There must be something you can give him that he wants badly enough to let you go. In fact, I know there is.'

'And so do I, but he'll not get it. Whilst there is an Argead on the throne, Eumenes will come to defend him.'

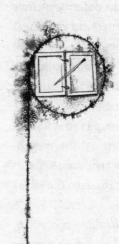

EUMENES.
THE SLY.

BUYING POPULARITY WITH *such extravagance is nothing short of foolish, Peucestas; you'll be obliged to keep on doing so until you've not a single drachma left,* Eumenes reflected as he looked, after a twenty-eight-day march, with a mixture of admiration and disbelief at the sight that greeted the army as they descended from the Persian Gates towards Persepolis nestled in the rugged, brown foothills below.

'There will be a huge sacrifice to Alexander and his father,' Peucestas announced as he and Eumenes gazed down on four concentric circles of tables set before the main gates of the city, 'so that they grant us victory in the campaign against the traitor. Then I shall feast the whole army together, all forty thousand of them. The common infantry will be in the outer circle; the veteran infantry, including the Silver Shields and the Hypaspists, in the next; then the cavalry and the junior officers in the third; and, finally, the senior officers in the innermost circle.' He looked down his nose at Eumenes, his countenance smug. 'I sent ahead to have this all prepared. The dining couches are made of piled-up leaves covered in carpets,' he said in a tone that invited Eumenes to coo with wonder.

Not much of a cooer, Eumenes did not oblige him, although it was, he had to admit, a magnificent sight: the outermost circle was at least a third of a league in circumference and could seat twenty thousand men; even the smallest inner circle could still seat over a thousand. And at the very middle of it all, a huge altar to Alexander and Philip had been erected around which were penned at least a hundred white bulls awaiting sacrifice.

Platters and cups had been laid out and fire pits smouldered all around beneath rotating carcases, sending up the mouth-watering aroma of roasting meat on the warm air as slaves scurried around distributing wine and bread amongst the tables now that the army was in view. *I'm going to have to find a way to outdo Peucestas if I'm to keep my leadership. Should he continue to splash money about like this he will make himself very popular indeed. Kudos with the men is what I need, without, of course, bankrupting myself in the process.*

With this in mind Eumenes endured, first, the lavish sacrifice and then dish after dish of sumptuous hospitality, seated with the other satraps on the high table of the innermost circle. The finest recipes from Persis and the eastern satrapies had been prepared by the best cooks Peucestas' stewards could find; and it was exquisite. All the subtle blend of flavours of the east presented themselves, whether it be fruit and meat in the form of a pigeon and dried apricot pasty or dishes of pistachios with fluffy rice and raisins or a spicy-hot meat dish, with a thick sauce that burned the tongue, from lands further towards the rising sun. And with each dish came a new wine chosen expressly to complement its flavour. Such was the variety and quality of the fare, especially at the innermost table, Eumenes felt he would never be able to re-establish ascendancy over Peucestas; he became more morose with every passing delicacy.

He soon noticed, however, he was not the only one to be put out by the extravagance of the gesture and its blatant purpose. On the table he shared with the other six satraps and Oxyartes' deputy, only Peucestas seemed to be genuinely enjoying himself. He was praising the food and jesting with his fellow diners, who returned his good humour with forced smiles and feeble banter as they picked at their platters with the enthusiasm of those who feared Roxanna had been allowed too near with one of her potions. Seeming not to notice the sullen atmosphere around him, Peucestas drank more and more of the crisp vintages that appeared with each new course as all about the noise level rose, fuelled by the juice of Bacchus, until the entire plain was throbbing with the din of good-humoured and well-fed inebriation – the whole plain, that was, with the exception of the host's table-companions.

Watching the wine slop from Peucestas' cup as he turned to toast tables close by, shouting greetings and exchanging boasts with comrades, Eumenes realised what needed to be done; as the feast drew towards to its riotous conclusion, well after midnight, he managed to slip away unnoticed and went in search of Parmida and Hieronymus.

'In Aramaic?' Parmida said, once Eumenes had divulged his intentions in his chambers in the recently rebuilt section of the royal palace – the original having been burned down some years previously by Alexander in a drunken frenzy, goaded on by a mischievous Thais and an inebriated Ptolemy.

Eumenes nodded. 'Indeed. It's meant to be from Peucestas' friend, Orontes, the satrap of Armenia. Normally he would write to a Macedonian in Greek but he well knows Peucestas is fluent in Aramaic; thus the letter will seem authentic if it is written in that language.'

Eumenes turned to Hieronymus as Parmida sharpened his stylus. 'Now, my friend, how shall we phrase this?'

The big man laughed. 'In my experience, if you tell people what they want to hear, they'll believe it.'

'Then we should make the lie so big and delicious the army swallows it whole without questioning its veracity.'

'Exactly.'

'I'll give them just what they want; and then, my friend, I'll need you to write a few letters purporting to be from Antigonos. But first, Parmida, begin with: To Peucestas, satrap of Persis, and Eumenes, commander of Asia, I, Orontes, send my fraternal greetings. Peucestas, I send this to you as I know it will find you quickly and that you will be able to pass the news onto Eumenes wherever he may be; for I have had no tidings of him since he left Babylon. What I have heard from Europe is momentous and needs to reach his ears as soon as can be.'

Eumenes paused. 'Now, how to phrase it?'

'"Olympias has triumphed,"' Peucestas read, translating from the Aramaic, to the assembled satraps sitting in the shadow of the empty throne. '"She has defeated and killed Kassandros and now Alexander sits firmly on the throne; there is no one left in Europe to challenge him."' Peucestas looked up from the letter at the audible intake of breath, frowned, and then carried on. '"Polyperchon has crossed to Asia with an army large enough to bring the satrapies loyal to the traitor, Antigonos, back into the royal fold, and is moving east with alacrity."' This was greeted by an enthusiastic cheer.

Eumenes joined in, wholehearted, with a look of joyous surprise. *They're loving the good news, and what's more, it's good news that completely justifies their refusal to go west. It'll make them all feel so much better about themselves; except, perhaps, the eclipsed Peucestas.*

Peucestas essayed a look of pleasure in Eumenes' direction; it did not quite convince. "'Meanwhile, Polyperchon's son, Alexandros, controls Greece with his army in the name of the king whilst Aristonous commands the army of Macedon. Kassandros' men have been divided between the three forces to keep their influence to a minimum. I, of course, will offer my army as a blocking force to the north to prevent Antigonos from extracting himself from his grave predicament in that direction. I wish you well in your upcoming campaign against the traitor and congratulate you, Peucestas, in choosing to ally yourself with Eumenes through whose endeavours this has all come to pass. He will be in high favour with Olympias and much patronage will flow through him to those who followed him.'"

This statement brought the largest cheer so far. Eumenes' shoulders were pummelled by those keen to show just how earnestly they supported him, all remembrance of their flat refusal to head west conveniently overlooked.

That seems to have got my kudos up; shame Peucestas doesn't seem to be sharing my joy. I'm looking forward to him reading out my favourite bit.

With a face that betrayed his inner mind, Peucestas held up a hand for silence. 'There is more.' Rapt attention was soon his. "'It is, however, my sad duty to warn you, one of your number in the eastern alliance has been passing on information to Antigonos. I know this to be a fact for I have a spy very close to Antigonos. If you do not unmask the traitor then it might be that Antigonos can still thwart your plans and defeat you. Be warned.'"

Silence ruled the room as each man began to eye his neighbours.

I won't keep them guessing too long; in the meantime I should press my advantage. 'I think such good news should be shared with the whole army. We should have this copied and sent to every officer so they can share it with their men – except, of course, the bit about the spy, that won't be good for morale. But it'll give them heart for the campaign to know we have the army of Europe on its way to support us.'

'I agree,' Antigenes said, slapping the little Greek hard on the shoulder. 'And we should find out soonest which of you is the traitor.'

Peucestas bridled at this. 'And why shouldn't you be a suspect? Or Eumenes for that matter?'

'Because, Peucestas,' Eumenes said in a helpful tone, 'it clearly states in the letter the traitor is one of the satraps in the eastern alliance. That excludes Antigenes and me as we've only arrived in the east this season. But please don't concern yourself with this, gentlemen. I suggest we all stay here whilst I ask someone impartial to conduct a thorough search of all our baggage, and yes, I include myself and Antigenes in that so there can be no complaints. If you have nothing to hide, there is nothing to fear.' He smiled his most innocent smile, daring any of the satraps to protest. None did. *Because you all know yourselves to be innocent in this matter, but one of you is in for a big surprise.*

'Sibyrtius?' Peucestas exclaimed after Eumenes had laid a sheaf of letters before him and announced in whose baggage they had been found. 'But he's my personal friend; he would never betray me.'

'It's a lie,' the accused professed, his eyes darting around the room, 'they must have been planted. I've never had any contact with Antigonos.'

Eumenes feigned surprise. 'Really? Well, gentlemen, that is obviously a falsehood because who here can truthfully say they've never had any correspondence with the traitor? None of us, naturally, because we would all at one point have liked to know what he could give us to entice us over to his cause. So to claim, as Sibyrtius does, a total lack of communication is ludicrous and therefore, to my mind, condemns him.' He picked up the letters and selected one at random. '"The information concerning the numbers of elephants Eudamos has brought from India is most helpful but I would be grateful if you would furnish me with the overall strength of the eastern alliance now Eumenes has joined with you. I remain, Sibyrtius, your good friend, as I hope you remain mine. Greetings, Antigonos."'

Eumenes turned to face the accused; Sibyrtius blanched and ran. 'After him!' Eumenes shouted; but there were no guards on the door for all had agreed to forego their personal security as a sign of trust between them. Eumenes sucked the air through his teeth and then tutted. 'I'll send some men after him. He won't get far. I think it's only right he should stand trial before the army assembly; it would be wrong for us alone to condemn the man without giving him a chance to defend himself – although, running like that does rather indicate his guilt.' Again he smiled his most innocent of smiles for Peucestas. *So let that be a warning to you.*

'I'll have the army assembled for his trial,' Peucestas said without much enthusiasm.

'Have the letter distributed whilst they wait,' Eumenes said. 'And have Alexander's throne set up; I think the lads feel better knowing it will be him sitting in overall judgement.'

But assembling the army for Sibyrtius was a pointless exercise, as there was neither sign nor word of where he might have gone.

'Perfect!' Eumenes exclaimed as he was informed of this by Hieronymus. 'The trial might have raised a few questions but his complete disappearance only goes to prove his guilt. I couldn't have planned it better.'

'Shall I tell Peucestas to stand the men down?'

'Yes.' Then a thought hit him. 'Wait, no, I think I'll have a chat with them first. Make sure the rest of the satraps are all present. I need to plan a little insurance for when the truth about Olympias and Kassandros is exposed.'

Eumenes stepped onto the dais in front of the raised empty throne and took the cheers of the assembled army. All praised him for they had now heard of the great victory to the west, and Eumenes' agents within the ranks had been quick to point out it was the little Greek himself who had been championing the Argead cause right from the beginning and this victory should be seen as a personal triumph for him. Long he let them cheer him for he was about to announce even more good news and he wished for them all to be in the best of moods.

Judging the time right, he raised his hands for silence; it took a while but eventually he could make himself heard. 'Soldiers of Macedon, the last stage in this war is about to commence. The west is held in the name of King Alexander, the rightful heir, and now it is our duty to rid the east of the scourge of treachery. It is down to us to defeat Antigonos and reunite the empire under the Argead royal house.' He let the men cheer this noble objective with his arms outstretched above his head. 'To this end,' he declaimed as the cheering died, 'to this end, my fellow satraps,' he indicated to the august group standing to his right, 'have offered to lend me personally the generous amount of four hundred talents each in order that I can keep your pay up to date throughout the rest of the year. They will deliver their loans here in front of you as witnesses tomorrow morning.' Eumenes resisted the temptation to glance at the eastern satraps but could well imagine their expressions – or, rather, expression as all would be the same:

outrage. 'We will assemble again two hours after dawn to witness this selfless act of charity.'

'How dare you force me into lending you money!' Peucestas fumed as he and the rest of the satraps gathered around him whilst the army was dismissed. 'I've no intention of lending you such an amount.'

'Nor I,' said every other man there.

Eumenes looked affronted. 'How will that appear to the army now they are expecting you to do so tomorrow?'

'But you lied to them by telling them we had agreed to lend you the money.'

'Would you have lent it to me if I had asked you first?'

Peucestas' silence spoke his answer with eloquence. Eumenes looked around their faces and smiled. 'I'll see you in the morning, gentlemen. With the money.'

'Why did you do that?' Hieronymus asked as he walked with Eumenes back through the city gates.

'What? Force them to lend me money?'

'Yes; you don't need it as you have the whole of the Susa treasury at your disposal.'

'Ah, but the Susa treasury won't keep me alive when it is confirmed the letter from Orontes was a fake. But now the eastern satraps all know if they were to kill me they would lose a small fortune each, it might well stay their hand.'

Hieronymus enjoyed the thought. 'Oh, that will go down well in my history; normally a man pays people not to kill him, but you, my sly friend, have people pay you so they don't kill you. That is a clever manipulation of human nature.'

'To human natshure,' Eumenes slurred, three days later, raising his cup for the twentieth time that evening and then downing it.

'Human nature!' his guests echoed as they tipped the wine, by this stage of proceedings unwatered, down their throats.

'And the vileness of us all,' Hieronymus added as he slammed his cup down on the table, letting out a resounding burp.

'You can speak for yourself,' Xennias said, reaching for the jug. 'Personally, I consider myself to be one of the finest examples of human nature around.'

Parmida wiped the excess wine from his beard. 'What gives you that delusion?'

'Who says I'm deluded?'

'Well, my friend,' Parmida said, considering the question as he held his cup out to Xennias for refilling, 'firstly, you have not been brought up in the ways of Azhura Mazda and therefore you haven't been taught to fight the Lie with the Truth and therefore you are open to terrible self-delusion. And secondly, you Greeks and Macedonians, for the same reason, never speak plainly and so will often exaggerate without being corrected by your family or friends; thus you come to accept as facts figments of an over-blown sense of self-esteem and thus become self-deluded.'

Xennias frowned, his wine-addled mind trying to work its way through the Kappadokian's reasoning; it failed. With a sudden smile, he raised his cup. 'To self-delusion!'

'Self-delusion,' Eumenes, Parmida and Hieronymus all echoed with gusto as they tipped yet more wine into their gullets.

'The life-shlong friend shof all men,' Eumenes added. 'And a comfort to ush all.'

It was relief more than anything that had caused Eumenes to organise this symposium with his only close friends and it was also relief that had caused him to drink too much. Relief the satraps had submitted to him and lent him four hundred talents each in the presence of the army assembly, thus binding themselves to him. And then there was relief at the news, which had arrived mid-afternoon, that Antigonos had left Ecbatana and was moving south-east into Paraetacene in the direction of Persepolis. He had immediately given the order to strike camp and be ready to march north at dawn; he had then invited his friends for a drinking session in celebration of the relief he felt in finally being in the position to defeat Antigonos. 'Hish almost fifty thousand men and sishty-five elephantsh against our fifty-three thoushand men and one hundred and twenty elephants; Antigonosh must be suffering from self-delusion if he thinks he can come shouth and beat ush.'

'Let him come,' Xennias said, again reaching for the jug. 'And we'll move north and face him on ground of our choosing.'

'It'll be the biggest battle ever between two western generals,' Hieronymus announced with wine-fuelled fire in his eyes. 'It will make a great tale in my history of the times.'

'The battle to end all battlesh.' Eumenes' voice faded into whimsy at the thought of such a momentous scene. 'The lasht battle.' The idea appealed to him and he held out his cup for a refill. 'The final battle!'

'The final battle,' all repeated.

'And may it be our victory.'

'The final victory!'

And the four cups were emptied in unison.

There was little else Eumenes could remember about the evening as he puked into a bowl held by his wife the following morning.

'What made you do such a thing?' Artonis asked, stroking his sweat-soaked hair.

Eumenes, eyes closed, emitted a pitiful moan followed by a copious surge of dark, reeking liquid, splattering her dress as drops ricocheted off the contents of the half-full bowl.

'I've never heard of you drinking this much in all the time I have known you.'

Again he could do nothing but moan in reply. *Why did I do that? What possessed me? I must try to get up.* He pushed himself up onto his right elbow and opened his eyes. Before the room spun out of control he caught a glimpse of Peucestas and Antigenes over Artonis' shoulder, standing in the doorway. But it was a mere glimpse as the rapid spinning of the walls forced his eyes to close and his stomach to convulse. Another jet of vomit shot from his mouth with such force it missed the bowl altogether, drenching his wife's garments and causing her to drop the sick-basin onto her feet, its contents sloshing over the floor.

'He can't be moved today, gentlemen,' Artonis said in a remarkably level voice for someone awash with vomit.

Eumenes slumped down onto his back, his chest fluttering with rapid, shallow breaths. He tried to contradict his wife but nothing but bile came from his mouth; he felt Artonis pull his head onto its side and open his mouth to allow the fluid to drain from it and was aware that had she not done so he would have swallowed it again, or worse. He was totally in her hands; he could do nothing for himself.

Oblivion took him.

'He still cannot be moved,' he heard Artonis say in his first period of lucidness.

'We have to leave today,' Peucestas said; at least, it sounded like him.

'He can't be moved. This is more than an excess of drink; a fever has crept over him whilst he was in a weakened state.'

'It's been three days; any longer and we will let Antigonos steal a march on us and he will be able to choose the ground.'

You must go; don't wait for me.

But there was no response to the order.

I didn't vocalise it.

His head swam and sweat rolled off his skin. As he faded back into unconsciousness, the image of Antigonos' disfigured face laughing at him filled his inner vision.

ANTIGONOS.
THE ONE-EYED.

'T HE LITTLE GREEK can't hold his wine!'

'No, Father,' Demetrios replied. 'At least that's what our spies in his column have reported. He got drunk and then caught a fever whilst he was severely incapacitated by a hangover the following day. They couldn't move him for four days and now the army is heading north with him in a covered litter at the very back, away from the baggage train so he can rest.'

This was too much for Antigonos, who dissolved into rumbling mirth.

'His wife is travelling with him,' Demetrios added with a smirk, 'constantly mopping his brow to keep the fever down and trying to feed him broth.'

'Broth!' Antigonos enjoyed this image even more and was obliged to sit down as his body was shaking so much; a high-pitched fart accompanied the manoeuvre. It took a while but eventually he had himself back under control. 'So, I'm facing an army whose commander-in-chief is being ministered to by a Persian princess with a wet towel and warm slops and travelling far enough behind the column so he doesn't take fright at the sound of the whores in the baggage train cackling and shouting lewd jokes at one another; is that it?'

Demetrios shrugged. 'It could be construed as such, Father.'

'Oh come on, Son, don't take everything so seriously. My arse, where's your sense of humour? I was exaggerating for the fun of it. But, however you look at it, the situation is most amusing as well as being greatly to our advantage.'

'There's one more thing in one of the reports which is not such good news, Father.'

'Go on.'

'Eumenes received a letter, purportedly from Orontes, satrap of Armenia, reporting a victory for Olympias over Kassandros, placing Alexander firmly on the throne and Polyperchon crossing with an army into Asia.'

'My arse, he has. We would have heard about it by now.'

'And yet the letter was distributed to the whole army.'

'Our people in Phrygia would have sent urgent despatches if that were the case.'

'Unless the magnitude of the supposed victory is so great they see the balance of power changed and have gone over to Olympias to save their necks.'

Antigonos made to dismiss the issue and then thought better of it. 'We should check this as it would completely change the objective of this campaign in the east; pointless winning it if our route back west is blocked.'

'I agree, Father; it's best to be sure.'

'Send a messenger to Orontes, asking him if he wrote this letter, and send men back west to find out the truth of the matter.'

'Yes, Father.'

'Either way, we need haste. Who's in command now in Eumenes' absence, and don't say Alexander because we all know that to be bollocks?'

'Peucestas and Antigenes hold joint command according to all the reports I've had.'

'Perfect: a Persian-lover with no experience of leading an army of that size and an old man who thinks only of his beloved Silver Shields.'

'You're not exactly young, Father.'

'But I lead armies; big armies, not detachments. No, Eumenes is the only one who understands what's required to lead a host that size and he is prostrate.' He slammed his fist into his open palm. *This is my chance. Gods, this could be good. Philotas, old friend, you will soon be avenged.* 'A series of forced marches, taking what we can on pack-animals, leaving the baggage behind to catch us up as and when. I want to strike them when they're least prepared and Eumenes is in no position to influence things with his unnatural luck. Speed, Demetrios! Speed is what we need; we must catch him before he leaves his sickbed.'

And speed had been the one thing that had eluded Antigonos in recent months. His march north into Media after the defeat at the Coprates River had been a demoralising affair: deciding to take the shorter direct route, he had ignored Peithon's advice and had failed to pay the Cossaei, the local tribe who considered that part of the Zagros Mountains as their own personal domain; consequently they had raided his column and massacred his foraging parties to the extent that, when they had finally arrived at Ecbatana, his men were so disillusioned with his leadership, it took all his gruff, old-soldierly charm, much time and not a little gold and silver to get them to forget their woes. Indeed, he knew from informers there was still a deal of grumbling in the ranks. Hence a quick and decisive victory had become imperative and this was a gods-given opportunity to gain it. Thus, with his insatiable desire for victory coupled with the urgent political necessity of achieving one, Antigonos drove his army south and east, down from the cool uplands of Ecbatana and onto the rugged plains of Media's interior, towards Persepolis, to intercept Eumenes before his faculties returned. On they marched, at a speed that would have impressed Alexander himself, grateful for the fading of summer's heat as the more tepid autumnal winds swept the dust into their eyes. Stripping the meagre land bare as they went with forage parties ranging wide, the thirty-seven thousand men, eight and a half thousand horses, sixty-five elephants and the host of followers of Antigonos' army swept down from Media into Paraetacene on the border of Media and Susiana. It was here a unit of Peithon's scouts reported the first sighting of the enemy to Antigonos, Seleukos and Demetrios at the head of the main column just behind the vanguard.

'Four leagues away and formed up behind a ravine with a river running through it! My arse! With both his flanks secure? My rancid, leaking arse! How are we meant to engage if he does that?' Antigonos' one eye glared at Peithon who had brought this unwelcome news himself. 'Well? How can we do battle if there's a fucking ravine in the way? You tell me that.'

Peithon looked blank and made no reply; his horse snorted.

'I rather think that's the point,' Seleukos said, indicating with his head that Peithon should move aside, out of range. Having been recently summoned north to report personally on the progress – or, rather, lack of it because of the few men Antigonos had left him – with the siege of Susa, he was well aware of the state of his commander's temper.

'What's the fucking point of having an army if you don't use it?' Antigonos turned his cyclopic wrath onto his subordinate, pulling on his mount's reins as the beast grew skittish at its master's rising temper. 'I'm here with my army and he's here with his; this will be the biggest battle since Alexander's final victory over Darius at Gaugamela, almost a hundred thousand men! It will be a proper battle, not that child's play we had in Cyprus or Kappadokia. We should just get on with it and decide the issue once and for all and not lurk behind ravines. That's no way to behave.'

'It is until he gets better.'

Antigonos opened his mouth to shout some more but then closed it and turned to glare in the direction of the enemy position. 'The little shit is stalling for time, is he?'

'Wouldn't you, Father?' Demetrios questioned, his face betraying amusement.

'What are you smirking at, boy? Do you think it's funny I can't get at the sly little Greek and finally finish off the bastard?' He gestured back down the column, tramping behind them, trailing off into the dust-clouded distance. 'The lads need a good fight and, fuck it, so do I.'

'Father, I *am* smiling at you; at your ridiculous inability to engage with what your opponent is doing and why. Come on, this is not like you at all and it's certainly not what you taught me: think.'

'Are you criticising me, Demetrios?'

'If that's the way you want to look at it, then yes. I've never seen you like this.'

'Like what?'

'So desperate. Yes, I know you want revenge for Philotas, but that's a private matter and shouldn't affect your judgement when commanding an army.'

'Be careful what you say, boy,' Antigonos growled, pointing a cautionary finger at his son.

Demetrios ignored the warning. 'But it's not just that: we all know there're some bad rumblings in the army about your leadership on the march north to Ecbatana, and Eumenes probably knows that too. So why should he rush into an engagement? Why not just let bad feeling grow, especially when he recovers with every passing day?'

'And he has his baggage with him,' Seleukos pointed out.

Demetrios nodded. 'Which we know for a fact as the reports say his litter was travelling behind it.'

'All right! Enough!' Antigonos drew a series of deep breaths, calming himself, thinking for a long moment. 'And he's probably got a supply line all the way back to Persepolis, which is far closer than Ecbatana, so we will have to survive almost entirely on forage in this benighted place, whilst he will feast his lads every night. No, you're right, Son: if I were him, I'd be lurking behind a ravine like the snivelling Greek he is.' Antigonos held his chin up. 'Forgive my outburst, gentlemen; my son's done well to correct me. I desperately need a victory and that clouded my ability to put myself in my opponent's place as a general always should.' He kicked his horse from a trot to a canter. 'But no more: I'll try to shame him into battle.'

'Evidently he has no shame,' Seleukos observed as, for the fifth day in a row, both armies formed for battle, filing out of their respective camps less than a thousand paces distant. But despite their proximity they might as well have been a thousand leagues apart since the ground between them was impassable for a close-formation phalanx in good order, as each had formed up with gullies, ravines and rivulets along their frontage. 'Mind you, I'd quite happily stand where he is and feel no shame rather than disorder my phalanx crossing that ground just to engage an army that's in as strong a defensive position as I already hold.'

Antigonos growled but said nothing. *The arrogant bastard's right. Only a fool would come forward from that position and I would be a fool to advance from here. No matter how many times we form up, nothing is going to change*. He closed his eye and cursed. 'That he should be so close and yet I can't get to him.'

'And we're running out of supplies, Father, even now the baggage has caught up with us,' Demetrios said. At the same time, to the shouted orders of its officers, a syntagma of two hundred and fifty-six men formed up as the furthest right flank of the phalanx right next to them, sixteen men deep, whilst the remaining eighteen thousand began to take their places from that mark, stretching way off into the distance; a formation bristling with pikes and burnished with bronze and iron. 'With his army and ours, as well as all the followers, there are well over a hundred thousand mouths to feed every morning, noon and night, plus the animals, and this is the fifth day. The only lads who see any action are our foragers skirmishing with those of Eumenes; and he has the shorter supply line so he can afford to stay whilst we begin to starve.'

'I know!' Antigonos roared into his son's face with an explosion that unsettled all the horses within range and caused Demetrios to recoil. 'There is no need to point out the fucking obvious. I'm well aware of just how long we can stay here.'

Demetrios spat on the ground, turned his skittish horse and kicked it away, calling over his shoulder: 'Then why didn't we move out yesterday and head west into fertile Gabene, which has as yet been untouched by the campaign?'

Antigonos thumped his thigh with his fist. 'You think you know everything just because you've taken the time off rutting and drinking just enough to pick up the rudiments of logistical military planning?'

'You told me to, Father; you should be pleased I can see you're making a mistake.' Demetrios cantered off along the rear of the phalanx towards his own cavalry command, taking up position, half a league away, on the left flank.

'The insolent young pup,' Antigonos muttered with a touch of pride in his tone. He turned to Seleukos. 'You do your best for them and before you know it they're all over you trying to prove they're better than you are.'

'Perhaps he will be, one day.'

'Perhaps he will; but he isn't yet and next time he does that in public I shall slap him down.'

'A bit late for that; you should have done it this time.'

Antigonos gave a vague smile. 'That's exactly what Philotas would've said.' Another deep breath. 'I miss the old bastard. The only reason I'm fighting mounted is that I haven't the heart to stand in the phalanx without him at my side – not yet, anyhow. No, it'll take some healing before I'm ready to enjoy myself in the front rank again. Really enjoy myself, I mean, not just play around with a few half-hearted stabs and parries but get really stuck in with good lads at your side and good lads trying to kill you.' He looked with regret at Eumenes' army, just that short distance away, and shook his head. 'I'll have you for taking away my pleasure like that, you sly little Greek. Once I have your head, I'll feel more myself and go back to the front rank.' He drew himself up in the saddle and nodded with conviction. 'I'm going to get Nearchos to have one last try at bribing or coercing Eumenes' men away from him.'

'And if that fails?' Seleukos asked in the tone of one who thought it would.

Antigonos clenched both his fists. 'It won't, not this time.'

'But if it does?'

'If it does, we'll slip away tonight. Warn the officers that as soon as we stand down we'll have a quick meal and then head into Gabene, resupply and wait for Eumenes to come to us.'

EUMENES.
THE SLY.

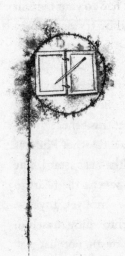

'**Y**OU HAD BETTER come quickly, old friend,' Hieronymus said, finding Eumenes eating a broth made by his wife whilst sitting in his campaign chair behind the rear rank of his Kappadokian cavalry; all along the line, the rest of the army ate their midday meal, standing-to. Slaves with water-skins walked up and down the files, bringing refreshment to the men where they stood, as, under a thousand paces away, Antigonos' army went through the same motions.

Eumenes put the spoon in the bowl, placed it on the table and looked with sunken eyes at his friend. 'What is it now, Hieronymus? Just as I'm getting my appetite back.'

'Well, this will dampen it again. Antigonos has sent another delegation over to talk to our lads; they're meeting in the ravine on our left flank.'

Not again, this is becoming so tiresome. What is it with the Macedonian military mind that it refuses to admit defeat? Deep was Eumenes' sigh and weary was his countenance; he heaved himself to his feet. 'Does the resinated cyclops never give up? Does he think the boys are stupid? Only a fool would trust a man who has no need of him.' He gestured to a couple of attendant slaves to follow. 'Let's go and see what he's offering this time.'

212

And it was the same offer as before but with a few minor improvements. So similar, in fact, Eumenes had to stop himself from laughing for the first time since he had been struck down with the fever, as he stood for all to see above the meeting place, listening to the proceedings.

'So,' Antigenes said, as the envoy finished speaking, 'Antigonos will let us keep our satrapies.' He gestured to Peucestas and the other satraps gathered around. 'Is that correct, Nearchos?'

'He will.'

'And all our officers will be rewarded with gifts of land, either in Asia or back in Macedon, and those who wish to serve in his army will also be given appropriate posts?'

'That's correct,' the Cretan replied, looking up at Eumenes. 'In return for him.'

'Really?' Antigenes did his best not to look incredulous. 'On top of that all my men in the Silver Shields will be promoted to officers in Antigonos' army.'

'To spread them around but in positions of honour, you understand. Antigonos wishes to neutralise them as a unit but utilise them as individuals.'

'Does he now?'

'You must see that Antigonos could not risk having them in his ranks all together.'

'And you must realise they've been together for fifty years, so you can imagine how they are going to take that.' Antigenes stepped forward and grabbed Nearchos' beard. 'Is there anything else Antigonos would like to promise, Cretan, before I send you back to him?'

'Those are his terms, which are more than generous.'

'And these are mine.' A knife flashed in his hand; Nearchos' beard came away, sliced through at the tip of the chin; a droplet of blood collected on the newly shaven skin. 'It's only for our past comradeship I send you back without a beard rather than without a throat. And ask Antigonos this: why would we go over to him when Polyperchon is coming east with his army? His cause is lost.'

'You don't really believe that, do you?'

'We've heard nothing to the contrary. Now go!'

Nearchos, eyes still registering surprise, held Antigenes' gaze for a couple of heartbeats and then turned away to climb back out of the ravine.

'I thank you for your loyalty,' Eumenes said, looking down into the ravine, 'although I never doubted it as you are all clever men and can see what's going on here. I'm minded of a story I once heard as a child: a lion fell in love with a maiden and spoke to the girl's father about marriage.' He allowed a smile to spread over his wan face. 'The father said he was ready to give her to him but he was afraid of the lion's claws and teeth, fearing after he had married her the lion might lose his temper about something and turn on his daughter in the manner of a beast. When, however, the lion had pulled out his claws and teeth, the father, seeing he had thrown away everything that made him formidable, killed him easily with a club.' He paused for the meaning of the fable to sink in, before adding: 'It's the same as what Antigonos is doing now: he'll only keep his promises until he has become master of the army and in that very moment he will execute its leaders.'

It was to pleasing shouts of agreement that Eumenes walked away to finish his broth.

'You must rest,' Artonis said, gently putting her hand on Eumenes' chest as he tried to rise from the couch, having finished his evening bowl of broth mopped up with fresh bread. 'There's nothing you urgently need to do.'

'There is plenty, woman,' Eumenes said, pushing away her hand, 'and I feel my energy returning.' He tugged her to him and kissed her mouth. 'Thanks to your nursing.' Raising himself to his feet, he rolled his shoulders, cracking them, before swinging his arms back and forth and stretching. 'Yes, Artonis, I'm beginning to feel like my old self; so much so I might even call for some wine.'

'You will not!'

Eumenes furrowed his brow. 'Grateful as I am to you, you still remain my wife and, as such, should not be giving me orders, especially so vehement an order.'

Artonis lowered her head.

Smiling, he lifted her chin. 'I was joking, Artonis. Of course I wasn't going to call for wine and you can give me as many orders as you wish – I just probably won't obey them, that's all.' He kissed her again before turning to face the huge amount of correspondence that had accumulated on his desk during his illness. *Once a secretary, always a secretary.*

It was as dusk was falling and he laid a letter onto the mounting dealt-with pile and broke the seal of yet another scroll that Xennias, his cavalry commander, was escorted into the tent.

'Xennias,' Eumenes said, laying down the scroll, 'if you've come to save me from myself and my suicidal urges to wade through piles of letters taller than me, then you'll find me more than grateful.'

'If informing you that some deserters have come over to us with some very interesting news will save you from yourself, then, sir, I look forward to your gratitude.'

'What news?'

'Antigonos is on the move tonight.'

'Is he now? Did they say where he's headed?'

'They're just grunts; no officers amongst them.'

Eumenes nodded, contemplating the news. 'Well, I don't think it's too difficult a conundrum: he needs food, as do we, and there's plenty to be found in Gabene; he means to get there first.'

'Then we should stop him.'

'We should,' Eumenes mused, 'indeed we should.' It was suddenly blindingly obvious. *Mercenaries!* 'Xennias, I need a dozen or so mercenaries who are willing to risk their lives for a great deal of money, half payable now and half upon their return. Bring them to my tent and have the army ready to move as soon as is feasible.'

With a smart salute, Xennias went about his business, leaving Eumenes smiling to himself. *I really do know how to enjoy myself – even when I'm not too well.*

'So, do you understand what's required of you?' Eumenes asked the leader of a dozen Greek peltasts after having briefed them.

The man grinned, displaying teeth that made Eumenes shudder, as he eyed the twenty-four heavy-looking bags of coinage lying on the desk. 'I think so, sir.' He turned to his mates. 'Are we good for this, lads?'

There was general agreement amongst the group; the man turned back to Eumenes. 'We go over to Antigonos' camp as if we're deserting and then make a lot of noise about you being about to spring a surprise night attack on him and we decided we wanted none of it because when we signed up with you no one said anything about fighting for an eastern army.'

'And what will you say if Antigonos questions you himself?'

'The same.'

'And if he offers you more money?'

To this the reply was but a shrug.

Well, that's a risk I just have to take, I suppose; but at least I've taken precautions. He pointed to the money on the table. 'Take a bag each and when – or if – you return, you can claim the other; and my advice, gentlemen, is to get out of that camp as soon as possible. Oh, and by the way, Xennias will be taking care of your women and children whilst you're away, for their own protection, you must understand.'

The looks that crossed the mercenaries' faces implied complete understanding of the threat. It was Eumenes' turn to shrug. 'Well, that's the way it is; take it or leave it.'

They took it.

'Now we move as fast as possible, Xennias,' Eumenes said, jumping to his feet as the mercenaries left the tent. 'It's three days' march to Gabene, have the men issued with sufficient rations. Each man carries his own. If we can steal a full night off Antigonos then we'll be able to choose our ground and he will have a choice between fighting us in Gabene – and most probably losing – or wintering here in Paraetacene with meagre forage or going back up the mountains to freeze his balls off in Ecbatana. I don't think any of those choices will go down well with his lads, which would be a pity for the resinated cyclops.'

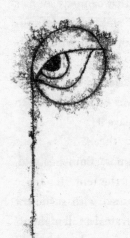

ANTIGONOS.
THE ONE-EYED.

'S OUND THE ALARM! Sound the
alarm!'

Antigonos paused, mid-thrust. *My arse, what's going on?* He jumped from his camp-bed, pulling the slave-girl beneath him to the floor, and ran to the entrance. 'What the fuck's happening?' he called to nobody in particular as men rushed hither and thither in what seemed to be growing pandemonium. The guards turned and looked at him with blank faces illumined by the almost full moon. 'Well then, find out. Who raised the alarm and why?'

'I did, Father,' Demetrios said, emerging from the gloom.

'You! What gave you the right to do that without consulting me? We're meant to be leaving.'

Demetrios looked beyond Antigonos at the girl, scrabbling for her clothes by the bed, and then raised his eyebrows at the sight of his father's dying erection. 'Yes, I know; although it would seem some of us were in less of a hurry than others.'

'Don't give me your cheek, boy, and tell me why you've caused all this panic.'

'Eumenes has evidently heard we're on the move and plans to attack as we leave. The moon's almost full and there's not a cloud in the sky; he has the light for it, and—'

'It's what I'd do.'

'Exactly.'

'How do you know this?'

'Some Greek deserters came in saying they had no wish to take part in a battle for an eastern army against one from the west and they wished to return to the sea rather than fight alongside Indians, Bactrians and other sundry barbarians.'

'Did they, indeed? And you believed them?'

'What choice did I have? The best part of the camp is struck and we were forming up in column to leave.' Again he looked towards the dressing girl. 'At least, most of us were.'

'Enough of that!' Antigonos surveyed the scene and realised at once what was occurring. 'So you've given orders to form up in battle line, have you?'

'Yes, Father.'

'Without consulting me?'

'Yes, Father.'

'My arse! And why the fuck not?'

'Because I was right on the other side of the camp and the deserters weren't brought to me until they had been here for over an hour. Eumenes could have come at any time so I thought it best to be safe rather than have him catch us ready to march. He won't care about the rough terrain disordering his troops if he catches us with our shields on our backs and our pikes on carts.'

'And what about Seleukos and Peithon? Well, Seleukos at least?'

'He was seeing to his men at the front of the column; I had no time to get a message to him either. I had to react quickly; with speed, Father, as you have always taught me. It was speed or risk a massacre.'

The young brat has a good point. I've only got myself to blame for allowing myself a little distraction. Antigonos grunted and slapped the girl's arse as she hurried from the tent. 'Well, it's too late to stop it now; it will be even worse chaos if we reverse the order. Bring me those Greek deserters once I'm dressed. I want a word with them.'

But there was still no sign of the Greeks as Antigonos left his tent, with slaves waiting, ready to dismantle it, and strode to his waiting horse where he found Seleukos already mounted. 'What do you think?'

Seleukos shrugged. 'I think we're facing a sly little Greek.'

'Hmph, so do I.' Antigonos swung himself up into the saddle. 'But, in the circumstances, I suppose the boy did the right thing. Are the lads ready?'

'All formed up, sir.'

'Good. Now all we have to do is wait. Stay with me.' He glanced to his left, along the rear of the phalanx. 'Where are those fucking deserters?'

The moon continued its journey across the night sky, bathing the army in its pale light, drawing all colour from it and its environment so all was either a soft moon-glow or deep shade. From across no-man's land came neither sound nor movement; the faint glimmer of fires from behind the camp stockade was the only sign of activity. Tension rose from Antigonos' men as they stood in silence, peering into the night. A distant wolf-howl or the occasional chatter of some nocturnal bird drifted through the otherwise still air.

Antigonos shifted his sore buttocks, and his mount shook its head, jangling the harness. He turned to Seleukos. 'We've been duped.'

Seleukos shrugged. 'Can we be sure, if we stand down and form a column, they won't come?'

'I wish I knew. Where are those deserters?' He again looked to his left, this time to see a small figure on a horse, racing towards him, in the distance. *That's Demetrios at a guess.* 'I think we're about to hear some bad news.'

'They've gone, Father,' Demetrios shouted as he pulled up his mount in a flurry of dust.

'I assume you're talking about the mercenaries on whose information we have based all our actions this night?'

'Yes. We've been looking for them ever since you asked me to send them to you. There's no sign of them; somehow they've just slipped out of the camp.'

'I wonder why? Did it not occur to you to have them placed under armed guard?'

Demetrios' silence was answer enough.

'Seleukos, send a patrol straight over to Eumenes' camp. I don't think you need be worried for their safety.'

'Nor do I.'

And Antigonos was correct in his assumption.

'There's no one over there,' the patrol officer reported upon his return. 'The fires have been built up and left to burn to dupe us.'

'Gods, what a fool I've been to let him trick me like that!' Antigonos slammed his fist into his palm. *That's the last time I enjoy a woman when I should be concentrating on the army. Philotas would never have let me behave like that; caught with my tunic up at my age. That'll get round the lads in no time. I need to retrieve the situation before I lose all respect.* 'He could have gone the moment we formed up at the beginning of this watch, which means he has a three-hour start on us. It will take us at least another watch to be ready to march, which puts him six hours ahead on a three-day march which he'll try to complete in two and a half if he pushes hard.' *If he does then he can choose his ground and keep me from Gabene with winter coming on. In that scenario I won't have an army left by spring; it would be the end of me. And all because of one girl. Speed.* 'Speed, gentlemen. Speed. Seleukos, delay your return to Susa, I need you with me and Susa can wait. Get all the cavalry ready to march as we must leave within the hour. Peithon! You and Nearchos bring up the rest of the army as fast as you can; leave the baggage to travel at its own speed. I'll chase him hard and stop him and then play for time as you join me. We can't let Eumenes get to Gabene; we must halt him here in Paraetacene.'

EUMENES.
THE SLY.

THE SUN ROSE, blood red, to the rear of the column, picking out on the horizon the verdant hills of Gabene at the far side of the plain below, less than twenty leagues distant; feature-less, apart from some low-lying hills about a league out, the plain offered the potential for a swift passage. Eumenes stood at the head of his breakfasting army, looking down the long slope they must descend if they were to cross to their objective. *I don't like it but I've no time to find a way around to a gentler slope; I have to take the direct path or have Antigonos catch me for sure before I reach Gabene. This is the point upon which the whole campaign must now rest.*

He turned to the satraps and officers gathered around. 'We've travelled fast through the night, gentlemen, but we must increase the pace now it's daylight. We need to be five leagues across that plain before we can rest at dusk; if not, we hand the initiative back to Antigonos. Get back to your men, they've just eaten so drive them hard for all they're worth. It doesn't have to be pretty so long as it's fast. Double pace.'

Not even the touchy Peucestas made any remark at the manner of this direct order, causing Eumenes a wry smile as he pulled himself up astride his horse. *I think we all understand the urgency of the situation at this point of the campaign. Self-interest is taking precedence over bruised pride. Interesting.*

Horns blared, the vanguard moved forward, down the hill at a jog, reinvigorated by the bread, sausage and cheese from their packs. Down they went, rank after rank of peltasts and sundry light troops, javelin-armed in the main, leading the way for the heavily armed van consisting of the phalanx, the Hypaspists and, of course, the Silver Shields. With rowdy whoops, mercenary Thessalian cavalry – in wide-brimmed, leather hats – flowed past the infantry on the right flank, sending up clouds of dust as they urged their willing mounts down to the plain. Thracian cavalry, wild hair and beards issuing from beneath bronze helmets, followed with leather- and fur-clad Sogdian and Bactrian horse-archers close behind, the fearsome Azanes riding at their head, and then the Persian cavalry, both light archers and heavy javelins, on richly caparisoned mounts, sporting the finely embroidered clothes of their homeland. On the right flank the brightly coloured Indian cavalry contingent, commanded by Ceteus, Eudamos' second-in-command, cantered by, their dark-skinned torsos naked and sheened with oil; earrings, arm-rings, rings for toes and fingers glistering in the rising sun; javelin-armed and with small shields of differing shapes, round, square or even two crescent moons back to back, decorated with strange devices of many-armed gods, both human and animalistic. Elephants with howdahs perched high on their backs lumbered through next, trumpeting as their mahouts coaxed them on down the hill, the men in the howdahs holding fast as their once-steady stations lurched forward in the descent. Light infantry accompanied the great beasts of war, armed with bows as tall as themselves and arrows longer than a man's arm.

It was a sight that gladdened Eumenes' heart as his army advanced down onto the plain with such speed and enthusiasm whilst he waited for his Kappadokian bodyguard, with Parmida at their head, stationed behind the mounted Indian contingent. On the far side of the infantry column, Xennias led the Companion Cavalry which had once formed a part of Krateros' army but had been with Eumenes ever since his defeat of that great general. And still they kept coming for the column was the best part of half a league long, even with the cavalry travelling to either side. Falling in, next to Parmida, Eumenes felt like himself for the first time since that near-fatal drinking bout. He sucked in a deep breath and defied Antigonos to do his worst.

With the gathering momentum of the hill, the army made good time and, keeping the pace up, the vanguard was soon far out on the plain as the rear ranks of the column began to descend.

And now it's a simple race, Eumenes thought, looking back over his shoulder and squinting into the newly risen sun, as the dark mass of the baggage train slithered down the shadowed slope.

And on they went, taking advantage of the cool of early morning to put distance between them and the ridge whence they had descended with a double-paced loping stride, heads lowered and lungs burning, until the heat of the day began to beat down and Eumenes was forced to call a brief watering halt, allowing the baggage to gain on the column.

It began as they were passing to the south of the low-lying hills. At first it was just the odd warning shout coming from various points in the formation, but it grew; it grew until all were staring at the skyline of the ridge, just under half a league distant, and pointing.

So here is where we'll decide it, then; not Gabene. Eumenes wiped the sweat from his brow as he surveyed the long line of tiny mounted figures, silhouetted by the sun, massed either side of the very point he had stood but two hours previously.

Antigonos had come – and he had come with more haste than Eumenes had thought possible.

'The question, gentlemen, is whether that is his whole army, or is it solely the cavalry?' Eumenes asked the assembled satraps and generals as they met beneath the empty throne set under a hastily erected awning.

All looked up to the large force on the hill; a force that had not moved since it was first sighted. Indeed, neither side had moved.

'If it's his whole army, why doesn't he bring it down to face us?' Peucestas wondered. 'He knows perfectly well there's no way we would ever consider attacking him up a long slope like that.'

'He wants to keep us guessing,' Antigenes said.

'And it's working,' Eumenes muttered. 'If his infantry is there and we move off, his cavalry will take the rear of our formation on the march. That will delay us whilst the infantry come down onto the plain, form up and attack a disordered column that'll have no chance of forming into line of battle.'

'If the infantry really is behind the cavalry,' Eudamos pointed out. 'But if it's not, his cavalry will be unsupported.'

'Indeed. But even if we try to screen our column with our own cavalry, there's no way we can make it to the hills in those conditions; we'll be forced to stand and fight eventually, by which time his infantry will definitely have arrived. He knows that, so my guess is he doesn't care one way or the other; he's going to sit on that hill pretending his infantry is there and we have to stay here for fear it is so.'

'And if the infantry is there, the elephants will be so too,' Ceteus added.

'All very true,' Eumenes agreed; he took another long look at the enemy but the force did nothing to betray its true nature. 'In which case I would say we have little option but to form up and wait for him to come down and meet us. But we can sneak a little advantage out of this by sending the baggage on ahead so if the encounter is inconclusive we can make a run for Gabene without being hampered.' He looked around the table for signs of disagreement and found none. 'Then, gentlemen, when the lads have finished their midday meal we form up and wait to see what Antigonos does.' He pointed to the low hills half a league to the north. 'They will anchor our left flank; a thousand light troops, both bows and javelins, should be enough to prevent anything coming through them. Peucestas, you have the most light infantry, see to that. Put your best man in command of them.'

It was with tight lips that Peucestas acquiesced.

'Eudamos, you take command of the left wing with your cavalry and a third of the elephants. The other eighty I want split between the centre, in front of the phalanx and on the right wing.'

Eudamos consented. 'Very well, Ceteus will see to the elephants.'

'Amphimachus will support you, along with Sibyrtius' former command, under Cephlon, as well as Stasander with his Arians and Azanes' Sogdians and the Bactrians. With the remaining Thracian and Paropamisadae cavalry acting as a reserve and a screen of light infantry across your whole front, you should have a strong position.' There was a general mutter of agreement as Eumenes turned to Antigenes. 'The centre is yours. Phalanx tight on Eudamos' command, then the Greek mercenaries to their right and then your Silver Shields with the Hypaspists outside them. Forty of Ceteus' elephants and a screen of light infantry will take the initial shock out of their attack.'

'Very good, Teutamus and I will see it done.'

'Good man. I'll take the right flank with Parmida and our Kappadokians, Peucestas and his Companion Cavalry and Tlepolemus and his Carmanians. Xennias will take his men, and the Thessalians and the rest of the cavalry to form a reserve behind us to prevent any attempted outflanking move. Peucestas, your light bowmen will form our skirmish screen along with the final forty of Ceteus' elephants. Is that all clear, gentlemen?'

'I have one question,' Peucestas said.

Eumenes sighed inwardly. *Why aren't I in command of a wing? Because Eudamos is a better general than you.* 'Yes, Peucestas.'

'Who will be guarding the baggage?'

For once, you surprise me; it's not about yourself. 'Antigonos has almost forty thousand men up that hill and we have just over forty-one thousand and therefore can be said to hold a slight edge over him. The baggage is travelling on and will be at least a league away, so if they were to capture it, we would already have lost. Let's not give up what little advantage we have to protect something that needs no protection.'

Peucestas assessed that for a moment and then gave a sharp nod.

'Good. Any other business?' When satisfied there was none, he turned to the empty throne and inclined his head. 'Form line of battle, gentlemen. We are dismissed.'

But as they turned to go, Hieronymus came striding forward. 'Our scouts have reported movement. It looks like they want to parley: Seleukos is coming down the hill.'

Eumenes turned to his officers. 'Tell your men to carry on forming up as we chat with this overgrown beast.'

'No, I'm not coming to surrender, Eumenes,' Seleukos said, anticipating the little Greek's sense of humour. 'Nor am I coming to have another failed attempt to bribe your officers into handing you over.' He nodded to the satraps and officers come to bear witness to the conversation. 'Even Antigonos has realised that will never happen.'

'Then why are you here?' Eumenes asked, with what he hoped sounded like genuine curiosity. *They've uncovered the truth about my forged letter from Orontes, I would wager; well, it was only a matter of time. Seleukos will try to trap me with a bogus offer from Antigonos, trying to force me to expose the lie myself. I'll have to play this carefully; let him think, for a while, he's going to surprise me.* 'I'm not going to submit to Antigonos and he won't submit to me so that leaves us doomed to fight it out until only one of us is left standing. Speaking of which,' he indicated to the chairs set in front of the empty throne, 'shall we sit, Seleukos?'

SELEUKOS.
THE BULL-ELEPHANT.

YES, IT WOULD *probably be better for you to be seated when I expose your lie to your friends.* Seleukos sat and surveyed the faces sitting around him; he knew each one. *Good friends of mine, some of them, too. We've been through so much together. It's criminal that it's come to this.* Taking a cup of well-watered wine from a slave, he sipped it; his eyes peered over the brim, assessing the mood in the camp as horns sounded and raised voices, far and near, issued orders and the army sprang to life. *So, they are forming up. They intend to fight here.*

'So please enlighten us, Seleukos,' Eumenes said, setting down his cup, 'to what do we owe this undoubted pleasure?'

First things first. 'It's simple,' Seleukos replied, 'Antigonos had a reasonable proposition. He—'

'Goes back west and leaves the east to us, provided we promise never to set foot east of the Zagros Mountains?'

How did the sly little Greek manage to finish that sentence?

'Because it's what I would offer if I were as untrustworthy as Antigonos, to answer your next question.'

'It's a genuine offer. He goes back west so he can deal with Polyperchon's invasion. Oh, and we keep Media. For Peithon, you understand?'

Eumenes laughed. 'Of course you do. Do you really think the offer's genuine, Seleukos? Really? Didn't Antigonos let you in on what he really means to do?'

What is he on about? 'No. He said I should make this offer and he hoped you'd accept it and save a lot of lads getting killed.'

'No, he thinks I have to accept it because not to do so would imply I know that Polyperchon hasn't invaded Asia and the report of Olympias defeating Kassandros was false.'

Seleukos looked around Eumenes' allies once more; shock was displayed upon every face. *He's anticipated me and that's the first time he's admitted it to them.* 'So you admit it then?'

'That Orontes was mistaken in his letter, yes. A message from him reached me yesterday to that effect. He was very apologetic.'

'And why didn't you tell us?' Peucestas was indignant.

Yes, wriggle out of that one.

'What would it have achieved on this march other than to lower morale? No, I was waiting to share the bad news until after we'd defeated Antigonos in Gabene, which is something we need to do whether Polyperchon has invaded or not.'

Now to do what I've really come for. 'Except it wasn't really bad news, was it, Eumenes?' Seleukos said in a light tone. 'Orontes never sent you that message saying he was wrong because he never sent you the letter in the first place, you made it all up. We know because Orontes denied all knowledge of the letter when Antigonos wrote to ask him about it.'

Eumenes dismissed the accusation with a straight face. 'And why should we believe that? It's a clever lie designed to undermine trust in me and I dismiss it out of hand.'

But Seleukos could see from the expressions around him that many were not so sure. *Time to press the advantage.* 'I'm sure you do, but it's not a lie; it's the truth. You made it all up to strengthen all these deluded gentlemen's support for you. You duped them.'

231

Eumenes gave a deep sigh. 'Oh, Seleukos, I do fear for your ability to keep Babylon, I really do. Don't you see, even if your outrageous accusation really were true it wouldn't matter one way or the other? These men stay with me because they know I need them and Antigonos doesn't. I won't execute them, whereas Antigonos will. I have no need to boost their support for me with lies.' He turned to his comrades. 'Do I, gentlemen? What do I gain by lying to you other than your ire when the lie is exposed? Why would I risk that?'

It was an impossible argument to refute and none made an attempt to do so.

They believe him. The sly little Greek has got away with it. To pursue the case would only make me seem too intent on proving something they now believe to be the truth as a lie and further under-mine my argument. Gods, he is good. Perhaps he was right and I should have sided with him – even though he's a Greek.

Eumenes addressed Seleukos again as a unit of Companion Cavalry cantered past, lances raised, heading to their position on the right flank. 'So, let's stop this pathetic attempt to drive a wedge between us and get back to your master's slippery offer which he says will save a lot of lives.'

'It will.'

'Except that it won't, will it? It'll save a lot of his lads getting killed, granted, but not mine. In fact, more of mine will get killed to make up for that, so in the end it won't save lives; and it certainly won't save mine.'

'I don't understand. Really, I don't.'

'Oh, Seleukos, how do you expect to hang onto Babylon if you can't see through Antigonos' schemes? You really should have sided with me. I may be sly but I like to think of myself as not being treacherous. Antigonos believes these gentlemen sitting with me have no interest in the west as their satrapies are all eastern and in that he is absolutely right. Indeed, when he went north into Media, I argued that it was the time to head back west but none of them would have it and we wasted, to my mind, a golden opportunity to snatch the initiative.' He looked at his colleagues and shrugged. 'But what's done is done and we are where we are. And Antigonos wants us to stay here. He thinks we'll say yes, you take the west, our resinated old cyclopic friend – and let's not worry for the moment about the veracity or the source of the news of Polyperchon's invasion – and we'll stay here in the east and wave you a fond farewell as you go – even if that means deserting the king; which, of course, I would never do. Only he won't really go, will he? How did he suggest we separate? We head south back to Persepolis and he crosses the mountains into Susiana and winters in Babylonia whilst you continue with the siege of Susa?'

Seleukos raised his eyebrows in surprise. 'Something like that, yes.'

'Something like that?'

'Well, exactly that, actually.'

'And did he mention the bit where he doesn't cross the mountains and, instead, falls upon our column as we form up to head back south? You know, Seleukos, the part where he massacres us in cold blood just to make himself feel better about Philotas? Did he let any of that slip when he briefed you on his generous offer?'

No, he didn't, and the sly little Greek has a point.

'So, to sum up: Antigonos wants us to move off south, in column, so he can pretend he's going back west but is in fact going to massacre us and, in the process of making this offer, has accused me of lying to my men.' He paused for a moment's exaggerated thinking. 'Does that sound like a fair appraisal of the facts?'

233

Seleukos got to his feet. 'It would seem I'm wasting my time.'

'All our time,' Eumenes said, also rising. 'We'll set for battle here. I assume Antigonos will come down off that hill once the infantry have arrived. Tell me, have they arrived?'

Seleukos gave a half smile. 'The first scouts had just come in to report its sighting a league or so back, when I left.'

'So this parley was not only disingenuous but also a delay?'

'What can I say?'

'Well, sorry won't do much good. You see, gentlemen, just what we're dealing with in Antigonos? He'll have you stripped of your honour and titles in no time. Remember that when we fight today. As should you on the other side, Seleukos.'

Seleukos walked away from the empty throne without a glance; keeping his posture upright and his face expressionless he hoped to hide the anger he felt. Not anger at Eumenes but, rather, anger at Antigonos for having put him in a position whereby he was not in possession of all the facts and was thus made to look a complete idiot. Was he truly now a mere creature of the resinated cyclops rather than a force in his own right? *Eumenes is right: Antigonos will discard me and take all I have as soon as he has no further use for me. I've been a fool.* He sighed and walked away.

'So, they don't trust me,' Antigonos said after Seleukos had reported the outcome of the parley.

'No, and I think they are right not to.'

'And what makes you think that?' The cyclopic eye fired with outrage. 'What even gives you the right to think that?'

'Because I could see that was what you intended to do.'

'And what if it was? It would've been better than fighting a pitched battle and losing a lot of my lads whilst also risking the possibility of being defeated, which is now what I'm obliged to do.' He glanced down at Eumenes' army as the phalanx swung from column to line like a series of bricks being mortared into position.

'But at least that's the honourable way of going about things. These are our old comrades.'

'They're not mine, Seleukos, not since I was left in Phrygia. These men mean nothing to me. I haven't seen some of them for almost fifteen years and then they were only puppies, and that includes you. What do I care for whelps like that? Or for you, for that matter? You can't even take Susa after three months of siege.'

This was too much for Seleukos. 'You stripped me of men when you came north, leaving me with just two thousand infantry. I asked for four thousand, five hundred of whom should be cavalry. So don't try and throw that in my face, Antigonos. How am I meant to stop supplies getting through if I haven't got the men to completely surround the city and the cavalry to scout the perimeter?'

'That's for you to work out!'

'And I have: you left me with just enough troops to contain the city. You don't really want me to take it because you worry I'd steal the contents of the treasury, seeing as Demetrios wouldn't be there to make sure I didn't because you wanted him to join you on this campaign. So instead you're just using me to make sure the treasury is still there when you go back down south and then you'll accuse me of failure so you can use that as an excuse to remove me from Babylon.'

Antigonos went to refute the statement but then chuckled, wagging his finger at Seleukos.

So I'm right, you old resinated cyclops. You're setting me up. 'You really are without honour, Antigonos. You really would've turned back on your word and massacred them.'

'Oh, just forget all that bollocks about honour. I'm here to win, and to win with as little loss of life to my lads as possible because they're the men I'm loyal to. And if you don't understand that then I don't know what you're doing here; in fact I think you should go and contemplate your position back at Susa whilst I go and win a battle now that my infantry have deigned to join me.'

Maybe I will. If I'm not wanted here and Eumenes won't trust me then there is only one place I can go; but not yet. 'I'll fight for you, Antigonos.'

'Good; you'll be in command of the reserve. Just make sure you do the job wholeheartedly.' Antigonos turned away.

'That I promise.' *But what I do afterwards depends on the result.*

Deep in thought, Seleukos watched Antigonos stomp towards his son, waiting at the command post.

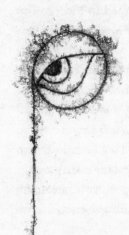

ANTIGONOS.
THE ONE-EYED.

'GET THE CAVALRY down onto the plain and form a screen whilst the infantry deploys, Demetrios,' Antigonos ordered. He pointed to the opposing army. 'You can see what they're doing: heavy infantry across a broad front, the best on his right, with cavalry to either flank but heavier on his right, and all screened by elephants and light troops; not at all imaginative but, no doubt, very effective. Therefore we'll counter with, seemingly, an equal lack of imagination to put him at his ease before I strike. Peithon with his Asiatic horse-archers, half the Tarantine mercenaries and Phrygian and Lydian cavalry will start off the proceedings by probing Eumenes' position on his right; negating the power of his heavy cavalry, by mainly using our lights, will give us an advantage. Meanwhile, our phalanx outnumbers his by nearly ten thousand. However, let's not deceive ourselves: his is of much higher quality what with the Silver Shields, the Hypaspists as well as all that veteran infantry, so we'll match him for frontage and deepen the formation on our left against his best troops to negate them.' Antigonos paused, his eye roving over the enemy phalanx, assessing his options.

'I'll place the Macedonians on our right, opposite his Greek mercenaries, and then the Asian troops armed in Macedonian fashion will face up to his similar unit, neutralising it. The phalanx will engage slightly angled from right to left, swivelling the enemy and tying them down, keeping it in position for us to strike. You and I will take the right flank and deal with the Indian contingent and assorted other cavalry on his left using those small hills to cover our flank. No doubt he has placed light infantry in them so I'll do the same. You'll have the companions; they, combined with the Thracian and Greek mercenaries, will form the main prong of our attack whilst I and my bodyguards, along with the remaining Tarantines, will take them in the flank, shattering them so that we can get behind the phalanx. And then…'

Demetrios smiled. 'And then, the job is done.'

'Job done indeed, Son.'

'Who commands the centre? Seleukos?'

'Seleukos, my arse! He may not be totally reliable. He'll command the reserve under the watchful eyes of a few trustworthy lads. No, Nearchos commands the centre.'

'Is that wise, Father? He's more of a naval general – you should command the centre.'

'And leave the right wing to you; you in your first battle?'

'It's not my first battle.'

'A couple of skirmishes in Kappadokia don't count, Demetrios; they weren't battles.' He extended his arm towards the huge army below, still going through its evolutions as it turned from column to line. 'Two armies that size facing each other is a battle, and this is your first. So no, I'll command the right wing and leave the centre to Nearchos. It's a simple enough job: he just has to go forward and keep it tight.'

But tight was not a word that could be used to describe the infantry as they descended to the plain below: exhausted after the forced march to catch Eumenes, they had neither time to rest nor eat before they were ordered to form line of battle at the top of the hill. Down they came at a steady but ragged pace, their legs aching, their backs sore and their stomachs empty, to face the biggest army many of them had ever seen, for most had been with Antigonos in Phrygia when the great battles of the east had been fought. Before them the cavalry patrolled the ground, chasing off light troops intent on disrupting the deployment of the huge force. Eight thousand Macedonians formed the right of the phalanx with a further eight thousand new troops armed in the Macedonian style to their left. Next to them were three thousand Lycians and then nine thousand – mainly Greek – mercenaries all armed with the hoplon shield and long thrusting-spear.

They're no match for the Silver Shields and the Hypaspists in normal circumstances, but in a much deeper formation their weight should stop them, Antigonos mused with some concern as he surveyed the deployment from above. *By placing them there I can concentrate all my might on the right and break that quickly; but if I don't…* Antigonos shook his head, refusing to contemplate the consequences of failure on his right flank. It was here he had to break the enemy and so get around his flank; everything else was but a holding action, using troops of lesser quality against the elite of Eumenes' army.

Slowly the infantry came down from on high, onto the dust of the plain, raising it with the crunch of thousands of boots. Forward they marched behind their cavalry screen; to their rear, on either flank, came the elephants, supported by their light troops, ready for deployment along the whole frontage of the army to counter their fellow beasts of war arranged along the enemy line, now just a thousand paces distant.

More horns blared and hundreds of raised voices sounded in righteous anger as the file-closers along the rear of the formation tried to get some order into what was fast becoming a ragged deployment.

With five hundred paces between the two armies, the call to halt was sounded. The cavalry streamed away to left and right as the trumpeting elephants thundered in the opposite direction, taking their places at prescribed intervals along the line and supported by the light infantry flowing after them.

Dust spiralled, dampening the shouts of the file-closers as they finally managed to instil some order into the twenty-seven thousand men forming the anvil of Antigonos' army and awaiting the hammer strike from his cavalry that would crush the opposing force with its ferocity.

Banners fluttered above each unit and peace began to descend as the cavalry on either flank rallied and then trotted into position. Soon the dust started to settle. Antigonos surveyed his disposition and found it to be to his liking. *The lads have done well; now it's up to me to get this over with as quickly as possible before their tiredness becomes a factor in the fight. Eumenes has had all morning to rest his men, and they've eaten.* With this thought playing in his mind, he slapped his horse's rump and cantered down the hill to his bodyguard of three hundred of the finest cavalry to be found anywhere in the empire. He took his place at their head on the extreme right of his line, abutting the hills, and breathed deep.

All was now set for the biggest clash of arms since Alexander.

Gods, this'll be good. Finally a battle worthy to be called so. Here I'll put an end to the little Greek's arrogance. Antigonos patted his mount's neck and tried to recall the last time he had fought mounted. *Back in Philip's time, it must have been; in his campaign against the Thracians. Well, Philotas, this is for you, old friend.* He raised his fist in the air and pumped it three times. His bodyguard cheered, brandishing their lances over their heads as signals rang out along the line, along both lines. The two armies bestirred themselves for combat.

But Antigonos did not move, indeed, all of his command remained motionless as the light infantry screening the two phalanxes filled the clear sky with arrows. Up they rose in great swarms, hissing as they flew, volley after volley along a frontage of half a league, to fall amongst their opposite numbers and, more importantly, on the great beasts within those ranks. Trumpeting and with stamping feet and shaking heads, the elephants endured squall upon squall of piercing hail; their hides, although thick and tough, becoming coats of increasing pain as shaft following shaft thumped into them. It was but a couple of hundred heartbeats into the iron blizzard that the first of the tormented creatures, on Antigonos' front, reared, throwing the men from the howdah as its mahout clung to the flapping ears to remain mounted. The infantry supporting it turned and fled, knowing full well a rampant elephant cares not which side a man is fighting for. Up went its forelegs and trunk, waving wild in the frenzy of its pain that increased as the archers opposite concentrated their attentions on the brute. To its left, another could stand it no more as, across the divide, one of Eumenes' great war-beasts, flying a spectacular banner from its howdah, reared up, its passengers falling screaming to the ground to disappear beneath stamping rear feet.

'Send to Nearchos to open his ranks and get the elephants out!' Antigonos shouted to the nearest messenger in the group of two dozen standing by. 'Fast as you can or the battle is lost before we've even started.' The man turned his horse and kicked it away with all due haste, leaving Antigonos cursing himself for his stupidity. *Putting elephants in front of the phalanx is asking for trouble; I should've seen that coming. I placed them there solely because Eumenes had done so. I must work out how to use them properly. Come on, Nearchos, surely you don't need a messenger to tell you what danger you're in?*

With massive relief Antigonos saw his trust in the Cretan, who had been so respected by Alexander, had been well placed. Right along the line, behind each of the beasts, the phalanx opened its ranks by sending half a dozen files to the rear to make a passageway wide enough for each of the beasts. Their mahouts needed no second invitation; they turned their charges and raced for the safety being offered, leaving the light troops supporting them to pour more pain on Eumenes' elephants until, with two of the beasts down and their crews crushed, they too could brave no more and the ranks of the phalanx opened and they were able to retire. Back they thundered, passing through the ranks of uneasy infantry. With the elephants gone, the light infantry on both sides lowered their aim and released another few volleys into the mass of heavy infantry beyond their opposite numbers. Disordered by the passing of the elephants, the infantry's long pikes that, upright, would have normally obstructed the flight of many projectiles failed in their purpose and the cries of the wounded rose to the air. Fearful of having provoked a stronger entity than themselves, both sides' archers then retreated back through the still-open lanes.

With the light infantry through, the files refilled the gaps; silence grew over the battle's centre as forty-four thousand men stood and stared at each other.

It was Nearchos who made the first move as the right of his phalanx, the eight thousand Macedonians, lowered the first five ranks of sarissas to horizontal, leaving the rear eleven ranks' pikes arranged over their heads at rising elevations. They moved forward with a massed roar to take on the Greek mercenaries opposite them.

Good man, Nearchos. Now let's see how Eumenes responds.

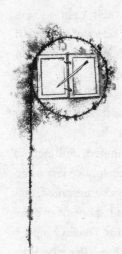

EUMENES.
THE SLY.

B UT, ON THE far side of the field,
Eumenes was leaving his centre to
Antigenes' judgement for he had a
fight on his hands on his right wing; a
fight he was slowly losing – if, indeed, it
could be called a fight as no contact had been made. Wave after
wave of horse-archers, mainly Parthians and Medes, swarmed in,
releasing as they charged and then releasing again as they
swerved away without contact, and then releasing once more to
their rear as they pounded off, making way for another such
attack. Shafts rained in on the elephants and archers lining the
front and flank of Eumenes' command, causing the same distress
as had already been witnessed in the centre as the hordes revolved
in endless circles, refusing hand to hand combat with the heavier
and slower cavalry or elephantry sent against them. Not even
Peucestas' Persian archers could make any impact on their
numbers; such was their speed and so powerful were their
compact bows of wood and horn, they were very rarely in range
for long enough for significant damage to be rendered.

'I've got nothing to counter them,' Eumenes shouted to
Parmida in frustration. Another wave flowed in, spitting death
as it came, bringing down a few of Tlepolemus' Carmanians,

who had been sent against them, as they retreated under the arrow storm to leave the elephants and their light escorts exposed once again to yet another withering series of volleys. 'If I withdraw the elephants and the Persian archers, their attention will fall on my heavy cavalry and that'll suffer woefully.'

'And if we charge them, they just run away,' Parmida said, shaking his head, 'leaving the unit exposed as it rallies and tries to return.'

'It's no good, Eumenes,' Tlepolemus shouted, pulling his horse up in a flurry of dust, 'we can't catch them. I've lost more than three dozen men in the two charges we've mounted; the bastards veer away, turn in their saddles and shoot over their mounts' rumps, before we can even get within javelin range. I don't think my lads will have the heart to go in again on such an obviously futile mission.'

Eumenes cursed and then cursed himself for a fool. *I left all my light cavalry on the left wing so that Antigonos would waste his heavy cavalry overcoming them, and now I find I'm in the position I tried to place him in. I can't withdraw without exposing the Hypaspists' flank. There is only one thing I can do.* 'Parmida, send a message to Eudamos. I want Azanes, Cephlon and Stasander with their Sogdians, Bactrians, Arians and Arachosians and any other horse-archers here at once.' He pointed to the ground. 'Right here, right now. Understand?'

With nothing to do but wait and endure, Eumenes looked to his left to see the great phalanxes stirring on either side. Away in the distance, Antigonos' right had already engaged his extreme left; and it was holding. Closer, the *pantodapoi*, Asian troops armed in the Macedonian manner, on either side clashed for the first time. *Those are his best troops, his Macedonians, being held by my mercenaries. If they can keep it that way and my Asian pikemen hold his then I would hope the Silver Shields and the Hypaspists should crack his Lycians and Greeks, despite them being in double deep formation.* Eumenes held his breath as the pantodapoi ground to a halt, pikes stabbing from each formation as both tried to push forward to get in amongst the enemy and break them. But stalemate soon ensued as the men realised they were of equal strength and there was nothing to be gained by attempting to gouge each other. So, as if by mutual agreement, the pikes were lifted and the melee turned into a shoving match of huge proportions where death by crushing asphyxiation was the worst that could happen.

And then the Silver Shields and the Hypaspists moved forward towards the left of Antigonos' line that had, so far, remained static, fearing to charge such superior troops despite their deep formations. On they came, the fifty-, sixty-, seventy-year-old veterans of countless campaigns and set-piece battles, with their younger – in their thirties and forties – comrades to their right. Sun flashed from their shields, clad in silver upon Alexander's orders as reward for the faithful and long service they had given to him and his father before him, a reward they repayed with mutiny in India. They roared their battle-cries, full-throated and filled with defiance, as they closed with an enemy that was visibly shrinking from them such was their fearsome reputation.

But Eumenes' attention was quickly drawn from the infantry battle as, with speed merited by the urgency of the situation, the horse-archers approached along the rear of the Hypaspists. 'Get the men ready to charge, Parmida, whilst I talk to Peucestas and Xennias.'

It was not a difficult task he set Peucestas but it would require careful timing and Eumenes cantered back to the head of his Kappadokians, praying the lover of luxury and all things Persian would be up to the job. Xennias, he was sure, would do as asked.

He pushed the worry from his mind as Azanes, Cephlon and Stasander reported. 'Take your men and clear those bastards away,' Eumenes shouted, pointing at yet another wave of Parthians racing in and unleashing yet more death on the hard-pressed Persian archers screening the right wing. 'I don't care how, just get rid of them so I can take the heavy cavalry forward and finish his left wing.'

Out from the right flank command, the horse-archers swarmed. Leather- and fur-clad Sogdians and Bactrians with their distinctive leather bonnets, long at the sides and back, Arachosians from the southern side of the Paropamisus Mountains, swarthier and wearing loose-fitting tunics of varying bright hues, and then the Arians, dressed in trousers tucked into high boots, woollen tunics and twisted turbans, from the mountain range itself, where the River Arius springs from the southern flank of the Paropamisus as it begins its journey to the great lake Ponticus. All had one purpose: to reap as many Parthian and Mede lives as they could, for it had been Peithon, the satrap of Media, killing the satrap of Parthia and installing his own brother who had brought war and they intended to punish him for that. They cared not who supported whom and had barely heard of the boy-king back in the west, nor were they acquainted with the extent of Antigonos' lust for empire. None of that mattered to the archers from the east as, controlling their mounts with their knees and ankles alone, they nocked their shafts and, in one fluid motion, released. Time and again they let loose a volley, receiving as much in return from the enemy as they chased the Parthians and Medes away to the south. But the tactic of a horse-archer is to remain out of contact whilst causing as much damage from long range as their expertise with the bow would allow, and thus the Parthians and Medes only turned to face the assault on rare occasions, to let loose a volley, before fleeing the superior numbers of their foes.

With relief Eumenes watched them as they were chased from the field. He turned to Parmida and his Kappadokians. 'Now! Now!' He urged his mount forward as he shouted.

And forward they went, five hundred troopers completely loyal to their satrap and burning with indignation that he should be forced to fight for his cause; before them was the source of much of their master's woe and they rode towards it with glad hearts. Shielded Tarantines, used mainly for ambush and skirmishing, were no match for the heavily armoured Kappadokians and, at the sight of their charge, now mounting in pace, they made the normal response for light, dispersed troops facing a frontal charge: they evaded, leaving the heavier colonist cavalry from Phrygia and Lydia, under the command of Peithon himself, to face the attack. Lance-armed, they numbered three times that of the Kappadokians; but that counted for nothing as Eumenes gripped his first javelin tight and felt the power of the force around him as five hundred horses thundered across the barren ground; great hearts pumping hard powered the beasts whose heads, necks and chests were protected with scale-armour. Soon they made it to a canter with their heavy loads and could maintain the pace as, knee to knee, in double ranks, their riders prepared for contact.

Ahead, the colonists rallied and set to counter. *Let them come, let them fix all their attention upon us.* Eumenes led his men on as the colonists charged towards them, lances extended forward, pointing the way, tongues lolling from the side of their mounts' foam-flecked mouths and cries of war issuing from the riders.

At fifty paces apart the Kappadokians hurled the first of their three javelins; up they reached to the sky to fall directly into the mass of horseflesh barrelling towards them. And mayhem they caused as beasts reared or tumbled, struck by weighty missiles that seared through their hide to reach the vitals. Men were thrown back, javelins juddering in them, to fall, blood misting, beneath the legs of the horses behind, entangling them so they nose-dived into the ground, furrowing the dust with ripping muzzles. Within a few heartbeats the second volley hit, increasing the chaos within the disordered ranks as further men and horses crashed down; many a lance was dropped as the riders attempted to get their mounts to jump the obstacles, thrashing limbs and screeching, on the ground before them. At the third volley the forces were barely ten paces apart and the Kappadokians sent their sleek bringers of death low and hard, further disorganising the counter charge, slowing it and turning it into a ragged collection of disparate groups now trying to band together for mutual protection against the wall of scale-armour pounding in. Impact was brutal as beast cracked in on beast, crushing the wind from lungs and casting aside the weakened; swords were ripped from scabbards and the business of slicing life from living began.

A flash of sharpened iron flicked past Eumenes' left cheek; with barely a jerk of his wrist, his blade severed the hand brandishing the lance that had come so close. The scream was lost in the din of contact; blood, pulsing from the stump, gushed into Eumenes' lap. He pushed his mount through the gap as the colonist fell, hacked from his horse by Parmida. With inchoate cries spewing from within, Eumenes ducked under a second, overarm, thrust and worked his sword with haste to slam the tip up into the exposed armpit, bringing a shrill screech of wincing agony from the rider as he jerked back, pulling Eumenes' weapon with him; slick with gore, the hilt was wrenched from his grasp. Grabbing his victim's falling lance as it fell from his dying hand, Eumenes swung the haft and cracked it into the face of a horse being driven at him; up the creature reared, forelegs beating, a bestial shriek rising. With no time to turn the lance, Eumenes rammed the butt, two handed, into the beast's exposed chest and drove his mount on, pushing with all the strength in his upper body whilst gripping on with his legs; over the horse tumbled, crashing down onto its back, crushing its rider's ribcage, as its limbs thrashed in the air. It rolled to its right, pulling its forelegs back under it and pushing itself up with a buck of the hind-quarters, to bolt away from the perceived danger, crashing through what was left of the rank behind it and opening it.

Seizing the moment, Eumenes pointed the lance at the opportunity, roaring to his men to follow. Punching the butt into the midriff of a screaming colonist, doubling him over and beating the wind from his body, Eumenes exploded through the gap with Parmida and a dozen men following; turning to the left, and shouting at Parmida to go right, he rode along the rear of the colonists to where resistance seemed stiffer and rammed the lance into unprotected kidneys, stabbing repeatedly as he raced along the line with his followers imitating his actions. With enemy suddenly behind them, the colonists wavered as the rear rank turned their horses to face the new threat, shouting and gesturing to the Tarantines who had rallied a couple of hundred paces behind them to come to their aid; but more and more Kappadokians flooded through the breach to face them and, with the advantage of momentum, charged into the make-shift defence.

A brief moment of unease ran through Eumenes as he glanced over his shoulder and saw the Tarantines move forward into a trot and then accelerate into a canter.

But the attempt at saving their comrades came too late. It was not the break in the line that finished Peithon's command as a shudder rippled through it from north to south. Peucestas' Companion Cavalry ploughed into its left flank, rolling it up with ease as the fight flew from the colonists who had come east to claim land for themselves and their families and not to die here, so far from their new homes. Turning, they fled headlong towards the hill they had descended so recently, taking the Tarantines with them.

Pausing only to rally his Kappadokians and Peucestas' Companions in order to pursue the enemy in good order and not risk his men's lives unnecessarily, Eumenes turned to see what he had been expecting: Xennias leading his command towards the exposed flank of the Lycians and Greeks, now struggling to hold their own against the Silver Shields and the Hypaspists, despite their depth in numbers.

But a deep formation is only of advantage when facing an enemy to the front; to a flank attack it doubles the points of contact and it was with vigour that Xennias thundered into the infantry's left flank as they scrambled to turn and face the threat. Leading with their lances and then drawing ringing swords, the cavalry penetrated deep into the ranks, their momentum unstoppable, their wrath unfaceable, as the Silver Shields and the Hypaspists worked their pikes with renewed vitality, using every bit of their long military experience to cleave gaps in their opponents' formation. And the gaps were soon forced and cohesion crumbled and the Lycians and Greeks fell in increasing numbers such was the infiltration of their ranks. Try as they might to escape the massacre, they were hobbled by the depth of their formation; they barged into one another in their desperation to flee from the scything blades of the cavalry and the piercing tips of infantry pikes, creating a fatal congestion that could not be eluded.

With the rally of his cavalry complete, Eumenes turned away from the infantry battle as Antigonos' line crumbled, shields thrown to the ground and weapons discarded, as full flight ensued. But he left the pursuit to Xennias as he and Peucestas set about driving Peithon's cavalry so far from the field that it would not be a part of the battle again.

He smiled as they moved forward, confident that Antigonos was as good as beaten.

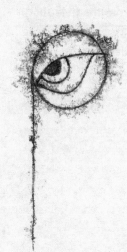

ANTIGONOS.
THE ONE-EYED.

N OW IS NOT *the time for faint-hearts.* Antigonos sat, grim, upon his horse as he watched his Macedonian infantry on the right of his phalanx give ground inexorably. The pantodapoi shoving match next to them, in the centre, was being decided in Eumenes' favour and they did not wish to have their flank exposed. There seemed very little hope as, from what he could make out through the dust, the Silver Shields and the Hypaspists had broken his Lycians and Greeks. As to what was going on with Peithon on the far side of the field, wreathed in the fog of combat, he could but guess, and it was not a pleasant answer that came to mind. There was naught he could do to try to change the tide of the battle, for Eumenes' light infantry had won their own private fight in the hills to his right and now threatened his cavalry with archery from higher ground; to get around Eudamos' flank on that side was impossible. As was a frontal charge, even against the much lighter and less numerous cavalry force, for the satrap of India had kept his elephant screen along his breadth. Antigonos knew his horses could not be induced to approach the strange-smelling giants, whereas Eudamos' Indian horses were used to the beasts and would happily charge with them or through them. *Even when Eumenes weakened Eudamos' command by taking away all his horse-archers I couldn't take advantage of the position. The little Greek has played me well, neutralising me and my best cavalry with forty elephants, a couple of thousand indifferent cavalry and a hill full of light infantry.*

'We should retire,' Nearchos shouted, bringing his mount to a skidding halt. 'The phalanx's left wing is collapsing and the centre is retreating step by step; I don't know how much longer the right of it can endure this pressure.' He pointed over to the Macedonians. 'I've ordered them not to give any more ground but it's futile; if they don't retire at the same pace as their neighbours, they'll be finished. If we all pull back together, at least we have some chance of an orderly withdrawal onto the higher ground behind us.'

'My arse, we will. That'll leave Eumenes the field and he'll claim victory.'

'But you'll have extracted your army for another day.'

'If I don't camp on the battlefield and control the burying of the dead there won't be another day. Now, get back to your command, Nearchos, and make sure your centre keeps on retiring, as fast as you like.' He looked to the sky. 'We've only about an hour of daylight left and I think I've seen a way to do Eumenes some damage.'

Nearchos looked incredulous.

'Just go!' Antigonos roared at the Cretan as Demetrios approached.

Nearchos turned his mount and galloped away; beyond him, the phalanx retreated another few paces.

'Not you too?' Antigonos said as his son drew up next to him.

'What do you mean?' Demetrios wiped the grime from his face.

'Telling me to withdraw.'

'Withdraw? No, Father; I'm getting ready to attack. We're about to get the best opportunity.'

'You've seen it? Good. Watch my lead, count to fifty and then follow me. I'll take the left and you take the right.'

Demetrios grinned. 'We may not win today, but we won't lose either.'

And it was with these encouraging words playing in his mind that Antigonos sent out his orders to the officers of his command, whilst he watched and waited for the moment he had foreseen to arrive. Step by step his Macedonian phalanx was driven back but he did nothing to retire his cavalry command with it, knowing it was not vulnerable to a flank attack from infantry it could easily evade. Furthermore, staying put made it look to Eudamos that he was planning to take Eumenes' phalanx in the flank, a move the Indian satrap would counter by his own similar manoeuvre once Antigonos was engaged; thus he would wait where he was to see what developed. *That's right, Eudamos, you wait there, just where I want you to be.*

Antigonos turned in his saddle and ordered his bodyguard to ready themselves; now there was a clear gap between the left flank of Eumenes' phalanx and the front of Eudamos' cavalry command. Bearded, like the commander they had served for all their military life, Antigonos' Companions checked harnesses before swinging back up onto their mounts, gripping their lances fast in their right hands. To his left, Demetrios' thousand Companion Cavalry, as well as the Thracians and mixed allied and mercenary troops, went through the same procedure; to his rear, the elephants waited with their attendant light troops.

Back the phalanx went, step by weary step, leaving a trail of bodies in its wake, each one skewered for a second time as the enemy stepped over, to make sure of death and not to leave the threat of an upwards stab to the groin to those in the ranks behind.

A hundred paces was now the gap between the phalanx and Eudamos' cavalry and still Antigonos did not move and still the satrap of India made no attempt to plug the hole. *You're still expecting me to do what you would do in the circumstances – fool.*

A hundred and twenty-five paces, a hundred and fifty. *Any moment now.*

A hundred and seventy. 'Now!' Up went Antigonos' fist, punching the air as it gripped his lance; a horn screeched and his standard was raised. He kicked his horse forward into a trot; three hundred men followed, heading directly towards the elephant screen protecting Eudamos' front. It was as he accelerated to a canter that he swerved his mount to the left to ride parallel with the enemy line. With mounting joy, he broke into a gallop, relishing the wind in his face and the thunder of the charge surging through his being as he led his men to the extreme right of Eudamos' formation, the flank that had once been protected by the phalanx. Turning now to his right, he headed at an angle that bisected the rear of the phalanx and flank of the cavalry as, behind him, Demetrios brought his men forward; following him, the thousand Thracians and thousand allied and mercenary troops moved towards the gap.

It was the sudden turn to the right, as Antigonos pushed ahead of his men now fanning out behind him in a solid wedge, which would have shown Eudamos the real objective of the charge, for, up until then, Antigonos had been careful to make his manoeuvre look as if it was aimed at the rear of the phalanx. But now he drove his full force onto the static flank of the Indian cavalry and Demetrios brought his men in next to him.

Gods, this is good; so different a thrill to that of the infantry. With this thought in his head and a grimace of a teeth-bearing smile on his face, he slammed his lance home into the throat of a dark-skinned Indian desperately trying to get his terrified horse to move forward to gain some momentum in countering. In a spray of blood, the man was jerked back off his saddle, his throat open and his head lolling to one side, the neck vertebrae pierced. In a flash, two more sleek lance-tips, his wingmen's, sliced into the Indians and then two more and two more as the wedge rammed itself deep into the heart of the enemy, its weight growing as more and more made contact, its solid core ensuring the velocity did not diminish. Horses whinnied, shrill, as they were tumbled to the ground, their riders, skewered, slithering from their backs. Ever forwards did Antigonos drive, feeling the weight of his men behind him push him deeper, as his arm ached with the repeated, random stabbing of his lance; no longer able to see clearly out of his one eye, such was the sweat and dust accumulated within it, and deafened almost to the point of insensibility, he now just lashed out at anything before him, relying on his wingmen to keep him from harm.

With a vicious jerk, the lance was yanked from his grasp; a burning flame sliced through his right forearm as his subconscious drew his sword. Ignoring all pain and living only for the joy of the moment, Antigonos roused his body to belie its sixty and more years and fight with a new and desperate strength. Now the momentum of the attack had stalled and he was in the midst of a huge swirl of men and beasts where chaos reigned and the normal rules and etiquette of life were forgotten. Blood, sweat, urine and faeces – of man and beast – assaulted the one sense still retaining some degree of function; his head swam with the stench as the muscles in his right arm, cramped with usage, sent pain searing through him, pain he ignored in the sure knowledge that to give in would be the last thing he would do before meeting with the Ferryman.

Two wild slashes of his blade met with no contact. He felt pressure ease to the front of his mount and noticed a change in the tone ringing in his ears. He felt a restraining hand on his shoulder and had to check himself from turning to bite it.

'They're gone, sir,' his wingman said, 'gone.'

It took a couple of moments before he had the sense to wipe his eye, to see the truth of the matter. The entire command, cavalry, elephantry and infantry, was in flight, either heading for the low hills to the north or fleeing west out across the plain; he had salvaged something from the day.

But there was still much to be done; whilst his arm was cleaned and bandaged tight, orders issued from him in a stream as he rallied his entire force facing back the way they had come, leaving the wounded to fend for themselves as time was now the issue. In the distance, almost half a league away, the dust rising from the infantry battle had increased, implying the steady retreat had turned into abject flight. Antigonos was a finished man – if not a dead man – if his infantry could not be extracted. And so, without rest, he drove his exhausted horse forward once more; great-hearted, the beast responded, its nostrils flaring, its chest heaving and, taking its example, the rest of its kind followed. Almost two and a half thousand stallions, mares and geldings thundered back across the plain, bearing down on the rear of Eumenes' phalanx as it, in turn, harried the fleeing remnants of the Macedonian pikemen broken upon its spear-points.

Urgency added speed to his pulse; he knew that, as the sun began to fall below the western horizon behind him, he might never see it rise again. In they closed upon the as-yet unaware block of infantry. With swords waving as most had lost their lance in the first contact, they were too ragged to form a wedge and, besides, they needed a broad frontage to cause maximum panic. So it was in small groups, or sometimes twos or threes, they ploughed into the file-closers, taking heads and arms, wading down the gaps until all knew of their presence and all were aware of the mortal danger they faced.

It was a simple question of self-preservation that caused the phalanx to break off pursuit of the fleeing enemy; and it was the same simple question that caused Antigonos to withdraw his cavalry before it was set upon and mauled to death, for in the final analysis it was grievously outnumbered and surrounded.

Thus, Antigonos led his exhausted command around the foe that stood eyeing them in the half-light and on to where his shattered infantry were rallying not far up from the base of the slope they had descended but seven hours earlier.

And still they had not eaten.

But it was not just Antigonos' army that regrouped and reformed, for Eumenes had returned from the pursuit of Peithon and the news of Eudamos' defeat had reached his ears: the horns blew along Eumenes' formation and the infantry, now completely disengaged from their broken foes, retired, at a weary jog, to form up five hundred paces from the foot of the hill.

'He's forming up again,' Demetrios said, unable to believe what his eyes were seeing in the gloom; the full moon, already risen, spread gentle light on the massed helms of both sides. 'He's not camping on the battlefield, he's forming up again.'

Antigonos rubbed his eye and shook his head, clearing the tiredness from it. 'Does he expect us to come again?' He looked to the sky. 'The moon is bright enough to fight until it sets.'

'Will the lads stand for it? They had a serious mauling.'

'Almost four thousand dead is the provisional number reported to me; almost one in ten with at least twice that amount wounded, no doubt. It's better to stand-to down here, rather than lick their wounds up the hill. It'll concentrate their minds away from dead comrades. Besides, Eumenes might attack and that would be a mistake.'

EUMENES.
THE SLY.

'HE'S FORMING UP to face us,' Eumenes said as he stood with Antigenes and Teutamus at the head of the Silver Shields. 'If he attacks now, it would be the mistake that finishes him.'

'What do we do?' Antigenes asked.

'We wait. We've formed up here to secure the right to camp on the field and bury the dead; I won't let him take that from me.'

And wait they did as the badly mauled troops of Antigonos' army were corralled back into line and moved forward from the lower reaches of the hill. Down they came, back onto the plain, and marched towards their enemy to halt within two hundred paces of them.

Silence descended across the field as exhaustion ruled out any attempts to hurl insults across the divide; exhaustion fuelled by hunger.

Gradually the moon rose, playing its silver beams on the iron and bronze of eighty thousand men's armour and weapons; a soft night breeze ruffled horsehair plumes, banners and tunic hems, whilst, now positioned on the flanks of each formation, the elephants stood swishing their trunks to clasp at any piece of vegetation they could find, however poor the quality.

'The lads have got to have something to eat,' Antigenes said, reporting to Eumenes after having made a tour of the whole army. 'They've been standing-to for three hours now and are getting mutinous. They don't understand what you're trying to achieve.'

'To camp on the battlefield and thereby claim victory. I want Antigonos to send to me for his dead and not the other way round.'

'I don't think any of the lads care who sends to whom for the dead; they just want to build fires and eat a hot meal washed down with as much wine as they can lay their hands on.'

Eumenes conceded the point. 'Very well; it looks as if Antigonos is not about to push forward. Give the order to stand down and prepare the evening meal. But we stay right here; have everything we need brought up.'

The signals rang out in the half-light and there was muted cheering from the ranks as they rested their weapons; the men opposite them did the same and the battle ended by mutual consent. But the men did not break formation and settle into small groups awaiting their supplies; instead they turned and, led by the Silver Shields and the Hypaspists, began to walk west.

'Where are they going?' Eumenes shouted. 'I gave orders to stay here. Antigenes, see what's happening.'

'I can guess: they're going to find the baggage.'

'The baggage? But that's a couple of leagues away; it'll take them two hours. Talk to them.'

Antigenes shrugged. 'If you think it will do any good; but you know what they're like and how much they prize the baggage. They won't be parted from it for long so I don't know what I can say to dissuade them. Perhaps you shouldn't have sent it so far in advance.' With a false smile Antigenes stomped off.

Why is it always about the baggage? You can't move with it and you can't move without it. I defeated Neoptolemus by seizing his baggage and I'm just as vulnerable as anyone to losing mine, but to lose a battle because the army won't camp on the field but, rather, retreat to the baggage is ludicrous.

But that was the cruel reality Eumenes had to accept as the entire army refused to stay where it was ordered and marched the two leagues west to be united with the baggage, shortly after midnight, leaving Antigonos to claim victory.

'We lost five hundred men and he had nearly four thousand killed and I had to send to him to retrieve my dead,' Eumenes complained to Hieronymus as the herald returned from Antigonos' camp the following day.

'What does it matter? The point is we're between him and Gabene, so either he fights us again or he has to slink back to Media, like a whipped hound, and winter there. So in all other respects you've won as you're going to do what you planned and he's going back to where he came from, having lost twenty per cent of his army either killed or wounded.'

And it was with that in mind Eumenes sat on a dais beneath the empty throne and presided over the funeral games with Eudamos and Peucestas next to him and the rest of the satraps to either side. The Indian satrap had been given the place of honour to Eumenes' right as more than half of the casualties had been from his command; his second-in-command, Ceteus, was amongst them, crushed beneath the feet of his elephant as it reared and threw him from the howdah. It was in sombre mood that the various foot races, jumps, javelin throwing and many other events were conducted before the pyres in which the bodies lay ready to make their final journey. But once the victory crowns had been dispensed, the gods had received their due and the time to light the pyres had come, a series of shrieks, high-pitched and full of malice, disrupted the proceedings; two women, clawing at each other and pulling at hair and clothes, ran headlong towards Eudamos.

The satrap of India let out a great sigh. 'I thought this might happen; it's Ceteus' wives.'

'What do they want?'

'One of them will burn alive with their husband on his pyre.'

'And both wish it to be the other.'

'On the contrary: they both wish for the honour and it'll be down to us to decide.'

Eumenes stared at Eudamos, incredulous. 'Why?'

'It's custom. It came about because in India, parents don't make the choice of spouse for their child. Instead, people get married by mutual consent, which, as you can imagine, often leads to mistakes being made and wives poisoning a husband who disappoints them.' Eudamos spread his hands. 'There you have it; it became the custom for wives who did not have children or weren't pregnant to die with their husbands to deter such murders.'

Eumenes shook his head in mute disbelief.

'Now it's considered a matter of honour to be burned on the pyre and if a woman fails in her duty she'll be shunned for the rest of her life.'

Eumenes looked at the two women as they drew near, still raging at each other. 'Why don't they both get on the pyre?'

'Custom decrees only one should burn.'

'Yet a man can have two, three or even four wives?'

'Indeed.'

'Well, I suppose it keeps the competition between them going after death as to who can best please the man.'

The women controlled themselves as they approached the dais. One was in her early thirties, the other, late teens. Both had wreaths woven around their heads.

'I demand justice, Eudamos,' the elder of the two said, kneeling before the dais and clasping the satrap's knees, 'for the friendship you showed my late husband whom I mourn with a deep yearning that may only be cured by cleansing fire.'

'She's pregnant!' the younger wife shrilled.

'She lies!' The first wife's talons flashed, narrowly missing the other's face.

The younger one extended her tattooed hands in supplication to Eudamos. 'She cannot take advantage of the law if she is with child. It should be me who has the honour of burning with my husband.'

'I am the eldest and as I have precedence in years I should have precedence in honour too. In all matters, those who are older are regarded as having greater precedence over the younger in respect and honour.'

'She's pregnant! I know it; her moon did not come this month.'

Eumenes looked at Eudamos. 'Well, what do we do?'

'We find the truth of the matter. There are midwives amongst the camp-followers; both women will be examined.'

It was a short process that took place in a tent erected behind the dais as the entire army, now fascinated by the argument and laying wagers upon the outcome, looked on.

'The belly is hard,' announced the crone of advanced years who was leading the investigation, as she came out of the tent. 'It is sure the older woman is with child, whereas the younger is most certainly not; she shows no signs. We also spoke to the two women's attendants and the younger's confirmed their mistress had just finished her moon whilst the elder's said hers had not come this month.'

A wail went up from inside the tent; the younger woman came out, a smile broad across her face and a skip in her step, followed by her rival tearing at the wreath around her head and weeping as if the worst thing that could possibly happen had just occurred.

'The honour of sharing Ceteus' pyre lies with you,' Eudamos said to the young wife.

She clapped her hands and jumped up and down a few times. Cheers rang through the entire army; even those who had bet on the elder one seemed pleased at the younger's perceived good fortune.

'We will honour her and Ceteus,' Eumenes declaimed. 'The army will form up and march around the pyre.'

Thus, with the smoke from the rest of the pyres wafting across the camp, the young wife was dressed as if for a wedding with fillets bound in her hair and golden stars woven around them. Her neck was draped with gold and silver necklaces, each progressively longer than the last, and rings with many precious stones decorated her hands and feet. Singing a hymn in honour of her virtue, her kinsfolk accompanied her to the pyre as the army continued its march past.

'That's her brother,' Eudamos informed Eumenes, pointing at a turbaned man holding her hand and smiling as if it were the happiest day of his life.

Eumenes once more shook his head in disbelief as he watched, mute.

As she reached the foot of the pyre she began to strip off her jewellery and distributed it around her kin as keepsakes, laughing with them as she did. Once ready, her brother helped her to mount the pyre; leaving his sister reclining next to her dead husband, holding his hand, he descended as the whole army came to a halt and watched on in amazement. He took a flaming torch and, with a prayer to the heavens, plunged it into the oil-soaked wood. Fire spread, flames licking their way up through the branches, catching them, crackling and hissing, as all observed in silence, waiting to hear the woman's screams. None came as she endured the ordeal without so much as a twitch.

Eumenes turned away, wondering what it could be that caused the women of India to behave in such a manner and how their families could celebrate their agonising deaths.

As the flames died down news came that Antigonos had taken his army back up from the plain and was returning to Ecbatana. Eumenes gave orders to prepare to march the following day. 'We winter in Gabene, gentlemen, and will renew the campaign against Antigonos in the spring. Once he's defeated we will turn west and relieve Olympias.'

OLYMPIAS.
THE MOTHER.

OLYMPIAS PUT HER hand to her mouth; once again, she gagged on the fetid air enveloping Pydna despite the stiff, early-winter sea breeze and the incense burning constantly in her chamber, which she had rarely left since her abortive escape attempt. Such was the state of decay of the thousands of bodies flung, without ceremony, over the city walls it was impossible to breathe without feeling nausea; sometimes it proved so much of a strain on the constitution that the contents of the stomach were voided. Not that there remained much to void as the siege entered its second year and supplies were almost completely non-existent: the horses and pack-animals had been eaten as well as those elephants that had survived on a diet of wood-chippings over the summer and autumn. Regular troops were getting enough grain for a few daily mouthfuls of bread, baked with additional sawdust; the irregular troops and citizens were issued with naught and had to survive on whatever rodents they could trap – dogs and cats having already been consumed – and, in some cases, whatever they could cut from a dead relative or friend before corruption set in.

Misery and lethargy hung over the city, like the stench from the dead. Beyond it, the army of Kassandros was still encamped outside the towering siege walls and the fleet continued to patrol the coastal waters, denying all but the most intrepid boats ingress or egress; the few that did get through could barely bring enough food to keep Olympias and her entourage in reasonable health, leaving nothing to spare for those who so desperately needed it.

And so it was with hope and joy, despite the constant nausea mounting in her gorge, that Olympias read the message from Polyperchon, giving the time and place to rendezvous with a rescue party he was sending in a quinquereme, a ship best suited to the choppy winter sea – the first time after the next new moon that there was a sea mist an hour after dawn. With a look of new purpose written across her gaunt, but still striking face, she handed the letter to Thessalonike. 'I'll head to Sardis.'

'You mean "we", surely, Olympias,' Thessalonike said, having finished reading with sunken and dark-rimmed eyes. 'You, me, Alexander and Roxanna.'

'Yes, yes, of course I mean all of us; I can't guarantee my safety without the king. If we can get to Sardis, I'll be safer there than with that traitor, Polyperchon, in the south.'

'That traitor is trying to rescue us.'

'He deserted me!' The shrill voice echoed off the walls. 'As did the other traitor, Aristonous! They both promised to bring their armies back here and yet here I still sit.'

'Aristonous is holding Amphipolis against Kassandros; Polyperchon and his son are occupying the Peloponnese; Aeacides is still with his Eperiot army in the west; and, on top of all that, Monimus in Pella is still refusing to bow to Kassandros. Traitors are people who desert to the enemy, not people who fight on.'

'They should be here!'

'Calm down, Olympias.'

'As should be Aeacides!'

Thessalonike wrapped her arms around her shrunken frame, lowered her head and drew a calming breath. 'The fact they're not here is because, had they come, Kassandros would have defeated all three of them, one at a time, before they could link up as he stands at their midpoint and controls the sea. They were all well aware that once Kassandros proved, by getting round behind Aristonous and thrashing him, that he was a strategist of some subtlety and could lead an army, he deserved to be treated with respect.'

'He's a pimply little toad!'

'And that pimply little toad defeated us and has an army and navy that has kept us in here for more than a year; whereas that *traitor*, Polyperchon, is going to get us out of Pydna using the weather as a screen now it's finally closing in. So, perhaps it would be better to focus on the realities of people's characters rather than calling everyone names in an emotional and blinkered manner.'

'And what do you know about the realities of people's characters?'

'As much as you know about letting your emotions rule your head: a lot.'

There she goes again, telling me the truth and baiting me with it; it's becoming intolerable. Olympias waved her adopted daughter away. 'Leave me.'

'No.'

'What!'

'You heard me, Olympias: I said no.' Thessalonike held her palm out to Olympias to silence her. 'And don't start shouting and screaming the way you normally do when someone fails to do what you want, but, instead, listen to me.'

Olympias met Thessalonike's gaze. *I don't have the energy to argue; where does she get her strength from? She has the same meagre fare as I do.* 'What do you want?'

'Me? I want nothing, but the army wants permission to leave and surrender to Kassandros.'

'They want what?'

'Just listen, will you, woman? Calm down and listen. They have been threatening for the last month just to walk out the gate but they didn't want to do it without seeking your permission first.'

'They should have come to me, I'd have—'

'Which is exactly why they went through me; I promised I'd find a time when you wouldn't force them to eat each other's testicles directly from the scrotum and listen with a positive attitude to their request.'

'Which will be never.'

'Which is now because it's in your interests to let them go; you don't need them any more. What use are ten thousand starving men who can barely lift a sword? We're going to be out of here very soon so why keep them here any longer?'

'To defend the walls.'

'Against what? If Kassandros was going to storm the city he would've done it already, as he knows, from agents, our men would be incapable of beating off an attack; yet he chooses to starve us instead. No, let them go and you may find a good percentage of them will remain loyal to you even after they go over to Kassandros, which could be vital if you ever face a Macedonian army in person again. Remember what happened against Adea?'

Olympias opened her mouth and then closed it. *She has such an annoying ability to be right.* Her face brightened. 'And I can stop paying them.'

'Exactly, not that you've paid them since we ran out of coin three months ago.'

'If they desert with me still owing them money, they'll lose it.'

Thessalonike gave a wan smile. 'Now you're catching on.'

'And if, in the future, I was to offer to repay the money I owe them, they would see me as the fairest of people, completely trustworthy and meriting loyalty, and they'd return to my cause.'

'Especially as you have so compassionately released them.'

Compassionate? That's something I've never been accused of; I rather like this argument. 'All right; tell them to come to see me.'

And so it was with the hope of the policy one day coming back to her with advantage, Olympias watched, from the high tower atop the gateway, what had once been a proud army shuffle out, past the piles of festering dead, some bloated with gas, others decayed and crumbling and all reeking to the heavens. Empty stomachs retched out drips of bile from dry throats as the pathetic lines of emaciated men filed past the heaps of carrion and crossed no-man's land to the gate now swinging open in the siege wall.

'Good riddance,' Olympias muttered to herself as the last of them disappeared into the camp beyond the siege works. She turned to Thessalonike standing, as ever since the slap, as far away from her as the situation would allow. 'So, tell me, my cunning little vixen, what happens if Polyperchon's ship fails to turn up on the first dawn of sea mist?'

'Then we are ready on the next.'

'And then it doesn't come?'

'We hope it comes on the next.'

'And if it doesn't?'

'Then we negotiate.'

'Negotiate! Over my dead body.'

'Yes, Olympias; there is always that option.' Thessalonike turned to go with, Olympias thought, a hint of a smile playing on her lips.

But the need for negotiation seemed to be avoided as Polyperchon proved good to his word. Olympias stood on the mist-shrouded deck of a swift lembus, watching the spectral shadow of a massive ship fade in and out of the miasma as the sun rose behind it to the east; she turned to Thessalonike, standing with Roxanna and Alexander, and pointed an aggressive finger. 'Never speak of negotiation with Kassandros to me again.'

Thessalonike kept her thoughts to herself as she had done for the last ten nights since the new moon, as they had waited in harbour for the dawn to break to see if there was sufficient sea mist for the operation to stand a chance of success.

And now, here they were, a hundred paces from the shore, halfway between the harbour mouth and where the siege wall met the sea to the south, barely fifty paces from their huge saviour and protected from the lookouts of the blockading fleet by a gods-sent mist whose fresh salt tang cleared away the months of stench and decay from their weary throats and nostrils.

A breeze billowed the mist, clearing it from the quinquereme's deck, revealing a group of about half a dozen men standing, peering towards them; the central one raised his arm in greeting. Olympias, forgetting her dignity, waved back with almost childlike enthusiasm. 'Bring us alongside,' she ordered the triarchos, her voice almost benign.

The full-bearded seaman shouted a series of orders in fluent nauticalese and the little ship eased away to the slow beat of the stroke-master's flute. Another gust of wind pushed in more mist and the two ships were momentarily obscured. Olympias leaned forward, staring towards the place where she had last seen her rescuer; there it was again, but still a shadow, although far closer now. Another time it dissolved, only, a few heartbeats later, to reappear in full clarity, the figure now clearly visible, smiling down at her with his pinched and pockmarked face.

'Good morning, Olympias,' Kassandros said in a voice full of cheer. 'May I help you aboard?'

Horror on her face and fear in her eyes, she looked up at the man she had not seen for many years and yet who consumed her to the core of her inner self with hatred; he was there, above her, and soon she would be in his power. 'Turn back! Turn back now!' she screamed at the triarchos, pulling away from the bow to put more distance between herself and Kassandros.

Orders flew; the swift little ship slowed and veered to larboard at the same time, its starboard oars clacking on those of the quinquereme.

'Oh, and if you're thinking of making a run for it I've strengthened the blockade; you won't get through.' Laughter erupted from Kassandros and those around him as the lembus turned and pulled away. 'Do you think I couldn't have taken you, Olympias? Do you think I couldn't still do so if I chose? Do you, Olympias? I intercepted Polyperchon's message and then sent it on to you; I knew when the galley was coming so I took it and came with it instead. It would've been the easiest thing to have captured you; but what fun would that have been, eh? So I'm letting you go; flee back into Pydna, Olympias, and stay there and rot. It's the easiest way of killing you without having the blame of your death lain at my feet.' Kassandros thumbed his teeth and spat towards the retreating lembus. 'Rot, Olympias! Rot or come and beg me for your life.'

It began as a growl, deep within Olympias' belly, and worked its way up through her vitals with gathering speed and growing strength until it exploded from her like a harpy's death-cry, inchoate but intelligible in its malevolence, shocking all on board that such a sound could emanate from a human being – even Olympias. As it tailed off she collapsed to her knees, her chest heaving, leaving only the sound of Kassandros' laughter, faint in the distance, and the creak and splash of oars as the lembus powered back to the harbour entrance.

He's got me; the pockmarked son of a toad has me completely in his hands. Sobs now welled up, shaking her body as she knelt, hunched over. 'I will not rot; I refuse to rot. I will not become a thing of no importance.' She looked up at Thessalonike. 'I will not fade; I will not!'

'Then negotiate; there's something you can give him that he wants badly enough to let you go. You know there is.'

Olympias made to object and then thought better of it and nodded her head. 'Alexander.'

Thessalonike narrowed her eyes and indicated over her shoulder to where Alexander stood with Roxanna gazing into the fog. 'And his mother. And one more thing.' She pointed to the Great Ring of Macedon on Olympias' hand.

'The regency?'

'Yes, Olympias, the regency; the boy is of no use to Kassandros without the ring.'

'But then I have no legitimate power.'

'You have no legitimate power when you're dead and that's the choice you are now facing.'

Olympias bit her lip as she looked down at the ring, her mind in turmoil as she tried to balance the arguments in her head. Gradually she calmed as she came to her decision. 'You're right: I must buy my freedom with this and those two.'

'*Our* freedom.'

Olympias looked at her adoptive daughter, the wind pulling at her wet hair. 'And why should I help you?'

'Who's going to negotiate with Kassandros? You? He'd kill you once he'd had the pleasure of hearing you beg on your knees. He needs to be made to swear an oath before you come out of here.'

She's right; I can't go anywhere near the little toad. She's got me. 'And your price for negotiating with him is that I buy your freedom too?'

'It is.'

'And what's to stop you from going over to him as soon as you sit down to talk in no-man's land?'

'And why would I go over to someone so abhorrent? No, Olympias, I would be more worried about him trying to seize me; I'll need to take a strong bodyguard.'

Olympias considered her position for a few moments as the rising sun began to break through the mist and play golden on the sea. 'If I give up Alexander then I've nothing with which to tempt Eumenes back from the east to fight for me.'

'Whilst you are locked up in here you've nothing to tempt Eumenes with anyway; at least you will be free.'

Olympias made her decision. 'Once I get to Sardis I'll work out a way of getting Eumenes back.' *It will have to involve marrying Kleopatra to someone powerful enough to be accepted as the consort to an Argead queen; just because we've never had one before doesn't mean we can't start now. As long as the Argead royal house sits on the throne, Eumenes will fight for it.* 'You're right, Thessalonike. Although it pains me to ask, make a deal with Kassandros.'

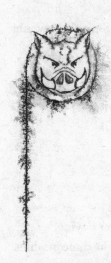

KASSANDROS.
THE JEALOUS.

I T HAD BEEN a good day already and
the hearty breakfast of cheese,
sausage, bread and lentils awaiting
Kassandros in his tent after he had disembarked, put him in an even better mood.
*The look on her face will stay with me to my
dying day and will still make me smile even then. As to that sound
she made: priceless.* He grinned at Philip and Pleistarchos, both
already at work on the breakfast, slapping Philip's thigh as he sat
upright on the couch next to him and grabbed a cup of wine.
'She'll be coming to beg me for her life in the next couple of
days, I know she will; and once I've heard her do so I shall slit her
throat.' Happy with the world, he drained his cup.

'You don't look like you need any further cheering up,
brother,' Philip observed, chewing with vigour on the sausage
gripped in his fist.

'You're right, Philip,' Pleistarchos said, 'we should save the
good news for another time; you know, when he thinks the whole
world is against him and he growls at anyone who comes near.'

Philip turned his full attention onto his sausage. 'That's a
good plan.'

Kassandros looked at the twins and frowned. 'What are you
two talking about?'

'Nothing,' they replied in unison.

'Tell me.'

'No; you're in too good a mood already,' Philip said. 'It would be a waste.'

Pleistarchos nodded.

'My mood will evaporate very quickly if you carry on like this.'

The twins looked at each other in mock terror.

'We can't have that, can we?' Pleistarchos said.

They both shook their heads.

'We'd better tell him,' Philip concluded.

'What, now?'

'It could wait until after breakfast.'

'Tell me now!' Kassandros yelled, his temper fraying.

Philip shrugged. 'Atarrhias is back in camp; he came in whilst you were out fishing for wicked queens.'

Kassandros was immediately interested. 'Where is he? Get him here, now.'

And it was with rising joy that Kassandros listened to Atarrhias' report over breakfast.

'More than half of Aeacides' army mutinied, wanting to go home when they heard I was approaching with a sizable force,' Atarrhias said with grim satisfaction. 'The idiot let them go, thinking he could face me in the narrow passes with fewer men as the terrain makes large numbers irrelevant. He was wrong. I blocked his path eastward and forced him to return to Epirus where the mutinous part of his army had rebelled and had already managed to pass a public decree condemning him to exile and making an alliance with you. I've brought the document they ask you to consider.'

Kassandros' eyes shone and he threw his cup to the ground in excitement. 'Ha! The way north is now open. I can send an army to deal with Pella and Amphipolis without fear of an Eperiot army getting between us.' He looked at Atarrhias with something bordering on gratitude.

'I told you he'd be pleased,' Philip confided in his twin, loud enough for Kassandros to hear.

'I never disbelieved you for a moment.'

Kassandros glared at the twins. 'Stop acting the fools and get Crateuas here; he can go to Amphipolis and deal with Aristonous whilst you two can take a well-needed lesson in generalship from Atarrhias and get me Pella.'

Thus, with his mood as buoyant as it had ever been, Kassandros watched the two large detachments leave the camp bound for Pella and Amphipolis, and it was with equanimity he received the request to take an oath preserving the person of Thessalonike should she come to negotiate. 'When does she want to come?' he asked the cadaverous messenger who smelt as bad as he looked.

'As soon as you've taken the oath that I am to witness.'

Kassandros stared at the man, amazed he was not ordering his immediate execution for daring to imply he was untrustworthy enough to need to have his oath witnessed – which, indeed, he was, as he knew full well. 'Very well, I'll take it now.'

It was with yet more amazement at his composure that he swore to protect the life and wellbeing of Thessalonike whilst she was within his camp as well as travelling to and from it. *I actually think I mean this and will abide by it.* The thought made him shake his head in surprise as he slit the goose's white throat to release the blood sealing the contract between him and the gods.

'You've witnessed it,' he told the messenger. 'So tell her I shall let her come.'

Kassandros watched with great interest as the gate in the siege wall opened to reveal a small party of bedraggled soldiers, led by the messenger, surrounding Thessalonike. At first glance, she looked as if she had prepared herself for the meeting in the royal palace at Pella and not in a town under siege for nine months. Beautiful she was, with her hair pulled into an intricate bun, plaited and woven on the back of her head, leaving a golden ringlet to fall to either side of her face; she wore jewelled chains of gold about her crown, matching the earrings glittering in each ear. A gown of finest linen clung to her frame, still of a reasonable shape and firmness despite the hardships she had endured in recent months. As she grew nearer, Kassandros felt a tightening in his belly for he beheld for the first time in his life a beauty that made him forget all else: lips full and painted in the tone of intimate female flesh; the rouge on her cheeks disguising their pallor as the kohl about her eyes hid their dark circles. Tall she stood as she walked towards Kassandros and at that moment he knew he would do anything within his power to possess this beauty. *She must be mine but not against her wish.* Once again he had surprised himself in not wanting to suborn someone to his will; for actually having consideration for another's feelings. Yet how could anyone desire to do anything that would cause this vision distress?

Ten years his junior, Kassandros had not seen Thessalonike since she had been a small girl in the court of King Philip, before she had gone into exile with her adoptive mother as Olympias feuded with his father, Antipatros. He had barely noticed her then and so had never imagined the woman who was walking towards him would take his breath away as sure as repeated blows to the solar plexus. Indeed, it was such a physical experience he almost staggered. *Control yourself; don't allow her to see this weakness.* For weakness it was to Kassandros' mind, yet it was a weakness in which he would willingly wallow. And then the practicality of the situation hit him with a force equal to that of her beauty. *Marrying her would make me the legitimate King of Macedon; no longer claiming the regency but actually wearing the crown with the half-sister of Alexander bearing my children. The argument would be over and I would've won.* 'Thessalonike,' he found himself saying, 'I welcome you and am honoured to receive you.' He held out his right hand to her and, to his amazement, she took it with a slight incline of her head. He turned, transferring her hand to his left, and in silence they walked to his tent.

It was pride he now felt as the gawping soldiery watched them pass, pride at having such a beautiful woman at his side, and he knew he would do everything to keep her there; he would make her the happiest of women.

The guards drew back the entrance of his tent and he led Thessalonike within, sneaking a sidelong look at her just to drink in some more of her beauty. She kept her eyes forward, allowing him some privacy as he drunk deep.

Kassandros gestured to a couch, thickly upholstered and covered with cushions. 'Please, make yourself comfortable, Thessalonike.' He stood attentive, as she sat and arranged her dress so it fell to the ground without creasing; all the time she did not meet his eye. Once she had settled he turned and shooed his guards away before looking back at her and smiling, again surprising himself as the smile was for genuine pleasure and not, as was normal, for someone else's misfortune. 'May I pour you some wine?'

Finally her eyes met his. 'I would be delighted.'

It was another punch to the solar plexus and again it was a struggle not to roll with it. Hoping she would not notice the shaking in his hand, he poured a cup and passed it over, before pouring himself one and sitting opposite her. 'To our negotiations,' he said, raising his cup.

'Our negotiations,' Thessalonike agreed.

She took a sip and he watched, transfixed by her lips, before hurriedly taking a large swig of his own to disguise his staring.

He set his cup down and entwined his fingers, his elbows resting on the arms of his chair. 'Do you bring a message from Olympias or are you here to negotiate in your own right?'

She smiled; it was as if the sun shone only for him. 'Both, Kassandros, both.'

'Then please begin with what Olympias has to say.'

Thessalonike took another sip, considering her next words. 'Naturally she wishes to live and naturally she wants to retain her power. She thinks that she can do this by offering you Alexander and his mother along with the Great Ring of Macedon in return for safe conduct to Sardis. She expects you to swear an oath guaranteeing her safety just as you have sworn an oath guaranteeing mine.'

'Indeed I have, and that oath shall be respected – for all time.' He cast her a nervous look to see how she had taken that: a brief meeting of the eyes told him she had understood. *And she has not rebuffed me.*

'And would you be willing to do the same for Olympias in return for Alexander and Roxanna and the ring?'

'I would not.'

'You wouldn't take the oath or you would take the oath but you wouldn't honour it?'

Again Kassandros smiled. *Could she be a woman who thinks like me?*

'And if I were to agree to the second option what would you say?'

'I would say it would not be unexpected and it would be understandable.'

'Would you approve?'

'Were I in your position I would do the same. She desecrated your family's graves and executed your brother, stepmother and two small half-siblings along with hundreds of your kinsmen and followers; she would be a fool to trust you and therefore her death would be her own fault.'

'You show a devious side to your character very early on in our negotiation.'

'Do I? I would call it practical not devious. Devious makes it sound like I'm a wily schemer who sets out to be deceitful as a matter of course; that is far from the truth. However, I do know ambition cannot always be satisfied by actions solely of integrity; occasionally one has to deceive.'

'To be practical.'

'Indeed.'

Kassandros' breath stuck in his chest as she bestowed upon him a smile that reached deep into his being. 'And are you here to be practical?'

'Oh yes, Kassandros; you won't believe just how practical I can be in order to get what I want.'

'And what do you want, Thessalonike?'

THESSALONIKE.
THE HALF-SISTER.

OH, I KNOW what I want only too well, Kassandros. The question is: do I want it enough to make this bargain? Thessalonike gave Kassandros another smile, seeing as the last one had had such a dramatic effect; she was enjoying herself despite the fact she was feeling naked under his intense and probing gaze. 'Let's put what I want to one side for the moment, Kassandros; I would rather hear what *you* want.' *It will be interesting to see whether he tells me the truth.*

Kassandros paused, taking his eyes off her for what felt like the first time since they met, such had been the force of his scrutiny. 'I want what is rightfully mine; that and no more.'

'And what is rightfully yours?'

'The regency of Macedon.'

'To be regent for Alexander?'

'Regent of Macedon in the presence or the absence of the king.'

A clever way of phrasing it.

'It's what my father was and he should have passed it to me at his death and not the nonentity Polyperchon. Now Olympias holds the Great Ring of Macedon and has offered it to me along with the custody of the king, I'll take it; once she has knelt at my feet and begged me to take them so she can live, of course.'

'Of course. You wouldn't want to miss out on that particular pleasure, would you?'

Kassandros cast her a confused look.

He thinks I'm mocking him; that will never do. 'I make no judgement on you, Kassandros; I would wish the same if I had someone in my power who'd done such wrong to me, as Olympias has to you.' She smiled and took another sip of wine to let Kassandros see she was at ease and not being confrontational and waited for him to relax.

'I'm pleased you understand,' he said.

He really is a most ugly man; like some kind of avian mistake crossed with a spindly giant. 'Oh, of course I understand. But what I don't understand is why you limit your ambition to the regency.'

She smiled inwardly at his shocked reaction to this question. *Now I've really got his attention; he wasn't expecting that at all. Time for honesty, Kassandros.*

'Do you mean… the crown?'

She remained silent and impassive, looking about the tent at his possessions to get a feeling for the man. *No books, so not much of a reader, but he appreciates the finer things, judging by this wine and some of the statuettes.*

Kassandros was hesitant. 'That would mean killing Alexander.'

'And you weren't going to do that anyway?'

Kassandros swallowed.

'Be honest with me.'

Again he swallowed, his enlarged Adam's apple grinding up and down his tight-skinned throat. 'It had occurred to me.'

'Occurred? Come, come, you can do better than that.'

283

'All right; yes, it's what I will do. It's the logical thing in my position because, should I be fool enough to let him live to take up his crown, the first thing he'll do is repay my mercy with execution.'

'Correct.' *I think I may be able to do something with him, so long as I can get over his physical appearance.*

They remained looking at each other for a few moments in silence.

'So,' Thessalonike said eventually, 'tell me what you want.'

'To be king.'

'And now ask me that question again.'

'Which one?'

'The one you asked earlier and I said we should leave it to one side for the moment. I think the moment has passed, don't you?'

He gave a shy smile, at least what passed for a shy smile on his pinched face. 'Ah yes. What do you want, Thessalonike?'

'Only what is rightfully mine; that and no more.'

'And what is your right?'

'To be queen.' *I think I'll get used to the way he looks; I may even surprise myself by starting to like him.*

Kassandros' eyes widened as the implication of what she had said registered. 'You mean...'

'Yes, Kassandros, I mean you will be king and I will be queen.'

'You would marry me?'

'How else do you suggest we accomplish it?'

'No, of course; I see.'

'Good. But to do it well, so we are both secure in our positions, we have to do things slowly and in order.'

'But why?'

'Because it mustn't look like we've seized the crown but, rather, it has fallen into our hands and to that end we must also have powerful friends who will back our claim: your brother-in-law, Ptolemy, for example, would find it very useful to have an ally against either Antigonos or Eumenes, neither of whom have cause to like him. Lysimachus is another—'

'No, I meant: why are you doing this?'

'Doing what, exactly?'

'Well, betraying Olympias and coming over to me in the full knowledge that I will kill Alexander.'

'I am not betraying Olympias because I'm not loyal to her; she murdered my mother, Nicesipolis, and this will be my revenge. Yes, there was a time, after Kleopatra had gone to Asia, I could have been considered Olympias' creature, but that was purely a defensive ploy on my part. She's a ruthless woman and had she suspected me of anything short of absolute loyalty it wouldn't have been long before I felt a burning in my stomach or a restriction in my breathing as I succumbed to one of her potions. Even now, although we aren't close any more, since she publicly humiliated me, she still believes I'm loyal to her or at least to the Argead royal house of which she considers herself to be the personification. No, she will be surprised and I look forward to seeing her face.'

'As she dies at my hand.'

Thessalonike sighed. *He evidently needs tutoring in the finer art of politics.* 'That must never happen, Kassandros; you – and by extension me – can never be seen as being responsible for her death. She must die condemned by Macedon's assembly as a murderess or traitor, or, preferably, both. She cannot be seen to die for our convenience.'

Kassandros went to reply but then thought better of it. 'Whatever you say, Thessalonike.'

'That's right, Kassandros: whatever I say.' *He looks at me like a lost puppy; I do believe he's smitten. Good.* 'And the first thing I say is you will grant Olympias her life – but not safe passage to Sardis – and swear an oath to it; how we get the assembly to rid us of her

285

later will become apparent in time. I shall go and inform her of your decision so we can get this siege lifted and concentrate on more important issues. I'll come back with her and the king later.'

Thessalonike rose and adjusted her dress as Kassandros stood, holding out his hand for her; she took it. Looking deep into her eyes, he said: 'I shall make you the happiest of women.'

Thessalonike squeezed his fingers. 'I can't promise to make you the happiest of men but I shall certainly make you the happiest of kings.' With that she walked past him and left the tent. *Where was the cruel coward I was promised? No doubt in there somewhere and no doubt I will see him in such light one day, but until then I'm quite content with a lovelorn puppy. I'd better brace myself for allowing him into my bed and feeling his bony body all over me.* She grimaced at the thought as she rejoined her escort to return and report to Olympias.

Olympias was outraged. 'He won't allow me safe passage to Sardis! Why not?'

Thessalonike closed her eyes as her ears rang. 'No, he says he could never allow that as you would be free to continue fighting against him.'

'Which I would, the pockmarked son of a toad.'

'So you can see his point of view, can't you?'

Olympias' face darkened; her fists clenched and unclenched. *She can, and she can't argue against it; how enjoyable.*

Olympias managed to prevent an outburst; she swallowed, controlling her temper. 'But he will swear to guarantee my safety.'

'Yes, Olympias; he will never harm you.' *Directly.* Thessalonike spoke with all the sincerity she could muster. 'We can walk out of here right now if you wish. You could be eating good food and drinking fine wine before sunset; although I doubt Kassandros will invite you to his table after what you've done to him.'

'That's what makes me suspicious. The pockfaced coward should be desperate for his revenge on me and yet he just rolls over and accepts my first offer. I should have offered him less.'

'I think he's very happy with what he'll gain: as regent of Alexander he'll have power for the next ten years.'

'And then what?'

Thessalonike kept her counsel.

'And what about me?' Olympias demanded. 'What will I be able to do if I'm not allowed to go to Sardis?'

'You'll have to ask him that.'

She'll take it because she believes she'll be able to escape to Sardis with ease.

'Very well, I will.'

Thessalonike tried to conceal her pleasure at the depth of hatred that passed between the two of them, as Olympias approached Kassandros with the sun falling into the west. Seated outside his tent so all his army might be witness to her humiliation, he glared with venom at the woman responsible for so many family deaths and for the desecration of his family's tombs – not to mention the murders of so many of his followers and kinsmen. But if he had murderous intent he did well to control it as Olympias halted in front of him.

'My oath is made,' Kassandros said, holding out his hand. 'Your person is safe.'

Olympias' eyes smouldered with loathing as she pulled the Great Ring of Macedon from her right forefinger. 'I hope it burns you!' She tossed the ring towards him.

Kassandros snatched it out of the air, slipped it on his forefinger and then held it out at arm's length to admire. 'It hasn't been too tarnished by your filth, I'm pleased to see.'

With a hiss, Olympias spat at his feet.

'Careful, woman, or I might forget my oath; remember, you are only alive because it pleases me to arrange things thus – for the time being.' He paused and turned his eyes onto Thessalonike. 'And because Thessalonike has spoken for you.'

A look of horror crept across Olympias' face as she saw the love in Kassandros' expression and the consequences dawned upon her. 'You bitch! You've deceived me.'

Thessalonike shook her head. 'No, Olympias; everything I've told you was true.'

'And seducing this toad?'

'I have not seduced Kassandros; but I've come to an arrangement with him.'

'What kind of arrangement?'

'That's between him and me.'

In a flurry of nails, hisses and attempted slaps, Olympias flew at her adopted daughter, screeching her betrayal; but Thessalonike had foreseen the event and, with a speed that shocked all, slammed her right fist into Olympias' face, arching her back, hair flying, arms flailing, to lay her out on the ground. 'I've wanted to do that for some time now, Olympias; don't make me do it again or I might start getting a taste for it.' She turned to Kassandros, who sat looking at her with the pride of one who loves unconditionally. 'You will have to send men into Pydna; Roxanna was not very keen on coming before you.'

But even the dozen soldiers Kassandros sent to apprehend Roxanna and her son seemed inadequate to the task as they dragged her across no-man's land and then through the siege works; screeching like a harpy, she gouged and snapped at any piece of exposed flesh in range as her son writhed in the grip of two powerful men, fighting for all he was worth for he realised, even at his young age, Kassandros was no friend to him and his grandmother had betrayed him.

'Olympias! You're a dead woman!' Roxanna screamed as she was hauled before Kassandros, her veil ripped away and her captors bloody from the exercise. 'You know he will never let any of us live; I just hope I survive long enough to kill you before Kassandros does.'

'Gag her!' Thessalonike ordered, standing now behind Kassandros' chair with one hand resting on its back. 'Gag her, you fools, and restrain her.'

Roxanna screamed again, and, breaking free from her captors with a wrench of her right arm, clawed at the nearest one's eyes; blood spurted, the man howled, backing away, clutching at a vicious wound. His comrades pounced on her, crushing her to the ground as they fought to get a gag around her mouth in the face of gnashing teeth. But, with the odds so stacked against her even Roxanna had to admit defeat and soon lay trussed up and silenced. Thessalonike put her hand on Kassandros' shoulder.

'You and your son have nothing to fear from me, Roxanna,' Kassandros said in a loud voice so all his army might witness how fair their general was; it was for no regicide they fought but, rather, a man who had been denied his rightful position and had now regained it. 'You are under my protection as regent of Macedon. Alexander will have all royal privileges and you will both live in the style that is right for the King of Macedon.'

This provoked a great rolling cheer from the thousands assembled as the words were relayed back through the crowd.

'Take her away and make sure neither she nor her son is harmed.'

'And what about me?' Olympias asked.

'What about you?'

'You promised me my safety.'

'I did; but I didn't promise your freedom.'

'I still wish to go to Sardis.'

'You can wish as much as you like, Olympias; but it is not your decision, nor is it mine. Your fate will be decided by the assembly.' Kassandros rose and Thessalonike stepped up to his side. 'You will be tried for your crimes committed whilst you ruled in Pella.'

Olympias looked aghast. 'I am Queen! I cannot be tried for there is no one fit to pass judgement on me.'

Thessalonike linked her arm through Kassandros'. 'That is where you are mistaken, Olympias: everyone who has suffered at your hands is fit to pass judgement upon you. Guards, take her away.' The sight of Kassandros' men obeying her order without question thrilled Thessalonike. *They accept me. If I can command his men then I can command Kassandros, and the first thing I'll need him to do is to make a treaty with Ptolemy. Between us we should be able to defeat whoever emerges victorious in the east.*

Ptolemy.
The Bastard.

MAGNIFICENT WAS THE only word Ptolemy could use to describe the new theatre overlooking the Great Harbour of Alexandria. *Absolutely magnificent; it will draw the best writers and actors in the world and make the city a cultural centre to rival Athens.* And it was with a good deal of satisfaction that he completed the sacrifice dedicating the huge construction, capable of seating more than twenty thousand people, to Serapis, the new god he had introduced into his domain. This god embodied both Egyptian and Greek trappings and in drawing from gods of both religions he had turned to Serapis in an attempt to unify the old and the new in Egypt. *And it seems to be working,* Ptolemy observed as he witnessed the religious awe the congregation – with the exception of the Jewish element, standing to one side during this unpure part of the proceedings – was displaying during the ceremony. *It's nice to have a god who has a part of us all in him, even the Jews if only they would accept him.* And that was just what Serapis was: an amalgamation of the Egyptian Osiris and Apis with the chthonic powers of Greek Hades and Demeter and rounded off with the benevolence of Dionysus. *Something for everyone; very convenient. I shall make*

him the guardian god of my dynasty and build a Serapeum in his honour. The thought was a pleasant one and he smiled to himself as he washed the blood from his fingers in a golden bowl and dried them on a linen towel.

Standing before the theatre's altar, the *thymele*, set, as always, in the orchestra, between the *skene*, or stage, and the semi-circular banked seating rising high above him, the *theatron*, he held his hands out, palms up, and recited a prayer hailing the deity as the king of all the dead and the god of the afterlife and resurrection, as well as healing, miracles, fertility, destiny and abundance. *Quite a healthy package; if you can't find something there to please you, you're more demanding than you have a right to be.* The prayer over, he turned to face the packed theatron, filled with many new arrivals to the city, Macedonian, Greek, indigenous Egyptian, Jewish and Persian, some already wealthy and some who had come to make their fortunes, and held out his arms as if to embrace them all. 'People of Alexandria, I give you this building, paid for out of my own purse, as a gift so you may enjoy our cultural heritage here on the shores of Africa.'

It was a short speech – and not necessarily true in that the construction had been paid for out of import duties in the now fully functioning commercial harbour, but Ptolemy was not going to let a little detail like that prevent him from making political gain – but it had the desired effect of an ovation for himself as he walked to take his place between the heavily pregnant Berenice and Eurydike, recently delivered of child. *I must get round to making her pregnant again,* he reflected as he caught Eurydike glaring at Berenice's hand patting his thigh in appreciation of his performance, *if only to give her something else to think about other than how to make Berenice's life difficult.*

Since the birth of Meleager, Eurydike's second child, she had been actively pursuing a policy of making her cousin and former friend's life as hard as possible in the palace by attempting to monopolise the building as if she were the senior female and all else were her underlings, including Berenice and Thais, Ptolemy's mistress. Thais, seated a row behind him with her three children, took no interest in playing Eurydike's games and responded to her ploys with indifference, keeping to her suite or her gardens and living her life as she wished, with no reference to the woman trying to set herself up as senior wife. This policy had, obviously, a grating effect on Eurydike which Ptolemy thoroughly enjoyed witnessing. Berenice, however, was more inclined to fight back as she too had ambitions to dominate, and this conflict caused a good deal of domestic disharmony which Ptolemy felt he could do without. Forever arbitrating in the arguments of his womenfolk was an onerous task and a constant drain on his energy. *Yes, I should enquire of Eurydike's maids which night this month she'll be at her most fertile and get it done; especially as Berenice is too fragile for rigorous enjoyment.* He gave a sidelong glance at Berenice's swollen belly and touched it in satisfaction. *Thais was so right to suggest I marry her; the fruit of her womb will be far less volatile.* He did not like his first son with Eurydike, his namesake Ptolemy, now almost four, as he found him wilful, vicious and disobedient, and he was beginning to think Meleager, despite being only a few months old, would turn out the same way such was his wailing and constant ill-temper.

His mind made up, he settled down, as the chorus filed into the orchestra and the actors took to the skene, for a performance of *Dyskolos*, a comedy in the new style by the rising star of Athenian theatre, Menander, which had won first prize that year at the city's Lenaia festival. Ptolemy had chosen it especially to flatter the playwright in the hopes of luring him to Alexandria; indeed, he had already sent a substantial bribe to Demetrius of Phaleron, Kassandros' creature in Athens, to help persuade the young man to cross the sea. *It won't be solely through military might and trading power that I'll forge this place into the greatest city in the world and in doing so make my name and legacy immortal.*

And it was with these pleasant thoughts he sat through the play, a pastoral, family comedy, with the god Pan driving the plot concerning love and marriage and a grumpy old man, the Dyskolos of the title. Exploring firstly the social class system of Athens at the time – a safe enough subject, Ptolemy considered, for the opening of his gift to the people of Alexandria – and secondly examining philanthropy, with each character displaying a different characteristic of such a noble impulse, Ptolemy felt it to be an ideal way to underline his generosity – something he was always keen to do.

The applause he received at the end as he departed, after he had so generously applauded and rewarded the actors, was most heartening and again he extended his arms to embrace the audience in thanks before he and his party left them to enjoy the rest of the day's entertainment of more conservative fare from the tragedy canon. With his two wives each taking a litter back to the palace so that one would not be seen to be less regal than the other, Ptolemy was free to stroll with Thais along the waterfront of the Great Harbour with just a couple of guards in attendance. Although many of the vessels were still stripped down for their winter refurbishment, there was much bustle in the port for the work of the fishermen in these southerly climes was not unduly affected by the season. But it was not the ships and boats that interested him as he stood with Thais on the edge of the quay and looked north towards the island of Pharos: it was the growing Heptastadion, the great mole which protruded from the island towards its twin opposite, extending out from the shore. Soon these two grand constructions would meet and divide the harbour in two: to the west, as was already evident from the huge number of warships moored there, military, and to the east, commercial.

'Dinocrates is meant to be meeting me here,' Ptolemy informed Thais as they marvelled at the scale of the work that could not be properly appreciated from the palace just over a third of a league away. The length of seven stadions – hence its name – it would be one thousand two hundred paces long and two hundred wide.

'Two more years, I estimate, Lord,' a voice said from behind the couple.

Ptolemy turned to see his chief architect, appointed by Alexander himself to lay out the city on a grid in the most modern of styles. 'I know, Dinocrates; and I wish it were less. There is so much to build in this city.'

'And such limited resources; so much of my labour and materials has gone into the harbour and this.' He indicated to either end of the unfinished Heptastadion where gangs of slaves laboured to unload rubble or large stones from wide-beamed, flat-bottomed transport ships directly into the water to form the base for yet another push forward of the growing mole. 'To have finished the harbour quay as well in the fourteen years since Alexander appointed me, not to mention most of the palace, Hephaestion's memorial and all of the theatre, is something I would have said was unachievable then.'

'And yet here we are having seemingly achieved the impossible,' Ptolemy said with a congenial smile. 'And look how well it's going. All the time, new people come to the city, building their houses along your grid system at a furious rate so every day there are more abodes fit for occupation and more small businesses producing goods for the markets. This, in turn, brings in more tax revenue for my coffers, a great percentage of which is passed onto you to keep the public building of the city growing, which in its turn brings more people here to build their houses on your grid system and create work, thus perpetuating the growth of Alexandria and ensuring it can grow faster.' He scratched his chin as if in thought. 'You can see what I'm getting at, can't you, Dinocrates?'

'I can, Lord; but I don't see how I can accelerate the building programme; especially as you are now freeing so many of the Jewish slaves you brought back from Hierosolyma.' Burly and in his fifties, with long, wavy white hair, a scraggy, grey-flecked beard on his leather-brown face with blue, piercing eyes squinting from it, Dinocrates looked more like a ship's triarchos than the foremost architect in the world.

'That's political, my friend: the Jews seem to be of greater benefit to the economy working for themselves rather than being forced into manual labour. Their religion makes them troublesome slaves, no matter how many you execute, as you know only too well, whereas they are very canny businessmen in general, and I wish this city to be, first and foremost, a commercial centre.'

Dinocrates cast a worried look at his patron. 'That may be good for the part of the city that's already constructed but I have such limited resources for what is required of me for the rest.'

Ptolemy put a comforting hand on the man's shoulder. 'But you shall have more, Dinocrates; you shall. The campaigning season will soon be upon us and you shall have all the slaves you need.'

Dinocrates looked uncertain but did not voice his doubts.

Ptolemy squeezed his shoulder once more. 'And to celebrate this influx of men and materials I would like you to put your mind to work on a new project.'

'A new project?'

'Yes, a temple.'

'Dedicated to whom?'

'To Serapis. I want a Serapeum of such grace and beauty that all who come will have no doubt he is Alexandria's god and the guardian deity of my family.' With another friendly squeeze of the shoulder he turned and left his architect with an even more worried countenance than before.

'You're putting too much pressure on that man,' Thais admonished as they strolled along the quay, past fishermen and their slaves unloading baskets of fish and haggling a good price with market traders, housewives and food-sellers.

'Nonsense; if anything, I don't put enough on him.' He paused to give a shaven-headed young lad a couple of drachmae for his father's catch, gesturing to one of the guards to pick up the basket. Delighted with a price well above the market rate, the fisherman's son whooped, then remembering in whose presence he was, he knelt and kissed the jewelled ring on Ptolemy's hand, before running off in case there was a change of heart. 'The faster we grow this city the more powerful Egypt becomes and the stronger we'll be. Stagnation is not an option for us, not if we want to survive the storm coming in the next few years.'

'And where will all these slaves you've so rashly promised Dinocrates be coming from?'

Ptolemy cleared his throat as he considered his answer, stepping over a coil of rope smelling of pitch. 'That depends upon who gets in my way as I move my army back into Syria and reinforce Cyprus.'

'And what about Crete?'

'What about it?'

'Well, when the Carthaginian embassy was here you neither confirmed nor denied your interest in the island.' She indicated back to the scores of triremes, quadremes, quinqueremes and smaller ships in the military side of the harbour. 'After all, you don't need all those to reinforce Cyprus and Tyros. I haven't been paying close attention but it seems to me every time I come here there are a few more and they all seem to look rather new.'

'And many of them are. As to what I will do with them, I need to wait until I know what's in the mind of Agathocles in Syracuse and I won't know that until the Exile-Hunter is back.' He placed an arm around Thais' shoulders. 'Knowing the sharpness of your mind, I think that has probably answered your question in full.'

Thais smiled up at him. 'Oh, it does; and you're absolutely right to wait. In the meantime, can I suggest you go to Eurydike either tonight or tomorrow? She is becoming unbearable and it would make all our lives a little more tolerable if she were pregnant; my source in her household tells me now is a good time.'

Ptolemy burst into laughter.

Thais frowned. 'What's so amusing?'

'I don't know what I would do without you.'

'That really is not funny.'

'No. I mean I was just about to send someone to question her maids about the very same subject.'

'Well, you don't need to bother now.'

'No, I don't. I shall go tonight.'

'Good. And remember the object is to get her pregnant so put it in the right place.'

'Eventually.'

Thais slapped his buttocks. 'Just make sure she gets pregnant.'

And so he did, very thoroughly, with a reasonable amount of satisfaction and the expenditure of a considerable amount of energy; and thus, the following morning, he was enjoying a hearty breakfast on his private terrace, served by his body-slave, Sextus, of Macedonian sausage, boiled eggs, freshly baked bread and watermelon, washed down with watered resinated wine. Feeling very content, he surveyed the city, his city, glowing golden in the soft morning light, appreciating the peace. It was, he knew, not long before military matters would call him away from this almost serene existence, but they had to be attended to if he wished to continue his life as it was at present, therefore he would not resent the intrusion. Nor did he resent the intrusion of Lycortas, his chamberlain, gliding in his long robe, his feet concealed beneath it, his arms folded and his hands up either sleeve.

'My lord,' Lycortas said, dipping his head, 'I trust you are refreshed.'

Ptolemy bit the top off an egg. 'Admirably.'

'It pleases me to hear you say so. If you will permit me, I would like to express the thanks of myself and all who try to run this palace smoothly for your pleasure, should you have been successful in your objective last night; and, if not, I trust you will have another, more successful attempt soon.'

Ptolemy smiled. 'The thing I like about you so much, Lycortas, apart from your excellent advice, is I can never tell whether you are being serious or having a dry little chuckle at my expense.'

'Serious, Lord; my attempts at humour have never amused anyone, not even myself.'

'I'm sorry to hear it.'

'I thank you for your consideration on the subject.'

He really is enjoying himself today. 'To what do I owe the joy of your company on this beautiful morning?'

'Alas that it should only be for a short while as I am sure you would wish me to withdraw once I've informed you that Archias the Exile-Hunter is waiting to see you.'

'Excellent; that being the case I take it you have already paid him and his men the outstanding portion of their fee?'

'As usual, he refused to do anything until that was done.'

'Then show him through.'

Lycortas bowed and turned.

Ptolemy raised a finger. 'Oh, and Lycortas?'

'Yes, Lord.'

'We shall obviously want to offer Archias refreshment.'

'Naturally, Lord.'

'So don't try to fob him off with the third-best wine again this time.'

With a puckering of the lips, Lycortas glided away.

'The second-best wine this time,' Archias observed, with a tilt of the head and a complementary expression, having sniffed the contents of his cup. 'That wouldn't have been a decision Lycortas would have willingly made for the likes of me. Socrates says that wine awakens kindly feelings; I would submit Lycortas is the exception to that rule.'

'He can be a little parsimonious with my vintages.'

Archias sipped his wine and swilled it around his tongue, before swallowing. 'You must have ordered him to serve this; I am to construe that I'm still in favour.'

Ptolemy chuckled, dismissed Sextus, his body-slave, with a wave and raised his cup. '"A friend for everyone to see is worth far more than wealth which you keep buried out of sight".'

'Menander, very good; *Dyskolos*, if I'm not mistaken. I saw it at the Lenaia festival in Athens and found it reasonably amusing; although I have to say I find most comedy trivial. Menander, however, has a talent and I think it made uneasy viewing for Demetrius of Phaleron: he won't have enjoyed being portrayed as a grumpy old man.'

Ptolemy hid his surprise. *I didn't see that; but perhaps it is no bad thing.* 'In which case, I hope it'll make it more likely that

Demetrius will help me in my effort to get the young man to Alexandria; I want him to accept my patronage.'

'I'd say that was an excellent idea, if you don't mind being constantly mocked, that is.' Archias took another sip of wine, closing his eyes in appreciation.

'Do you really think he would do that?'

'What, mock you? Of course he would. Not a full-on slap-stick, vicious mocking, but a gentle mocking. A mocking with a degree of respect but a mocking nonetheless. That's what comedy is, after all: getting people to look at their situation as represented by the playwright and to laugh. The two neighbouring families in one play might represent Athens and Thebes or Athens and Macedon, or two fathers struggling with unruly children could be allusions to Alexander and Phocion or Demosthenes and Philip; it doesn't really matter, it's always based on somebody, and so, should you invite this ambitious young man to Alexandria, brace yourself for a regular mocking – no matter how much you give him and in what style you put him up – because that's how he will get the Alexandrians laughing.'

'Do you really think so?'

Archias once again savoured the vintage for a few moments, thinking. 'Consider this: a brand new play in Alexandria by Menander called *The Persian Husband*. The scene opens with a husband, in Persian attire, so that there can be no mistaking his origins, and a mask of distress on his face. His problem – a very Persian problem, not a normal Macedonian one at all, except for an elite few – is that his wives are at odds with one another and he gets no peace, only his mistress brings him comfort. And yet he loves one of his wives but is unable to make her happy because he will not give up his mistress and cannot control the machinations of the other wife. Need I go on?'

Ptolemy wiped his nose free of wine he had spluttered as Archias outlined the plot. 'No, I get the point. I see what you mean: very fruitful ground for comedy.'

'Isn't it just?'

Ptolemy gave Archias a hard look but the Exile-Hunter's round, boyish face was a picture of innocence. *I can't hold him to account for giving me a fair warning of my potential folly.* He raised his cup and smiled. 'I thank you for being so blunt, Archias.'

'My pleasure.'

'I'm sure it was. However, despite your warning, I still intend to make this city the cultural capital of the world.'

'And I wish you well with that noble objective. As you know, I'm a great admirer of the theatre and would be still on the stage were it not for the fact I was fed up with poverty and make far more money in my current profession.'

'At which you shine above all else.' Ptolemy spread his hands. 'So how was Syracuse?'

Archias indicated to the jug of wine on the table between them. 'Be my guest.'

'Busy,' Archias said, refilling his cup. 'I'd say I arrived at precisely the right time for what you had in mind for me to do.'

'Agathocles had ample work for you?'

'He was delighted to see me. I had met him once, a dozen years ago or so, before he had come to prominence, and so it wasn't hard to get an audience with him; my reputation is, shall we say, of interest to a tyrant such as him. I arrived by ship from Tarentum having sailed there from Crete so there was nothing to link me with you; as far as he was concerned I was just a travelling assassin with my seven associates on the hunt for a bit of business. To his mind it made perfect sense I should come to him as he knows his own character better than anyone. He did not suspect for one moment I was a spy.'

'Excellent.'

'Yes, it was. His problems were mainly Carthaginian, although I can't say his ambition impressed me. I helped him out with a couple of leading citizens from the Punic enclave as well as some middle-ranking army officers and the entire family of a Greek merchant in the enclave suspected of trading with the Carthaginians – leaving the miscreant alive, naturally, the way Agathocles likes to do business.'

'Naturally.'

'What I will say, though, is his position seems to be very secure; he has substantially reduced the number of people opposing him.' Archias paused for reflection. 'Perhaps that's why his ambition seemed to be lacking somewhat: he's got rid of most of the people who mattered, either by executing them or murdering their entire families.' He shrugged. 'Either way, "fear crushes men's spirits".'

'Yes, quite. So did you have much to do with him privately?'

'Yes, I managed to have dinner with him on a number of occasions.'

'And did you get to know his mind concerning Africa?'

'The Carthaginians are right in their analysis of his position if they were looking into the mind of an intelligent and cunning strategist; unfortunately – or fortunately – for them, he is no more than a lucky and ruthless thug. He doesn't see the bigger picture and didn't mention Cyrene or anything about Africa once. He sees his battleground as Sicilia at least for the next couple of years.'

'Excellent, I can concentrate my energies in the other direction.'

'I would think so; longer, perhaps, as he is also concerned about the growing power on the Italian mainland of a city called Roma.'

'I've heard of it, I have a slave from there.'

'Well, they have been expanding the territory south as far as Neapolis in the north of the Greek colonies. Agathocles can see them being interested in Sicilia in the next decade or so.'

Ptolemy clapped his hands and then rubbed them together. 'Good, let him deal with the Carthaginians and then look to the north. How did you leave it with him?'

'You mean: how did I leave Sicilia and come here to report to you without him suspecting I had been spying for you all this time?'

He does so understand the niceties of diplomacy. 'Exactly.'

'It was quite simple: he expects me to come to Egypt as he's paid me to assassinate you.'

Ptolemy froze, searching the Exile-Hunter's eyes for any sign of a joke. There was none. 'And?'

'And when you pay me not to kill you one drachma more than what Agathocles paid me to kill you, I shall send his fee back to him with apologies saying you and I had come to an agreement. He has the type of mind that will understand completely.'

Ptolemy felt relief surge through him but remained outwardly calm. 'How much?'

'Five talents in gold.'

'What are you going to do with all this money?'

Archias shrugged. 'I don't know. Buy an island and fill it with women sounds like a good idea. In the meantime I think I'll spend the rest of the winter here wallowing in luxury.'

'I'll make some arrangements. But tell me, Archias, why did Agathocles want me dead when you said Africa doesn't figure in his plans?'

'Because whilst I was there a report of your meeting with the Carthaginian embassy here in Alexandria arrived and Agathocles was none too impressed; he assumed, because he can only see the Sicilia picture, they were trying to get you to use your not inconsiderable fleet against him in conjunction with a Carthaginian invasion. For obvious reasons I couldn't put him right on the subject as that would have implied I had been in Alexandria at the same time as the Carthaginians.'

'No, I quite understand; so when he paid you to assassinate me in order to stop me aiding the Carthaginians against him in Sicilia you had no choice but to accept.'

Archias' face was a study in innocence. 'You have the matter entirely. For Agathocles, your death, with no heir old enough to succeed you, would take Egypt out of the reckoning, leaving him free to concentrate on Carthage alone.'

'It makes complete sense if you think the way he does. I suppose I'd better pay you then.'

'It would help ease my conscience for turning down a commission for the first time ever.'

Ptolemy stood to show the audience was over and also to be ready should Archias change his mind and decide to take Agathocles' money after all. *I may like him but it would be foolish to trust him.* 'Lycortas?'

'Yes, Lord,' the chamberlain said, gliding onto the terrace at a speed implying he had been eavesdropping all this time.

'I take it by your prompt arrival you know how much to pay our good friend for not assassinating me?'

'Indeed, Lord,' Lycortas said with a look showing he entirely disapproved. 'Might I suggest it would be cheaper to just throw Archias off the terrace onto the rocks below?'

Ptolemy went to the wall and looked down. 'It's the height of twenty men.' He turned back to Lycortas. 'Yes, it should do the trick.' He smiled inwardly, as he saw Archias tense, and then made a show of considering his options as the Exile-Hunter flicked his eyes from him to the chamberlain and then back again. 'But, after due consideration, Lycortas, even though I completely agree with you and, as you know, am always searching for ways to economise, I think we should pay up.' He smiled at a visibly relaxing Archias. 'After all, if you were gone, who would do all the underhand work I might need as I move north into Syria in the spring to reinforce the area in preparation for the arrival of either Eumenes or Antigonos?'

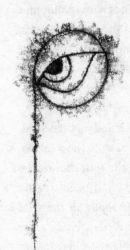

ANTIGONOS.
THE ONE-EYED.

ANTIGONOS BREATHED WARM air onto his hands and then rubbed them together above the brazier burning in the centre of his tent. Stamping his chilled feet, he cuffed away a slave bringing him a towel. 'It's hot wine I need, not a fucking rubdown!' Cursing the cold, he continued to warm himself by the fire, snatching the steaming cup as soon as it was offered him. He took a huge gulp and roared with pain, spraying the contents of his mouth, fizzing, into the fire before hurling the half-full cup at the retreating slave. 'Not *that* fucking hot!'

Muttering more curses as he felt his scalded tongue, he continued to stamp his feet, which felt like solid blocks of ice despite the woollen socks impregnated with pork fat; he was not in the best of moods. 'Demetrios! Demetrios! Someone pull my son out of Phila and get him standing here in front of me!' He turned and glared with his one eye at the couple of junior officers standing by for moments such as these. 'What are you fucking waiting for?'

With haste that merited the gravity of the situation they scampered from the tent, leaving the entrance flaps loose so a flurry of snow blew in. 'Close the fucking tent!' A slave ran to obey his master's wish as another one approached, with all reasonable caution, holding a cup of not-so-hot wine. Antigonos took it and gulped it down, before looking at the empty vessel in appreciation and then at the slave who had brought it. 'Just right; why couldn't you have done that the first time?'

The slave bowed his head in contrition.

'Get me another.' Turning his attention back to the fire, Antigonos contemplated the information he had just received, having mustered his army for a headcount, despite the weather. Indeed, everything that had been done in the four months he and his men had spent wintering in Media had been despite the weather. *And Eumenes is sitting very happily in the mild Gabene climate gorging himself on lamb and fresh bread every day.* Again he cursed and rubbed his hands together, beginning to feel the warmth come back to them. Taking the new cup of wine proffered by the slave, he held it in his palms and sniffed in the steam.

'You wanted to see me, Father?' Demetrios said as he came through the entrance.

'Of course I wanted to see you, I wouldn't have sent for you otherwise, would I? In fact, I wanted to see you at the headcount this morning but you consistently turned up missing.'

'I didn't think you would need me.'

'Need you! Need you, my arse! I didn't need you but I had the whole fucking army standing in ranks for over an hour, freezing their bollocks off, so the least you could have done was extracted yourself from Phila and come to share the men's pain like a decent officer. I'm sure Phila would have made sure your bollocks didn't stay cold for too long seeing as you've done nothing but plough her ever since she was delivered of your daughter.' He downed his wine and glared at his son. 'Well? What have you got to say for yourself?'

Demetrios glared back, unrepentant. 'If you think that getting cold unnecessarily would make me a better officer then I'll come next time. However, if you expect me to apologise, you'll be having a long wait as I wasn't enjoying Phila's favours. Rather, I was debriefing the scouts who have just returned from Gabene, seeing as you were busy lining everyone up in freezing conditions so we can lose even more men to fevers and frostbite. How many did you count?'

Antigonos grimaced. 'Thirty-one thousand.'

Demetrios let out a low whistle. 'That's more than two thousand lost to the cold over the winter; the total is three-quarters of the number of men we came east with. We've lost one in four.'

'I can do arithmetic!'

'Sorry; I was just letting the enormity of the loss sink in.'

'Let it sink in by all means but don't rub it in.'

'Yes, sorry, Father.' Demetrios held his hands over the fire as they stood in silence, contemplating their situation.

'Well?' Antigonos asked after a while. 'Aren't you going to tell me what the scouts said?'

'I was but I was waiting for you to calm down a bit.'

'I'm perfectly calm! Get on with it!'

'Well, it seems Eumenes has billeted his army all around the place in little communities rather than have two or three centres.'

Antigonos' eye gleamed. 'Are you saying he's completely spread out all over Gabene?'

'Yes, Father. But he's got advance scouts along the road we must take to get there who will report back, giving him enough time to muster his army.'

Antigonos rumbled a belly laugh. 'Only if we oblige him by going that way.'

'What do you mean?'

'Why go the long way round, a road that takes a month, when the direct route is far quicker?'

'It may be far quicker, but it's a flat desert at least eight days across covered in snow and ice at this time of year; we'd lose scores of men even if we wait until the spring.'

'I know; and we'll lose even more if we go now in this weather.'

'You're not serious, are you?'

'Perfectly. Look, Son, we're down to eight thousand men fewer than Eumenes, maybe more; if we oppose him in open battle in the spring we won't stand much of a chance. Face it: he's a talented general. But if we surprise him in the winter by coming from a direction he wasn't expecting whilst his army is all over the place, that puts the odds back in our favour. What do you think?'

'I think it's a risk.'

'So do I; but I want to win this war and get back to the west this year. Crossing the desert makes both of those things possible.'

'And if it goes wrong then it makes the chances of us being dead this year very high indeed.'

'We'll be dead if we wait until spring and face Eumenes with his superior numbers; and we'd be dead if we decide to run back to the west without facing him.'

'Put that way, it would seem we have no choice in the matter.'

'And now we've all the facts in front of us it becomes easy to make a decision. Tell Peithon to give orders to have the men issued with dry rations for eight days; we'll be lighting no fires, day or night. This has to be a complete surprise.'

'Then might I suggest we let it be known we intend to head north into Armenia?'

'But why would I do that?'

'Does it matter? Any spies in our army will report to Eumenes that's what we're doing and he'll have to take it at face value and, whilst he's wondering why, we'll appear.'

Antigonos grinned and slapped his son on the shoulder. 'I'll make a general of you yet. We'll do just that and to make it authentic have Peithon issue the lads with twelve days' rations not eight.'

And thus it came as a surprise to Peithon and all Antigonos' officers – and those of his men who had a vague knowledge of geography – when, on the second day of the march north-west, Antigonos turned his army due south and, through miserable, driving sleet, led it across rugged hills, slashed with gullies and populated by sparse copses, towards what they knew to be a heartless wasteland; a destroyer of armies.

On he drove his men, riding up and down the column, urging them to more haste, for the quicker they went the sooner the ordeal would be over. Down they came from the hills onto the featureless plain, similar to the one upon which he had confronted Eumenes in Paraetacene, but higher, much higher, and far more desolate; a place of winter snow and ice where all life struggled in the best of seasons and very little grew; a place in which one did not linger.

Wind, racing down from snow-swathed hills to the north, ripped over flat ground without restraint to claw its way into the clothes of thirty thousand men, chilling them to the bone and compounding their misery as they strove to understand what objective this madness had. At night they huddled together in great piles of humanity, sheltering under snow-flecked cloaks on frozen ground. Fires, banned throughout the hours of darkness, were lit at dawn to provide an hour's respite from the biting chill gnawing their bones and freezing their extremities. And each night there were more executions for fire-lighting for, despite being aware of the capital punishment for the offence, desperation drove the men to it in greater numbers as the march progressed so that by the fifth night, as if by mutual consent, the entire army set to lighting fires and the desert was aglow.

'What shall I do? Execute the whole lot of you?' Antigonos slammed his fist into his palm as he stormed through the camp kicking out fires. 'I said no fires! You've lit up the place like a feasting hall!' He stamped on another burgeoning flame, sending sparks into the faces of the men sitting around it; up they got, all eight of them, and surrounded their commander. With cloaks wrapped tight about them and scarves tied around their heads and necks, their steaming breath clouded what few exposed features remained of their faces.

'I'd be very careful, if I were you,' one of the shrouded figures growled. 'Sir. Very careful indeed about what you do next.'

Antigonos put his hand on his sword-hilt. 'Are you threatening me, soldier?'

'No; just giving you some free advice. We've had no warmth for the last five nights; I know of two of the lads who froze because of it and I'm sure there have been many more. Now, you can either just go back to your tent and keep warm yourself or try and kick a few more fires out and find out exactly what it means to have a very pissed-off army on your hands.' He paused. 'Sir.'

Antigonos took a step back, looking at his adversaries. *I can't recognise any of them; there's nothing I can do but swallow my pride.* 'You realise we'll be seen and Eumenes will be alerted to our arrival?'

'You realise we don't give a fuck.'

'I should have your head.'

'You should have every man's head in this army but then where will that leave you? No, sir, I think it would be much better if we all just pretend this little chat never happened.' He stepped forward and his mates moved to stand shoulder to shoulder.

Antigonos strained to control his temper; he knew all too well how dangerous mutinous troops could be, having saved Antipatros from them just before the Three Paradises conference. *If I say anything it'll just make me look even more impotent.* He turned and walked away.

'It's your own fault,' Demetrios said, once he had been acquainted with the incident. 'You should've taken your bodyguards with you.'

'And how would that look, me protecting myself from my own men?'

'Better than being humiliated by them.'

Antigonos slumped down in his chair, shaking his head. 'All the surprise is now lost; you'll be able to see this many fires from leagues away. Because the lads have lost their discipline, Eumenes is going to have time to gather his army.'

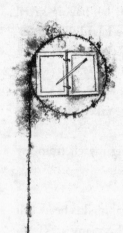

EUMENES.
THE SLY.

'HOW LONG AGO was this?' Eumenes asked Peucestas as he and the other satraps met in the audience chamber in the palace at Aspadana, the principal town of Gabene, the empty throne, as ever, presiding over them.

'Two nights ago,' Peucestas replied. 'He's out-thought you. I suggest we retreat south, gathering the army as we go.'

Eumenes looked at his rival for command of the army, feigning studied interest. 'Do you? You think the best thing to do is bravely run away?' He turned to the others around the table. 'Who else agrees with the satrap of Persis? Should we run away before we even know what's coming?'

Antigenes banged his fist on the wooden surface. 'We haven't even got a reliable estimate of their numbers; this could be a feint to bring us north.'

Hieronymus nodded in agreement. 'The goatherds who reported this to you, Peucestas, where are they? Perhaps they could be a bit more specific?'

Peucestas dismissed the thought with a wave. 'They're outside, but you won't get any sense out of them.'

Eumenes gave Peucestas his most sympathetic look reserved

for Macedonians of particularly painful intellect. *The poor man really is an idiot; thank the gods I've managed to keep him down or we would all be dead by now.* 'So your grand plan of running away is based on information from some goatherds out of whom you can get no sense. Is that it? Have I understood correctly?'

Peucestas looked with unconcealed hatred at the little Greek. 'Antigonos' army is coming out of the north and could be here in a day or so; meanwhile, our army is spread all over Gabene, with some elements, such as the elephant herd out in the west, six days' march away. He's pulled a very clever move whereby he'll be able to engage us piecemeal, rolling up the whole army unit by unit. What do you suggest we do?'

'Pull a clever move back and make sure he's not here in a day or two; and if it is his whole army, make sure he's not here until we're ready for him.'

'And how do you propose to do that?'

Eumenes gave his mysterious smile. 'Gentlemen, will you allow me to try to divert Antigonos away from us on the understanding that should my idea not work then we shall follow Peucestas' well-thought-out stratagem of running away?'

Eudamos looked around the table at his colleagues. 'I think it would be rash not to try to buy ourselves some time.'

The nods and voices of agreement heartened Eumenes. 'Excellent. Antigenes, assemble as many of your lads who are in this area as possible, at least a couple of thousand, more if you can, and issue them all with a sack of firewood each; and arrange for there to be none of our units between the edge of the desert and the north-eastern province of Gabene.'

Antigenes frowned, alarmed. 'But that's the area that we've saved to provision the army for the spring offensive.'

Eumenes nodded. 'Indeed. In the meantime, everyone else, call your men here with all due haste. We have an army to muster.' He rose and turned to bow to Alexander's throne. 'We are dismissed.'

It did not take long after their arrival, the evening of the following day, at the hills marking the southern edge of the desert, before the scouts could report the exact position of Antigonos' army to Eumenes. Far out on the plain they were, about half a day's march away; Eumenes and Antigenes stood on a high cliff as the day began to fade, studying the dark trail that was the enemy column in the distance.

'We got here just in time,' Eumenes said, having done some mental arithmetic. 'I would say he's come with his entire army; this isn't a feint to distract us whilst he does something clever elsewhere.' He looked to either side; the hills rolled up and down west and east, gentle along the length of the cliff for half a league to either side. 'This is as good a place as any.'

Antigenes looked around. 'For what?'

'For a camp. How many of your lads have you brought?'

'Almost three thousand.'

'Excellent. Have each one of them make a couple of fires at least ten paces away from each other and on different levels of the hills; have them tend them for the first four hours of darkness and then let them fade as they do when we sleep so that from a distance it will look like an entire army is waiting for Antigonos. In the morning, have the lads move around as much as possible so there are many glints of metal reflecting down to confuse Antigonos even more.'

Antigenes grinned. 'Do you know that many people call you a sly—'

'Little Greek? Yes, I had heard something along those lines; I can't imagine why.'

'Perhaps it's to do with your size.'

'Antigenes, I think you might be right. Oh, and make sure you capture any patrols he sends forward to have a closer look at our position. We wouldn't want him knowing the truth, would we?'

Eumenes' mood was made even better by the beauty he beheld as the sun dipped west and the hill-range came alive with thousands of points of flickering light. Although he had seen massed campfires on many occasions in his life – most nights, in fact, in recent years – they had always been accompanied by the constant rumble of thousands of men going about the business of cooking the evening meal; but here, this evening, with one man tending two fires a distance from his comrades, there was virtual silence. It was as if the stars had fallen to the earth and had come to fight for him. *The army of the firmament.* He smiled and looked north to the glow that was Antigonos' camp. *Well, old friend, what are you thinking as you look up to this hill? Do you think my whole army is here? I do hope so. And how will that affect what you do tomorrow?*

'He's heading east,' Hieronymus informed Eumenes, sticking his head through the entrance of the tent, soon after noon the following day.

Eumenes looked up from the wax tablet he was writing on. 'Is he, now? How gratifying.'

'It worked.'

'Yes, it certainly seems to have.'

'When his scouts failed to return, that must have convinced him he faced our whole force.'

'Then he has no one to blame but himself for not being more thorough and sending out more scouts. I thought he'd be down there for at least a couple of days before he made his mind up. Ask Antigenes to join me, would you?'

Amazed Antigonos had taken the bait so quickly, Eumenes carried on with his work until Antigenes arrived. 'I'd like you and your lads to shadow Antigonos until he gets into the unplundered area of Gabene in three days or so; I'll send you some cavalry for support. Once he's there, let him re-provision for a couple of days and then arrange for him to find out we've tricked him; I want him coming at me in a rage, so as he's more likely to make a mistake. Meet me on the road heading north from Aspadana, in six days. I'm going back to see how the muster is going; hopefully I'll have most of the army assembled by then.'

The older general chuckled. 'And then it will be a bloody day.'

'That it will, my friend; that it will.'

'And will you win that bloody day?' Artonis asked, looking with concern at her husband as she teased the hairs on his chest, curling them around her little finger a couple of days later.

Eumenes pulled her closer and kissed her forehead. 'It's in my own hands, provided I can get the army together quickly enough. It's coming on well; almost three-quarters of the troops have already arrived and the rest should be here in two days, three at the most. I need to be ready in three days at the latest as Antigonos will probably find out he's been tricked by the day after tomorrow.' He inhaled deeply through his nose, enjoying his wife's scent. 'I'll be back before you realise I'm gone.'

'Liar.' Artonis plucked out a hair.

'Ow!'

'You know perfectly well I'll miss you as soon as you're gone.' She reached up and kissed his cheek, entwining a leg around his. 'So I'd better make full use of you now I have you back briefly.' With that she straddled him, looking down at him with dark eyes full of love as she rubbed his shoulders and then kissed him on the lips.

Eumenes responded with enthusiasm as he always did to her sexual advances even so soon after the completion of the last bout. Since their reunion in the previous spring he had grown in his feelings for her to the point where his analytical mind wondered if he was truly in love with the woman. He certainly desired her body above all else – except, perhaps, victory for the Argead royal house – and he had come to dote upon her, wanting only to make her happy and see her smile, and he enjoyed her company above all others, even his old friend Hieronymus. *I suppose I must love her; how strange at my age to fall in love.* He ran his hands down her back and then smoothed his palms over her buttocks, feeling his arousal strengthen. *This is another reason why I cannot afford to be defeated; I would not want to lose this.* And with that thought he lay back and let his wife have her way with him.

And thus he spent his spare time in the final two days of the muster, in between the provisioning and organising of the army flooding in from all directions with a speed Eumenes found reassuring. *At least the lads seem to be keen,* he mused, as he, Hieronymus and Eudamos watched a unit of Xennias' cavalry, who had been posted in the far south of the country, clatter through the gates of the military camp to the north of Aspadana. *I expect they all sense the end to the eastern campaign.* A dark thought clouded his mind for a few moments. *One way or the other.* Dismissing the gloom, he checked the list etched onto a wax tablet and then turned to Eudamos standing to his right. 'Apart from stragglers, it's just your elephants and their support troops to come, I believe.'

'Yes, that's correct.'

'How long?'

Eudamos shrugged.

'Do you think—'

'That they'll be here by the end of the day? No.'

'It's normally my annoying habit to finish people's sentences for them.'

Hieronymus, standing to Eumenes' left, looked down at his friend. 'Now you know—'

'How it feels.' Eumenes made a show of considering. 'Yes, and I don't understand why people get so uptight about it; it seems quite innocuous to me.'

'That's because you don't have it inflicted upon you relentlessly.'

'That's a fair point and I'll tell you what; my victory present to all of you when we beat Antigonos will be to cease the habit.'

Hieronymus looked sceptical. 'Really?'

'Yes, really. Unless, of course, I'm dealing with a Macedonian military mind on a par with Peithon's; it would be impossible to restrain myself under those conditions.'

'Then I shall redouble my prayers for your victory.'

'If you feel it will help, do that, my friend. Personally, I'd rather have the help of Eudamos' elephants than that of the gods; although, of course, we will perform the Lustration ceremony tomorrow morning, before we leave, with the whole army parading outside the camp.'

And so it was with great relief, a couple of hours after the following dawn, that Eumenes, having completed the ceremony to purify the army before it headed north, heard Eudamos report the elephant herd was no more than a day away to the west. 'If they now head due north they should intercept us in a couple of days before we meet Antigonos; their pace is slightly quicker than the baggage,' he said to Eudamos. He looked over at the baggage train with its oxen and mules harnessed to heavy carts and wagons, assembling to the rear of the ranks. *Such a cumbersome thing; anyone would think we are going away for a whole season's campaigning and not just a few days. Baggage, can't move with it, can't move without it.* Shaking his head, he turned to his generals and satraps gathered around. 'Gentlemen, give the orders to move out.'

It was with a heavy heart that Eumenes held Artonis in his arms as the column formed and the vanguard headed off; each parting grew progressively harder and for a moment he was tempted to take her with him. *No, I must be free to concentrate my whole mind on victory. It would be too much of a distraction having her waiting for me in my tent.* He lifted her chin, her eyes, brim full with tears, met his; he kissed her lips, soft and with love. 'I will win that bloody day.'

Artonis tried to smile. 'I will pray to Azhura Mazda it will be none of your blood that's shed.'

'There seem to be a lot of gods being petitioned on my behalf.'

'It can never harm to have the favour of the gods for the man you love.' She took his face in her hands and pulled him into a forceful kiss. 'Come back to me.' Once more she kissed him and then turned to walk away.

Eumenes watched her go, admiring the sway of her hips, with a knot in his stomach. With a deep breath, he brought his emotions under control, called for his horse to be brought to him and steeled himself for the final campaign against Antigonos.

ANTIGONOS.
THE ONE-EYED.

'TRICKED! AND SO easily too.' Antigonos was fuming as he strode, with his son, along the growing column, in and out of ranks of forming units; indeed, he had been fuming ever since he had parleyed with Antigenes, at dawn, three hours previously, and the Silver Shields' commander had told him of the ruse used to convince him Eumenes' full force awaited him. 'Tricked by a Greek! A sly little Greek at that.' He stamped his foot and bellowed at a mercenary officer: 'Form your sluggards up quicker; what do you think I pay you for? Standing around and stroking each other's cocks? My arse, I do; get in line.' He shoved a dithering youth in the chest. 'Get in line and stop holding me up.'

Demetrios closed his eyes in exasperation as they continued their progress through the muster. 'Father, ranting at men who might soon be dying for you is not going to make things any better. Look at the positives.'

'What positives? The element of surprise is totally gone. Eumenes will have mustered his forces by now and therefore outnumbers us; and I'm still trying to get these bastards ready to go out to meet him.' He gave his one-eyed glare at a unit of Thracian peltasts, standing in formation but resting on their shields and talking amongst themselves; they snapped to attention. 'I'll have to be very lucky to find ground that suits us and then force him to engage when it's not in his favour. So tell me, just what are the positives?'

Demetrios dodged out of the way of a messenger galloping up the column. 'Well, for a start, we've been able to completely re-provision the army; this is fat, unplundered land and we can survive here for a couple of months, therefore we don't have to rush into a pitched battle but bide our time and strike when we have the advantage. Don't forget, Peithon knows this ground very well, as he campaigned through it when the eastern satraps rose against him.'

'Peithon! Peithon is as subtle as a Bactrian's fart; yes, he's handy in battle but useless when it comes to thinking strategy. And don't forget the eastern alliance whipped his arse and it's mainly that same army we face again, so by your logic they know it very well too.' He kicked a soldier, bending over to adjust his greaves, up the arse, sending him flying. 'Your kit should be fully functional before you come on parade!' He growled his approval as a unit of light cavalry thundered past, heading up to take their place in the vanguard. 'No, it's Philotas I miss; someone with whom I could discuss ideas and be sure of a sound response.' Shaking his head in regret, he took his horse's bridle from a slave. 'And Seleukos; I miss him too; not because I like him, I find him far too arrogant. No, I miss his organisational abilities; perhaps I shouldn't have been so hard on him and kept him here rather than send him back to carry on besieging Susa.' *Or perhaps I should've killed him instead of letting him go; then I'd have no cause to miss him.*

'You've got *me*, Father.'

'You?' Antigonos just managed to stop himself from scoffing and saying anything derogatory about his son's military abilities whilst he was in such a foul mood. 'Yes, Demetrios, you're right, I've got you.' He paused to control his temper and clapped his son on the shoulder. 'You're right. Now stay here and get this column ready to leave as soon as possible whilst I go to tell Peithon not to wait but to lead the vanguard out once it's formed up.' Antigonos swung himself up into the saddle and then looked down at Demetrios. 'And forget about any baggage we may have acquired; we got across the desert without any so there's no reason to weigh ourselves down with it now. It can follow at its own pace. We can at least be faster than Eumenes.' He turned his mount and kicked it away up the column as the elephants, trumpeting and flapping their ears, joined its rear.

The vanguard was, at least, in some sort of order as Antigonos arrived at the head of the column to find Peithon in the process of sending out scouts to either side of the road heading south. 'I want to know everything that moves on both flanks of Eumenes' column,' Peithon told the four cavalry commanders. 'Keep regular reports coming back to me; there must be no chance of him getting around our flanks. Now, get going.'

Good man, Peithon, there's nothing wrong with your day to day technical abilities. 'Are you ready, Peithon?'

Peithon turned his horse and acknowledged his superior's presence with the vaguest of salutes as the four officers hurried to rejoin their men. 'It's been a rush, but Macedonians will always get there; we'll leave within the hour. I'm just sending the scouts out, one unit close to the road on each side and one further to the east and west.'

'I heard; good. Judging by the speed at which the chaos is being sorted out back there I should be ready to move out with the main army an hour later. I left Demetrios to sort it out.' Antigonos could tell from his look just what Peithon thought of his choice, but let it go. *No point in aggravating him at the moment*

I really need him. 'Move fast, and if you come into contact with the forward units of his army show yourself to them and retreat, drawing them on until I bring the column up.'

But it was a good two hours, almost noon, before the main body of the army was ready to move; slow did it start with massed calls of horns from along its length as each unit moved forward in turn, stretching the column until it was more than a league long. However, with the late winter sun falling behind the mountains to the west, almost as soon as the rear had covered two and a half leagues, the head of the column caught up with the vanguard, which had stopped to make camp for the night.

'I told you to move fast, Peithon,' Antigonos said, his tone belying the anger he felt as he looked down from his horse at his general seated by a campfire with a cup in his hand. 'Instead I find you roasting pork and drinking wine, barely four leagues down the road when there is still daylight enough left.'

Peithon looked up, his expression unconcerned. 'I've had reports in from the scouts: Eumenes is a day to the south-east coming up from Aspadana. Antigenes blocks the way four leagues from here with his Silver Shields and cavalry support.'

Antigonos felt the rage well up within him as his eye burned down on his erring commander. *I should kill the bastard here and now.* 'Then why didn't you send a message back to me informing me of the situation? I would have told you to fucking well press on!' He jumped from the saddle, able to control himself no more.

Peithon threw his cup down as he leaped to his feet. 'And I would not have taken any notice of the order; I would still have camped here.' He grabbed Antigonos' wrists as he went to clasp his throat. 'Listen to me!'

'Father, stop!' Demetrios shouted, pulling up his horse next to the burgeoning fray.

Peithon, arms bulging with fur-covered muscle, slowly pushed Antigonos' hands down until the two of them stood almost nose to nose. 'Listen to me, Antigonos.'

'What excuse could you possibly have for being so negligent?'

'Listen to him, Father,' Demetrios urged. 'Listen before you come to a false judgement and do something neither of you can back down from.'

Antigonos stared into Peithon's face, feeling the loathing that came with the discovery of blatant insubordination. *You might just have lost this whole campaign and with it my life.* But again his son shouted, 'Listen to him!' This time it seemed to pierce his consciousness through the hate and anger.

Slowly Antigonos turned to look at his son, his wrists still clasped in Peithon's iron grip. 'Why should I?'

'Because he asked you to; because he must have a reason for stopping here. You said yourself – well, you know what you said.'

'I said he's handy in battle but not in strategy.' He turned to face Peithon. 'So, surprise me.'

Peithon remained motionless as he digested Antigonos' remark. 'I should kill you for that.'

Antigonos pulled at his locked wrists. 'Killing me won't help you; you'd be dead before my body touched the floor.' He gestured with his head to the large group of his men who had gathered around the confrontation.

Again Peithon thought for a few moments, before releasing Antigonos. 'Very well.' He brushed down his tunic, more to gather his thoughts than because it was soiled or rumpled. 'Very well, Antigonos. Seeing as you don't think I'm much of a strategist, judge me on this: I didn't go forward because it would be best if Antigenes stays where he is.'

'Hmph, and why is that?'

'Because my scouts to the west have reported a major part of his force is yet to join up with him and have changed direction to head right this way. Therefore, the further to the south-east Eumenes is, the further away he is from his elephants and the more time we will have to capture them before they can reach him or he can send a relief force to them. As it stands, they are south-west of us, closer to us than they are to Eumenes.'

Antigonos felt a new surge of hope. 'How far?'

'Oh, so I did do the right thing, did I?'

The bastard has made me lose face in front of all these men; the whole army will hear of this. And yet how can I afford not to take advantage of the position Peithon's contrived? There's no choice but to swallow my pride. 'Yes, you did, and I apologise for doubting you. Far from losing the campaign, you could well just have won it.'

Peithon's dark eyes remained emotionless as ever. 'I don't need you to think well of me, Antigonos, but I insist on being treated with respect. Respect! And I will kill you if you ever talk to me like that again even if I die doing so.' He leaned in closer and whispered: 'I may not be a subtle man but I know enough not to ask you, in public, if you understand me, forcing you to reply and making you look like a small boy in front of all these men.' He cracked a grin that was more grimace, his eyes remaining dead, and slapped Antigonos on the shoulder. 'Now that we understand one another, we can be friends,' he shouted for the benefit of the onlookers, drawing an uncertain cheer. Peithon lowered his voice to answer Antigonos' question: 'Eumenes' elephant herd is four hours' swift ride from here. One hundred and fourteen elephants and three hundred light infantry, mainly archers; and, crucially, only a small cavalry support. I have sent word to Anatolios, commanding the scouts, to keep them in sight.'

'A small amount of cavalry? How many?'

'No more than four hundred.'

Antigonos could barely contain his excitement. 'We'll overwhelm them. Demetrios, I want you to take six hundred light infantry south now; you're to march through the night. I'll catch up with you in the morning with a large force of lancers and Tarantine light cavalry. Understood?'

Demetrios, realising the urgency of the situation, set off immediately to fulfil his mission.

Antigonos turned to Peithon and indicated to the jug of wine. 'Shall we?'

Peithon spat on the ground. 'I may have to fight with you, Antigonos, but I don't have to drink with you.'

Antigonos walked away. *That, my dull friend, was your death warrant. As soon as you're of no more use to me, that is.*

Hence he drank his resinated wine alone that night, having seen off Demetrios and given orders for two thousand lancers and two hundred Tarantines to be ready an hour before sunrise. And it was as the pre-dawn glow hit the wisps of higher cloud that Antigonos led his cavalry detachment south, accompanied by the scout who had reported the sighting the previous day.

'Anatolios, my commander, will be sending men back to intercept us,' the scout said in response to Antigonos' question as to how he would find their quarry now it would have moved further east.

'What makes you so sure?'

'Because Peithon told him to start doing so from first light this morning in the message he sent back yesterday.'

'Did he now?' *I really can't fault his technical abilities.* 'Then guide us south as fast as you can.'

*

With the meagre heat of the late winter sun beginning to warm through their cloaks, the cavalry detachment slowed as a lone rider approached them. The man drew up his mount and then swallowed hard when he recognised Antigonos.

'Well?' Antigonos asked.

The scout pointed to a line of hills a league to the south and slightly east. 'They're just beyond them, sir. Demetrios is tracking their progress from the high ground.'

'Very good. Lead on.'

'They're down there, Father,' Demetrios said as Antigonos dismounted and went to lie next to his son peering over the crest of the hill.

Down the slope, less than a thousand paces away, the herd made its way east with their mahouts keeping a purposeful, but not rushed, pace with the escort cavalry following behind. Some carried howdahs containing a couple of bowmen and another man armed with a pike, others just a pikeman astride the beast's back; light infantry screened them from the hill but they did not concern Antigonos. *We'll lose a few of the lads to their arrows but that's a price worth paying to capture those beasts.* 'All right, Demetrios, I'll leave you half of the heavy cavalry and all the lights; I'll take the rest through the hills to get ahead of the herd. As soon as you see me breaking out onto the flat ground have your light infantry clear away as many of their archers as they can. You bring your lancers up behind their cavalry and send your Tarantines around to the south to block any retreat that way. Then deal with their cavalry whilst I stop the herd. With luck we'll surround them and, if they've any sense, they should surrender.'

Demetrios nodded. 'After all, what does an elephant care which side it's on?'

Antigonos laughed as he slid backwards and then got to his feet. 'If only it were left up to them.'

Through the hills, Antigonos led his thousand lancers at a canter; gradually they drew level with, and then overtook, their prey down on the grassland below. Judging a fifteen hundred pace lead sufficient for what he had in mind, Antigonos halted in a wide valley sloping down towards the flatter ground, giving orders for his men to form up in four ranks. Savouring the upland air, he breathed deep before throwing his arm forward and kicking his horse into action. Off he went at a trot; he soon accelerated into a canter, enjoying the sound of four thousand hooves pounding the ground beneath him. Down the hill he led his men, down onto the grassland and there he turned to the west in the face of the elephants he would capture.

And as he turned and sped towards the surprised herd, a storm of arrows rained down from the hills onto its screening light infantry; despite their loose formation, many fell dead or wounded as the survivors looked up the hill to try to locate the source of their ordeal. Again and again the clouds of death rose to the sky, forcing the skirmishers to run back to the protection of the beasts they were meant to shield for there was no cover to be had out on the grassland. As they ran, in the distance the two hundred Tarantine mercenary cavalry – shielded and javelin-armed – raced across the open ground and circled around the elephants whilst, with a mighty war-cry and a flamboyant rearing up of his stallion, raising his lance above his head, Demetrios initiated the charge of his thousand lancers aimed at the cavalry to their rear.

Thunder trembled the ground as Demetrios and Antigonos charged from opposite directions; with massed trumpeting as the sense of danger registered in their elephantine minds, the herd, surrounded on all sides now the light infantry ran down from their concealed position in the hills, did the only thing it could do other than surrender: it charged forward as its supporting cavalry turned back towards Demetrios. Lumbering at first but soon building momentum, the hundred and fourteen huge beasts added depth to the thunder rumbling below as they accelerated towards Antigonos and his lancers, archers nocking the arrows and the pikemen readying their long weapons capable of reaching well beyond the extreme range of the beasts' trunks. On they both came, cavalry and elephantry, rapidly decreasing the distance between them as their pace increased, and it soon became apparent to Antigonos that the mahouts had no intention of backing down; they intended to drive their charges directly into his formation, which would result in but one outcome, and it would not be a good one for him. He glanced to either side and he could already see uncertainty on the faces of his two wingmen and the other riders nearest him as all knew that their mounts could not tolerate the smell of the elephants; even if they could, what could they possibly gain by charging straight at a wall of the brutes? Yes, they might get a few lucky lance-tips in the eyes but they would be thrown aside by the weight of the charge; thrown aside or trampled underfoot or skewered on a pike.

With two hundred paces left until impact, Antigonos raised both arms into the air and pointed to either side. 'Split!' he roared, hoping at least the men nearest him would hear him. He gestured to his wingman on the left to head off in that direction whilst he took his mount to the right. Down the middle the unit parted, sweeping away to the left and right as the herd surged through the gap, with just a few paces to spare to either side.

But to escape the trampled death beneath the feet of beasts was to expose themselves to the attentions of their light infantry desperately sprinting behind. Although they had been left some way distant, the archers nocked arrows and released on the run, sending scores of missiles into the flanks of the cavalry as it sped past.

Antigonos felt his mount judder and then kick out behind as an arrow slammed into its rump with another glancing off his helmet. He hunched down over his horse's neck as it galloped on despite its wound until the hiss of swift projectiles faded as the range grew too long. He ordered a halt and turned to survey the situation: the herd had slowed enough for its light infantry to catch up, but was still heading north-east with the Tarantines shadowing it to the south as half of Demetrios' command chased what remained of the opposition cavalry from the field, bringing many down with extended lance-thrusts as they went. Demetrios brought the other half of his cavalry to a halt close by to Antigonos' position with his archers following up behind.

'They won't be troubling us again, so what now?' Demetrios asked, riding up to his father who was examining the shaft of the arrow embedded in his mount.

'First I need a new horse.' He gestured over to a trooper to bring his mount over.

'And what then?'

'Then?' Antigonos looked round and pointed to the herd. 'Then we have to surround them and take down their mahouts with arrows.' He yanked on the arrow, pulling it free from bloodied and ripped flesh, causing the horse to screech and buck; he drew back out of range of the flying hooves until the beast calmed down. Taking the bridle of the trooper's mount, he left his wounded horse in the man's care and mounted up. 'We'll ride up behind them and take their light infantry down.'

'And then offer the mahouts money to come over to us?'

'Something like that.'

But the mahouts had other plans, and as Antigonos and his two thousand cavalry approached the herd, they formed a square with the light infantry on the inside shooting out, protected by a wall of thick, greyish-brown skin.

Antigonos led his cavalry round and round the herd, but never a gap could he find as the square stood firm and the archers in its centre and in the howdahs kept his men at a distance. Despite repeated advances, all requests for a parley were refused.

'How long do they think they can stay there without water?' Demetrios asked as another advance from the light infantry was beaten back by waves of well-aimed arrows.

'I don't know, but if they stay like that until nightfall then we'll have a good chance of infiltrating them. I can't afford to wait here until then, though; I need to get back and move forward. You stay put with the light infantry and your cavalry; keep them surrounded as I engage Eumenes. At least if the herd remains here it's of no good to him.'

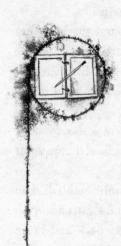

EUMENES.
THE SLY.

'ANTIGENES REPORTS THAT Antigonos hasn't moved towards us all morning,' Xennias told Eumenes as he dismissed his scouts back up the road. 'He's just stopped, four leagues from Antigenes' position. Apparently a large body of horse left, heading due south, at first light; but there has been no movement since.'

Eumenes scratched the back of his neck as he trotted along at an easy pace just behind the vanguard of his column. 'Has he found good ground?'

'It appears not: it's flat with nothing to recommend it to either side or to the front or rear.'

'Then what's he doing?'

Xennias looked nonplussed.

Eumenes took off his helmet to rub his head and then looked to the west. 'Have the scouts reported any sign of our elephants?'

'No; but they should be with us today.'

'Just in time, I'd say. Especially with Antigonos sitting there doing nothing. Now every pace we take north-west brings us closer not only to Antigenes but also to the elephants coming from the west.' But as he uttered these words Eumenes felt a knot develop in his stomach and he saw a geometrical image in his mind. 'South did you say?'

'What's south?'

'South? Did you say the large body of horse went south this morning?'

'Yes.'

'How many?'

'It was estimated at around two thousand.'

'And today the elephant herd should arrive with us from the west; meanwhile, Antigonos has stopped ten or so leagues to the north-west of us and sent two thousand cavalry due south. I'm no expert on these matters but I can see a very disturbing triangle.'

Xennias looked at his commanding officer in alarm. 'He's gone for the elephants.'

'Yes, and they've only got an escort of four hundred cavalry and a few hundred light infantry; I'd say two thousand cavalry would do the job, wouldn't you? Should he capture them, he will effectively have wiped out our superiority in numbers. Oh, that is clever.'

'What do we do?'

'We stop him. You with your men and me and my Kappadokians had better head west immediately; our three thousand to his two.'

With haste, and no time to issue provisions, the troops were mustered, peeling away from the column and heading west as the sun approached its zenith. Having left Antigenes in command of the column – much to Peucestas' disgust – Eumenes rode hard for he knew this was an existential threat which needed to be dealt with immediately. Scouts were sent out along a broad front, for the precise location of the herd was uncertain. That it was coming from the west was the only information Eudamos had been able to supply; yes, it had been sighted by long-range scouts but that had been a day ago and it would have needed to change direction so as to rendezvous with the main body of the army as it moved north-west. And so it was with blind hope Eumenes led his men in search of the heaviest component of his army, across the rolling pasture and farmland that was the fertile Gabene as it began to swell back into life with the coming of spring. On they went without let-up, eating the leagues and slowing only to ford streams and allow the horses an opportunity to drink.

With the sun now low enough to shine in his eyes, Eumenes squinted towards a small dot up ahead. Within a few heartbeats it became clear a rider was approaching; without slowing, the man swerved his horse as he came close and fell in, next to Eumenes.

'About a thousand cavalry and three hundred light infantry under Demetrios' command have them surrounded about a half hour's fast ride from here,' the scout reported.

Eumenes looked at him in surprise. 'Just a thousand cavalry? Where're the rest?'

'I don't know; that was all I saw. The elephants are in a tight square with their light infantry inside. I think when night falls it'll be the end for them.'

Eumenes thanked the man. 'Stay with me and guide us.'

Good to the scout's word the surrounded herd came into view half an hour later as the sun reddened and turned the few high clouds a glorious range of colours. With no time for any elaborate thinking, Eumenes placed himself and his Kappadokians on the right wing with Xennias' men in the centre and on the left of his line. *We'll head straight at them and watch them fly.*

But as the line formed, Eumenes found himself becoming more and more surprised by Demetrios' tactics, for he did nothing but send his light infantry running for the hills; he kept the cavalry surrounding the herd, riding around it, as if he were unaware of Eumenes' arrival. Regardless, Eumenes raised his sword and urged his men forward at a canter. And still Demetrios did nothing, keeping the herd encircled as the charge neared. With a hundred paces to go, Eumenes stretched his mount into a full gallop. It was then he realised what Demetrios had been waiting for: his cavalry suddenly streamed away, exposing the elephants facing the charge to the shock of seeing three thousand horses heading directly for them. For, although the mahouts, high on their animals' shoulders, had been able to see the oncoming cavalry, the beasts themselves had not, as the screen of riders revolving around them had taken all their attention. Thus it was with renewed panic that they absorbed the situation they were in, for they had no concept this was a rescue – all they saw was hostility and reacted accordingly. Taking no notice of their mahouts, they turned and bolted, spooking those elephants that had, as yet, no sight of the danger speeding towards them. Chaos multiplied, howdahs tipped, spilling the passengers beneath trampling feet, as man and beast struggled in what was becoming a very tight place despite all of the open ground. The screams of the crushed and the trumpeting of terrified beasts, rearing and tossing their heads, had a spiralling effect and the panic fed upon itself. Eumenes slowed his charge and then ordered his men to back off so as not to aggravate the situation further.

It was not until the ground was a thick mush of bloodied flesh and spilled innards that the mahouts managed to gain some order in the herd and extract it from what had been a living nightmare for all involved. Eumenes looked at the carnage and was reminded of the time Perdikkas had had the three hundred ringleaders of Meleager's opposition to him trampled to death by the elephants; it had not been pleasant then and it certainly had not improved over time. Cursing Demetrios for such a nasty trick, he looked to the hills where Demetrios' cavalry was now disappearing and saw a lone rider waving from a high point, his horse rearing. Shaking his head, but having a grudging admiration for the young man's audacity and inventiveness, he returned the wave. *I shall see you on the battlefield, you cocky little sod.*

After giving orders for the bodies to be scraped from the turf and burned, Eumenes gathered his men and, leaving a good force to guard the slower-moving elephants, headed back to the column with the rest, now determined to use what he had retrieved to forge a victory against Antigonos and his young pup.

It was not until mid-morning the following day that Eumenes caught back up with his army to find that Antigenes had just ordered a halt.

'Antigonos stole a night march on us and is camped a league away by a ruined town surrounded by farmland which was sowed with salt centuries ago; nothing's grown there since. It looks like he's going to try to exploit the one superiority he has in his cavalry as he seems to be preparing the ground by removing large stones.'

'That would make sense from his point of view.'

'I didn't want to get any closer to him in case he attacked before you and the elephants were back.' He looked beyond Eumenes. 'They are coming back, aren't they?'

'Yes, but they won't be here much before the end of the day, so we must do everything we can to delay the battle until tomorrow. Let's ride forward and take a look at what he's up to.'

It came as no surprise to Eumenes that Antigonos had picked ideal ground: flat and barren with a gentle slope; he had the ruins of the town on a low hill to his left and open ground to his right. 'Perfect for cavalry,' he observed to Antigenes. 'He'll place most of it on his right, skirmishers in the ruins and on the hill to the left, and do his best to hold our centre with his and then try to outflank us and take us up the arse.'

'Feint to our right and load the left?'

Eumenes grinned and looked up at the veteran commander, fifteen years his senior. 'We'll make a general out of you yet, Antigenes.'

Taking the remark in the spirit it was intended, Antigenes continued: 'And I'll make sure my lads make quick work of whatever's opposite them and get it over before his cavalry superiority begins to tell.'

'I'd be most grateful if they would.'

Antigonos did not move for the rest of the day, nor overnight, the early part of which saw the arrival of the elephants without further incident. As the sun broke the eastern horizon on the new and fateful day, Antigonos continued his preparations whilst Eumenes held a final meeting beneath the empty throne as his army broke its fast. 'Gentlemen,' he said, looking around the satraps and generals, 'I think we all agree the outcome of today's battle will affect the way our world develops. We will either stay as a united empire under the king, each of us with our own satrapies free to do what we like, within reason, so long as we remain loyal to the Argead royal house. Or, if Antigonos triumphs, the empire will disintegrate into constituent parts for he will never be able to command the respect and loyalty the heir of Alexander can expect. If that occurs, there will be decades more of civil war and that'll be bad for us all; if we want to make ourselves fabulously wealthy, it's a peaceful climate we seek.' He looked from face to face; all seemed to be in agreement. *Appeal to their sense of greed; it's always the quickest way to a man's heart.* 'Therefore we must ensure we're victorious, for if we're not, it won't be only the dream of riches we shall lose but, most probably, our very lives.'

'Now we have the elephants back, we cannot lose.' It was Eudamos who had so rashly tempted the gods and all around the table clasped their thumbs between their fore- and middle-fingers to ward off the evil eye.

But it's too late, the damage has been done and I'm not even superstitious; but the rest are and that piece of stupidity will play on their minds for the whole day. 'Let us hope that's the case, but we shouldn't depend upon it. To win we have to beat Antigonos militarily and not just rely on numbers.' *Although they do help.* 'Antigonos is a league away waiting for us on ground of his choosing; it's advantageous to his superiority in cavalry. Should we, therefore, refuse to go forward as conventional wisdom would dictate?' The question was rhetorical as Eumenes had no intention of letting another answer it. 'Of course not; to pause now would have our lads asking themselves what we're afraid of. They can do the arithmetic; they'll know we have a ten-thousand-man advantage as there has already been much toing and froing between the camps despite our efforts to curb the practice. No, we go.' This time he did leave a pause for anyone to gainsay him; none did. Indeed, Antigenes, Teutamus, Xennias, Eudamos, Tlepolemus of Carmania, Stasander of Aria and Drangiana, and Androbarzus, Oxyartes' deputy from Paropamisadae, all thumped the table in support, causing Hieronymus to make a note of the names for his history.

It was just Peucestas, unsurprisingly, who seemed reluctant. 'I say stay here and let him come to us: we've got the wealth of Gabene behind us, whereas he is camped on salted ground and has only a few leagues of fertile land behind him before it turns into desert. He will start to feel hunger before we do.'

Eumenes studied Peucestas for a few moments as if seriously considering the argument. 'And what do we do whilst we sit here waiting for him to advance? Do we reinforce ourselves with more troops? No, because we have no more troops, unless we can persuade Seleukos, who I presume is back at Susa, to lift the siege so Xenophilus can send us his garrison; which I doubt he will as he'll now remain studiously neutral until there's a result here. And what about Antigonos? Will he be reinforced? The answer is we don't know. There may be more troops coming down from Media as spring gathers pace, which might be why he has chosen to stop where he is and wait for them – or it may be not. Should we take that risk? Or should we just go and try to beat what is already there?'

This got the table-thumpers going again, causing Peucestas to raise his hands in submission. 'I can see I am a minority of one.' He spread his palms. 'I therefore concede defeat; we go.'

That was remarkably easy; what's he up to? 'Thank you, Peucestas. So, gentlemen, it is with infantry, specifically the Silver Shields and the Hypaspists, with which we will win this battle and it is with cavalry, all of it, that we will prevent ourselves from being defeated until that time. So I will ask all of you with cavalry contingents to join Xennias and me on our left.' He raised a hand to stifle any protest from the more status-minded of his satraps. 'I know the place of honour is on the right but it's from Antigonos' right his main force will come and so we need a strong left to nullify that. We shall refuse with our right; Antigonos is more than welcome to keep his ruins. To that end we shall station peltasts and light troops there, screened by four-teen of the elephants. Also, to make a show of looking aggressive, and to perhaps give Antigonos something to think about, the remnants of the cavalry who were mauled whilst protecting the elephants will reinforce it; about two hundred and fifty have come in so far and they are of not much use other than being for show.' He turned to Antigenes. 'How will you arrange your centre?' *It always helps to seem inclusive; the others will never know we've already discussed the subject, but it'll make them feel far more a part of a team.*

'The Asian pikemen on the right. Then come the Greek mercenaries who will form the bulk of my centre; I imagine Antigonos will either have his mercenaries or his Lycians opposite, so it'll be evenly matched and therefore shouldn't move forward or back. I'll be next to them with the Silver Shields, and Teutamus will be outside me with the Hypaspists, and it's here we shall break them.'

Eumenes nodded. 'Excellent. Peucestas will provide a screen of five thousand of his Persian archers interspersed with forty of Eudamos' elephants.'

Teutamus grinned. 'That'll please the lads; they love to watch the enemy being softened up – provided the beasts don't get pushed back and pick on the wrong army.'

'Indeed,' Eumenes said, wishing these sorts of observations would be kept private. 'Peucestas, you'll command the main bulk of the cavalry next to the centre and I'll command a further formation outside you, specifically for countering a flanking move. I'll take my Kappadokians and the Thracian and Thessalian mercenaries as well as Azanes and his Sogdian horse-archers and their Bactrian counterparts. You will have the rest: your Persian companions, Xennias' men and then the eastern contingents and Eudamos with his Indian cavalry. With them you'll hold off Antigonos until our centre has broken through. Understood?'

Very much to Eumenes' surprise, Peucestas said he did understand and was delighted and honoured by the importance of his role. 'Good, Peucestas. The whole wing will be screened by the sixty outstanding elephants and your remaining five thousand archers.'

'And what about the baggage?' Antigenes asked. 'My lads are always very concerned about that, as you know; their entire fortunes and families are there.'

'We'll leave it here; it's far enough away to be safe and I'm going to prevent any outflanking move anyway so nothing should threaten it unless our whole line breaks, in which case we won't be needing it again.'

Antigenes grunted. 'Fair enough.'

Eumenes looked around the table. 'Any more questions, gentlemen?'

'Yes,' Eudamos said. 'What do we do with Antigonos when we capture him?'

'If we capture him, he should be treated with respect.'

'Really?' The satrap of India bared his teeth. 'I'd say we kill him; what do you think he'd do if he were to capture you?'

Eumenes did not have to think about the answer. 'I imagine he would execute me after what I did to his friend, Philotas. But that is no reason why I should wish to kill him.'

'You should; and his son, otherwise this will never be over.'

'If there are no more questions?' No one spoke. Eumenes stood and bowed to Alexander's throne. 'Then we are dismissed in Alexander's name to go and face Antigonos.'

Antigonos.
The One-eyed.

'H E'S DOING AS I'd hoped,' Antigonos declared to his son as they watched Eumenes' army deploy from column to line, 'refusing his right, placing his best infantry on the left of his centre and massing his horse on his left flank. Perfect!' He rubbed his hands together. *This is going to be good; gods, this'll be good.* He surveyed his army, which had been standing-to for the past couple of hours and was now being watered, and felt he was ready to overcome the ten-thousand-man disadvantage. He had given the left wing to Peithon with orders to do nothing unless the enemy went into retreat. The centre he had stiffened as much as he could but he knew none of his troops would be able to withstand the Silver Shields or the Hypaspists, and so it was here, on his right wing, he must grab victory. Ever since he had found this ground he felt it could be achieved.

For two days the ground had been worked on to make it suitable for his purpose and, as he looked up at the high white clouds, with not a low, grey rain-bearing one in sight, he smiled with inner confidence. Yes, he had fewer elephants, and although he had weighted them on his right, they still would not suffice to nullify their opponents. 'It's the cavalry, my boy,' Antigonos

344

said, yet again. 'It's the cavalry that'll win this; which is why I'm not fighting in the front rank of the phalanx today.'

'I don't need you to keep an eye on me, Father; I can manage perfectly well by myself.'

'My arse, you can; this is going to take precise timing, if we're going to get around his back and pay him out in his own currency.' Antigonos pointed over to where Eumenes was stationing a smaller cavalry command further out and behind the main body of his cavalry opposite. 'You see, he has sensed the danger and is trying to counter it.' He stared harder at the deploying unit. 'That's his Kappadokians; Eumenes himself is commanding the force that's meant to prevent us outflanking him. Ha! My arse, you will, you sly little Greek.' Antigonos tapped his nose. 'What I have in mind will make his move useless.'

Demetrios did nothing to hide his frustration. 'I wish you would say what you have in mind, Father, rather than just endlessly going on about it and then tapping your nose and chuckling.'

'Now, if I had divulged that, Eumenes would have heard about it in no time at all.'

'I wouldn't have told anyone, you know that, Father.'

'Of course *you* wouldn't. I'm keeping it from you for another reason: I want you to guess, Demetrios. Why have I had the ground cleared of stones and raked over?'

'To make it smoother for the cavalry, of course.'

'Of course it has had that effect, but that'll be just as much help for Eumenes, more even, as he has far more horse-archers than I do.' Antigonos played the part of the disappointed father. 'No, Son, if you can't see it, you'll just have to wait.' He carried on watching the deployment, nodding his satisfaction every now and again as Eumenes did exactly as he wanted him to do. *Well, my vicious little friend, today decides it; and by the end of it I shall be rich enough to buy you – if you're still alive, that is.*

But even as the thought passed across his mind a horseman appeared from the ranks of the Silver Shields and rode, carrying a branch of truce high in the air, towards Antigonos' Macedonian phalanx. Halting before them, he raised his voice: 'What do you suppose your fathers think of you now you sin against them, the men who have conquered the whole world under Philip and Alexander?' He pointed back to the Silver Shields. 'For there they stand opposite you; your fathers and indeed, in many cases, your grandfathers. Are you going to force them, once again, to kill their own progeny, for that's what they'll have to do if you move against them? You've faced them before and lost and you know their reputation: they have never been defeated and they will do their duty again. Look at yourselves now and see yourselves for what you are: wicked men who, for one man's vanity, would die on your fathers' pike-tips. Look at yourselves! I feel your shame if you fail to reconsider.' The messenger spat on the ground, turned his mount and walked it back to his own lines, leaving a low murmur emanating from Antigonos' Macedonians, sounding anything but happy.

Antigonos did not wait; there was every reason not to. Now all was set he gestured to his signaller, who raised his horn to his lips. Up went Antigonos' fist and a note, high and clear, issued from the instrument and with it the elephants and their light troops moved forward. The cheers of the men and the trumpeting of the beasts soon drowned out the unease of his Macedonian phalanx as the first volleys of arrows hissed through the air, rising from both sides, for Eumenes, too, had given the signal to attack – although his order had been more general. The Silver Shields and the Hypaspists followed behind the elephants, screening them as they trundled forward, dust rising from their heavy footfalls, closing with the beasts to the front of them. Antigonos glanced over to his phalanx and felt relief that they were still standing; indeed, they were checking their gear and preparing to advance.

Concentrating, once again, on the action ahead of him, Antigonos saw the first of the elephants make contact with each other. Pikemen in the howdahs thrust their weapons forward, either at the mahouts or their opposite numbers, and the archers shot, close-ranged, at one another as the huge engines of war clashed with tusks and bronze-reinforced heads with such ferocity that it always amazed him. But it was not the struggle between the elephants which really interested Antigonos, it was its result; and the result pleased him mightily: for the heavy beasts and their supporting infantry raised clouds of dust that plumed into the air in differing shades of umber and spread out on a light breeze.

It was dust that would win him the battle.

And through the dust he could just make out Eumenes' main body of cavalry moving forward. *Excellent, more dust.* However, looking further to his right he could still clearly see Eumenes' secondary cavalry command preventing the outflanking manoeuvre. 'Not long to go, now.'

Demetrios turned to his father. 'It's dust, Father; that's how you plan to get around his back.'

Antigonos chuckled and tapped the side of his nose and then called a messenger over. 'Tell the Median and Tarantine cavalry to follow me and to be ready for my signal; three rising notes of the horn.'

The young man galloped off to the two cavalry units, stationed a couple of hundred paces behind Antigonos to his right. He turned back to his son. 'Dust it is; which is why I spent two days having the ground raked: it wasn't to smooth it, it was to loosen it. The only way I can ultimately defeat Eumenes is to buy him. And the only currency I can buy him with is baggage; if I have their baggage, the Silver Shields and the Hypaspists will do a deal. They will sell me Eumenes for all their possessions.' He rubbed his hands together, turned his face to the sky and breathed deeply. 'Gods, this will be good. Go back to your unit, Demetrios; let's make more dust.'

And so, with Demetrios to his left, Antigonos led the entire wing of his cavalry forward into the rising dust of the elephant melee as the unmistakable sound of phalanx clashing with phalanx rose from his left, now completely shrouded. Around the elephants they skirted, leaving them to their own dust-raising struggles, and on to where he had last seen Peucestas' now veiled command. But there was very little he could see to guide him and he smiled as the dust thickened. He pointed to his signaller with a nod. 'You'd better blow that thing whilst you can still breathe.' Three ascending notes wailed from his horn, again and again, so there could be no doubt. But doubt remained in Antigonos' mind for, although the signal had been given, he could not see if it had been obeyed. Then he calmed himself with the thought that if he could not see the Medians and Tarantines go by, nor could Eumenes. And so he relaxed and began to concentrate on enjoying a good cavalry battle.

Forward he led his men into the heart of the dust cloud, forward with abandon on the verge of recklessness as he was as good as blind. He still had a picture in his mind of the field before the dust enveloped it, and he knew opposite him stood the main body of Eumenes' cavalry and that they had started to advance. *We shall hit them hard.* And hit them hard they did: like wraiths, materialising where once nothing had been, they emerged from the miasma to crash into the enemy with a roar on their lips and death clasped in their fists, punching their lances before them. Although the contact was equally a surprise for Antigonos' men as it was for Peucestas' Persian companions, the former had been advancing with intent, whereas the latter had, through the caution of their commander, almost come to a standstill. And so it was with greater momentum that Antigonos led his charge into the belly of the enemy formation, slashing and stabbing as they went, casting the surprised first and second ranks aside with ease and falling on the rear ranks as many of them turned to flee.

With joy in his pounding heart and a wild grin on his face, Antigonos took life after life, working first with his lance, thrusting and stabbing, and then, when that had snapped, with the butt-spike, slashing it, forehand and backhand, like a pointed mace to crack skulls and slice open faces. It was with an arm-juddering jerk that what remained of his lance was cracked out of his grip by a blade swooping down from his right. With no pause to look, as the weapon sliced on down, glancing his thigh in a spray of blood, Antigonos swept his sword from its scabbard and swung it with one fluid motion to cut up through the jawbone of his adversary. Back went the Persian, spewing blood from an open throat as his jaw hung loose, attached only by the flesh of his cheeks; his severed tongue slithered down his chest. Pulling back his blade, Antigonos kicked his horse forward, ignoring the searing pain of his thigh; he felt his wingmen surge after him, shouting death as they came, and dealing it out to all who opposed them. On Antigonos worked through the half-glimpsed world of silhouettes writhing in a swirling cloud, and filled with cries of pain and roars of battle-joy, all dampened by the overbearing atmosphere so that the microcosm of violence a man inhabited in a battle became even smaller and more claustrophobic. But there was no time for Antigonos to wonder at the conditions, although he fleetingly registered them, for he felt the pressure before him lessen as more of his adversaries turned and fled. Indeed, it seemed as if the whole line was in flight, for all he could make out were the occasional hind legs of retreating horses. And he pursued in the hope of breaking Eumenes' entire cavalry wing.

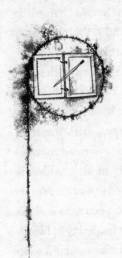

EUMENES.
THE SLY.

'Now I can see what the one-eyed bastard has done,' Eumenes said to Hieronymus as they moved forward from his stationary command, trying to make out what was occurring. 'Or, rather, I can't,' he added with a grim smile as he tried to penetrate the literal fog of battle enshrouding them all.

Hieronymus sucked the air between his teeth and shook his head; behind them the stamping of a thousand horses and the jangle of their tack fell deadened by the conditions. 'Clever, very clever. That's why he stayed on the salted land: it was dead and he knew it would exude dust. With that one move he has negated our numerical advantage.'

'And I didn't see it coming.'

'No one did. What now?'

Eumenes had been considering that question ever since the dust had enveloped all of Antigonos' cavalry and left him guessing. 'I have to go forward and support Peucestas, assuming it's his command we can hear in contact. I know I risk letting Antigonos outflank me but what can I do? If he does, he will fall on Peucestas' rear and therefore I need to be there, and if he doesn't then I should still be there to keep Antigonos from breaking this wing whilst hoping Antigenes and his lads don't take much longer in defeating the centre.'

Hieronymus indicated to the swirling dust all around. 'And that's just guesswork.'

It is, but the Silver Shields have never yet been defeated so I must have faith in them. Eumenes took another couple of moments to reflect on his decision. 'We go,' he said, more to himself than his companion. He turned in his saddle and looked back at Parmida, just visible at the head of the Kappadokians. 'We go! But we go without horns and war-cries. We'll use the dust to our advantage.'

Parmida shouted in his own language as Eumenes sent messengers to the Thracian and Thessalian mercenaries on his right flank and the Sogdian and Bactrian horse-archers on the left, to support the heavier cavalry in any way they could, despite knowing that skirmishing would be impossible in the thick of the pall. *But better to have them there than not; it may be they could tip the balance.*

Hence, with little noise, Eumenes' wing moved forward towards the sound of battle somewhere in the haze conjured by Antigonos. Without undue caution, Eumenes accelerated into a canter, for the ground had been raked smooth and was rid of large stones and he knew, judging from the last positions he remembered before the luxury of clear vision was withheld from him, if he travelled directly towards where his centre had been he should hit Antigonos in the flank should he have come forward to engage Peucestas.

With surprising rapidity the sound of battle close by died away just as he felt he should soon collide with the source. Still he led his men on and still he seemed to get no closer to combat. It was with the first of Peucestas' Persian bodyguards flitting by, intermittently visible, that it became obvious why: *he's broken; he's running away.* With a renewed urgency, Eumenes pressed on, now hampered by Peucestas' fleeing command. But he and his Kappadokians did not make way for the routers and either they swerved away, out of the line of advance, or they went down beneath them, as now was no time for pitying the weak. 'Forward!' Eumenes shouted for he knew they would soon contact the pursuers and this was an opportunity for surprise. *This will be your dust working against you, Antigonos.* And as that thought crossed his mind the enemy came from the shadow directly at him, but he was prepared and threw his javelin with all his might; his Kappadokians followed his lead. Hissing through the cloud, five hundred missiles plunged into the oncoming cavalry, crunching men back and bringing horses down or rearing them up with death embedded in chests and necks. Out flashed the swords and up went the cries, for stealth was no longer an issue. To work Eumenes and his men went and hard did they labour as they harvested the lives of Antigonos' cavalry caught unawares at its moment of triumph, its enemies vanquished and the unit in disordered chase.

Again and again Eumenes worked his blade, taking no pleasure in the killing and maiming but having a detached interest in the result of the process, as if he were looking down from above and his body was being controlled from afar. And he saw himself struggle forward, all the time swiping and stabbing at those around him whilst controlling his mount with his knees. Through the crush he moved, Parmida to one side and Hieronymus to the other, parting the enemy who had lost all cohesion in their pursuit of Peucestas. Time and again he killed as he felt the weight of man and beast behind him press him forward until there was nothing but brown dust ahead and he burst through the last rank. It took a few moments before what remained of the opposition turned from the hunters to the hunted as they fled. But Eumenes knew better than to fall into the very same trap as he had just set. 'Halt!' he cried. 'Halt! Do not follow them up. We don't know what is ahead. Halt!'

And his cries were heard and passed on, for his men drew up, their frontage bowing as the message travelled along it so they ended with the left and right wings ahead of the centre, but what had happened to his light cavalry on either flank he could not tell for they were lost in the dust.

Blind to all but the closest details, Eumenes struggled to understand the position he was in: he had routed the cavalry which had routed Peucestas, but that was all he knew for certain. What of the rest of Antigonos' cavalry? Were they all in front of him, or had some managed to outflank him and, if so, where and when would they hit him? And what of the rest of Peucestas' command, Xennias and Eudamos; were they still intact somewhere over to his right between him and the battle of the phalanxes? And how was that battle going? Had Antigenes and his men triumphed and were they even now rounding on the rest of Antigonos' infantry as his, Eumenes', Greek mercenaries came forward to crush the enemy between them and the Silver Shields and the Hypaspists? And was his extreme right command still refusing?

Not for the first time he cursed Antigonos' cunning, but not without admiration for the ruse: it was one of the most ingenious he had ever witnessed. He turned to Parmida. 'We need to probe over to our right. I can't make any decisions until I know what's happening with Antigenes' command. Send some scouts ahead of us to act as our eyes and ears. I don't want to blunder into Xennias or Eudamos and lose lads unnecessarily, for the sake of good scouting.'

Parmida made the arrangements, sending out men as the Kappadokians began to move forward at a trot towards the distant sound of battle.

Through the dust Eumenes took his cavalry, slow and painstaking so as not to trigger an attack by his own men; but the further he went the more it became obvious that Xennias and Eudamos' cavalry were not there, for surely he would have run into them. And then he did run into them, or, rather, he ran into a few of them, for they came across the bodies of a dozen or so of Xennias' men. But they had died not from proud wounds of battle to their front; no, they had all had their throats slit. Eumenes jumped from his saddle to look more closely; a couple of the bodies were lying on their bellies, so he turned one over and knew before he saw the face whose it was. 'Xennias. Who did this to you?' But the dead give no answers and Eumenes could not afford to waste time on the puzzle. He clambered back onto his horse and led his men off, now convinced there were none of his cavalry left on this wing other than those following behind him.

Nor did the scouts, when they returned, give him any reason to think differently; indeed, one had reached as far as the left flank of the Hypaspists and reported that they, and the Silver Shields next to them, had the enemy phalanx moving back at a speed at which its formation must surely rupture soon and Eumenes' infantry would break through; meanwhile, the elephants were still getting the better of their opponents. *I've no choice but to gamble,* he decided as he weighed the news in his mind. *I must assume Antigonos has somehow got behind me and is coming to take the Hypaspists and the Silver Shields in the rear to prevent them breaking his line. I must take my cavalry forward to prevent that.*

As he turned to give the order, his left flank was shattered. Made up of lightly armed horse-archers mounted on the smaller ponies from the east, the Bactrian and Sogdian cavalry protecting the Kappadokians' flank were no match for the heavy lancers under Demetrios' command. And nor did they need to be, for they were far fleeter on their hardy little ponies, and at the first contact they turned and sped away across the Kappadokians' frontage, leaving them exposed to a follow-up charge that smashed into their side, sending a shudder through the whole unit. As the Bactrians raced past, Eumenes tried to make out the damage to his men but the part in contact were lost in the shroud. Shouting orders to face the unseen enemy, he tried to turn those as yet untouched into line and take them forward. However, it soon became clear the unit was wavering and unwilling to respond to his commands as they began to pull away from the hidden fight.

'We need to get out of here, sir!' Parmida shouted as the first Kappadokian fugitives came into view, some bloodied and all without their weapons. 'We need to regroup; we can't fight like this.'

And he was right, Eumenes knew; to stay was to condemn his most faithful troops to certain obliteration and, with that in mind, for the first time in his career he gave the order to his Kappadokians to retreat.

Thus Eumenes led the majority of his men to safety – for Demetrios did not give chase as he had heard what had befallen his father – and the further they went the more the dust thinned until they came into open air once more to find the sun shining down on the umber blanket concealing a battle.

Eumenes looked around as Parmida rallied his men along with the Thracians and Thessalians – the horse-archers now too scattered to be effective any more – and his heart jumped, for way over to the west, and well out of the dust, was what could only have been Peucestas' command and it was heading away from the fight, back towards the camp. *I need to get Peucestas back, and with him, and my cavalry on my right, try to* turn Antigonos' weaker left wing. 'Parmida, send a messenger to Peucestas ordering him back here immediately.' He looked back south again and felt sick. It was not so much the sight of his retreating men heading back to the camp which caused the bile to rise in his throat, it was what was coming from that direction to face them: blocking their way was a strong force of cavalry, cavalry he did not recognise as his. *He did manage to get a force around my flank though it wasn't to take me in the rear but to take my camp. Antigonos played me at my own game. I've always hated baggage and now it could be the death of me. Unless I get it back, whatever the outcome of the battle, Antigonos has won.* As that realisation dawned on him he turned away to look north to see the spectral figures of Antigonos' cavalry emerging from the dust.

ANTIGONOS.
THE ONE-EYED.

WITH CAUTION NOW did Antigonos move through the cloud with his recently rallied Companion Cavalry, with caution for he did not wish a repeat of what had very nearly proved to be his last fight. It had been just by a hand's breadth the javelins had missed him, all four of them in quick succession. How he had survived the surprise collision with the enemy just as he was pursuing Peucestas' broken command, he did not know, but he was thankful he had for now he could feel the tide of the battle turning in his favour, despite what was happening to his phalanx. If the message he had received from his son, up ahead of him, was reliable – and he had no reason to think it was not – then there was no more of Eumenes' cavalry left on this side of the field as the little Greek had taken his command over to his right with the presumed intention of attacking Peithon's small command. But even so, Antigonos proceeded with caution until the dust began to thin.

It was as if a veil had been drawn from his eyes as, for the first time since he ordered the initial charge, he could now see more than twenty paces in all directions and what he saw was all to the good: Demetrios had formed up opposite Eumenes, preventing him from rejoining the main part of the battle, whilst the rest of the enemy cavalry, away to the south, now had the Medians and Tarantines before them, which meant he had taken Eumenes' camp for sure. But if this was not enough for him, then the sight of Eumenes' cavalry on his right wing leaving their position and coming across to join their commander in facing Demetrios made him whoop with joy. *Peithon can get through!* He turned to a messenger stationed behind him, and pointed to where he assumed Peithon's position was beyond the dust. 'Tell Peithon to bring his cavalry around as soon as possible and threaten the Silver Shields and Hypaspists' rear.' He looked deep into the eyes of the young man. 'Make sure that is perfectly clear: threaten the rear but not attack it unless I give the order. They will most probably form square and move off. He's to follow them until I come to speak to them. Understand?'

'Threaten, not attack, unless you order it. He's to follow them once they form square. Yes, sir.'

'Good. Now be quick.' Rubbing his hands together with more vigour than usual, Antigonos cast his eye over to where Peucestas, a thousand paces away, was now changing direction and heading west to avoid contact with the Median and Tarantine cavalry blocking his way back to the captured camp. With another whoop, he kicked his horse forward towards his son. 'Peucestas has given up the fight,' he said to Demetrios as he reached him. 'Eumenes hasn't a hope.' He surveyed Eumenes' position. 'He's stuck there and can only retire. We won't lose any more of the lads by attacking him unnecessarily; we'll only respond if he attacks us. My guess is he'll withdraw to Peucestas, which is exactly where I want him.'

'And what do we do in the meantime?'

Antigonos grinned. 'I'm going to watch Peithon set in motion a trail of events that will end in my purchase of Eumenes and you are going to speak to Eumenes' Greek mercenaries. Offer them their baggage and any back-pay owed them by Eumenes if they sign on with us. Oh, and get a message to our friend to sound out Teutamus; he will prove a useful ally in what is to come.'

As the breeze freshened and the fighting lessened, the dust dispersed to reveal a field strewn with dead, both man and beast, for many had fallen. The Silver Shields and the Hypaspists had between them killed over five thousand of their opponents, and such had been their superiority they'd received only flesh wounds in return, but now they were unsupported infantry out in the open and vulnerable to cavalry and surrounded by the bodies of their sons and grandsons. It was, therefore, no surprise to Antigonos when they formed square at the sight of Peithon's command approaching from their rear, and he smiled to himself as they began to move south-west, heading to where Peucestas was now setting up camp next to a small river – if, indeed, it could be called a camp as they had nothing that would add to their comfort, it now being entirely in the enemy's hands, including their women and children.

And so, as the sun began to dip over Peucestas' camp and the Silver Shields and Hypaspists slowly made their way in square formation to link up with him, Antigonos watched Eumenes withdraw his cavalry and ride off. *There's only one place you can go, my little friend; and I can promise you it won't be a safe haven. But then, I imagine you know that perfectly well by now.* Again he rubbed his hands with vigour, his mood improving by the moment as he saw his victory would be as inevitable as it would be final. And so he followed Eumenes and surrounded his camp.

'They've agreed, Father,' Demetrios said as he returned from his mission. 'All of the mercenaries, including the peltasts and light infantry. I've sent them back to our camp to wait for their possessions and have told them we will supply them with rations. They seemed very pleased with the outcome.'

'And so they should be. They're alive, they are now fighting for me and I am about to be victorious because, with their defection, I now outnumber Eumenes so there is no way he'll be able to fight to get his baggage back. His men will just have to buy it off me. Let's see just what they have to say on the subject. Send some of our lads into their camp and tell them what I propose: the baggage for Eumenes and all his satraps and generals. They can send a delegation to come and talk with me as soon as they like. I'll be only too pleased to see them.'

If Antigonos was expecting a quick conclusion to the matter, he was disappointed for it was a full three days that the Eumenes' men held out, discussing their options according to the deserters who came in most nights. But eventually at noon of the third day after the battle a delegation from the Silver Shields slipped into Antigonos' camp. He saw them in private.

'And how can we trust you that, firstly, our possessions and our women and children are still untouched and you'll give them to us once we have done as you ask?' It was a fair question the leader of the Silver Shields delegation asked and the grizzled, grey-bearded veterans behind him growled their approval.

'I will take you, and your companions, to the camp personally, Aeropos,' Antigonos replied, looking up at the old man standing before him, 'and you can be the judge of the first part of your question. I have forbidden any looting so your possessions are intact, although I can't guarantee your women are unsullied.'

'No, we didn't think so, but we don't want them spending another night in the beds of our enemies.'

'Friends, now, Aeropos, friends. As to the second part of your question: why would I go back on my word and lose the chance of having the greatest fighting unit in the world join my army?' And this was true, Antigonos freely admitted to himself as he surveyed the faces, many of them older than himself, standing before him in the flicker of torchlight. Every one of the two dozen delegates had been under arms since their sixteenth birthdays – in some cases that was more than sixty years – so that they were so hardened in the ways of war none could stand against them. However, Antigonos also knew this knowledge had made them arrogant to the point of blindness and he fully intended to use that fault against them by flattering them into obscurity where they could never again be a danger to him. 'It would be an honour for me to consider you as one of my supporters.'

Aeropos considered the statement for a few moments before turning to his mates. 'Well, brothers, what do you think? Do we turn Eumenes over?'

'And the others, mate,' a mere stripling in his early sixties reminded him. 'Besides, it's his fault we lost our baggage.' This statement received yet more growls. 'But what about Antigenes? Now, he may be a cunt but he's our cunt and he's always been fair with us: share and share alike and none of us can deny it. Are we to hand him over? Peucestas, yes, I have no problem with that; it's because of him that we are in this situation. Had he not retreated we would have won the day. We had won, remember, only to find ourselves without cavalry support because Peucestas had decided he'd had enough, the soft Persian-lover.' He paused to spit on the floor, emphasising his point as his mates growled again in agreement. 'And then, as if running away wasn't enough, he refused to come back when Eumenes ordered him, having seen that our camp had been taken. Had he done so we could have regained it and wouldn't be negotiating for our worldly goods at this moment, but, rather, minding the funeral pyres of our sons and grandsons who still lie out there untended.' That point hit home with all his comrades, who nodded and growled deeper. 'As for the other satraps, personally, I couldn't give a fuck: give them over if we have to, and Teutamus, Hieronymus and any other generals Antigonos wants. But I say we keep Antigenes.' This brought the deepest bout of growling of the meeting.

Aeropos turned back to Antigonos. 'We agree to everything but Antigenes; he's our general, and we keep him.'

Antigonos inclined his head a fraction. 'And so you shall; of course you shall, I guarantee that. However, before you keep him, he must come to me to swear his allegiance. If he fails to do so then how can I trust him? But trust me, you will get him back. And if you don't give me everything I want, how can I be expected to give you everything you want?' He shrugged with upturned palms, regret on his face. 'It's all or nothing. Besides, I have a man here who will guarantee my word that you will get him back.' He gestured to the darkened depths of the tent. 'Won't you, Teutamus?'

Teutamus, Antigenes' deputy, emerged from the shadow. 'He had made that promise to me, Aeropos. I trust him to keep it.'

The Silver Shields looked at their second-in-command in surprise. 'What are you doing here, sir?' Aeropos asked.

'The same as you: looking after my interests. Eumenes has fed us so many false promises, leading us astray, it's time to put an end to him and ensure we have a place with Antigonos. I've sworn loyalty to him, and once Antigenes does, he will be given back to *us*, Antigonos has promised that.'

'I have,' Antigonos reaffirmed.

Aeropos considered the matter and then turned to his mates. 'Well, brothers, I don't know what our comrades will think of betraying Antigenes; they won't be happy about it, I'm sure. We should call the assembly and put the matter to them.'

Antigonos inclined his head. 'You do that and I look forward to hearing the results of your deliberations.'

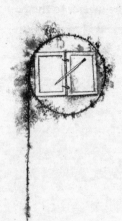

EUMENES.
THE SLY.

'WE CAN STILL win through,' Eumenes insisted again at the council of satraps and generals meeting beneath a rough substitute of Alexander's throne – the original being with the baggage in the hands of the enemy. 'Antigonos' phalanx was smashed and we are now equal in cavalry and still have more elephants than he does. If we act now with a surprise night attack and retake our baggage then we can fall back to less dust-prone ground in a position of strength.'

'No!' Eudamos again replied. 'That strategy has too many risks, and besides, our Greek mercenaries have all gone over to him almost to a man.'

'Even so, we can still retake the baggage.'

'Fuck the baggage!' Peucestas spat.

'Yes, fuck it,' Eudamos agreed. 'We forget the west and fall back on the upper satrapies. Leave Antigonos to his own devices and secure what we have. He will have to come to an accommodation with us at some point.'

What these men refuse to understand is Antigonos will never come to an accommodation with anyone as he's in the thrall of his own ambition. He won't stop until there's no one left to want to make an accommodation with him even if he would. 'We must stick together; together we can beat him,' Eumenes argued. 'If you go back to your satrapies he'll go east and defeat you one by one, just as Alexander did to your Persian predecessors when he made the same journey. Most of you were there and so can remember how easy he found it.'

'Antigonos is no Alexander,' Tlepolemus said.

'Nor does he need to be,' Eumenes countered. *Because none of you have the ability to beat him; but it would be politic not to point that out.* 'Because he will always outnumber any one of us who stands alone, don't you see that?'

'We must secure what's ours,' Peucestas asserted.

'And isn't the baggage ours?'

'No, it's the men's. I mean securing what we have in our satrapies in order to keep them now that Antigonos has won.'

'I agree,' Stasander said. 'I intend to go back to Aria and strengthen my position with the nobles and wait to see what happens. I'll wager Antigonos will head back west to secure Macedon and then begin a war with Ptolemy; it'll be years before he looks to the east again and by then much may have changed.'

Eumenes pointed at Stasander, wagging his finger as if he were admonishing a slave or small child. 'If you want to gamble Antigonos will head back west before he has settled the east then you understand less of strategy than his arse he's always swearing by.'

Stasander stood, knocking his chair backwards. 'You insult me in public!'

'No, Stasander, I say the truth! Now, is our alliance going to crumble and we hand power to Antigonos, leaving our fate and the fate of the Argead royal house in his untrustworthy hands, or are we going to make a stand here, now, and defeat the resinated cyclops?'

But there was no time for a response as the clash of weapons from without the tent caused all to turn to its entrance; the flaps were stripped back and armed men rushed in, two dozen at least.

Too late; I'm a dead man. 'What do you want?' Eumenes demanded, knowing the answer.

'Only what is ours,' their leader replied.

'What's the meaning of this, Aeropos?' Antigenes asked. 'You know how you are meant to go about asking for a meeting with your commanders.'

'Yes, I do, General. But I ain't asking for a meeting; it's got beyond meetings. We're not negotiating, we've already done that and now we're taking the price we negotiated.'

'And that is?' Eumenes asked, again knowing the answer.

'You, all of you – and don't try to resist because the tent is surrounded by all our lads and the Hypaspists.'

Eumenes shook his head and sighed. 'And you think Antigonos will give you your baggage back, do you, if you pay his price?'

'We've agreed.'

'Oh, you've agreed, have you? How gratifying. And do you really think he'll keep his word? Do you? Whereas if you persuade these gentlemen here to fight and stand with me, in return for not handing them over to Antigonos, then together we can get the baggage back and you won't have to worry about anyone keeping their word.'

'How can we rely on any of you?' Aeropos pointed at Peucestas. 'Look at him: he was once a man we could all follow, ten years ago, but look what Persian luxury has done for him. One sniff of danger and he fucks off leaving us in the lurch. How can we trust him? How can we trust any of you? No, you're all coming with us, and remember, us and the Hypaspists have the whole camp under our control.'

Eumenes felt vice-like, callused hands grip his wrists as they were bound with a leather strap; in the certain knowledge he had lost the argument, Eumenes tried a different approach. 'Then by Zeus, who protects soldiers, and the gods, who enforce oaths, kill me yourselves. Antigonos will not blame you. Or, if you're reluctant to, leave me one hand free so I may do the deed. And if you don't trust me with a sword then throw me bound as I am under the elephants. If you do as I ask, I'll release you from all blame and would consider you most just in your treatment of me.'

But his pleas fell on deaf ears. 'Our women have already been raped,' Aeropos said, 'and no doubt they are being raped again. You're the price that will halt our humiliation which, ultimately, was caused by you allowing our baggage to be seized. Take him!'

Eumenes was dragged away and did not resist for he knew his bid for power was over and in the end it had all come down to the baggage. *Can't move with it; can't move without it. And now I won't live because of it.* He allowed himself a wry smile as he was led away. It was, after all, an amusing notion that he should have made his military reputation against Neoptolemus with the shrewd taking of his baggage and that his career ended with the same done to him.

With the thought going through his mind, he and the other satraps and generals were taken before Antigonos. And it was with shock that Eumenes beheld his captor, for he sat, with his son, in an open space surrounded by men holding torches, with his army all around, beneath the empty throne, complete with its breastplate, sword and diadem.

'You think you have the monopoly of Alexander's support?' Antigonos asked as he noticed Eumenes' reaction. 'Well, if you did, my sly little friend, I think it's safe to say he has now abandoned you.'

367

'Just because you have his trappings doesn't make you his heir, Antigonos.'

'Oh, so you still think you're his heir, do you?'

'I never did, and you know it: because I'm a Greek and a little one at that.' He raised his voice so that all around could hear. 'I have always fought for the rights of the Argead royal house. I have never asked for anything for myself, only for the kings, when there were two, and now for Alexander, the fourth so named.'

'Gag him,' Antigonos ordered. 'It's not his views that interest me but, rather, the views of his comrades.'

Again Eumenes did not struggle as the leather was tied around his head. He stood and slowly turned so everyone could witness how Antigonos treated those who disagreed with him. *There, my friends, look at me; this will be you soon.*

Antigonos seemed unaware of the negative propaganda image he had created as he surveyed the captives arranged before him, until his eye rested on Eudamos. 'There you are, Eudamos. Now something very interesting came to my ear, something you said about what to do with me, were I to be captured. Can you remember what it was?'

Eudamos took a deep breath and stood to his full height. 'How did you hear?'

'Does it matter? Well, I suppose it's only fair you should know.' He smiled at Peucestas. 'Would you care to tell him of your treachery?'

Peucestas turned white.

Antigonos' smile broadened. 'Yes, I know I promised not to tell anyone but I think it's only fair that a man should be aware of who his accuser is.'

Eumenes was not surprised by the revelation. *I need look no further for Xennias' murderer. Peucestas must have done a deal with*

Antigonos to take his men from the field either after a token fight to disguise the treachery or if the battle started to turn in Antigonos' favour. That's why he didn't fight against me, as he normally does, when I suggested we go forward to meet Antigonos on his chosen ground; he'd already made the arrangement with Antigonos by then. Xennias objected and paid the price, murdered under the cover of the dust. It was just a case of summoning him for a briefing – or some such excuse. He stared at the satrap of Persis as his mouth opened and closed, trying to find the words to admit his guilt. *I'll not live long enough to avenge Xennias, but I'll find someone who will.*

'Come, Peucestas,' Antigonos cajoled, 'surely you can tell a comrade the truth?'

Peucestas could not meet anyone's eye. 'I told him, Eudamos. I told him you advocated executing him, should he fall into our hands.'

'Why? What for?'

Antigonos provided the answer once it was obvious Peucestas would not. 'Because he'll do anything to hold onto his satrapy, won't you, Peucestas?' Antigonos' smile was chill. 'Which is why I'm taking it away.'

Peucestas' eyes widened in horror. 'But you promised!'

'I know; but surely you must be a canny enough politician to realise a man who betrays his friends as easily as you do cannot be trusted and therefore any promises made to him are null and void? No? You're not so canny? Never mind; I'll find something for you that will fit with your limited intellect and pumped-up vanity. How about I make you general in command of Asia in place of the little Greek? That sounds important, don't you think?'

'Antigonos, you promised me Persis!'

'Silence! Feel lucky you've escaped with your life, which is more than Eudamos will do.' He pointed to the satrap of India. 'Take his head.'

He's really going to do this.

From the shadows behind the empty throne three men emerged, evidently prepared for the order as one held a drawn sword. His two companions grabbed Eudamos by the arms, but he shook them off and addressed Antigonos in a calm voice. 'Yes, I did advocate your execution, and yes, I quite understand why you now call for mine. But I would have allowed you to die with dignity and I would hope you'll allow me the same.'

Antigonos paused for thought and then nodded. 'Very well. Don't hold him.'

Eudamos looked to the night sky and breathed deep of its air for one final time, settling himself before he got to his knees and, after a brief hesitation, lowered his head to offer his neck.

Quick it was, and clean. Eumenes closed his eyes as the head shot forward, propelled by a burst of dark blood shooting out and slopping to the ground for the body to splash into. *I've seen the manner of my death. That will be me before the hour is through. I've always been short but in death I'll be shorter still, by a head.* He opened his eyes to see Eudamos' body being hauled away and then bundled without ceremony into a pit, especially dug for the occasion, Eumenes judged by the earth piled up next to it. The severed head was thrown in along with a couple of torches; fire soared immediately, announcing the presence of oil splashed on the wood now burning so bright.

'Let him burn and there let his ashes lie,' Antigonos declaimed. 'Like so, I treat my enemies! Like so!'

I am well out of this world if it is to be ruled thus by Antigonos.

ANTIGONOS.
THE ONE-EYED.

H E WAS ENJOYING himself, he could not deny it. The power he now had over the men who had come so close to defeating him, shattering his dreams and thwarting his ambition, was exhilarating; the smell of the roasting flesh of a man who had advocated his death sent a warm feeling throughout his body. *And now I have Eudamos' elephants, I shall be unstoppable.* His eye roved over his captives. It rested on Eumenes. 'Take him away and lock him up safely.' *I should just kill him now, but I've a feeling I may find a use for him before I take his life.* He watched Eumenes being escorted, unresisting, through the crowd. *He's resigned to his fate, but what's it to be? The same as Philotas or worse?*

Resolving to consider the matter for the next few days, Antigonos returned to the prisoners, in particular the satraps standing all bunched together. 'Other than Peucestas and Antigenes, I confirm you all in your satrapies. There will be no need for further conflict, provided you swear loyalty to me and protect the eastern empire in my name.' *That's surprised them.* 'Androbarzus, you can tell your master, Oxyartes, I also confirm him in his satrapy of Paropamisadae. You will take his oath by proxy for him and I will consider it to be as binding as if he were here to take it himself.'

'I will, Antigonos,' the huge Bactrian said, stepping forward. 'And it would greatly honour my master if he could be the first to so swear to you.'

'Then so be it.' He smiled inwardly as the fire on the altar was lit and the satraps had their bonds cut and swore their loyalty not only to Antigonos, but also to his son. *Now I have birthed a dynasty; now the young king in the west is irrelevant. I wonder what Oxyartes will do to Androbarzus when he realises his proxy has just signed his daughter's death warrant? That's not going to be a comfortable end.*

When it was done Antigonos addressed Eumenes' remaining generals. 'Gentlemen, I am ready to offer an amnesty if you will join with me. Hieronymus, I know it will be difficult for you seeing as I hold your friend and countryman, but I hear you are writing a history of these times, are you not?'

'I am,' Hieronymus confirmed.

'Then in my service you can continue to do so. What is more, I will not interfere; you may write what you please.'

'You'll not force me to paint Eumenes in a bad light?'

'As long as you don't glorify him unjustly, then no.'

'Then I'll be happy to serve under you.'

'Good. Parmida, you and your Kappadokians may return to your country and will answer my call whenever it comes. Is that acceptable to you or does honour decree you prefer to die by my hand rather than receive my mercy?'

Parmida stood straight, his chin raised. 'Our honour was satisfied when we broke your cavalry, Antigonos. We were not defeated so can go back home with our heads held high. And yes, we will answer your call should it come.'

'An oath to that effect will satisfy me.' He turned to Azanes.

'I need the services of your horse-archers whilst I stay in the east; you will be released when I head west.'

The Sogdian bowed his head but said nothing. As to what was going on behind the fearsome dark eyes, Antigonos could not tell; he grunted as he wiped the red fluid seeping from his scarred socket and then turned to Antigenes. 'I suppose you're wondering why I have left you to last?'

'No, I can guess,' Antigenes said, looking at his tied wrists. 'I don't imagine you are going to cut these. I expect they were Teutamus' price for helping you to convince my lads to hand me over.'

Antigonos chuckled. 'You've guessed well.'

'It wasn't a guess. I've known ever since Teutamus slipped out of the camp shortly after we brought our lads back in square formation; I haven't seen him since.'

'Well, he's now busy taking your lads back to their baggage, and once they've been reunited with their women and gold I'm going to start sending detachments of them on *special* postings to shitholes in the east.' He turned to the satraps. 'Yes, gentlemen, to your satrapies. You will all be getting some of the Silver Shields, and my advice to you is to kill them as quickly as you can by sending them on suicidal missions before they start sapping the morale of your other men by their constant complaining and arrogance.' He turned back to Antigenes. 'The Silver Shields will never fight as a unit again and, therefore, nor will they cause trouble as a unit again. They betrayed Alexander, they betrayed Eumenes, but they won't betray me.'

'You'll be losing the best fighting force in the world.'

'I'll train another.'

'And what will you do with me?'

'Ah, well, that is a problem; you see, I promised your lads I'd give you back to them.'

It was Antigenes' turn to chuckle, only his was wry and far darker. 'And, I suppose, you didn't specify in what condition you would give me back?'

'Sadly for you, no.' He gestured to the guards. 'Take his head and then throw him into the fire-pit. His lads can have his ashes if they can manage to separate them from those of Eudamos.'

The men moved forward and grabbed the veteran general, forcing him to his knees.

'Wait!' Antigonos snapped, standing and looking around at his audience. 'I've a better idea. This will be a demonstration of what'll happen to anyone who breaks faith with me: let this be a warning to you all. Guards, forget taking his head, just throw him in the pit.'

It was not just Antigenes who looked at Antigonos in disbelieving shock, all present did. That a Macedonian general could be executed by a fellow Macedonian in such a manner was unthinkable; and yet the order had been given.

Let them fear me for it'll make them less likely to oppose me. 'What are you waiting for?' he snarled at the guards around Antigenes who stood, motionless, unable to process such an order. 'Throw Antigenes into the pit and then chuck some more fuel wood in on top of him.'

Still the guards did not move.

'You can't do that to me, Antigonos,' Antigenes shouted, his voice tight with fear, 'I am a Macedonian.'

'I know you are, but you're also an example. Take him!' Such was the power of his roar and such was his terrifying cyclopic countenance in the torchlight, the guards jumped to their mission. No longer were they concerned about the inhuman nature of the punishment being meted out to a Macedonian general of renown who had followed Alexander and his father before him faithfully for so many years. They

374

dragged a struggling Antigenes towards the fire-pit; all watched on with horror.

'This is what you now have,' Antigenes shouted, 'this is the kind of justice you can all expect. You'll be nothing but slaves under this man and his arrogant pup. Tell the world how Antigonos treated me! Tell the world!'

In he was hurled, to fall on his back onto Eudamos' burning cadaver. It took but two heartbeats before a scream of unbearable pain issued from the flaming depths of the pit, chilling the core of all who heard it, and such was its volume few in the camp did not.

Too terrified to disobey, the guards heaped more wood into the furnace, which flared high with the boiling fat melting from Eudamos, igniting as the temperature rose, adding to Antigenes' agony but, at the same time, curtailing it. The screams died in an instant as burning air collapsed his lungs, leaving only the sound of crackling wood and hissing fat, for no one watching made a sound.

That's got their attention. Antigonos turned to address the satraps and generals recently sworn to him. 'You are dismissed but you are not free to leave the camp.' None of them uttered a word of complaint as to the manner with which he had addressed them and it amused Antigonos mightily to see them cast nervous glances over their shoulders in the direction of the flaming pit. With the satisfaction of a good day's work well done, he rubbed his hands together and then clapped them in anticipation. 'Come, Demetrios, it's time for the cyclops to resinate himself.'

The cup was full to the brim and was emptied in one long gulp; with a resounding burp, Antigonos wiped his mouth with the back of his hand and slammed the empty vessel down on the table. 'Fill it!' he ordered a slave standing behind him with a jug.

'And then leave the wine and go.' With his cup refilled he now sipped at it, enjoying the warmth creeping through his body from the first draught as the temperature in the tent grew with newly lit braziers.

'What will you do with him, Father?' Demetrios asked, placing a plump, green olive in his mouth.

Antigonos did not answer immediately, gazing instead into the heart of the fire. 'I don't know. I should kill him immediately, after what he made me do to Philotas, but something in the back of my mind is holding me back from the deed. He's shown himself to be an extremely clever politician and would be a great advantage to me in bringing people over to my cause without always having to resort to violence – not that I mind doing things that way, it's just the lads may well start to feel they have deserved a rest in order to enjoy what they've already won. But can I trust him after his breach of our agreement at Nora? Of course not, he's a sly little Greek.'

'But surely his loyalty is always going to be to the Argead royal house, especially whilst Olympias and Alexander are still alive?'

'But for how much longer? It's only a matter of time before Pydna falls, if it hasn't already fallen. I can't imagine Kassandros will let either of them live too long after that: he hates Olympias to his bones and the young king is of no use to him. Who knows, but with winter finally coming to an end, we may soon get news from Macedon confirming that very thing.'

'And until then?'

'Until then?' Antigonos took another sip whilst considering the matter. 'Until then I'll keep Eumenes locked up and allow any friends he still has left to visit him.'

'So you know who they are?'

Antigonos smiled in appreciation. 'You're learning, my boy. In the meantime we'll wait for the rest of the army and our baggage to come down from Ecbatana before heading south, on our way back west, and helping ourselves to the treasury in Susa which Seleukos has been keeping safe for us. Peucestas reckons there were at least fifteen thousand talents in there at the beginning of last year.'

'We'll take it west and leave the east to itself.'

'I think that would be the best strategy. We retain nominal control over the east and take whatever money we can from it, but I have no intention of coming out here again.'

'Another reason why you should kill Eumenes. If you keep him alive for his advice but know you can't trust him, you'll always be afraid he'll slip away again, and unite the east against you once more. He's too dangerous.'

But he's the one person who has the intellect to be able to help me deal with Ptolemy. 'I'll think about it.'

And he was still thinking about it when Eumenes' wife, Artonis, came into the camp.

'She wants to see her husband,' Demetrios told his father as he inspected the latest new arrivals from Ecbatana on a warming spring morning.

Antigonos waved the suggestion away. 'I can't let her do that.'

'She says you've allowed Hieronymus to see him as well as Parmida and some of his Kappadokian officers.'

'Why doesn't she come to me and argue her case herself?'

'Out of pride; she won't beg. Either you let her see him or she'll take her petition to the army. You know, the weeping wife routine, faithful but weak, thus helpless. The lads always seem to like it. What harm can it do, Father? It's not as if she can break Eumenes out.'

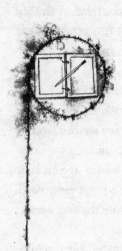

EUMENES.
THE SLY.

H E HAD GROWN used to the half-light of his prison, a cabin built in the centre of the camp. Strong, well-founded and windowless were the walls, and barred was the door; barred by two great rods of iron, wedged into sockets that took much to manoeuvre on the few occasions he had a visitor. And his curiosity was piqued as he heard the familiar sound of the bars being hammered out.

For just under a moon he had been kept a prisoner in this portal between one world and the next, in a limbo not of his making and beyond his understanding. What did Antigonos have to gain by keeping him alive? The question kept him awake through long nights which differed from days only by the lack of light filtering through the few small cracks in the ceiling. Lying on the heaped pile of straw in a way such that his manacles and leg-irons did not rub, he would search his mind for the reason he was still alive so long after he had seen the manner of his death. But no answer came. Not even Hieronymus could provide one that satisfied in the three times he had visited.

'Perhaps he likes you too much to kill you,' he had suggested the last time he had sat with Eumenes at the rickety wooden table sharing the food and drink he had brought.

'He's not so stupid as to let personal feelings get in the way of business,' Eumenes had replied through a mouthful of freshly baked bread, 'even if it were true, which it's not after I killed Philotas. No, he must be thinking of using me as a bargaining chip, but with whom I can't imagine.'

'Olympias, perhaps?'

'I very much doubt Olympias is in any position to make bargains. Pydna must have fallen by now and she's either dead or in Kassandros' hands – which amounts to pretty much the same thing.' He ripped another chunk off the loaf and dipped it into the bowl of olive oil. 'And I can't think of any reason why Kassandros would want me, so I'm worthless on that account.'

'Seleukos?'

Eumenes almost choked on his mouthful. 'Oh, come on, Hieronymus, you're meant to be writing a history of the time and you suggest Antigonos will negotiate with Seleukos? As soon as he's through the gates of Babylon he'll remove him and Seleukos will flee to Ptolemy – assuming he gets out alive.'

'Ptolemy, then?'

Eumenes shook his head. 'Again, why would he want me? What use would I be to him?'

'Advice?'

'Advice? I'd be advising Ptolemy on how to beat Antigonos. What would Antigonos be doing giving Ptolemy that sort of help? Not that Ptolemy needs advice, he should know perfectly well how to beat the cyclops now he's taken Asia: intrigue with his brother-in-law, Kassandros, rekindle the ambition of the eastern satraps, especially Peithon, and get Lysimachus to stop worrying about these tribes of monsters to the north and join the confederation for a year or two, then attack Antigonos from all sides. One big coalition will see the end of the resinated cyclops' ambition; an ambition that's taken us all by surprise.'

Eumenes tutted and shook his head in disbelief. 'Who saw that coming when Alexander gave his ring to Perdikkas, neglecting to say who he meant by "the strongest"? It certainly wasn't Antigonos, the half-forgotten satrap of Phrygia at the time. Phrygia! Where the fuck was Phrygia? We'd all forgotten about Phrygia, having seen how big the world really was. And then out he comes of his rugged valleys with an ambition to make himself greater than any of us. Who of us ever saw it coming?'

Hieronymus had considered the question. 'It would certainly be worth exploring in my history: the rise of Antigonos' ambition. Yes, you're right: he came from nowhere to beat us all by playing Antipatros so well. That's how he got his power, by pretending to be the supporter of the regent after Perdikkas had been assassinated. Do you remember, he and Seleukos saved Antipatros from the Silver Shields at the Three Paradises? After that he was made.'

'Well, it doesn't matter much now how he got to where he is. I just wish I understood how I got to where I am and why I'm still here.'

And the answer still eluded him as the door to his prison opened to reveal the unmistakable silhouette of his wife. She stood there for a few moments as her eyes got used to the light. 'Hello, Husband,' she said, walking forward once she could make out his shadowed figure.

'Artonis,' Eumenes whispered, audibly moved, getting to his feet. 'You should have stayed in Aspadana. When did you get here?'

'Three days ago. I've been petitioning Antigonos to let me see you; he was reluctant and then some news arrived which made him change his mind. He's let me come so long as I bear his message.' She stopped before him and held out a hand to caress his cheek. A slight wrinkling of her nose betrayed distaste for the smell of the hut; his slop-bucket was changed irregularly and he was unwashed and unchanged since he had been taken prisoner.

'You've seen me in better conditions,' he admitted, showing her his manacles to emphasise the point.

The sight of them brought home the reality of the situation. Artonis sobbed, collapsing to her knees, before letting go a quavering wail. The door closed and the bars slammed into place.

Following her down, Eumenes put his manacled hands over her head and embraced her, caring not for his unsavoury state. 'You must be brave, Artonis; this will soon be over, one way or the other.'

Artonis struggled to control herself, her chest heaving as she drew in ragged, high-pitched breaths. Eumenes held her close, relishing the freshness of her scent after so long in fetid accommodation. 'Thank you, Artonis. Thank you for coming, even though I would have forbidden it, had you requested my permission.'

'I wouldn't have obeyed you,' she whispered, hoarse with tears.

'Come, sit down.' Eumenes struggled to his feet, weak from lack of exercise, and helped his wife up and to one of the two chairs by the table. 'I'd offer you something to eat or drink, only...'

She indicated to the door. 'The guard should have left a bag inside before he closed up.'

Retrieving it, he placed it upon the table for Artonis to open, producing a cheese, some bread and a sausage. 'They wouldn't allow me to bring a knife so we'll have to tear or bite chunks off.'

'That's how I've been eating ever since they locked me in here.'

She held up a skin of wine and offered it to him. 'This, however, will be easy to drink.'

Eumenes took it gladly, and drunk deep to balance the strong emotions surging through him: desperate though his situation was and irretrievably lost his cause might be, the sight of his wife filled him with a rich desire to live. They sat in companionable silence for a few moments as Artonis did her best to serve her husband a meal that did not look too primitive.

'Well?' Eumenes asked after he had swallowed a few mouthfuls. 'What's the news that's prompted Antigonos to send me a message?'

Artonis set down a half-eaten piece of cheese and drew a deep breath, lowering her eyes. 'It's the worst news, Husband.'

Eumenes reached his manacled hands across the table and took hers. 'News from Pydna?'

'Yes: Kassandros has captured Olympias and Alexander.'

As expected. 'Are they still alive?'

'It was the first messenger to make it through from Macedon since the thaw who brought the news. They were when he left, but it's neither here nor there because they've become irrelevant.'

'Irrelevant? How?'

'There's no easy way to say this, Eumenes.' She met his eye in the dim light. 'Kassandros is to marry Thessalonike.'

It was as if she had reached over the table and punched him in the solar plexus. His mouth fell open as he mentally reeled from the shock.

'It's true,' Artonis said, 'Antigonos swore it.'

Who'd have thought that of Kassandros, the pimply coward? That's the act of a formidable politician: the son of the regent marries the half-sister of Alexander and I never saw it coming. Marrying Kleopatra, yes, but she would never have accepted the match. But Thessalonike? What made her do it, to betray her family like that? She has handed the crown to Kassandros and he will have the legitimacy of the Argead royal house behind him. 'That can't be allowed to happen.'

'We can't stop it. Kassandros is attempting to have Olympias tried for her crimes whilst regent; with Thessalonike, her adopted daughter, supporting the action he may well get a sentence of death passed.'

'Even if he doesn't, he has inveigled his way into the royal house and it won't be long before he feels strong enough to murder Alexander and proclaim himself king with Thessalonike as his queen; and it's a strong claim.'

'And Antigonos wants you to support it.'

Eumenes stared at his wife in disbelief. 'He wants what?'

'He wants you to support Kassandros and Thessalonike's claim – in return for your life. That was the message he wanted me to bring to you. He said if you were to support the move then it would unite the families who support Kassandros and those who've always supported Alexander's heirs.'

'Me? Support Kassandros against the rightful heir? After all I've been through to protect Alexander's rights, Antigonos wants me to support a move against the king.' He stopped. 'Wait. Why would Antigonos wish me to do that when he desires all the power for himself? Obviously he would like to see Alexander dead but why would he want to set up a more powerful figurehead in his place? Kassandros would be much more of a challenge for him to remove.' *This is why he's been keeping me alive: to be a supporter for any move against the natural order of the Argead royal house. But he couldn't have imagined this one in his most ambitious dreams.* 'So how will it help him, me supporting someone whom, logic decrees, he must soon eliminate?' And then it came to him with a flash, so obvious it was. 'Ptolemy! Of course, it's because of Ptolemy.'

Artonis frowned. 'How do you mean, Husband? How does it affect Ptolemy?'

'It leaves Antigonos free to deal with Ptolemy without having to worry about Kassandros. Don't you see? If he sends me to

Macedon to support Kassandros and Thessalonike and declare them the rightful Argead heirs and say the matter is now settled, he then places Kassandros deep in his debt. Meanwhile, Kassandros will spend a good couple of years securing his position with his new wife, no doubt forcing his progeny upon the world. Once he has a son he will kill Alexander, whilst Antigonos is leagues away in the south and is thus completely innocent of the crime; the one crime even he would not dare to commit. If he manages to defeat Ptolemy – and that's a big if – he will then be so strong he'll come back north, brush Kassandros aside, in the name of vengeance for Alexander's murder, and have it all. If he doesn't defeat Ptolemy, he will, no doubt, come to a peace accord with him whereby they both head north and brush Kassandros aside together and share his possessions; a state of affairs that'll last for a while until they decide to go to war again to see if they can settle the matter. But either way, Kassandros gets brushed aside after having killed the only legitimate heir to Alexander: his son. Antigonos can rightly claim his innocence but I will have been seen as being part of the conspiracy: the ultimate traitor to the Argead cause.'

Artonis squeezed his hands. 'You cannot do it. I can see that, Eumenes. I can see it.'

'No, I can't.'

Tears seeped from her eyes and, once more, she gave in to a series of sobs.

Eumenes knew her grief's source. 'If I don't, I am to be executed, is that right?'

Artonis screwed her eyes shut and nodded her head harder than necessary; her tears rained down on the table. 'But he will grant me your ashes,' she managed to say in a strained voice.

'How gracious of him. And my execution is to take place immediately after you leave this prison with my answer?'

Again her head moved at a frantic pace, her eyes still squeezed tight but emitting copious tears.

He felt his neck, soon to be severed. 'And they're waiting directly outside?'

She could not respond but Eumenes knew it to be the truth; it would have been what he would have done so that he would not have time to change his mind.

'Then we had best say our goodbyes, Artonis.'

A howl of misery burst from her and she shook without control.

I must get this over with as quickly as possible for both our sakes. He got to his feet and walked around the table to kneel next to her. 'Listen, Artonis. Listen to me.' He shook her with gentle force to get her attention.

With a few more sobs, she calmed enough to look at him.

'There is a way we can turn this against him.'

Her expression was of disbelief.

'There is, believe me. I'm dead, it is unavoidable, so let's not dwell upon that but think to the future. It will be down to you, Artonis. What are you meant to say to the guards as you leave: yes, he will go to Kassandros, or no, he won't go to Kassandros, or is it just a plain yes or no?'

'Just a plain yes or no.'

'Good. So who else is aware of what conditions Antigonos has set on my life?'

She shook her head. 'I don't know.'

'My guess is just Demetrios. But you must make sure both Ptolemy and Kassandros get to hear of the bargain he tried to strike with me, so they can see Antigonos' dishonesty for what it is. That will help them forge an alliance for long enough to be rid of him, despite their mutual hatred. After that, I don't care what they do so long as we have had our vengeance through them. Do you see?'

Artonis sniffed. 'Yes, but how?'

'Ask Antigonos for his protection; he'll grant it to you as he doesn't wage war on women and children – unless they happen to be kings or queens in his way. Tell him you want to take my ashes back to Kardia and you wish to travel with him as he heads west for your own safety. He will never question that. Antigonos will go first to Susa to clear out the treasury and then he'll come to Babylon to claim it for himself. You must tell Seleukos what's happened here. When, as is inevitable, he is forced to flee for his life, travel with him, if you can, for he'll go to Ptolemy. Seleukos will understand the value of your information and the importance of it reaching Ptolemy's ears. Ptolemy will know how best to get you to Kassandros because he'll see it's in his interest to do so.' He took her face in his hands and kissed her lips. 'Do this for us, Artonis. We will thwart Antigonos and he will never know how.' A brief smile cracked his mouth and he kissed her again.

She responded with a faint sigh and a suppressed sob. 'I will, my love, and I'll do it with great joy.' She leaned her forehead against his and managed to raise her eyes to look into his. 'I'll go now; now I can see a purpose to my life after you've gone I shall be able to carry on.'

'I could ask for no more.' He got to his feet and helped her to hers.

Artonis brushed his lips with a finger. 'Goodbye, and wait for me.'

'I will. I'll be there on the other side.'

She walked past him and knocked on the door. Eumenes did not turn to watch her go.

He heard the bars come off; a shaft of light flooded into the room.

'No,' Artonis said as she walked out.

Eumenes braced himself for the final journey he had seen so

many make before him; he felt his head, he did not want to lose it. He could see it in his mind's eye rolling across the floor; he wished there could be some other way, poison, perhaps.

Footsteps came up behind him.

'You are to execute me?' he asked.

'We are, sir.'

The respect in the man's voice surprised him. 'Then let's get this over.' Still without looking round, he knelt. 'Give me a few moments.' He drew breath and composed himself. *I may not have been able to save the destruction of the royal house but I hope I shall have contributed to the destruction of its destroyer. Go with all my love, Artonis.*

With his heart beating fast enough to make him light-headed, he exposed his neck.

'That won't be necessary, sir,' his executioner said from behind him. 'Stay as you were.'

The noose slipped over his head and he almost felt grateful to Antigonos even though he had meant it to be a crueller death than by the sword: he would keep his body intact.

As the handle of the garrotte turned, twisting the rope ever tighter, Eumenes did not struggle; now his time of struggling was at an end and he accepted it. He was satisfied that during his life he had done all in his power to repay his debt to Alexander and his father, Philip, before him, for raising him to such heights. And as the last breath was squeezed from his lungs and his mind floated away, his final conscious thought was of gratitude to the Argead royal house of Macedon, the house that had been so abominably and unaccountably betrayed by Thessalonike.

Thessalonike.
The Half-sister.

I T WAS DONE; the assembly had been called and the hearing was now in session. Thessalonike stood at a high window in the royal palace of Pydna, to the west of the city, looking over to the two hundred men sitting in the agora, three hundred paces away, who were listening to testimony from the victims of Olympias' time as regent. The maze of streets surrounding it and leading down to the port, crammed with shipping, were all still bustling with victorious soldiers spending their long-overdue back-pay on the usual vices: women, boys and alcohol in the many taverns and brothels to be expected in a harbour town. It had been Thessalonike's idea to give the troops their back-pay on the first day of Olympias' trial. It was imperative to keep the men occupied whilst the mother of Alexander was, hopefully, condemned to death as there was much awe and respect for her still in the ranks. Judging by the chaos throughout the town, the men were far too busy enjoying themselves to worry about what was occurring in the agora.

With a sense of deep satisfaction, she turned away from the view and sat back down at her desk to read the reports sent to her husband-to-be from the armies besieging Pella and Amphipolis.

It had been easy to persuade Kassandros to allow her access to the paperwork, as easy as getting him to take her advice about the back-pay and also not to allow Olympias a right of reply at her trial before the assembly. Indeed, getting Kassandros to do anything for her was easy for he was in love with her to a depth she could not fathom. And that being so meant she could do no wrong nor be denied anything, and thus she had pushed herself to the very heart of power.

The hardest part of putting Olympias on trial had been to assemble enough of Macedon's aristocracy in Pydna, with so many of them still holding out with either Aristonous in Amphipolis or Monimus in Pella. However, it had been managed using families from Kassandros' family's heartlands – and the clans affiliated to them – and then others who had previously supported Olympias – or, at least, the Argead royal house – and could see which way the politics of the country was heading. They had made the simple choice of self-preservation over loyalty.

Thessalonike frowned as she read the report from Amphipolis by a spy within Aristonous' garrison. It was completely different to the despatch received the day before from Crateuas, the general commanding the siege. He had stated he had pressed two attacks on the city's walls, whereas the spy reported nothing had been done as yet other than make camp before the gates and dig a few ditches as a defence against sorties; the fact the report had reached Pydna was proof indeed of the porousness of the siege. Resolving to speak to Kassandros about the lack of development in the north, she took up Atarrhias' report from Pella which showed better progress – the city had been surrounded and the inlet leading to its harbour blocked; it was now completely cut off and destined to slow starvation. *Excellent. Soon Macedon will be ours, and from here who knows how far we could go. Now the sea lanes are opening up it's time to start preparing the ground.* She picked up a pen and a blank wax tablet but paused before she began the letter to frame it in her mind. *Now, Eumenes, how best to convince you we should still be the best of friends, if you emerge victorious from the east?*

It was Kassandros who interrupted her train of thought as she reached the climax of her appeal to the little Greek who had always supported her family but might not now approve of her actions; but, as ever, she did not mind the interruption. In truth, she was becoming rather attached to her little pet, as she liked to think of him, although what she had researched of his sexual habits implied he would be anything but that once she let him into her bed. That was something to endure in the future, though, once they were married, and that was a day she knew she could no longer postpone once Olympias had met her fate.

She looked up and smiled at Kassandros as he walked from the door and sat down across the desk opposite her. 'I thought you were at the assembly.'

'I was. What are you doing?' Kassandros asked, his eyes looking more at her breasts than her face or the letter before her.

'Writing a letter,' she replied, putting her pen down.

'To whom?'

There's no need to let him in on all my secrets. 'My half-sister, Kleopatra,' she lied. 'I want her to formally recognise our union.' *As if she ever would, her hatred of Kassandros being rivalled only by her mother's.*

'Do you think she will?'

'One can but ask.'

Kassandros scratched the stubble on his pockmarked cheek and nodded. 'I suppose so. It would be a propaganda coup for us if she did, but I can't see it happening.'

Thessalonike shrugged. 'I'll write the letter anyway.'

'You do that.'

Again this was addressed to her breasts rather than her face, but she was used to it now, and had come to find it stimulating. She had always enjoyed her breasts getting a goodly amount of attention in bed and had begun to hope – forlornly, perhaps – Kassandros would prove a caring lover in that area. 'What is it you want, Kassandros?'

'Hmm, oh, good news.' He raised his gaze to the nearest he could get to meeting her eye; on the occasions he managed he would blush a bright red, almost matching his hair. 'Philip and Pleistarchos have just ridden in, bringing Monimus with them; that's what called me away from the assembly. He has surrendered Pella. He did so as soon as he heard Olympias was to be tried by the assembly.'

'Very sensible of him.'

'Atarrhias occupied the city at dusk, yesterday. The twins rode through the night to give me the news as soon as possible and to take Monimus' surrender in person.'

'He could be useful for us. Where is he?'

'Dead, of course; I had him executed immediately.'

Thessalonike bunched her fists and closed her eyes. *I must try not to call him a fool; I need to choose my words carefully.* 'Really? And why is that?'

'I had no use for him; he was a traitor.'

'And what sort of message do you think that sends to anyone else holding out against us? Aristonous, for example.'

Kassandros frowned. 'Why should I care what sort of message it sends?'

'Because, my dear, surely it's better for people to surrender to us with the hope of keeping their lives; that way they're more likely to come over to us. If you execute everybody who stands against us, we would halve the population of the country.'

Kassandros dismissed the idea. 'Strength is what's respected, not clemency. I can't afford to let Aristonous live either; he would become a rallying cry for the north and I'll just have to execute more people in the future. I believe it's best to have a short and thorough bloodbath now, rather than a protracted one later.'

I do see his point and perhaps it has merit. 'Let's discuss each case as they arise. Perhaps, with hindsight, we might think it was better keeping Monimus alive until Aristonous surrendered and then execute the two together?'

Kassandros' eyes narrowed. 'Yes, I see what you mean. Monimus could've been bait; it might have worked.'

'But we'll never know now as Aristonous will fight to the death unless he's captured.' She picked up the spy's report. 'Not that there seems to be much chance of that according to this; it seems Crateuas has done next to nothing, which is not how he's presented it in his despatch.'

'I'll send the twins to have a look. If they sail to Therma across the bay they'll be in Amphipolis in two days.'

'They should leave as soon as possible.'

'Tomorrow after the verdict. Seeing as they're here they can join the assembly and help get the bitch convicted.'

'How are we going to execute her when that happens? Have you thought about that?'

'I'll send an execution party to her rooms.'

'And you think they'll go through with it when they stand facing the mother of Alexander?'

Kassandros slammed his palm down on the desk. 'Alexander! Alexander! Why is it always about Alexander?'

'If you need me to answer that question then you really don't understand what has been going on in Macedon for the last seventeen years.'

Kassandros hit the desk again, screwing his eyes tight as he fought to rein in his temper.

'You must learn to control your emotions, my dear,' Thessalonike ventured. 'I know you hated him but it mustn't affect your judgement every time you hear his name.'

'All right! I know.' He composed himself. 'The men I choose will do their duty.'

'Will they? Perhaps I might be able to come up with a better way.'

And so it was with a plan formulating in her mind that Thessalonike joined Kassandros at the assembly; made up solely of men, it differed from the army assembly in that it was rarely called and there was a property restriction, thus making it a more elite gathering. Traditionally it had always been used to try members of the upper class, mainly for treason. This trial, however, was about more than treason: it was about Olympias' abuse of power for personal vengeance, and the wholesale slaughter of her enemies, real or imagined.

Throughout the trial, witness after witness came forward to testify to her bloodlust, whether it be relatives of the five hundred prisoners she had had executed or the lamentably few survivors from whole families she had all but wiped out. On and on this had gone from the first day to the second, and yet Thessalonike could sense an unease among the assembly to bring a conviction, let alone a death sentence, for the witnesses were continually being questioned as to their veracity or motivation.

'These are mainly your people,' she whispered to Kassandros, 'and yet they seem reluctant to go for a conviction.'

Kassandros scowled and muttered something under his breath as he looked around the assembly sitting three-deep in a semi-circle at the southern end of the agora so as to benefit from the strengthening spring sun. 'Perhaps we should've let her have a right of reply. Her arrogance and spite would have done more to condemn her than excuse her.'

'No, Kassandros, we were right with our first decision to keep her hidden away. She still has the power to overawe the populace.'

'If the assembly doesn't convict her, what do you recommend we do?'

That's it, get used to asking my advice, Kassandros. Soon you'll come to rely on me completely. 'How would it be if she were killed trying to escape?'

Kassandros' avianesque face cracked into a tooth-bearing grin. 'It would be a marvellous thing. It would leave me in the clear and it would take away the chance of her being acquitted.'

'Then have a fast ship at the far end of the harbour ready to sail at dusk, and have men aboard it who are prepared to kill her and her escort as she embarks.'

Kassandros considered the plan. 'Yes, that would work. We could display her body, saying she was caught trying to flee from the judgement of the assembly and was killed in the fight between her escort and the guards in the harbour – or something like that.'

'Yes, something like that.'

'And how would we get her to go to the harbour of her own free will?'

Thessalonike rose to her feet. 'I'll go to see her and offer, for old time's sake, to spirit her away. I think she'll go for the idea. After all, nothing is more precious to Olympias than Olympias.'

With her mind focused on the act she was about to put on, Thessalonike walked with purpose along the corridor leading to Olympias' suite in the palace. 'Open them,' she ordered the guards on the doors. They did not for a moment question her right to enter.

Through the opening doors she marched, her shoes clacking on the marble floor, into the main reception room of Olympias' suite.

'You!' Olympias shrieked as she looked up from a letter she was writing at her desk. She stood. 'You bitch!'

Thessalonike ducked the flying inkpot that followed the expletive. 'If you want to live, listen to me!' She leaned to her right, dodging the pen hissing past her left ear. 'Olympias! You're a dead woman unless you listen to me.'

This seemed to penetrate the hate emanating from her adoptive mother. Thessalonike pointed to the statuette in Olympias' hand. 'Put that down and listen.'

'I should kill you,' Olympias hissed, not dropping her weapon but making no attempt to hurl it.

'Perhaps you should, but if you did you would have no chance of surviving the day, whereas if you do as I say then maybe, just maybe, you might.'

'Why should I trust you?'

'Because you have no one else to trust.'

This hit the mark. Olympias sat back down, letting the statuette go. It thudded onto the desk.

'That's better.' Thessalonike sat in a chair a safe distance away from the woman who had brought her up.

'Well? What have you got to say?'

'Only this: tomorrow the assembly will find you guilty.'

'They wouldn't dare; I'm the mother of Alexander.'

'As you keep on endlessly reminding everyone; and as I keep on reminding you, that counts for far less now that he's dead.'

'I'm still his mother!'

Thessalonike held up a hand, palm out. 'Yes, Olympias, you are. But the assembly will still find you guilty and pass a sentence of death upon you. You will be on your way to the Ferryman by this time tomorrow. Unless you run.'

'Run where?'

'To Sardis, to Kleopatra.'

'I need a ship.'

'I'll have one ready by dusk.'

Olympias looked hard at Thessalonike, suspicion in her half-closed eyes. 'What? And I just walk on down to the harbour and get on it?'

'Yes. I have that power.' *That hurt her; what she would give for power.*

'And the ship will take me across the sea to Ephesus?'

'Where you can get transport to Sardis, yes.'

Olympias slowly shook her head. 'No, there's something not right about this. Why would you help me? Why would you get me closer to Eumenes?'

'That's assuming Eumenes will beat Antigonos.'

'He'll beat him!'

'If he doesn't, I'll be helping you get nearer to Antigonos. That may not be quite so attractive to you but it'll still be better than being dead tomorrow.'

'And what if this is a trap to kill me whilst I try to escape?'

'Then you'll be no worse off than if you stay. You'll still be dead.'

'What about Alexander and Roxanna?'

'They stay; without Alexander under his care, Kassandros ceases to be regent. They stay. Stop trying to bargain, Olympias. It's yes or no.'

OLYMPIAS.
THE MOTHER.

TRAPPED. GUARDS ON the doors, guards in the courtyard below, her letters read and then not sent, and all visits prohibited; until now, until this very strange visit from her cursed, adopted daughter. *Could this be a way out?* Olympias considered her options, staring at the hated face of Thessalonike. *Why does she want to save my life? It doesn't make sense. She knows I won't rest until she and Kassandros are dead. And yet, this could be my only chance of slipping away from Kassandros' grip. The bitch is right in that respect: he will have me killed, whether legally by the will of the assembly or with a knife in my ribs by Archias the Exile-Hunter, or some such lowlife. What have I to lose?* 'What assurances do I have?'

'None,' Thessalonike replied, her face expressionless.

She's giving nothing away. 'I suppose assurances are worthless anyway; either you are playing straight or you're not. There's only one way to find out. All right, perhaps I'm being foolish trusting you, but I'll come.' *And perhaps I'll get the chance to stick a dagger in your ribs before I get aboard.*

'Good.'

She looks relieved; why? 'How will you do this?'

'I'll come for you with an escort as it gets dark. Wear a cloak with a hood.'

'And we'll just walk out of here and then through the town to the harbour? Just like that?'

'Yes, just like that. People obey me and don't question what I do.'

'My, haven't you come on.'

'I learned from the best.'

Flattery? There is definitely something wrong here. 'Very well.'

She cleared her mind of all else bar this one question. She had spent the last couple of moons since her house-arrest, trying to decide on her best course of action. To escape was, of course, her dream, but she had looked into all possible ways to get out of her fine prison and all were too well guarded for a woman acting on her own, for she had no slaves or companions – they had been denied her and she was forced to do her own toilette and coiffure. The guards on the doors were changed regularly and were rarely the same on the few occasions she got to see them; they were therefore impervious to a subtle and lengthy period of wooing. Her food was brought by different slaves each meal and each delivery was accompanied by an officer from Kassandros' personal guard; men of such loyalty to the pockmarked toad that to try to bribe them was unthinkable. No, there was no other way out, so why had Thessalonike offered this avenue? And if she was playing false, the result would still be the same as staying in Pydna waiting for the blade. *Dying on a ship having been fooled into trying to escape or dying at the executioner's hand. What's the difference?* And then her fingers stopped working her temples. *All the difference! So that's what the little bitch is playing at: she wants my death to be laid at my feet not at hers and her toad's. Killed trying to escape justice. That's what she and the pockmarked reptile will say. Look, we had no hand in the death of the*

398

mother of Alexander; no, in fact we were planning on pardoning her, but now, how can we? We very much regret this tragedy. 'Bitch!' She hurled the statuette towards the door. It fell short, hitting the marble and sliding along the floor to crack into the wood. It did not make her feel better.

I'll stay here and take my chances.

'I'll stay here and take my chances, Thessalonike,' Olympias told her adopted daughter as she arrived with the escort. 'I've seen through you; I won't let you wriggle out of being responsible for my death. And don't try to embarrass yourself with pointless denials. Just go.'

Thessalonike sighed. 'The problem with you, Olympias, is you've never trusted anyone in your life so you cannot see a genuine action when it's right in front of you.'

'I said don't embarrass yourself. And you're wrong. There are two people I trust: Alexander and Eumenes. Although my son is dead, I still trust his memory.'

'Both are dead.'

Olympias looked at Thessalonike in shock. 'What did you say?'

'I said both Alexander and Eumenes are dead. A merchant vessel came in from Tyros whilst I was at the harbour organising your ship. Antigonos defeated Eumenes two months ago and executed him just after the last full moon.' She turned to walk back out of the door. 'There's no one you can trust now, Olympias, and there's no one who's going to come to your aid. You're finally on your own.'

And she was. She was finally on her own, that she could not deny. It hit her like a punch to the belly. She slumped to a seat as Thessalonike turned and walked, unhurried, to the door. *I'll not beg you to allow me to change my mind, bitch.* She seized another statuette and hurled it at Thessalonike. It cracked into her shoulder, knocking her off balance. Stumbling, she fell forward, her hands slapping onto the marble, just preventing her from measuring her length on the floor. Remaining on all fours, she breathed deeply for a few heartbeats, before pulling herself to her feet and turning to face her attacker, rubbing her shoulder and wincing with pain. 'That was foolish, Olympias.'

'Maybe, but it made me feel good.'

'It's the last time you will.' This time she backed a few paces, before turning and making her way at speed to the door as a vase shattered upon it.

With satisfaction, Olympias watched her go. It was a small victory, but a victory nonetheless to see Thessalonike scuttling from her apartments in such an undignified manner.

But then the brief elation faded and she was left with the reality of her situation: unless she could think of a plan, she was sitting awaiting her death. *With Eumenes dead, Antigonos will control the whole of Asia; Kleopatra will have to come to some accommodation with him. There really is no one to whom I can turn. Ptolemy will have his own problems when Antigonos tries to bring him to heel and so will, more than likely, form an alliance with Kassandros. Perhaps I should've taken my chances with Thessalonike's attempt to have me murdered. I might have been able to face the killers down, shame them into turning their blades against Thessalonike instead.* She hurled another statuette at nothing in particular, realising, as it got entangled in a curtain and then dropped harmlessly to the ground, it was a good metaphor for her predicament. She was lashing out at naught, trapped by her own impotence.

She had become irrelevant.

Bile rose in her throat as the truth screamed at her; saliva accumulated in her mouth. With a jolt, she retched, vomit spraying onto the floor, her body heaving with each fresh gush, until, exhausted and wretched, she collapsed into the former contents of her stomach, sobbing as she had never done before.

Self-pity, however, was not something Olympias had ever indulged in, and it did not take long for her to pull herself together and prise herself out of the pool of sick. Stripping off her clothes, she walked to her bedchamber and dipped herself into the tepid bath kept ever full. Sluicing water over her face and swilling it around her mouth, she cleansed herself whilst relaxing her mind so she could sleep, for she knew she would need all of her powers in the morning.

It was with the dawn that Olympias woke, refreshed and determined. Having dressed in the finest of her gowns, she took time over her coiffure so the dyed locks were piled high on her head, held by jewelled pins and decorated with a fine net of many and varied precious stones.

She walked into the main reception room and crossed to the window. The assembly could be seen in the agora with Kassandros sitting on a raised chair before it, delivering a speech with strong gesticulation. *Demanding my death, no doubt.* She turned to where her breakfast had been left upon a table – the vomit and soiled clothes had been removed – and sat to break her fast.

It did not take long, in fact it was quicker than expected: a cheer erupted from the agora; a cheer whose meaning was obvious. Olympias set down her cup of pomegranate juice and crossed once again to the window. It was as she had expected: a body of armed men now stood before Kassandros as he briefed their officer. She knew the man, for he commanded her guard, and knew him to be totally loyal to Kassandros, being of the same clan. *So, the pockmarked son of a toad is sending the men who guard me to kill me. Good; let them try.* As she watched, the officer snapped a salute, turned and led his men off towards the palace. Her death was travelling towards her at a steady jog.

Using all her strength, Olympias pushed a solid, high-backed chair across the floor so it stood at the far wall, directly opposite the doors to the suite. Composing herself after the effort, she sat down, arranging her gown so it fell with grace, and waited.

The clatter of many leather-shod feet mounting stairs heralded the arrival of the most desperate time of her life. She took a couple of flared-nostril breaths, bracing herself. With a resonant crunch, the door was kicked open; men spilled in, many of them.

'How dare you!' Olympias raised her arm and pointed her finger at the intruders. 'Halt!'

And halt they did, such was the force of her voice, such was its ease of command.

'Who sent you and why?' she demanded, now in a low and threatening tone, her eyes penetrating those of each of the men in the forward ranks; none escaped her gaze.

'We act for the regent. The assembly has sentenced you to death; Kassandros has demanded the sentence be carried out immediately.'

'The assembly!' She rose and sliced her hand through the air. 'The assembly is nothing to me. The assembly is a collection of old women pretending to be wise men. They do not represent Macedon. I am Macedon! Me!' She thumped her chest, glaring at her would-be assassins. None moved. 'How many are you?'

The officer cleared his throat. 'Two hundred.'

The ludicrousness of the number surprised Olympias and she let out a genuine laugh. 'Two hundred?' Some of the men grinned, looking sheepish at the obvious absurdity of the situation. 'Two hundred men to execute one woman? Is that what Macedonian manhood has come to since the death of my son, Alexander? Are you, men of Macedon, now so feeble you need to hide behind numbers to kill an ageing woman?'

The impugning of their masculinity and the mention of the sacred name of Alexander in the same sentence had a visible effect on the soldiers – even though many of them had not served under him, having remained behind in Antipatros' army. They looked around at their comrades as if registering for the first time just how many there were, for the crowd went right through the door and on down the corridor. Their numbers were excessive, and it shamed them.

'Look at you, huddled together like sheep with no clear purpose. And you are meant to kill me? Pah!' She stepped forward. 'Is there one amongst you who would dare to thrust his blade into me, the vessel that bore Alexander? Is there?' She turned the full power of her glare onto the officer, now looking far less confident than when he had kicked down the door. 'Well? Do you wish to be known, to the shame of all your family for generations to come, as the man who murdered the mother of the greatest man Macedon has ever known, and will ever know?' The man's eyes lowered under the weight of her scrutiny. 'Do you?' It was obvious he did not. She turned her attention to the men he led. 'Well? Are there any here who would step forward into infamy, for here I am?' She ripped her gown asunder, the pieces falling to either side onto the floor, and stood naked, her arms extended.

None could look at her. The front rank began to back away, pushing into the men behind who, in turn, gave ground, sending a concertina effect through the crowd as it began to retreat.

'Go! And trouble me no more. And tell your master and new mistress I do not accept the validity of the assembly's verdict.'

With great satisfaction and a fast-beating heart she watched the failed executioners withdraw, even surprising her by closing the doors behind them. Drawing breath into a tightened chest, she picked up her gown and went in search of another.

Her next move would be far more difficult to accomplish for she knew, despite seeing off Kassandros' men, there were still guards on her door who – even if they would not kill her – would prevent her from leaving; and she desperately wanted to leave as the assembly was still sitting in the agora and she would give anything to address it. As she contemplated her options whilst finishing her interrupted breakfast the solution presented itself in the form of her soon-to-be seven-year-old grandson, Alexander, being admitted by a guard, accompanied by his mother, Roxanna, with a guiding hand on his shoulder.

So astonished was Olympias that for a few moments she said nothing until she collected herself. 'Well, this is a surprise.' Ignoring the mother, she held out her hand to the child. 'Come, Alexander, kiss your grandmother.'

Obedient to her will, he came forward and placed a kiss on her cheek; she ruffled his hair, her eyes narrowing as she formulated her plan. *No one would stop me if I had a knife to the boy's throat. Even if Kassandros wants him dead, his men would never call my bluff. I need to disable or kill Roxanna so I can use the child as a hostage to get me to the agora.*

'I have a message,' Alexander said, rousing Olympias from her scheming.

'You do, child? A message from whom?'

'From Kassandros and Thessalonike.'

Olympias looked, with suspicion, at Roxanna. 'Why is he being used as a messenger?'

Roxanna's eyes burned with hate behind her veil. 'They didn't tell me, but they promised to make our conditions more comfortable if he came. Since you sold us in exchange for your life we have not been allowed outside our quarters.'

'Nor have I.'

'No, but then we weren't the traitors.'

'No, Thessalonike was, not I.'

'I'll still never forgive you.'

Olympias shrugged. Roxanna's feelings were neither here nor there. 'What's the message, Alexander?'

The boy screwed his eyes shut, remembering his words. 'If you wish to come to the agora, you may address the assembly.'

Olympias took Alexander by the shoulders. 'Are you sure that's what it was?'

'Yes, Grandmother.'

Olympias looked up at Roxanna, who nodded in confirmation. *Why would they let me address the assembly when it has already passed sentence on me?* She hurried to the window. The assembly was still there. *Even if they intend to execute me when I arrive, I'll still have the opportunity to speak and do what I do best. I'll make them see the difference between Kassandros and me.* With one more glance through the window, she made up her mind; the temptation was too strong. 'Very well. I'll come.'

In silence Olympias, Roxanna and Alexander walked through the palace gate under heavy guard. In silence on Olympias' part because she was composing the speech for her life, and, besides, she had nothing to say to her daughter-in-law.

Thus Olympias' mind was occupied as the party came through the winding streets to the agora, dominated by the temple to Poseidon, the port's guardian god. And it was there, in front of the temple, the assembly sat.

She cast her eyes across their faces, looking for men who were in her debt or owed her familial loyalty, but to her great surprise

405

and disbelief she could see none. Indeed, she barely recognised more than a dozen, and they were all prominent members of Kassandros' extended clan.

'Welcome, Olympias,' Kassandros said from his raised chair, behind her, as her escort halted in the middle of the semi-circle.

She swivelled around to see her enemy with Thessalonike standing behind him. 'It is not you I have come to address.'

Kassandros' smile was thin. 'Indeed not. I shall make way for you.' He rose to his feet and came down from his chair. 'There, take it. If you wish to appear before the assembly then you should do it as your rank deserves, despite the sentence hanging over you.'

Olympias' eyes narrowed. 'Why would you give me your chair?'

'Because I asked him to,' Thessalonike said, coming to stand next to Kassandros. 'I thought it best.'

'Best for whom?'

'For everyone.' She motioned the guards to stand aside, allowing Olympias through.

Olympias regarded the raised chair: it was her due as queen to address the assembly thus, and yet the manner in which it had been given felt suspicious. But what could she do? Should she stand before the assembly like some common petitioner or should she sit in state before it like a queen?

Her vanity got the better of her and she mounted the steps.

Her guards moved away, taking Roxanna and Alexander with them. It was the triumph in Roxanna's eyes that gave her a jolt of warning. She glanced around.

Thessalonike smiled at her. 'Are you ready?'

Olympias frowned and then looked towards the assembly; something was not right: they were now standing. 'What are they doing?'

'They're waiting for you to say you are ready so they can start.'

'But I'm here to address the assembly.'

'Oh dear, Olympias, I think the message must have got muddled along the way.' Her smile was all innocent concern. 'Perhaps I should have made Alexander repeat it another couple of times to make sure he had it right. You see, this is not the assembly, this is the new assembly and you are not here to address them but, rather, they are here to address you.'

'Address me?'

'Yes; you see, the new assembly is made up of the relatives of those five hundred prisoners you executed. Not for them is the squeamishness displayed by Kassandros' soldiers earlier. These are men with grudges that outweigh any awe or respect they might feel for you or what you are.'

Olympias' heart jumped. She was trapped. To run would be unthinkable; the act of a coward. To stay was the act worthy of the mother of Alexander. She sat straight in the chair and faced her enemies.

Thessalonike inclined her head in acknowledgement of her bravery. 'I commend you, Olympias, especially as you don't know yet how you are to be addressed.'

Olympias closed her eyes. 'Just get on with it. I'm ready for the knife between my ribs.'

'Oh, I'm sure you are but, you see, Olympias, that would be far too easy, and I've thought of a better way. In fact, it was you who gave me the idea yesterday when you started hurling things at me. I thought that, seeing as you seemed to enjoy throwing things at me so much, you might appreciate having it done to you. Begin!'

Olympias opened her eyes, dreading what she might see: a death by degrees. Stones were hefted in the hands of the three hundred men as they took aim, advancing towards her, but they did not release a volley. It began with a single stone thumping into the leg of the chair; an instant later her ankle was shattered. A near miss to her shin told her the worst. *They will not go for the killing blow to my head until I'm broken.* Her right shin then cracked as the hits on her chair, and the steps leading up to it, became more frequent. Stone after stone from the advancing mob now hurtled in, thudding into her with the dull report of a hammer tenderising meat, but still she uttered no sound. Her bones broke one by one as the aim was lifted. The fingers on both hands were crushed against the arms of the chair as she gripped them, her ribs then snapped, as did her forearms, and still she sat silent as her body jerked and rocked with multiple impacts as if suffering a series of fits.

It was as the first blows came close to her shoulders that she knew her head was next. With one final effort against the pain, she raised her mouth to shout: 'I am Macedon!' A hit took away her lower jaw before she could cry out again. Her eyes looked with horror at the bloodied bone and shattered teeth hanging down her chest for a moment until, with a flash of searing pain, one side of her vision darkened. Another crack to her head and she saw no more.

Olympias sank beneath the agony as her body continued to jolt and judder, pummelled by stones. No longer did she care for Macedon, as oncoming death took away its significance, for she had one thing in mind as her thought left her and she drifted away: it was to see her son again, after all these years; it was to see Alexander.

AUTHOR'S NOTE

This work of historical fiction is based on the writings of Diodorus, Plutarch and fragments of Arrian, all of whom used the lost history of Hieronymus as their primary source. I have kept mainly to what are the accepted facts – in as much as any historical detail can be considered factual as there is so much that is uncertain over such a period of time. Where I have blurred things is in the timeline: as the High and Low timelines differ by a year I have created an amalgamation of the two to best suit the narrative.

Most of what occurs in the book has been reported by the sources; however, I have embellished events now and again and have added bits of my own fiction to tie things together or to add motive. For example, Kassandros falling hopelessly in love with Thessalonike is my fiction; we are told that he forced her to marry him, something I find unlikely and suspect it was propaganda written to discredit him even further. I find it far more likely that Thessalonike entered into the marriage willingly as she would have seen in the power of the union, a daughter of Philip and a son of Antipatros, the ability to claim Alexander's inheritance. Making her the dominant party is very much my fiction – but who really knows?

The duel in the east between Antigonos and Eumenes is pretty much as it happened, although Antigonos having to execute his friend, Philotas, is my fiction. The battles of the

Coprates River, Paraetacene and Gabene are accurately described; however, the site of Gabene on ground around a destroyed town salted centuries previously is my embellishment; it was probably a natural phenomenon. I did credit Antigonos with using the dust from the salt as a prearranged tactic and, although this is not reported, I think it was probably so. As to the rest of that section, Peucestas' great feast, his betrayal at the battle of Gabene, Antigonos' bid to capture the elephant herd, Eumenes' fake letter and his forcing his allies to lend him money to safeguard his life are all reported and were, no doubt, in Hieronymus' original, which is why I have placed the soldier-historian at the heart of events. He would have witnessed Eudamos' execution and Antigenes' frightful death as well as the argument between Ceteus' wives as to who had the right to be burned alongside him.

Roxanna's and Olympias' attempted escapes from Pydna are my fiction but likely enough.

The Carthaginian embassy to Ptolemy is my fiction but I'm sure there were diplomatic missions between the two at this time, especially with the rise of Agathocles in Syracuse, which would have been a concern to them both, Carthage more than Egypt.

Eumenes' fate was, indeed, the garrotte but not immediately after his capture, which leads me to think Antigonos did have a deal he wanted to put to him that was evidently refused.

Olympias' death was as described: stoned to death by the relatives of her victims, of whom there were many.

I am indebted to many modern histories of the time, especially the excellent *Ghost on the Throne: The Death of Alexander the Great and the Bloody Fight for His Empire* by James Romm, *Dividing the Spoils: The War for Alexander the Great's Empire* by Robin Waterfield, *Antigonos the One-Eyed and the Creation of the*

Hellenistic State by Richard A. Billows, *Antigonos the One-Eyed: Greatest of the Successors* by Jeff Champion, *The Rise of the Seleukid Empire, 323–223 BC* by John D. Granger and both volumes of *The Wars of Alexander's Successors, 323–281 BC* by Bob Bennett and Mike Roberts.

My thanks go as always to my agent Ian Drury, at Sheil Land Associates, who loves this period of history and whose opinion I greatly value. Thanks also to Gaia Banks and Alba Arnau for their excellent work in selling my books abroad.

My gratitude to my editor Susannah Hamilton for her insightful input and to Will Atkinson, Sarah Hodgson, Poppy Mostyn-Owen, Hanna Kenne and all at Atlantic Books and Corvus. Also my thanks to Tamsin Shelton for a thorough copy-edit and her great attention to detail.

Finally my love and thanks to my wife Anja whose map and chapter symbols add so much to the book.

Alexander's Legacy will continue in *Babylon*.

LIST OF CHARACTERS

(Those in italics are fictional.)

Adea	Daughter of Cynnane and Alexander's cousin Amyntas. Wife of Philip, formerly Arrhidaeus.
Aeacides	The young king of Epirus.
Aeropos	*A veteran.*
Agathocles	Tyrant of Syracuse.
Alexander	The cause of all the trouble.
Alexander	Alexander's posthumously born son by Roxanna.
Alexandros	Polyperchon's son.
Androbarzus	Deputy for Oxyartes, satrap of Paropamisadae.
Annias	*Polyperchon's second-in-command.*
Antigenes	Veteran commander of the Silver Shields.
Antigonos	Satrap of Phrygia appointed by Alexander.
Antipatros	Regent of Macedon in Alexander's absence. Father of Kassandros and Philip.
Artonis	Eumenes' Persian wife.
Apama	Seleukos' Persian wife.
Archias	A one-time dramatic actor turned bounty-hunter.
Aristonous	The oldest of Alexander's bodyguards.
Atarrhias	A Macedonian general.
Azanes	*A Sogdian chieftain.*
Babrak	*A Pathak merchant.*
Berenice	Antipatros' niece and cousin to Eurydike. Ptolemy's third wife.
Ceteus	Eudamos' second-in-command.

Crateuas	A Macedonian general. Father of Peithon.
Deidamia	Daughter of Aeacides, King of Epirus.
Demetrios	Son of Antigonos.
Demetrius of Phaleron	De facto Tyrant of Athens.
Dinocrates	Ptolemy's architect of Alexandria, first appointed by Alexander.
Eudamos	Alexander's satrap of India.
Eumenes	First Philip's and then Alexander's secretary, a Greek from Kardia.
Eurydike	One of Antipatros' daughters, married to Ptolemy.
Hephaistion	A deceased Macedonian general; the love of Alexander's life.
Hieronymus	A soldier turned historian; a compatriot of Eumenes.
Iollas	Antipatros' son, half-brother to Kassandros.
Kassandros	Antipatros' eldest son, half-brother to Iollas.
Kleopatra	Daughter of Philip and Olympias, Alexander's full sister.
Krateros	The great Macedonian general killed in battle with Eumenes.
Lycortas	*Steward to Ptolemy.*
Lysimachus	One of Alexander's seven bodyguards.
Mago	*Representative of the Sufetes of Carthage.*
Menelaos	*A Macedonian cavalry officer.*
Menelaus	Governor of Cyprus. Brother of Ptolemy.
Monimus	Commander of Pella.
Nearchos	A Cretan, Alexander's chief admiral, now in Antigonos' pay.
Nicanor of Sindus	A Macedonian noble and supporter of Kassandros.
Olympias	One of Philip's wives, mother to Alexander and Kleopatra.
Oxyartes	Satrap of Paropamisadae. Father of Roxanna.
Parmida	*A Kappadokian cavalry officer.*
Patrokles	Seleukos' envoy.

Peithon	One of Alexander's seven bodyguards, son of Crateuas. Satrap of Media.
Perdikkas	One of Alexander's seven bodyguards, now deceased.
Peucestas	One of Alexander's seven bodyguards. Satrap of Persis.
Phila	Antipatros' daughter, widow of Krateros, now married to Demetrios.
Philip	Son of Antipatros and *Hyperia*, twin brother of Pleistarchos, half-brother of Kassandros.
Philip – formally Arrhidaeus	The mentally challenged half-brother to Alexander.
Philotas	Friend of Antigonos.
Phthia	Wife of Aeacides, King of Epirus.
Pleistarchos	Son of Antipatros and *Hyperia*, twin brother of Philip, half-brother of Kassandros.
Polyperchon	Krateros' erstwhile second-in-command.
Ptolemy	One of Alexander's seven bodyguards, perhaps Philip's bastard.
Pyrrhus	Son of Aeacides, King of Epirus.
Roxanna	A Bactrian princess, wife of Alexander and mother to his son Alexander.
Seleukos	Satrap of Babylonia.
Sibyrtius	Satrap of Arachosia.
Stasander	Satrap of Aria and Drangiana.
Stratonice	Wife of Antigonos and mother to Demetrios.
Teutamus	A Macedonian officer, second-in-command to Antigenes.
Thais	Long-time mistress of Ptolemy.
Thessalonike	Daughter of Philip the second and his third wife Nicesipolis, in the care of Olympias.
Tlepolemus	Satrap of Carmania.
Xennias	A Macedonian cavalry officer.
Xenophilus	*Warden of the royal treasury in Susa.*